PRAISE FOR *REASONS FOR WAKING*

"A compelling novel of grief and family secrets."

KIRKUS REVIEWS

"Compelling, unexpected, and unpredictable, Karen Foster's beautifully written story illuminates how misunderstanding can lead us down a dark, lonely path. And then it shows how, by talking and listening to one another, we can find our way back."

LYNNE RAE PERKINS   Author and illustrator
of many books for young people, including the
Newbery Medal-winning book *Criss Cross*

"Karen Foster's gripping *Reasons for Waking* draws readers into the tale of a political family shattered by unimaginable loss. The author's skillful unraveling of events, detailed character portraits, and sense of place create a compelling story. The shocking secrets revealed in this retelling of a long-ago tragedy force a fractured family to finally face its past together. Movingly told and beautifully written, *Reasons for Waking* gives you a legitimate reason to stay up all night–you will be reading this engrossing novel until dawn breaks."

HEATH HARDAGE LEE · Author of *The League
of Wives: The Untold Story of the Women Who Took on
the US Government to Bring Their Husbands Home*

"*Reasons for Waking* is a true testament of the author's fortitude and endurance and overcoming all obstacles. It is a story of tragedy, secrets, and healing. Once you open the cover of this compelling story, you won't want to put it down."

DENISE JELINSKI-HALL   Author of *From the Prairie to the Pentagon* and Chief Master Sergeant, 3rd Senior Enlisted Advisor of the National Guard

"*Reasons for Waking* is a page-turner! With so many unsuspecting plot twists, this novel has all the elements of a masterful mystery: political power and intrigue, multiple suspicious characters, gumshoe detective work, and suspense. It is unputdownable!"

TAYLOR BALDWIN KILAND   Coauthor of *Unwavering: The Wives Who Fought to Ensure No Man Is Left Behind*

". . . *Reasons for Waking* is a wonderful read, and I'm certain those who pick it up will feel the same."

JAMIE MICHELE   Readers' Favorite (5-star review)

Mom,

Jun 2023

Reasons
for
Waking

Hope you enjoy this. It looks very interesting. :)

Love,
Karen

Reasons for Waking

a novel

Karen Foster

BOLD
STORY
PRESS
WASHINGTON, DC

Bold Story Press, Washington, DC 20016
www.boldstorypress.com

This is a work of fiction. Names, characters, places, and
incidents are either the product of the author's imagination
or are used fictitiously. Any resemblance to actual persons,
living or dead, events, or locales is entirely coincidental.

First edition published June 2023

Library of Congress Control Number: 2022901375

ISBN: 978-1-954805-22-4 (paperback)
ISBN: 978-1-954805-23-1 (ebook)

Text and cover design by KP Design
Author photo by Telia Fleming Hanks

Printed in the United States of America
10 9 8 7 6 5 4 3 2 1

In loving memory of our sister, Karen,
who poured her heart into writing this story.
What a privilege and joy it has been for us,
her siblings, to see it through to completion.
Her greatest dream is now realized.

CHAPTER 1
TUESDAY, DECEMBER 8, 2015

SILHOUETTED IN A slice of moonlight, her muzzle aimed at the window that had been cracked open, Dilsey whimpered. I pushed myself up and looked at her and then glanced at the nightstand clock—1:18—before flinging away the covers and catapulting from bed. I reached Dilsey in an instant and rested my fingers on her head, hoping to steady her until a seizure hurled her to the floor.

But as soon as I touched her, I knew she wouldn't seize.

Without averting her gaze, she pressed against me, snorted, and sneezed. And immediately I smelled the smoke too.

Not a minute later, sirens blasted the night. Two or three at first from the general direction of the university, then so many they must be arriving from jurisdictions outside of town.

Whatever was happening, it was big.

When you think you've lost something, usually it's right where it should have been all along.

But Dilsey wasn't.

On a normal morning, one without an overnight campus fire, she'd never leave my office even with the door wide open and even if I'd stepped out. This wasn't a normal morning, though, and she and her tennis ball had disappeared.

After searching the corridors and classrooms of Braxton Hall and the attached academic buildings, I hustled back to my office in Braxton to pack up. I stuffed Dilsey's leash into my jacket pocket and my laptop into my backpack and headed for the stairwell. If she got outside, maybe she went home. She wouldn't need to cross many roads, and the police had cordoned off the busiest one, Central Avenue. Today, Central was a parking lot for news vans, fire trucks, and police cars. Still, any road my dog crossed alone was one road too many.

At a trot, I rounded the landing between the second and first floors and almost tripped over a young woman. She sat with her feet on the step below her, arms hugging her torso, head bowed to her knees.

"Sorry." I sidestepped and continued down. When I hit the first floor, I spun and retraced my steps. "Have you seen a black Lab?"

"Please go away."

I took that as a negative and left her.

But wait. She wasn't supposed to be there. In a text to the entire university community, President Randolph had directed students to remain in their dorms to give emergency crews and investigators space around the residence hall that had burned. I climbed the steps again. "Why aren't you in your dorm?"

She lifted her head.

Kate Appleby. One of my English composition students. From my position several steps below her, we were eye level. Her eyes were bloodshot, her dark hair a tangled mess. She wore a sweatshirt, cropped pants, and no socks with her untied running shoes.

"I live in Carter."

The dorm that had burned in the night. "Are you hurt?"

"No."

"I'll walk you to the dean's office. They'll relocate you." Consoling her wasn't in my wheelhouse, but I'd find someone to deal with her—though the longer I spent with her, the farther Dilsey could wander.

"Leave me alone."

"Alright . . . Whatever you say." I'd tried to help, but I wasn't going to beg, and I empathized with her desire to be left alone.

Outside, I pulled on my jacket despite the spring-like temperature of the December day. Residual haze from the fire draped the campus. I couldn't see the damaged building, but the odor of scorched wires and wet wood smoke made it impossible to doubt a structure *had* burned. Despite the number and types of vehicles on Central in front of me, the area was oddly quiet, except for the *whup-whup-whup* of a helicopter. I'd make one quick pass of the grounds before walking towards home.

Along a deserted sidewalk, I turned toward the heart of the campus. Because my hike to the office took me only to the edge of campus, I hadn't yet seen the fire site. Carter Hall sat almost dead center.

Along the quadrangle formed by Carter, a second dorm, and the history and business buildings, I stopped short. What appeared to be most of Grainger University's student body and a large number of my colleagues had congregated on the lawn in front of the building opposite Carter or on the porticoes of the other buildings. A few panned their cell phones at the charred end of the historic red brick structure or at their peers or the responders or the helicopter, but most simply stood quietly, well behind fluttering yellow caution tape. Reporters toting cameras and microphones inserted themselves among clusters of spectators. Only the occasional calls of the firefighters and the percussive rumble of their vehicles disrupted the eerie silence.

Blown-out windows flanked intact windows still decorated with Christmas tree and Santa decals. From one jagged fourth-floor window, a single metallic snowflake, dangling by tinsel and glinting in the sunlight, spun in the smoky breeze.

The fourth floor had won the residence hall holiday decorating contest. I knew that because Scottie Marston, the English department admin assistant, had volunteered me for the judging panel. I'd protested, but she'd rebuffed me. "It's no big deal, Philip. You'll have fun."

I hadn't come to Grainger to have fun. I came to teach and to be left alone in a town where no one knew me or cared to. When I mentioned the teaching part to Scottie, she studied me coolly and said, "Okay, here's why you're doing it: Trish told me to put you on the panel."

So the previous afternoon, for no reason other than our department chair's insistence, I'd accompanied my four overenthusiastic panel mates on a tour of dorms to judge hallways and suite doors. I'd also gotten a firsthand view of where the students' priorities lay. It wasn't studying for finals. Even the cookies and cider that the fourth floor residents had laid out for us—a setup complete with greenery and cinnamon-scented candles—didn't beguile me. Our judging panel leader scolded the students about the lit candles, and one grumbling student blew them out.

I'd suspected even then that someone would relight them after we left.

These students were eighteen, nineteen years old. They knew the dangers of candle flames and combustible decorations, but that didn't mean they believed the danger was real. They'd never consider that a single decision could alter their lives. Or end them. At their age, I hadn't either.

A light tug on my sleeve diverted my attention from the building. I noticed the tennis ball before I identified the woman holding it. Scottie.

"I got a little concerned when Dilsey showed up without you." She flipped the ball to me.

I allowed myself a relieved smile as I caught the ball, and looked around for my dog, puzzled. "Where is she?"

"She came trotting along the sidewalk like she was on a mission. Shoved her way through and settled among the students as if she belonged there." She pointed toward a small group, but I still didn't see Dilsey. "Gravitated to Nicole."

"Is she okay?"

"I don't know." She wrinkled her brow. "She and some friends smashed open a window to get air, but her roommate panicked and jumped; she died on the walkway."

I winced.

"The firefighters rescued Nicole and the other two. Nicole seemed okay until she saw the dorm again, and then she fell apart."

"Sorry, I meant Dilsey—she's okay?"

Scottie frowned. "You're asking about your dog when . . . Yeah, she's fine."

My cheeks tingled, and I shifted my gaze from her to the ball in my hand. "I was worried about her."

"I get it. Everyone's upset about every little thing."

As I looked around at the crowd, the police, and the media, I felt a strong desire to be somewhere else. I wanted only to collect my dog and leave the blame and emotional turmoil to others. If people wanted to grieve in private, fine, but they'd be better off moving on with their lives. I kept my opinion to myself, however. Scottie wouldn't understand what I'd long ago learned. She was all optimism because reality hadn't touched her world yet. Reality had long ago crashed into mine.

I pulled the leash from my pocket and started toward the group that Scottie had indicated.

She tugged on my arm. "Leave Dilsey with the kids. Please. They need her more than you do right now."

"I don't *need* her. I just want to go home; it's been a long day." I pulled away, and she turned and merged into the crowd.

I followed Scottie to the perimeter of the group and finally spotted Dilsey. She faced away from me, relaxed among a dozen students sitting on the ground with her. Each one touched some part of her dense coat–a finger doodling on a hip, a hand on her back, a leg shoved against her side. Dilsey rested her chin on the shoulder of a girl who had wrapped her arms around her and buried her face in her neck.

In my pocket, my phone vibrated against my hand. It was a text blast from President Randolph.

Please return to your dorms.

With scattered complaints as they looked at their phones, the crowd shifted and dispersed, but the students around Dilsey remained. Two women, one with a camera–who either didn't get the word from Randolph or chose to ignore it–advanced on us.

"That Lab. I understand it's yours," one said to me.

I bristled at the question. "Yes, she's mine."

"I'd like to ask you a few questions."

For years I'd watched my father deal with news media requests regarding his trials and elections. He'd handled them masterfully. Probably still did. And imitating him was easy.

"Sorry, but I really have to leave. Dilsey, my dog, doesn't do well in crowds."

I pushed past, but she grasped my arm.

"Look at those kids. They've glommed on to that dog like it's something special. There's a story there."

The fire would generate many stories from people who relished the limelight or at least didn't mind it. I was not one of those people. "I'm afraid that you'll have to find another story."

"Will you at least talk off camera?"

"No." I stepped around her.

Now all the students rose, except Nicole. Scottie crouched beside her and Dilsey, and the students let me through.

"–Can stay with you," Scottie was saying. "I'll stay with you too. We're going to Braxton Hall till your parents get here, okay?"

Nicole couldn't move with Dilsey plastered on top of her.

"Dilsey, come here," I coaxed.

When she uncharacteristically ignored me, I circled the group to face her and flashed her ball. She flicked her ears and blinked as sole acknowledgment. I stepped forward and pulled her away by her collar. Scottie and one of the guys eased Nicole up. When she started to fall, the young man tightened his arm and pulled her upright.

I leashed Dilsey.

Scottie motioned toward Braxton and asked me, "Could you come with us to the office?"

"I really need to get home."

"Please. Could you leave Dilsey here?" Her tone was soft, but left no room for argument.

I couldn't leave Dilsey with them. She rarely seized during the day, but *rarely* didn't mean *never*. Resigned, I followed Scottie and Nicole and the others through the milling media crews, the clusters of students who hadn't yet returned to their dorms, and the scurrying faculty members and staff futilely trying to make better what they couldn't.

En route to Braxton, Nicole melted into a sobbing heap. Scottie leaned over her, all encouragement. "We're almost there, just a little farther."

Nicole's friends watched silently.

I fidgeted, uncomfortable with the girl's outburst.

Dilsey bumped my leg. When I ruffled an ear, she lifted her muzzle, but her gaze remained on Nicole. I'd assumed Dilsey's natural friendliness had enticed her to the quad, but maybe canine intuition had drawn her there.

No, Dilsey was just a big, friendly Labrador retriever. No extra abilities were required. When Dilsey wedged herself between Scottie and Nicole, Scottie said to Nicole, "Dilsey's come to help you." The girl braced herself on Dilsey to stand and balanced against her as we shuffled the rest of the way to Braxton.

In the reception area of the English department suite, Scottie settled next to Nicole on the couch. Dilsey hopped up and lay across both women, her head on Nicole's shoulder, her thick tail dangling over the armrest. Nicole hugged her hard.

Hands in my jacket pockets, I leaned against the door-frame and waited for Nicole to release my dog. The other students sprawled on the chairs or on the floor by the Christmas tree or hovered around a table laden with cookies. I had no doubt that Scottie had baked the cookies. There was always food in the suite. Everyone loved the food—and her. She was vivacious, cute, and kind. I avoided her whenever I could.

She waved me over. "Make yourself comfortable. Dilsey will be here a while."

"How long is a while?" I asked, impatient.

"However long it takes Nicole's parents to get here."

Unless I wanted to make an ass of myself in front of the students, and I didn't, waiting was my only option. I draped my jacket over the back of Scottie's desk chair, the only un-occupied seat, and pulled a book from my backpack.

The students murmured among themselves, replaced an empty cookie tin with a full one, and tinkered with their phones. I opened my book and read the same two pages multiple times.

"Hey," one guy said, waving his phone. "They're about to stream the press conference."

Within minutes, President Randolph was droning all the expected responses: *an event of monumental propor-tions, we'll cooperate fully with investigators, make sure this never happens again.* He listed statistics: eight confirmed dead, eleven hospitalized with six in critical condition, five unaccounted for. He cited notification of next of kin as his reason for not identifying the casualties.

But the students knew who had died, or guessed, and whispered names among themselves while they hugged each other and cried quietly. I recognized a few as my students, but before I could process that information, Randolph began the inevitable, insipid, cover-your-ass platitudes about the emotional ramifications elicited by every *event of monumental proportions*.

I disconnected. The investigators had yet to speak, the reporters yet to query. Perhaps I'd skim a transcript later. Such events all seemed the same, though. We survived them and got on with our lives.

I opened my book again and concentrated through multiple chapters until a shift among the students interrupted me. A middle-aged couple hovered just inside the door. The students scrambled to their feet, directed goodbyes and thanks to Scottie as they edged around the couple, and filed from the office.

"Nicole?" said the man I presumed was her father. He sounded worried. "That dog . . ."

"She won't bother you," I said.

He shook his head. "Nicole's always been terrified of dogs."

Scottie freed her arm from around Nicole and caught my eye. "Dilsey's special."

I stood, and Nicole's parents approached their daughter. Together, Scottie and Dilsey relinquished their spots on the couch. Dilsey trotted to me, and when she leaned against me, I scratched her ears. After a moment, I leashed her, collected my jacket and backpack, and finally we headed home where the drama and angst of the fire couldn't touch us.

CHAPTER 2

SIX DAYS LATER, the scorched air from the fire had mostly dissipated, though when the wind blew right, I caught whiffs of its ghost. In my office early on that Monday afternoon, Dilsey had settled on her cushion under the windows with a bone.

My office, the only one on the third floor, was a long, narrow room with three-quarter-length windows. When Scottie assigned it to me late last summer, she'd apologized for its remoteness and assured me of a more accessible space when one became available. But I didn't want another office. I relished the seclusion and the way the shadows fell on the walls, and, for no other reason, Dilsey and I walked there almost every day, even after the fire cleared my academic calendar and eliminated my end-of-term responsibilities.

I scrolled through my university email. The administration had bombarded us with demands camouflaged as suggestions to modify our second semester course plans to incorporate the grieving process or allow students to express their feelings. They promised us information about identifying students who needed referrals for counseling– in other words, surrender the students to *authorities* who believed they must dictate how others should feel and for how long they should feel it. I couldn't delete those emails quickly enough.

Several students and a few parents had emailed about grades. I cut and pasted the information already outlined in the administration's correspondence from late last week.

The university public affairs director forwarded his latest press release. Delete.

The town's mayor pledged her support to the entire community. Delete.

Nothing to keep Dilsey and me from a stroll around campus.

A millisecond before I closed my email program, a new message popped up with the subject line *Looking for Info—November 20, 2005.*

My heart slammed in my chest, and despite the sudden blackness edging my vision, an afterimage—a deep purple morning in rural Tennessee—blazed sharply before fading. That morning's hard freeze should have melted into a sunny, brisk day, but for me, November 20, 2005, ended just before dawn.

I blinked away the image and the darkness and knew I would read the message even though every instinct warned against it. At a visceral level, I needed to know why, after ten years, *anyone* would mention that date.

When Dilsey nudged my hand, I scratched the groove between her eyes, and with my other hand I opened the email. The sender was Emily W. I didn't know an Emily W. The note contained no salutation.

> *I'm looking for information about a man named*
> *Vincent Gardner who died in Tennessee on*
> *November 20, 2005. All my internet searches link*

him to your family. I need to know why he attacked you. All I can find are news reports like the one I've attached. Because of the circumstances of his death, I should be able to at least find the police reports, but I can't. Please call or email me with whatever information you have. Thanks. Emily Warner

She included a phone number.

I drummed my fingers on the desk. Vincent Gardner. A name I'd heard a few times long ago. A name, I assured myself, I'd forgotten. But who was this Emily Warner? Why, so long after the fact, would she ask about Gardner? How was it any of her concern?

Reluctantly, as if the decision were out of my control—and appalled I was doing it—I clicked on the attached PDF: *Shooting News Article*.

The scanned article led with a banner headline—"South Carolina Senator, Oldest Son Remain Hospitalized After Shooting"—and a November 21, 2005, dateline. The splashy layout suggested the article was a feature, not straight news. The first two columns displayed a color photo of our family taken six weeks before that November date, when we'd gathered to celebrate our parents' twenty-fifth wedding anniversary.

I'd never seen the photo, a portrait from the formal dinner, my mother radiant in an emerald dress and the rest of us in jackets and ties. The caption identified each of us. My parents, seated, holding hands, gazing at each other rather than at the camera. Fanned behind them were my brothers, Jamie and Teddy, then me, and then our friend Henry, taller than me and despite the contrast of his ash blond hair with the various browns of the rest of us, as much a part of our family as if he'd been born into it.

"Aww," a dinner guest had called out, "the perfect family."
We had been.

Scattered throughout the article were other photos. My
father's official Senate portrait: navy suit, red tie, requisite
US flag lapel pin, and flag backdrop. My father speaking on
the Senate floor, stabbing an index finger at some point or
person. My parents at a parade they'd marshaled. A candid
of them, young and beaming, with all of us, as well as Henry,
picnicking on the lawn of the executive mansion when my
father was South Carolina's governor.

The smallest picture was of our assailant, Vincent Gardner. He'd been a decent-looking young man in what must
have been an old photo—frowning, but without the wild-
eyed expression I'd have imagined if I'd ever imagined him
captured by a photographer.

Only when Dilsey shifted position did I realize I'd dug
my fingers into her head. "Sorry, girl." I switched to scratch-
ing an ear.

I zoomed in to read the scanned article, but the words
blurred. I zoomed out and squinted. Should I even try to
read it? I'd never read any of the write-ups. Nor had I listened to or watched any coverage. No reason to; I'd lived the
events of that horrible day in person. Besides, by the time
the hospital released me five weeks later, the event was old
news and I refused to look back.

Never googled it. Whatever questions I might have had,
the news media couldn't answer.

Never brought it up with my family. Like me, they
never discussed what had happened with outsiders or
one another.

And early on, when college friends had asked, I'd shut them
down so emphatically, they never raised the subject again.

And yet I was looking back now.

I swept damp hair from my forehead and focused on the words.

South Carolina senator Bennett Rutledge expected to spend Thanksgiving break with his family, first on his annual hunting trip, then at his horse farm outside of Spartanburg. Instead, he'll spend it in a Nashville hospital with a gunshot wound to the chest.

On Friday, November 18, the senator, 49, his sons Philip, 20, Jamie, 15, and Teddy, 10, and family friend, Henry Linden, 20, traveled to a private hunting property in rural Sumner County, Tennessee.

Unnamed sources close to the investigation told The State *that shortly before dawn on Sunday, November 20, Vincent Gardner, 37, confronted the senator and Philip as they left the cabin. Jamie and Teddy, along with Linden, were inside at the time.*

After allegedly shooting Bennett and Philip Rutledge, Gardner was shot multiple times. Also shot was Teddy Rutledge. Sources declined to provide additional details, citing the ongoing nature of the investigation.

Teddy Rutledge and Gardner died at the scene. Bennett and Philip Rutledge were airlifted to a Nashville trauma center. The senator remains hospitalized in serious but stable condition. His son is in critical condition with gunshot wounds to the chest and shoulder.

Police initially detained Walter Driscoll, 57, caretaker of the hunting property, but released him after questioning. The State *reached out to him, but he didn't return our calls.*

*Sources declined to comment on a motive
for the shooting. Local authorities have turned
the investigation over to the Tennessee Bureau of
Investigation.*

*The senator's wife, Laurel, was not with her family
at the time of the incident.*

Without finishing the article, I scrolled back to the anniversary photo. *Also shot was Teddy Rutledge.* Teddy stood grinning between Jamie and me, like the rest of us, oblivious to the fact he had only six weeks to live. Thrilled to spend an extra weekend with older brothers who'd been away at college and boarding school, he'd badgered us into joining him in the hotel's stuffy, unoccupied indoor pool for multiple rounds of water polo—Teddy and me against Henry and Jamie. Teddy had even brought a ball.

I sagged in my chair and stared at my laptop, sucked in by the images of the perfect family juxtaposed with the narrative of the shattered one. How could they be the same family? What the article didn't say, what no one knew at the time, was that the family never glued its pieces back together.

For a few moments and then a few more, I breathed deeply and stared out a window, replacing images of a smiling Teddy with an empty blue sky. I could get a grip if I figured out who Emily Warner was and why she'd contacted me now.

She'd found me; I could find her.

I turned back to my laptop. When I googled her name, none of the hits proved that one of those women was the Emily Warner who'd emailed me. If I knew what she looked like or where she lived, I'd have quicker success.

I considered registering for a Facebook account to search for her there, but immediately dismissed the idea; I wasn't *that* desperate. I'd ask Henry to check her out.

Without thinking, my fingers typed *Vincent Gardner* into the search bar. On the three pages of results I scrolled through, every mention of him also referenced the shooting. I couldn't bear to read any of the articles to learn whether, as Emily Warner said, they mentioned our names. But how could they not?

I reread the email. Not only did I have no idea how to respond, I didn't know whether I should. I didn't have anything to tell her. Truthfully, from the articles she said she'd read, she'd learned as much as I knew.

I clicked on Reply.

Dear Ms. Warner:

I deleted the salutation; she hadn't used one.

My next attempt resulted in *Sorry, I'm unable to help you. Good luck in your search for information.* But I deleted that message too. I wasn't sorry and didn't wish her any luck.

Third time should have been that clichéd charm, but it wasn't. My inability to manage one buzz-off email to a stranger was ridiculous.

The shooting wasn't open for discussion. It never had been. I'd moved on from it. Thus, the most efficient way to ensure she'd drop the subject and leave me the hell alone was to call her and demand that she not contact me again. I punched her number into my office landline. It rang five times and, to my relief, rolled to voicemail.

"Hey, you've reached Emily Warner." The accent was familiar, the voice young. "Obviously, I'm unavailable, so please leave a message."

"This is Philip Rutledge, responding to your email. I have no information for you. Please *do not* contact me again. Not by email. Not by phone." Setting the receiver on its stand took two tries.

The woman's request shouldn't have rattled me. I'd created a life after the shooting that freed me from ever having to think about it. I refused to let even the residual effects of my injuries conjure memories of that day. I'd boxed up the details—the physical pain, the feelings—and shoved them all into the remotest corner of my psyche, and that was why I resented the swirling emotions she'd raised. She had no right to meddle. What was the *point*? After all that time, what was left to know? And why would anyone care?

Dilsey nudged my elbow. I swiveled toward her, grateful for the distraction, and hugged her. When I pulled away, she bounced her front half onto my lap and licked my face. I pushed her head aside, and she pressed it against my chest and sighed deeply, as only dogs can. We stayed like that for a few moments until my cell phone rang. Given the timing, it had to be Emily Warner. Except, I remembered with relief, she didn't have my cell number.

It was Henry.

"I'm backing out of our weekend plans. I can't gracefully miss the office party, and I have too much to wrap up before I head out."

"I understand." I could hardly complain. He'd spent practically every weekend with me since early October helping refurbish my fixer-upper of a house. In exchange, though it wasn't a fair one, I fed him and paid for season tickets to live theater in Richmond.

"Also, I'm bugging you, again, to go home for Christmas."

"I am home."

"You know what I mean. The farm. I'll even drive."

"And I'm telling you yet again . . ." I paused for effect, to make sure he heard me. "No. And not just no but hell no. I have nothing to say to them. I'm sure they have nothing to say to me." Instead of enduring days of tension-filled silence at the family farm, I'd enjoy a comfortable, familiar silence in my own home. That scenario had worked well for a decade.

"Everything's different now, though. You're so close." He laughed a little. "Geographically, anyway."

"Nothing's different." He needed to stop acting like he had a personal stake in whether I visited my family. I asked, "You know anyone named Emily Warner?"

"What?"

"Emily Warner. Ever heard of her?"

After a long pause, he asked, "Should I have?"

Only if she'd written to him. Maybe I was the first on her list. I hoped I was the last. "Probably not. Never mind."

After we disconnected, I was ready to get out. I shouldered my backpack, adjusting the straps on the right side until it was as comfortable as possible against my right shoulder and chest—which ached more than usual because Emily Warner made me think about the shooting—and walked with Dilsey out of Braxton and toward home.

I lived a mile northwest of campus. Once we left Central Avenue, the neighborhood streets narrowed and Victorian cottages were interspersed among 1950s bungalows. Dilsey and I maneuvered over cracked slabs of concrete distorted by the roots of old maples and dogwoods and around the occasional red wagon or Big Wheel, with her sniffing everything and me encouraging her to hurry along.

Walking usually cleared my head, but not today. *All my internet research for him came up with other names as well.* Those names would be my father's, Jamie's, Henry's, mine, and possibly even my mother's. Did Emily Warner write to everyone named in the article? Maybe she pursued me because the others hadn't responded in a way that satisfied her—or hadn't responded at all. If they hadn't, why not? Given my lack of any relationship with my family, I'd have no idea whether she'd contacted them, but Henry would've acknowledged a contact when I mentioned her.

Henry and the others aside, why couldn't she find information about Vincent Gardner and the shooting from sources other than media reports? Perhaps she didn't know how to conduct research, though between Google and Wikipedia, any idiot could find almost anything. I was pretty sure police reports were public domain. Sex offender records were available online, so why not records for the attempted murder of a US senator?

By the time I arrived home, I'd worked myself into enough of a nervous state that I carried a full bottle of cabernet and a glass onto the screened back porch. While Dilsey zoomed around the yard chasing real and imagined critters, I drank wine and talked myself out of worrying about Emily Warner. Since she hadn't bothered to mention who she was, why she was interested, or why she'd reached out now, she didn't warrant that much space—*any* space—in my head.

By the end of my second glass, I'd drifted on to considering the best time to raze the dilapidated detached garage behind the house. It annoyed me every time I sat out there, and it needed and deserved my attention far more than Emily Warner did.

But that question in her email skulked among more mundane thoughts and my plans for the garage.

Wouldn't you think I'd be able to at least find the police reports?

CHAPTER 3

ON THE COLD overcast Monday afternoon four days before Christmas, Dilsey and I took our routine seven-mile brisk walk around town. Despite the fire, Grainger had decked itself out for the holidays. Evergreen garlands wound against fences and porch railings, and holly and balsam wreaths adorned the doors of most businesses and private homes. Dilsey woofed and play bowed at a life-size inflatable Rudolph. Except for the occasional black band around a post or pinned to a wreath, no one would guess anything out of the ordinary had happened. Certainly nothing like a fire that had taken the lives of sixteen college students.

As we passed Braxton Hall, a silver Ford Focus crept by, then accelerated and continued along Central. Drivers often slowed to admire Dilsey.

The driver must have made a U-turn because a moment later the Focus approached from behind again and paralleled us in the wrong lane for a few yards before stopping. A girl, twentyish, popped out. She was short and whippet lithe with a blond ponytail.

"Need directions?" I asked. Dilsey, tail waving, smiled through her panting.

"No." She extended her hand. "I'm Emily Warner."

I gaped, caught so off guard that I couldn't speak. Finding my work email address was one thing. Showing up in Grainger and accosting me on the sidewalk was something else entirely.

"I was hoping you hadn't left for the holidays yet," she said, lowering the hand I'd ignored.

I backed onto Braxton's brown lawn, leaving Dilsey between us at the end of her leash. "I told you not to contact me."

With a perfectly straight face, she replied, "You said, 'Not by email. Not by phone.' You didn't mention in person."

Unbelievable. "What do you want?"

"I'm—" She flicked her eyes sideways, meaning she was about to lie. My students betrayed themselves that way all the time. "I'm working on a research project for my, um, criminal psychology class. I read about that shooting. It sounded, um, interesting. So I decided to write about it. I want to interview the actual people involved."

"Some of those actual people are dead."

She grimaced. "Please. I just want to ask you a few questions."

"Ask someone else."

"I tried. They never answered."

They? My family? "That's your answer."

"I wasn't *totally* sure you were the right Philip Rutledge, but after the fire, when you and your dog went viral and—"

"What are you talking about?"

"All those videos all over the internet. You looked about the same in those as in the pictures from the articles about the shooting. I *thought* the Philip Rutledge I'd found in the online faculty directory was you, but there wasn't a photo. I was trying to decide if I should call anyway, but then the fire happened, and well, I was sure." She pressed a hand to her chest. "I'm sorry about all that, the fire, I mean. That was really awful." She tucked both hands into the back pockets of her jeans and resumed talking without taking a breath. "So, I figured if you were sharing your dog with the students, you must be pretty nice, but then when you called me—"

"What's your *real* interest in that old news?"

"I told you. I—"

"Bullshit. You're a reporter, right? Writing an exposé to stir things up because of next year's elections or some political vendetta against my father?" I pushed into her face. "Money. Media attention. Selling yourself to your paper or some blog by tracking down old news and making it new again."

She backed up. "No. I just—"

"You're stalking me for the sheer hell of it?"

She flinched at my raised voice. "I'm not stalking you. I—" She straightened, and her body went rigid and still. "Vince Gardner was my father."

In the distance, a car alarm shrieked. No way. The man who shot Teddy had a child? I'd always considered him one-dimensional. A murderer and nothing else. It was inconceivable that he might have had a life outside that day—friends, a job, hobbies. A daughter.

"I don't believe you."

Dilsey swiveled her head between us, then stretched toward Emily Warner and nuzzled her hand. The young woman patted her without shifting her gaze from me.

"Prove it," I said.

She reached into her car, into her purse, extracted her wallet, and from that she pulled a small, tattered object that she held out to me.

Suddenly afraid she *could* verify her identity, I hesitated before reaching out my own hand. It was a photo, faded and crinkled, of a grinning Vincent Gardner standing behind a young girl, her wide smile illuminated by the candles on a birthday cake. Eight candles. The girl might or might not be the woman in front of me, but the resemblance was undeniable.

"Surely you can do better than *this*." I waved the photo.

"It's all I have of him," she said softly as she plucked it from my hand.

My gut told me she was telling the truth this time. "Why weren't you honest with me?"

"And *guarantee* you wouldn't talk to me? Because why would you"—she broke eye contact, as if seeking a way to escape what she threw at me next—"since you're the one who shot him, right?"

I stared at the sidewalk. A simple question no one had ever asked me. The people who needed to know always had known. There on the sidewalk, in a place I'd never have imagined addressing that question, the truth slipped out as easily as if I'd rehearsed a response I'd waited all along to say aloud. "Yes."

She clenched her fists and blinked repeatedly, but the tears I expected didn't materialize. In the nanosecond I contemplated that she might attack me, Dilsey jerked the leash from my hand to press against her, and Emily Warner focused on stroking Dilsey's head.

After a moment, she turned her attention back to me. I stood unmoving as she studied my face, searching for . . . I had no idea what.

"None of the news reports ever said who shot him, just that he died at the scene. I knew if your father had done it, the reporters would've been all over him. It could've been the caretaker, but the news would've said that, right? Your brothers and friend were inside. I was never totally sure, though, with you getting hurt and all."

Unexpectedly, I sympathized with her. She'd have been so young when her father died. What he did wasn't her fault.

But what I took from her wasn't my fault. What choice did I have? My father down and bleeding. Me, down and fading, but firing the shotgun I'd lost the mental and physical capacity to aim. I might have wounded Gardner by then, and Gardner had to have already killed Teddy by that point, because the additional shots between him and me tripped over each other, mine striking him in the face or forehead—exactly where, I never knew. Lucky shot for me, for us. Not so lucky for his daughter.

Not wanting to hear the question I needed to ask, I asked hoarsely, "What do you want from me?"

"I want answers. How'd your family know Daddy? Why would he want to hurt y'all? Where exactly in Tennessee did the attack happen? How'd he know where to find you? How'd it all happen? What did he say?" The questions gushed so rapidly, she had to stop to breathe. "And why can't I find anything official about the investigation?"

"I don't have answers to any of that. And even if I did, what next? You'll blackmail me or my family?"

Her hand on Dilsey's head froze. "What? No, I'd never do that."

For the second time, my intuition told me she was sincere.

The tears she'd managed to contain finally escaped. "I know you must think I have some nerve asking you for *anything* after what my father did to your family. But what he did left me without anyone at all, and I need to know why your family was more important to him than I was."

I turned my gaze away to give her privacy to pull herself together. Or to pull myself together.

"I get that that's not your problem, and you probably don't care. I know you don't owe me anything. But please. Let me show you the information I've found, get any that you have, maybe some leads. Then I'll leave you alone."

As much as I hated to admit it, in some warped way I *did* owe her. And I felt betrayed, as if by having a newsworthy fire, that Grainger University had violated its promise of anonymity to me. But that promise was entirely in my head, an assumption on my part that what Henry said was and would forever be true when he nagged me to move from Los Angeles to Virginia. *Grainger's perfect. A nondescript little place, hardly more than a crossroads. Nothing ever happens there. You can be as isolated as you want. And you'll never have to deal with earthquakes or fires!*

I'd accepted the position Grainger University offered, bought my house, developed lesson plans and taught my classes, politely but firmly declined social invitations, and settled into the relative isolation I craved and anticipated enjoying for the rest of my life.

Emily Warner wanted one discussion. I could do that. It would be short because I remembered little about the shooting and knew nothing about her father, including why he would have come after my family. Then I'd be done with her. She could hassle someone else or abandon her pointless quest for nonexistent answers, and I'd return to my peaceful life in quiet little Grainger and let her, and Teddy, recede into the past where they belonged.

I'd repay the debt that was no debt, and we'd both be satisfied.

"All right," I said.

She wanted to talk immediately, but I needed time to sort my thoughts, squelch my trepidation. We settled on seven thirty the next morning at McDonald's. She pulled away, revealing her car's license plate.

South Carolina. Where I grew up.

CHAPTER 4

WHEN I ARRIVED at McDonald's at seven ten the next morning, the silver Focus already sat in a parking spot by the entrance. I circled the nearly empty lot a few times, torn between getting the meeting over with or ditching it entirely, reminding myself why I'd agreed to meet Vincent Gardner's daughter. On my fifth loop, I parked on the far side of the building, cracked open the windows for Dilsey, and trudged inside.

She waved from a front corner booth. A thick loose-leaf teal notebook lay on the table beside her tray of food. I ordered coffee and oatmeal. The heavy smell of eggs and grease compounded my anxiety. My stomach churned.

Until that moment, I hadn't fully realized how intimidating the discussion would be. I couldn't rehash any part of the shooting in any way, not even for a girl who had a stake in it. Especially for her. What few details I remembered, I'd never shared with anyone and eventually had not only stopped mentally replaying the events, but also found myself almost denying the shooting had happened. And because it no longer seemed real, I was able to quit LA and return to the familiar southeast. And now this. I needed Emily Warner out of my life.

At her table, I tossed my jacket over the back of the booth and sat. "Didn't expect you here yet."

"Saw you circling."

I inhaled the steam from my coffee. "Ms. Warner–"

"Emily."

"I can't do this. . . . It's not–"

Quick as a striking snake, she gripped my wrist, almost knocking over my coffee. "Don't! It's taken me . . . You promised!"

I steadied the cup with my free hand and tried to pull away. She was stronger than she looked. "I'm sorry. I can't." Did she really not understand what she was asking? "You want me to talk about a shooting where I killed your father and he killed my little brother. Do you not get how upsetting–" No, this was far beyond upsetting. "How horrifying that all was?"

Her face went white, but she said, "Please, you don't have to say anything. Not yet. Just listen."

I shook my head.

She pursed her lips but didn't stay silent for long. "Is there something you're hiding?"

I jerked away and grabbed my jacket. "Don't be ridiculous. *He*–your father–attacked *us*." Not wanting to alarm the kid behind the counter, I leaned across the table. "He came to the place we were staying. *He* was the intruder. Hell, we didn't even know him."

"There's no way to confirm what happened, though, is there? Since apparently police records don't exist. Why would that be?"

"How the hell would I know? Maybe you're a shitty researcher."

She glared so intently, I focused on the empty counter. Usually the place was full of rowdy students, but even without the fire, they'd already have left for Christmas break.

"Please," she repeated.

I turned back to find her frowning.

"You met me here, so that must mean you know something."

"I don't. I've never talked with my family about the shooting."

"You have to. You were there. Most of your family was there. You can't expect me to believe that for ten years you've never discussed this!"

I wouldn't expect her to believe it, but it was true. From almost the moment of the shooting, our collective avoidance had defined our reaction to it: silence. The four of us who survived, and my mother, never discussed it, never mentioned the two who didn't survive, as if they existed only in a mutual nightmare that didn't bear remembering. And not talking about the shooting, not talking about Teddy, had left us unable to talk about anything else.

I slouched against the back of the booth. "Say what you have to say."

"Thank you." She nudged the notebook toward me. "Look at this."

I wrapped my hands around my warm cup. She popped the cover off her Big Breakfast and prepped her pancakes, meticulously placing a pat of butter in the center of each layer of the stack, crisscrossing through them with her plastic knife, and dumping two tubs of syrup over everything, including the eggs and sausage. She attacked the sticky pile, following each bite with a mouthful of soda.

I drained my coffee and reluctantly reached for the notebook. The D-ring binder was three inches thick and had an unadorned cover. The first five pages were a table of contents, a handwritten list of cities, states, and dates. Some entries ended with an asterisk. URLs filled both sides of the last table of contents page.

The binder contained originals of published articles taped or glued to notebook paper and hole-punched copies of others. There were printed screenshots. Everything concerned the shooting.

So many articles dating back so many years—the inch-high headlines of newspaper articles and colorful graphics from websites, my family's faces gazing from familiar photographs, that same photo of a young Vincent Gardner—and all I'd ever seen was the one article she'd emailed to me. Each page proved more difficult to turn than the previous one. All of this was so public and yet so intimate; I wanted to slam the notebook shut and walk out.

Instead, I shook my head. "Wow." The amount of information she'd collected astounded me.

"Mostly, they all say the same thing. I starred the most detailed ones."

"How long have you been compiling these?"

"Almost from the beginning."

I'd never considered the shooting as any kind of beginning. For me, it ended everything that mattered. "The beginning of what?"

"When I started looking for information. The beginning of all the changes in my life." She swirled her drink, grating the ice against the sides of the cup. "Anyway, even now, every few weeks I search again, hoping to learn something new."

"So, after years of collecting articles, why are you pushing so hard and approaching my family now?"

"Because I finally got old enough to do something about it."

Was it that simple? I closed the binder and slid from the suddenly claustrophobic booth. I needed a refill. More than that, I needed space between that notebook and me.

"Don't leave."

I nodded to my jacket on the back of the booth. "I'm not. Yet."

She flashed a quick smile and waved her cup. "Diet Coke, no more ice."

When I returned with our refills, she stabbed her straw into the lid and jiggled it up and down, an off-key instrument played by a novice.

"What happened that day?" she asked.

"I don't remember."

She raised her eyebrows but pressed on. "The last night Daddy and I were together was a week before that Thanksgiving. It was his bowling league night, and he let me take more of his turns than usual. Afterward, he let me have *two* orders of fries and Coke. For once, he didn't make me drink milk or eat any vegetables. I remember thinking, Wow, this is great! When he said he had to go out of town on a business trip, I was like, that's cool. I didn't think about it then–I was eleven–but he never had business trips. He managed local construction projects. He'd arranged for me to stay with friends. The next morning he dropped me off at school. I never saw him again."

Her mouth twitched. I busied myself with the oatmeal, tossing aside the lid and stirring in some sugar. *Don't you dare cry.*

She swallowed. "Thanksgiving break was the following week. On Monday afternoon, a social worker showed up, and more matter-of-fact than sympathetic, she told me Daddy died in a hunting accident. I was just another client, you know? And just like that, everything changed forever."

She opened the notebook and in two page flips apparently landed exactly where she wanted. "I know now where he's buried, but I didn't go to his funeral. Guess why? There wasn't one. And . . ." She turned the notebook around so I could read the simple obituary: name, city of residence, dates of birth and death. The photo was the same one from the article she'd emailed. "This obituary doesn't even mention he had family. Me."

Like she didn't exist. My long-held bitterness toward my parents for burying Teddy three days before they told me he'd died seemed petty by comparison.

I'd been in the ICU in Nashville. My mother perched on the edge of my bed, one arm around me, her other hand holding my hand. The one that didn't have an IV snaked into it. Beside her, my father supported himself on crutches. As medicated and sick as I was, I barely understood her words. They were murky and nonsensical, a dream. A nightmare. They stayed with me for what seemed like a long time. A nurse tried to usher them out, but they didn't leave. I drifted to sleep eventually, and when I woke, they were gone. When I remembered they'd visited and why, my anxiety triggered alarms that brought the nurses running.

No matter how awful that was, it was better than how Emily learned the news of her father's death.

"I'm sorry." I meant it.

She set her notebook upright against the wall, piled her napkins and utensils on her sticky tray, and pushed it aside. "The thing was, Mr. Rutledge, Daddy didn't hunt. But I was too scared and upset to mention the discrepancy between his supposed business trip and the supposed 'hunting accident' to that social worker or to anyone else. I didn't even know where he died. As soon as I could, I went to the library. Claimed I had a research project for school. I used a computer there to search the internet. The only reason I found anything about my father was because *your* father's famous."

I concentrated on my oatmeal. The injustice wasn't lost on me.

"Here's what I came up with for Daddy attacking your family. Political reasons, but I don't remember him ever mentioning politics. Jealousy—but of what? Or maybe he just snapped, but he was always so calm. Some personal disagreement, but there's no way he could have known any of you. Self-defense, but—"

"That's ridiculous."

"So are all the others."

"You left out the obvious one. Your father was a very bad guy." That was what I'd always imagined. Vincent Gardner was an evil man.

"No way." She sat back, folded her arms. "That's not how I remember him."

"You were a kid. Your memory is off. Besides, look at the facts, at what he did."

"But that's just it—I don't *know* the facts." She thumped the notebook, rattling our trays. "I know hardly anything. When Daddy died, I had no one else. You still had your parents and a brother and the same house and your nice cushy life. Daddy's death changed everything for me—how I lived and who I lived with and where. I never got to know what happened. Daddy lied to me and the social worker lied to me, and my foster families never said why. Maybe they didn't know." Using a crumpled napkin from her tray, she wiped her eyes.

I heard the despair in her voice. For a brief time, I'd yearned for facts too. But I'd shoved that longing aside so I'd be able to survive hour by hour, day by day, and year by year until I no longer needed, or wanted, answers. Meanwhile, a little girl fought through her confusion and loneliness and God knows what other overwhelming obstacles to stay motivated to uncover the facts behind stories she never understood. A begrudging sense of admiration seeped into me.

"Where was your mother?"

"I never knew her." She bounced her straw in her drink, as if deciding whether to say more. "She left when I was a baby. The one time I asked why, Daddy said it had nothing to do with me, and he'd tell me when I was older. I didn't get to be that old before he died."

Shit. It only got worse. "Why couldn't other relatives help you figure things out?"

"There aren't any other relatives. Daddy had a brother, but he died, and anyway, I never knew him." She sucked a mouthful of her Diet Coke. "When I was thirteen, I ended up with the Warners. They adopted me a year later. I couldn't have asked for better parents."

"Clearly you were better off without your father."

The fury in her eyes shocked me.

"How *dare* you say that. I'd never expect you to understand. *Your* father's still alive."

She was right. Again, I fought against the urge to apologize, and again I lost. "I'm sorry."

"Maybe I did have advantages with the Warners I wouldn't have had with Daddy. I'll never know. But that's not the point. He was a good father, the best. I loved him so much, and I was so hurt and angry at him for leaving me. How would *you* feel if your father did something terrible, without any warning, and it messed up your whole life forever, and you never knew why?"

"*My* father wouldn't."

"Yeah? I thought that about mine too. That's why figuring out why he shot at y'all is the most important goal in my life."

I finished my coffee, considering a response that never materialized. Emily and I existed worlds apart in every imaginable way, but long-unanswered questions about a single life-changing event bound us together. I'd discarded those questions, but Emily had fueled her life with them.

"There has to be *some* link between our fathers. Attacking a family isn't something Daddy would just do."

I shook my head.

"You know what I mean. If you think there's no connection, you'll help me prove it."

"You can't prove something that doesn't exist."

She folded her hands on the table. "Okay, I get it. It was awful for you, and you have this mental block about it or something." She tapped her notebook. "I think you hadn't seen a lot of these articles before, so either you're a psychopath who doesn't care or there's something else going on, but that mental block, that's your thing, so you don't need to tell me." She leaned forward. "But it could be that you're holding back because you're covering up something or for someone. I hoped you'd at least talk more, maybe use your connections to help me find people who might know or tell me why the police records are unavailable or exactly where it happened so I can go there. Maybe even go with me."

"It's private property." Or it used to be. "And why the hell would I go anywhere with you?" She wanted me to show her the scene of a multiple shooting—where her own father had died *by my hand*—and *I* was the mental case?

She lifted her chin. "Never mind. I'll figure it out without you. It'll be harder, but whatever it takes, however long it takes, I'll do it."

Exasperated by her stubbornness, I slid from the booth and snatched my jacket. "Just drop it. Nothing can fix what happened to you." *Or to me.* "Move on with your life."

"So, that's a no?"

"Correct."

When I reached the door, I glanced back. Her gaze struck me as wistful, defiant, and determined all at the same time.

And it haunted me long after I arrived home.

CHAPTER 5

BEEP-BEEP.

From my perch on the top step of the front porch, I jerked up my head, expecting Emily. She'd never left my thoughts, though I hadn't figured she'd need four hours to find me after I walked out on her that morning. But the car waiting on the driveway apron was bright blue, not silver.

I strode down the drive with Dilsey loping figure eights around me, and slid open the electronic gate. I'd enclosed my yard in a six-foot-high wrought iron fence for a reason. No one came in unless I knew who they were and allowed them in.

Scottie Marston leaned out her window. "You need a remote opener."

"I have one."

"Someone needs to show you how to use it." She grinned.

Dilsey bounced up on the window and spat her soggy ball into Scottie's lap. I pulled her off by the collar.

"I guess she wants me to throw it."

Scottie eased open her door and tossed the ball into the yard. She wore red jeans and a bright snowman-patterned polo, and she hadn't bothered to conceal the dark shadows under her eyes. Scottie's eyes were usually bright. *Scottie* was usually bright. Usually unfailingly upbeat. She was grieving for the students, the dead and the injured, and the ones hurting for the dead and the injured.

"Can I help you with something?" I sounded like a stuffed shirt, even to my own ears.

"Happy to see you too." She yawned. "Special delivery. Since the fire, I can't sleep through the night, so I bake. And I can't eat *all* of the goodies myself."

"Why can't you sleep?"

"Thinking about the kids—the ones who died and the survivors. The emergency crews. And Grainger, town and university both."

In the hours after the fire, when she helped Nicole and let the other kids hang out in the department's suite, I'd assumed she was just doing her job or what she considered her job. I hadn't realized the fire had affected her so personally.

"A few weeks from now, everyone will be all right," I said.

She shook her head. "How can you even think that?"

When I didn't reply, she opened the Kia Soul's back door.

Two suitcases topped by a garment bag lay across the flattened back seats. Behind them, a mountain of wrapped gifts. When Scottie faced me again, she held a rectangular tin, long and deep, decorated with Labrador retrievers wearing Christmas bows and holly sprigs. She thrust it at me. "These are for Dilsey, a thank-you for helping out with the students. No corn, wheat, sugar, or preservatives."

"Wow." How nice. I had no idea she knew how carefully I guarded Dilsey's diet. More likely a lucky guess.

She stacked a second tin, round and green with silver snowflakes, on top of the first. "Couldn't bring treats for her and not you. Note that yours aren't as healthy. Except for no preservatives." She smiled. "Merry Christmas."

"Thank you."

"You're welcome." She called to Dilsey, walked to the front of her car, and studied my house. "It hardly looks the same."

"Same as what?"

"The same creepy *Addams Family* house as when I was in college."

"You went to Grainger?"

"Class of '07. We had a whole lot of fun here. Someone had jimmied open a few windows. The house had water but no power; we partied anyway. Rumor was, Grainger students had been doing that long before my time."

No surprise there. The paraphernalia I'd found while cleaning up the property and the house's interior—T-shirts, pantyhose, shriveled condoms, and enough empty beer cans to fill an NFL stadium dumpster—had revealed my home's apparently not-so-secret history.

The modified red brick Craftsman, 1919 vintage, was spacious and architecturally distinctive, and it sat on nearly two acres. Every other house the agent showed me seemed to scream *pick me, pick me*. But this one had hunkered, abandoned and forlorn beneath the old hardwoods guarding it, never expecting to be chosen. Only rodents, insects, and at least three snakes had occupied the house. Inexplicably drawn to its charm, I'd purchased the house inexpensively four months earlier. It needed considerable professional attention to make it habitable, so Henry's place in Richmond remained my home base until early November, when I moved in. Since then, he and I had chiseled away at the finishing touches.

"Can I get the grand tour?" Scottie asked.

"It's not finished yet." I hoped my curt response impressed on her that, cookies notwithstanding, I didn't want anyone in my house. Henry didn't count.

Dilsey delivered her ball to me, and with my left hand I balanced the cookie tins against my chest to free my right one to throw it. *Lob* it, more like. I hadn't been able to throw anything on that side for a long time.

"It's still a cool house. I'm so glad someone finally loves it. *Please* give me a tour when it's finished."

I hesitated, then shrugged. "Sure." Since she didn't get the hint, what else could I say, holding the homemade goodies she'd delivered? Most likely she'd forget her request, and I'd never have to follow through.

She cocked her head. "I'm curious. Why does a single guy need such a huge house?"

"It has a big yard for Dilsey."

"Okaaaaay." She pitched the wet ball Dilsey presented her. "What're you doing for Christmas?"

"Staying here."

"Alone?"

"With Dilsey. Working on the house."

"That's so sad."

I shook my head. I always relished the uninterrupted block of time the holidays provided. This year I'd read, mask the guest bedrooms so Henry and I could paint them after New Year's, and maybe do a little yard work. I'd settled on Christmas dinner too: steak on the grill, baked potato, and a big salad. "Not at all." Politeness dictated that I inquire about her plans, but hoping not to extend her visit, I didn't.

"I'm leaving from here to drive home, northern Virginia. On the twenty-sixth, we're flying to Miami to board a cruise ship to the Caribbean."

She did a happy wiggle, letting me know she was hoping to enjoy her cruise. Or maybe that she was planning to live it up for a few days while touring the islands. Okay for her, but being confined in close quarters on a ship made me shudder. "Have fun."

She laughed. "Don't look so appalled. Not my idea, though it sounded fun when we planned it. Since the fire, I'd rather stay home and just *be* with everyone. You never know when it'll be the last time you'll see them, you know?"

"I do know." I didn't mean to respond aloud and changed the subject before she noticed. "Thanks again for the cookies."

"You're very welcome. Enjoy. Gotta run. Merry Christmas and Happy New Year."

After she left, I returned to the front steps and peeked inside Dilsey's tin. Scottie had taped an impressive list of healthy ingredients to the inside of the lid. The treats themselves were shaped like snowmen, Christmas trees, bells, and dog bones. I prepped Dilsey's food from scratch, but I'd never made her anything so special.

Dilsey sat on the bottom step, her eyes pleading. The gingery snowman I tossed her was gone in two chomps. Her tail swished hopefully until I covered the tin. She flipped around and streaked away.

Baking struck me as an odd replacement for sleep. Maybe what actually made Scottie feel better wasn't the baking per se but rather the baking served as a way to interact with others. She was always doing that. Maybe her presence or her attitude, not the goodies, was why the students liked her. In the case of the Carter Hall fire, though, engaging with the students was tantamount to immersing oneself in misery. Better to brace against the drama and misery, which would end. They always did.

I'd never understand people like Scottie, but that wouldn't stop me from enjoying the cookies she'd brought.

My tin contained no ingredients list but a variety of basic cookies like chocolate chip and oatmeal plus thin lacey snowflakes, peppermint bark, and fancy sugar cookies with colored sprinkles. And *fudge*. I lifted the top cookie: oatmeal raisin with red and green M&Ms. The raisins resembled flies. I should've been repulsed, but I bit into it, remembering Henry's first Christmas at the farm when we were twelve and how he'd horrified Jamie with the insects he'd frozen into ice cubes and sneaked into his Cokes.

I'd caught Henry in the walk-in freezer, door ajar, tweezing dead horseflies—abundant on a horse farm even during the winter—into four plastic ice trays. He poured bottled water over the insects and stashed the trays behind stacked packages of steak.

"Hey," he'd said, apparently feeling not the least bit guilty.

We both got punished: Henry for terrorizing Jamie, me for tattling. Henry's "you're-not-my-father" whine earned him additional kitchen chores for the duration of Christmas vacation. My smirk earned me whole-house vacuuming, and our house was big.

Henry never divulged how he'd managed to sneak his special ice cubes into the drinks. "You don't get to know everything," he'd said more than once.

I swallowed the last bite of cookie and had another. Scottie had packed the tin so full that even with two cookies eaten, I had to thump the lid to seal the tin, but not before I inhaled the drifting sweetness.

Our house had always smelled like that during the holidays, and suddenly I wondered whether my mother still baked holiday cookies. And that had me wondering about all the other holiday traditions. Who selected the Christmas tree now? Did they even have one? Did they still wrap the photos and artwork on the living room walls with Christmas paper, ribbon, and frilly bows? Did they still garland the fences along the road with cedar swags and decorate the barns with wreaths?

An overwhelming longing to be at the farm pummeled me. I attributed the yearning to nothing more than my conversation with Scottie, Henry's prodding, and the scent memory of the cookies, and I tried to shake it off. The reality of being there could never measure up to the memories. The memories couldn't even measure up to themselves.

Panting, Dilsey scrambled up the steps to sit beside me and groaned with pleasure when I scratched her shoulder. Whatever Scottie's family was like, mine was nothing similar. My feelings of nostalgia and yearning would pass.

I thought again about Emily Warner, questioning why her plea for help affected me so deeply. And it *had* affected me. Was it because, like me, she was a casualty of her father's actions? Because I felt protective of her, as I would a little sister? Because I respected and even admired her need to learn the truth? Because now that she'd asked them, I couldn't unhear her questions? Or maybe I was disturbed because of the not-insignificant fact that I had killed her father. That might be all that my uneasiness was, nothing more than guilt exacerbated by her heartrending story. The fact that I'd never told anyone that I'd killed a man, forcibly hiding the secret, might also be a factor. Not that I remembered killing him. But after my father went down, it was only me and the silhouette of an armed man a few yards in front of me. I'd been able to connect the dots.

I couldn't imagine how Emily must feel, being the child of a man who'd perpetrated such a terrible crime, especially when that crime was inconsistent with what she believed about him. Perhaps she was correct in suggesting that if my father had, with one action, altered so many lives, I'd be as intent as she was to find answers. For Emily, maybe having answers was the only way to move on.

By telling her she was on her own, I'd done the only logical thing. She'd figure it out or not. As I rose with cookie tins in hand, Dilsey bolted after a squirrel. I leaned on the brick post, giving her a few more minutes to play.

Perhaps I should ask Henry again, and my father and Jamie, too, whether Emily had contacted them. No way she'd get my father's personal contact information, but his Senate email was accessible. She said that no one had responded, so perhaps she didn't actually reach them or she asked inappropriate questions or, like me, they just wanted to forget everything to do with that time. And maybe they simply had no more information than she had.

I shifted when an unwelcome thought hit me—maybe someone was hiding something. I could simply ask them what they knew, and then I could dismiss Emily from my thoughts.

That would be perfect.

As consolation for the uneasiness I felt, I brushed crumbs off my shirt and indulged in a third cookie. Maybe I *should* go to the farm, get some answers. I hadn't been there, hadn't even seen my parents or brother Jamie in more than nine years, not since I'd left for my senior year of college in August 2006. I could leave tomorrow. An easy five-hour drive, not like when I lived in LA. No need to make a big deal of it. Work in a question or two about the shooting, but otherwise stay out of everyone's way. Just be there, as Henry had suggested. If nothing else, Dilsey would enjoy a new place to explore.

My mother had never allowed dogs in the house, but Dilsey needed to stay with me. And maybe she had loosened the rules.

If I were really curious, I could shoot emails to my father, Jamie, and Henry. If they responded, fine. If not, fine. But with email messages, I'd miss nuanced evasions or outright lies. In person, I wouldn't.

Damn it, why would I expect an evasion or lie?

Only one way to find out.

Henry was at work, but so he could reply at his convenience—or perhaps so I didn't have to deal with his smug teasing—I texted him.

I might have changed my mind—if I can be sure Dilsey can stay inside.

My phone rang immediately. "It's that simple?" Henry asked incredulously.

"You know it isn't. But I won't go if she can't."

"Stay tuned," he said.

Henry would call my mother, and she'd say yes or no. Saying no because she didn't want Dilsey there was one thing. Saying no because she didn't want me there was quite another. At least I wouldn't know the difference. Not that it mattered. Visiting the farm hadn't been in any scenario I'd imagined.

Five minutes later, my phone pinged with a text from Henry forwarding a text. I read it twice, hardly believing my mother's response.

OF COURSE his dog can stay in the house.

Underneath, he'd provided her cell number.

I didn't need it, though, because the text that followed his was from my mother herself. *Tell me when you'll be here.*

CHAPTER 6

THE NEXT AFTERNOON, Henry arrived at my house straight from an early departure from his office. I'd have preferred to meet him at the farm, but he insisted on riding with me. No doubt he expected me to back out, and I'd lain awake the previous night considering that very idea. If it weren't for Emily Warner, I would have. On the other hand, if it weren't for her, I'd never have considered going in the first place.

Henry often knew me better than I knew myself.

He transferred his suitcase from his sleek red Mercedes coupe to my cavernous white Expedition. Dilsey hopped into her crate and trampled her blankets into a messy nest. My gate slid shut behind us.

Henry held up an audio book, Grisham's latest. "I'm a third of the way through. You mind?"

"Not enough legal thrills at work?"

"In real estate law? Hardly."

"Still amuses me that a bad boy like you ended up practicing law."

"The joke's on my clients."

I laughed, and as we drove south through the rain into the approaching dusk, I tuned out the book and reflected on how much more uncomfortable I'd be about the visit without Henry as a buffer.

In the Virginia boarding school we'd attended as young children, everyone knew Henry Linden because he was always in trouble. He and I hadn't spoken, though, until one January afternoon in the headmaster's office. Henry had burned my American history report with a contraband Zippo lighter. He'd also accessed my computer and deleted the report from that. His actions weren't personal. My name just came up in his mental list of kids he hadn't bullied yet or enough. He wouldn't have known I carried the entire report in my head and that it was no big deal to simply rewrite it, which I did immediately after the headmaster dismissed me.

A few weeks later, some administrator decided I'd be a good influence on Henry and made us roommates. Complaining got me nowhere, so I ignored my new roommate. No matter what he said to or about me, no matter what he did, I pretended he didn't exist. Ignoring a bully who tried all sorts of craziness to get my attention wasn't easy—I was only eleven—but my attitude proved to be a good lesson in handling adversity. As a bonus, my total disregard of him infuriated him. Short of physically harming me, which wasn't his style, he had no recourse.

When my mother picked me up for Easter break, Henry blustered that *he* was allowed to stay at school because he didn't need parents to babysit him. Mom raised her eyebrows and obtained whatever permission she needed to bring him to the farm for the week. He didn't protest. I did.

Inexplicably, we became nearly inseparable. During the following years, he spent every vacation with us. We rode and hunted together. He improved my tennis game, and I improved his study habits. We lusted after the same girls. He dragged me into trouble I'd never have found alone, and on more than one occasion I dissuaded him from pranks that might have gotten him expelled or worse. He learned how to survive among siblings. Eventually, we chose the same university and roomed together.

Even after the shooting.

Hard as I tried to withdraw from everyone, I couldn't shake Henry. He visited me frequently during the semester and summer of my rehab. When I returned to school the following August intending to live alone, he spent so much time loitering in my dorm room that I gave up and let him move in. The truth was, I relished his obnoxious humor and found our mutual memories surprisingly comforting.

He attended law school at the same university where I attended graduate school, and we shared an apartment. Even after that, I couldn't dodge his relentless attempts to stay connected, however remotely, through the series of moves that ultimately landed him in Richmond to practice commercial real estate law and me in Los Angeles to teach literature and composition at a community college. He never stopped urging me to move back east, even sent me the job posting for the low-level instructor vacancy at Grainger. LA, Grainger, whatever. It was all the same.

Abruptly realizing the audio book had gone silent, I glanced at Henry.

"Want me to drive? We'll get there sooner," Henry said.

"Can't go faster than the flow of traffic." Which at the moment wasn't particularly fast.

"Unless you create the flow."

"Uh-huh. What makes you think my father would be more likely to bail you out for speeding today than he was the first time?"

"Why do you always bring that up?"

"You'd get more than a night in the county jail now."

Henry laughed. "The worst part wasn't even that. It was all those farm chores to repay our fines and no driving for the whole damned summer. We weren't going *that* fast, and there weren't any other cars on the road."

"We were racing, Henry."

"He should have taken pity on us. Sixteen with new licenses and a deserted country road! But no, he had to prove we weren't entitled to special treatment just because he was a senator."

We motored along for another forty-five minutes, again listening to Grisham, until Henry ejected the book. "I'm starving."

It was seven. Thanks to the weather and the holiday traffic, we still had three hours to drive, mostly on four-lane highways and surface roads. I should've brought Scottie's cookies instead of stashing them in the freezer.

At the Chick-fil-A we found a few miles later, the parking lot was full and the drive-through line wrapped around the building. I dropped Henry off to order inside and created a parking space by the dumpster so I could feed and walk Dilsey. When I finished, I circled the building to wait for Henry.

Without meaning to, I pictured Emily Warner as I'd left her the previous morning at McDonald's. She hadn't looked defeated, but she had been crushed.

I'd agreed to meet with her out of politeness—and some guilt—and I'd done that. I hadn't promised her anything, hadn't even hinted I'd help answer her questions, the same questions I'd raised with my parents a decade ago. Yet more guilt, as if I'd lied to her or abandoned her, crept over me. And that was on top of the emotions that still churned in me for having killed her father.

After all those years of repressing the shooting, now I imagined it being anything from some random or convenient crime of opportunity by Gardner the psychopath to a meticulously executed plan by Gardner the brilliant strategist. Even if Emily wasn't objective about how good a parent he was—and I assumed she wasn't—why would he abandon her to either his death or permanent incarceration? If he had a specific target, who had it been? Most logically, my father, but my assumption could have been off base. And if it had been him, even my father didn't seem to know why. That lack of a reason troubled more than just Emily.

Psychopath or not, Gardner had found us. So, that had to mean something. The private hunting property in central Tennessee was so remote, it's a wonder that my father's friends had found it to purchase.

On the day of the shooting, there were few people around, even fewer vehicles, so why hadn't at least one of us spotted him? Surely he hadn't waited outside through the frigid November night. Even if he had, the pointers in the kennel adjacent to the cabin should have alerted us. They barked at everything else.

I pressed my palms against my throbbing forehead. When the rear hatch opened, I flinched. Dilsey's tail rattled the sides of her crate, and she smacked her lips.

"Henry, don't give her anything."

"Just a fry. It won't kill her."

As soon as Henry settled into his seat, I headed for the interstate. By the time the smell of fast food enticed me to unwrap my lukewarm sandwich, he'd nearly finished his second and had devoured his fries and some of mine.

"What happened between the time I went into the restaurant and the time I came out?" he asked around a mouthful of chicken.

"What?" He'd always been able to read me.

"You're regretting the trip already."

"Yeah, well, I need to ask my parents about the shooting."

Henry shifted in his seat. More low than quiet, he said, "*What?*"

I braced my phone on the steering wheel and logged into my email. "Read the note from Emily W." I handed him the phone.

"'Thanks for meeting yesterday morning. I know I laid a lot on you, but I hope you'll at least think about it some more. I'll be in touch. Merry Christmas. Emily.'" He shook the phone in my face. "What is this?"

Wonderful. I blew out a lungful of air, annoyed at the new message I hadn't read. "I meant the one from the four-teenth. Read that. And the attachment."

"Yeah, so?" He responded so quickly, he could have only scanned them.

I described our two encounters, who she was, what she wanted and why, and he listened without interrupting. I finished by asking, "Did she contact you?"

"Her name's not familiar." He balled up our trash, stuffed everything into one bag, and tossed it to the floor. "How did you leave things with her?"

"I basically told her to get lost. Except—"

"Good. Though apparently she didn't listen."

"Except I feel guilty." I'd admitted that truth to Emily, a stranger, but before that I'd never said the words aloud, not even to Henry. I focused on the road, then took a quick look at him. "For killing her father." It was easier that time.

When he said nothing, I looked at him again.

His eyes were wide, his face frozen. He eventually opened his mouth, but immediately snapped it shut.

"Don't look so shocked. You thought I didn't know? I figured it out in the hospital, around when Mom and Dad told me about Teddy."

He leaned against the door, arms crossed, his anxiety evident even in the darkness. A time or two he started to speak but never finished, and he eventually jammed the thriller back into the CD player. We rode without talking until we turned onto the road to the farm.

"Don't ruin everyone's Christmas by mentioning that girl. Or the shooting."

"I won't ruin anything."

"Can't you just celebrate Christmas with your family?"

Celebrate? That wasn't possible, but perhaps I *should* drop the whole Emily thing and politely endure the holiday. After ten years of silence, how could I possibly mention the shooting? I certainly didn't need to. I'd never contact Emily, and maybe she'd never contact me again. If she did, I'd ask Henry to send her a cease-and-desist letter, though a damn letter wouldn't erase the questions she'd raised.

Questions that even now raced nonstop through my mind.

CHAPTER 7

THE PAVED DRIVE to the farm's main entrance diverged abruptly from the road and headed into dense pines and hardwoods. Iron double gates flanked by brick columns connected the wrought iron fencing that stabbed upward on either side of the drive. Lights in the guardhouse outside the fence meant it was manned and that one or both of my parents were on the premises. At least, that's what it had meant in the months after the shooting. It hadn't always been that way. The shooting changed everything.

The rain had slackened slightly when, right after ten, Henry and I pulled up beside the shack. A short stocky guy wearing a holstered sidearm approached. He'd worked private security for my father for fifteen years.

I lowered the window. "Hey, Zack."

"Evening, Henry," he called across me.

"Helloooo," I said, annoyed. Just because he hadn't seen me in a while didn't mean he couldn't be polite.

He squinted. "Being as how you're a stranger here, I should run your ID and search your vehicle."

Henry laughed. "I'll vouch for the loser."

Zack retreated to the shack and triggered the gates.

"Merry Christmas to you too," I called as they clanged shut behind us.

I flipped on my brights and crept through the red maples lining the half-mile drive that wound to the house. They'd have shed the last of their leaves six weeks earlier, and the drive was clear of debris. At the fork, I bore left toward the house, away from the road to the barns and the horses, the arenas and pastures, and beyond them the pond, our tree house, and the family cemetery.

The house gleamed in the strategically placed spotlights, and I stopped to absorb the sight.

Rich red brick accented by fat white columns. Four steps, wide and deep, rising to the covered front porch that wrapped around the sides and the back. Floor-to-ceiling windows with working shutters and double doors adorned for the season with enormous red-bowed evergreen wreaths. A second-floor balcony with doors off each bedroom. Above that, dormers to the high-ceilinged attic that was actually a third story.

Finished in 1813, the house had been updated with modern conveniences by every Rutledge generation since. Nothing added to the house, and nothing that happened to its occupants through the years, detracted from its architectural beauty.

"Miss it?" Henry asked.

I jerked the Expedition forward. Had I missed it even a little? It was lushly elegant, with a detailed history–a history that I'd loved discovering–going back almost two centuries. It contained hidden nooks and recesses where as children we'd invented our own happy little worlds, worlds that grew and expanded as we'd grown and our interests had changed.

I was practically an adult when Teddy was old enough to enjoy those spaces. With him, I'd rediscovered them. I turned away. Miss all that? "Why would I?"

The parking area around back glowed like a sports stadium. The only vehicles there were a black Lincoln sedan and a couple of golf carts. I pulled in beside the Lincoln.

Henry stretched and yawned. "I'm finishing my book before I go in."

"You can do that later." I hadn't expected to have to greet my parents alone. "Don't abandon me."

"I'm almost at the end." He smirked. "Besides, they're *your* parents. I'm giving y'all a few moments of alone time."

"I don't want alone time." I couldn't imagine what I'd say to them—until I asked about Emily Warner.

Henry pushed the audio book into the CD player. "Go."

I dragged my suitcase along the brick walkway. Maybe it was better this way, me alone with them, and no Henry to increase the stickiness with banter only he considered funny. Spotlights illuminated the back porch, still lined with oak rockers and side tables and sheltered by the balcony above it. At the northwestern corner of the house, lamplight shone from the bedroom that used to be mine.

Standing on the porch, I turned the doorknob but hesitated. *I should knock.* No doubt Zack had called in our arrival, but I was a stranger now, and one with no idea how welcome I might or might not be.

On the other hand, my mother *had* sent that text about Dilsey. And there was still Emily. Remembering why I'd come, I opened the door.

The live Christmas tree stood in the exact center of the wide hallway that ended at the front door. Even the tallest trees fit there without touching the ceiling. Until Teddy died, we always selected a Virginia pine as a family and decorated it together. As we grew, we hung our special ornaments on the branches we were tall enough to reach.

Even when Jamie and I attended our distant boarding schools, we'd always returned for that tradition. Teddy had never gotten old enough to leave.

My fingers tightened around the handle of my suitcase.

This year's tree, a cypress, was lush and dark green-gray. Ornamental balls of varying size and color reflected light from tiny blinking bulbs. Nothing personal embellished the token acknowledgment of a time when the intimacy, festivity, and joy of the holidays was authentic.

At least they had a tree. I'd never bought one for myself.

The last time we'd all decorated a Christmas tree, the year Teddy was nine, he declined to hang his favorite ornament, a ceramic Santa reading a book. I'd given it to him right before that Christmas, which turned out to be his last. He placed the ornament on his desk and would've left it there all year if Mom hadn't insisted he add it to the ornament box when we stripped the tree. We did that as a family, too, every New Year's Day.

Centering the trees in the hallway provided unlimited space for the fountain of gifts, but this year the floor around this cypress was bare.

"We stopped giving gifts," Henry had told me years ago. "After everything that happened, what's the point?"

"Welcome home." The words came from behind me. My mother always could sneak up on us.

I turned slowly, blinking away the memories.

She stood alone by the sweeping, open stairway to the bedrooms, one hand resting on the banister, as unpretentiously camera-ready as always. But now she bore a few unfamiliar lines at the corners of her kind brown eyes and across her forehead. The instant the thought formed that I might have been partly responsible for those, I dismissed it. She wouldn't have worried about me that much.

"Thank you," I said without approaching her.

"You had a good trip?" She inched forward.

"We did."

"And traffic?"

"About as you'd expect."

"Henry helped you drive?"

"I drove."

She stepped forward again but offered nothing else. Since she didn't ask about Henry's whereabouts, she must have conspired with him to greet me alone.

I struggled to bridge the chasm of years of silence before she reproached me for my long absence or my need to bring Dilsey or whatever she might choose to pounce on. "Anyone else here yet?" Then I remembered that the parking area contained only my Expedition and one other road vehicle.

"Jamie arrived yesterday, but he's out with friends tonight. Dad flies in early tomorrow afternoon."

So I had to endure the awkwardness twice. I hadn't planned on that, and I didn't like it. On the other hand, at least I could ease into my return with my mother before having to deal with my father.

"The fire at your school—you're handling that okay?"

"Nothing to handle." I might have sounded terser than I intended.

"It's okay to feel sad about it, Philip. Such a terrible thing and right before the holidays."

She edged close, and when she laid her hand on my right shoulder, I flinched.

"Any more physical problems?"

"I'm fine." She'd always seen right through the half-truths I'd spun about my injuries, but they were what they were. To distract her from additional questions, I swiveled my suitcase toward the staircase. "I should finish unloading the truck. If you'll tell me where I'm sleeping . . ."

"Where you're sleeping?"

The instant she realized what I meant, that I didn't assume that my childhood bedroom was still mine, that I considered myself a guest, she reached out and hugged me as desperately as Nicole had squeezed Dilsey after the fire.

I inhaled the sudden comfort of her still-familiar citrus perfume.

She kissed my cheek and looked me in the eye. "Don't ever insinuate you don't belong here. Ever. Do you understand me?"

"Yes, ma'am. I—"

"Hush. Your room is ready and waiting for you. Leave your bag here, and let's get Henry and your dog and finish unloading."

"It's raining. He and I'll bring everything in."

"I won't melt." She smiled and accompanied me into the chilly drizzle.

Henry hopped up from his perch on the edge of the cargo hold beside Dilsey and hugged my mother. "Merry Christmas."

"Thank you, Henry."

Dilsey twirled in her crate and woofed softly. I leashed her, and when I eased her to the ground, she sat in front of Mom, perfectly still except for her tail. I relaxed. Mom couldn't help but love her.

"Nice manners," she told Dilsey. To me she said, "Henry explained she has seizures. Is that why she needs to be in the house with you?"

"It is. Usually they happen overnight. Not every night or even every week. But sometimes she needs medication to stop them, so I keep a close eye on her."

She petted Dilsey's head but studied me intently enough that I blinked uncomfortably. "I see." She tapped her chest, and Dilsey bounced up on her and snuffled her ear.

"She's not allowed to jump on people."

"Don't be so rigid. I invited her." Right in front of me, my mother bonded with my dog. That boded well, considering she had agreed to allow Dilsey into the house. "She looks so healthy."

Healthy like the dogs and cats we'd always had around the farm and like the horses that appeared to be healthy until they didn't. So many times our mother repaired, or tried to repair, the broken wildlife we presented her. Some of them looked fine too. Some of them survived.

"Other than the epilepsy, she's incredibly healthy." And I intended to keep her that way, no matter the cost or inconvenience.

Henry and my mother unloaded the truck, and I walked Dilsey to the grassy edge of the parking area. I'd let her loose tomorrow, in the daylight, when I could find her if she chased anything.

As Henry lowered the hatch, my mother gestured toward Dilsey's crate. "Crib bumpers?"

"Just keeping her comfortable."

If she seized, they'd prevent her mouth and legs from catching in the wire sides. I'd hunted for the softest generic bumpers I could find, but the best I could do was ducklings and lily pads. Labs are duck retrievers, but the bumpers may have looked a bit silly.

We hauled Henry's bag, the large wheeled cooler with Dilsey's food and bowls, the tote bag in which I stored her medication—red, so in an emergency anyone could identify it—and her ball, brush, and travel bed into the house in one trip.

My mother chuckled. "Dilsey has more luggage than you boys do."

"Miss D has more and better everything," Henry said. "It's crazy."

I stowed Dilsey's food in the refrigerator, and she trotted away to explore the downstairs. Henry unwound at the kitchen table with a beer.

My mother set a plate of cookies in front of him. "Jamie will be home shortly. He'll be so happy to see you, Philip." She patted Henry on the head. "And you too."

"He'll have to wait till morning." I yawned so widely, she rolled her eyes. "It's way past my bedtime."

I declined offers of help and carried my suitcase and Dilsey's water bowl and bed up the stairs. She dashed ahead to the second floor. On the landing, I stopped to examine the unfamiliar artwork. When I'd returned a few weeks after the shooting, our numerous family photos had disappeared. The wall had remained blank when I was last there. Two landscapes had since commandeered the space.

There'd been so many photos—the best of the silly candids we took of each other, and the matted and collage-framed hanging adjacent to the annual professional portraits my parents insisted on. A series of photographers, alternately frazzled and supplicating, prodded us reluctant children—at first just me, then Jamie, then Teddy, and finally Henry, too—into traditional portrait configurations and then commanded the bursts of rehearsed smiles we rarely coordinated.

My favorite portraits were those with the horses. When my brothers and I each turned ten, we posed with our first big horse. The portraits of Teddy and me were nearly identical: boys with wavy light brown hair and root-beer eyes, each of us looking shyly away from the camera, right hand grasping the reins just below the bit on a gentle-eyed gelding. Their heads rested on our shoulders, ears attentive. But those photos—and horses—were long gone. Had my parents stored the photos and now forgotten where they were? No, they'd have discarded them altogether. I squeezed the handle of my suitcase and wondered whether I'd ever ask.

I finished my climb when Dilsey barked from the top of the stairs. Doors to six of the seven bedrooms were open. Diagonally across the hall from my room, the door to Teddy's room was closed. I faltered a step but didn't try the knob. The door had been closed when I returned from the hospital and through the next few months and appeared to have remained closed. I might ask about it too. I might not.

In my room, the lamps on the nightstands flanking the queen bed illuminated the large space. Except for an unfamiliar comforter, everything seemed identical to the day I departed for my senior year of college and the extra courses I needed to compensate for the semester lost to surgeries and rehab. August of 2006, I couldn't wait to leave behind the family that no longer was part of me.

I tossed Dilsey's bed against the brick hearth, dropped my bag in the middle of the room, and opened the French doors to the balcony. The rain had intensified. Even with Jamie still out, someone had extinguished the stadium lights around the parking area. The farm below—the barns and other outbuildings and the pastures rolling into the foothills—spread dark and quiet. Dilsey snorted at the unfamiliar scents, and I scratched her head.

I reentered the room. Directly across from me was the oak bookcase filled with the stories of my childhood. On the third shelf, my Stevenson section, a book-wide gap marked the only empty space. I'd forgotten about the book—or rather, its absence. After all those years, no one had attempted to fill the space with another book or to conceal the gap. Maybe because no one knew what belonged there. Or maybe because they did. If the space hadn't been free of dust, I'd have assumed no one noticed anything missing at all.

Treasure Island was the last book Teddy borrowed from me. He'd expected to finish reading it in the hunting cabin the evening of the day he died. I never saw the book again.

I averted my eyes, overwhelmed by Teddy's unfinished business: never learning how young Jim Hawkins, despite the greed and evil in the world and the fear within himself, mustered the courage to do the right thing.

So many other good books. I read every one on my own and reread them as I shared them with Teddy. Later, I helped him work through them, and later still I listened while he read them aloud to me. After I left for college—Teddy was eight—we talked every week, more often than I spoke with my parents and Jamie. "Philip's standing date," my friends teased. We never missed our call.

When Dilsey nudged my hand, I playfully tweaked her nose and set a bowl of water in the shower stall of my bathroom. When I undressed and collapsed into bed, I marveled that after so long, it all felt achingly familiar.

I didn't fall asleep right away. The wreaths on the front door, the tree, the spicy-sweet holiday aroma of baking—my bed—all suddenly reminded me of the Christmas I was ten. Late Christmas Eve, I lay in bed reading. I no longer believed in Santa Claus. Jamie, age five, believed with an evangelical fervor that our parents neither encouraged nor discouraged but which they cautioned me against spoiling for him. Infant Teddy knew nothing.

That night I must have dozed over my book, because I awakened abruptly to a clatter of hooves, the jingle of bells, and a jolly *ho-ho-ho*. I lay rigid, taking in the clomp of boots on the roof, a grunt, and a resounding *thump*, as if someone had dropped something heavy. A bag of gifts? A few indistinguishable bumps and mutterings followed and then a clear and enthusiastic *yummy*, and then I heard the return of steps on the roof, a repeat of the jingling bells, and a low but boisterous *Mer-ry Christmas!*

I lay awake for a long time, mortified that I might have been mistaken about Santa. By daylight, I'd convinced myself I'd dreamed the whole thing until Jamie confirmed I hadn't.

Years later, our father admitted the fun he'd had with his elaborate wiring and recording scheme, and he had shared my mother's joy in giving their children the gift of wonder. Still, my belief in the miracle of making the impossible possible remained—until fallout from the shooting stole the playfulness and joy from our lives and proved the only wonder was that we managed to survive at all.

CHAPTER 8

AT FIVE FIFTY the next morning, Christmas Eve, Dilsey and I stole through the upstairs hallway, down the stairs, and outside for her morning pee. The back porch thermometer read sixty-nine degrees. Although northwestern South Carolina got snow at Christmas only once every half century or so, at least it was usually chilly. The ridiculous temperature exacerbated the strangeness of waking in my childhood bedroom.

Dilsey tugged on her leash, asking to run. After hesitating, weighing the consequences of her bolting into the darkness, I freed her. She was safe, at least around the house. Too late I wondered whether anyone had covered the pool for the winter. Dilsey knew how to swim, of course, but I wasn't certain I could wrest her from danger if she seized in the pool.

She snuffled around nearby, then zipped across my path and in and out of the aura cast by the gas lamps that lined the walkway as I curved to the parking area to retrieve her towels from my truck. If the forecast held, for the foreseeable future I'd be drying her each time she entered the house.

I'd stacked the towels on a porch rocker when Dilsey barked twice. A light bobbed through the grassy rise between the main barn and the house. She bounced through the circle it cast on the ground.

"You must be Dilsey." The voice was deeper but still familiar.

Jamie.

I was surprised he was awake, especially given how late he'd probably gotten in last night. Even as a little kid, he'd resisted mornings. He ignored his alarm clock or didn't hear it at all. When Mom or Dad sent me into his room to wake him, he buried his head under the covers, whining that he had no reason to wake up. Just being alive in a family that loves you, our parents repeatedly told him, is all the reason you need.

By the time I reached the bottom step, he appeared on the walkway, Dilsey prancing beside him and mouthing his hand. The bobbing light was a headlamp, and he switched it off.

"What're you doing here?" I asked.

"I live here occasionally and visit often. You?"

"That's not what I mean."

He balanced on his right leg and grabbed his ankle to stretch his left quad. "Running." Despite being wet, his T-shirt hung loose and shapeless on him, and shadows highlighted the hollows below his cheekbones. He'd never been overweight, but he'd never been so gaunt either.

"In the dark?"

He switched legs and wobbled when Dilsey bumped against him. With his free hand, he steadied himself on her head, seemingly oblivious to her tail lashing the calf of his standing leg. "If you'd told me you were coming, we could've ridden together."

I scrambled for a response. "It was a last-minute thing," I finally said. That was true. "Besides, it's not like you planned to drive with Henry, and I screwed up your plans."

"Not the point."

He removed his headlamp and pulled his T-shirt over his head. Definitely too thin. He wiped his face and torso with the shirt. When he dropped his arm to his side, Dilsey snatched the shirt and ran off. He laughed at her, but when he addressed me, his tone was serious. "Driving here's the least of it. Between Henry's place and yours, you've lived fifty, sixty miles from me for what, six months? You've never invited me to visit you, never asked to visit me, nothing. I've left you phone messages you didn't return. I've texted–"

"I responded to those."

"You don't seriously consider a one-word reply or a thumbs-up thingy a response."

"Five months."

"Huh?"

"I've been in Virginia for five months. Not six."

He glared at me.

"Jamie, I've been busy. New job. Old house."

"Not to mention all the socializing with your plethora of friends."

He reclaimed his shirt from Dilsey and pushed past me up the porch steps. At the door, he yanked off his wet Adidas and socks and wrapped them in his tee. "We should be honored you managed to fit us into your busy sched-ule." He hurled the words and disappeared inside, the door banging behind him.

I leaned on the porch railing and rubbed Dilsey's ear as she pressed against me. I had no issue with Jamie, but I'd long since fallen out of the habit of including him in my thoughts, much less my plans. Living an easy distance apart didn't alter that. If I'd returned his calls, what would we have talked about? Perhaps I should have felt regret. But I felt nothing.

The coffee was percolating when a towel-dried Dilsey and I entered the unoccupied kitchen a few minutes later. I pulled Dilsey's food from the refrigerator—raw beef mixed with finely chopped vegetables that I spent one weekend every month freezing in batches. Since I hadn't let her food warm to room temperature as I usually did, I ran hot water in the sink and soaked the freezer bag there for a few moments before mixing warm water, her supplements, and a cocktail of anticonvulsants with the food in her bowl. When I found myself flexing the tingling fingers of my right hand for the third time, I cursed under my breath. Riding with my arm virtually immobile most of yesterday hadn't done it any favors.

Dilsey, sitting in the middle of the kitchen—ears up, head cocked, watching—whined at me. Or maybe at her breakfast. I mock-whined back. Behind her, Jamie, in dry clothes, leaned against the doorframe, bouncing his phone in one hand and mine in the other. I hadn't heard him come downstairs.

"Orthopedics and PT have come a long way in ten years," he said gently. "Stem cell procedures too. Maybe—"

"No." Zapped by a flash of memory from the ICU, I concentrated on Dilsey's bowl to prevent it from shaking as I set it on the floor. "I'm done with all that."

Dilsey wagged her tail and dove in. When I looked at Jamie and he averted his gaze, I realized he'd tossed me a bone to atone for his harsh words earlier. "I'm sorry, Jamie. I'm sure they've made great advancements. But I can't go through it again."

"As I walked by your room, your phone dinged." He tossed it to me.

An email from Emily Warner. Irritated, I deleted her message without reading it.

Jamie nodded toward Dilsey. "What's she eating? It looks gross."

"How can a med student consider dog food gross?"

He wrinkled his nose, and in a comfortable silence we watched Dilsey wolf down her breakfast. When she finished, she lay on the floor gripping the empty bowl between her forepaws and licking every remaining particle of food.

Jamie carried two mugs of coffee to the table, and I washed my hands and joined him with the cream. A sealed tub of what turned out to be my favorite cranberry-orange muffins sat in the center of the table. I placed one on a plate and slid it and a napkin onto the place mat in front of Jamie. He laid aside his phone.

"Expecting a call so early?"

"Used to being tied to it, I guess. In case the hospital calls." He pulled apart the muffin and visually dissected it before popping a chunk into his mouth. "So . . . How did you decide to come back?"

I ate the top of my muffin first, not unhappy to have a reason to stall. It was firm, crunchy, full of berries and orange zest. During Christmas break, my mother had always baked the cranberry muffins especially for me.

"Mom still makes these," I said, awed.

"She does every year. She used to ask—" He leaned back and pierced me with a glare. "She used to ask if she should freeze some so if you came home later in the year they'd be there for you. We always told her yes. But a few years ago, she stopped asking."

Imagining a freezer full of muffins in heavy-duty Ziploc bags, labeled with the year and my name, I sipped my coffee. She should've assumed I wouldn't be back. She shouldn't have kept hoping. "I'm sure they didn't go to waste."

After a moment, Jamie asked again, "Why'd you come?"

I nibbled a piece of soft muffin body, debating what to tell him. No point in hedging or lying. He'd find out soon enough. "Emily Warner. Name familiar?"

"Shit." He slammed one palm to the table. "I should've known you didn't come because you wanted to spend time with us." He stood and paced around the kitchen, his face taut.

"Jamie—"

"She emailed me in early November. I was so deep in my classes and clinical work, I couldn't deal with her."

"She contacted the others too?"

He flipped his hands in an I-have-no-idea gesture.

I pressed. "No one mentioned her to you?"

"What do you think?"

Our eyes met. We both knew the answer. No one in my family would discuss anything as important as Emily Warner and her questions.

"She attached a news article to her email," Jamie said. "I hadn't ever read or seen any media coverage."

He pushed back against one of the counters, gripping tightly with both hands in a pose I recognized. He was bracing for something.

"When I came back here with Henry, when you and Dad were in the hospital, we rarely watched TV. And if it was on and the shooting came up, Henry or whichever family friend happened to be checking on us turned it off." He inhaled a long shaky breath. "I don't know if you know this, if Henry ever told you, but when I saw anything of Teddy's, even everyday things like the photos on the landing, his bedroom, his horse—even from a distance, like out in the pasture—I pictured Henry entering the cabin, soaked in blood, not saying anything. Soaked in Teddy's blood. And I'd puke. *Every damn time.* So no way could I handle any news."

He rubbed his eyes, but they were dry.

I circled a finger inside the handle of my coffee mug, shocked that his aversion to coverage of the shooting matched mine. "I didn't know."

"Anyway, the article she attached was the first I'd seen."

"First one for me too."

"Really?" He returned to his chair and twirled his coffee mug on the place mat. "I keep telling myself it doesn't bother me that she found me. The whole mess is ancient history. I can't let it affect me for the rest of my life."

"Except her interest in it does bother you."

"It does. The fact that she can't find any information—how weird is that?"

"Maybe she sucks at research."

"You believe that? Given Google and everything?"

"No. Still, Dad's high profile and police records are public, I think, and yet she claims she couldn't find any official information. That assertion's easy enough to prove or disprove."

Jamie scattered his muffin pieces into a crumbled, inedible mess.

"What'd you tell her?" I asked.

"Nothing. I read her note and deleted it."

I drummed my fingers on the table, debating whether to admit I'd met Emily in person. I had nothing to lose by telling him. "I left her a voicemail telling her not to contact me again. Then she showed up in Grainger."

"You're shittin' me."

"Her side of the story's compelling." I finished my muffin, waiting for him to ask for specifics. He didn't. "I'm asking Mom and Dad about the police records, or apparent lack thereof. That's why I'm here."

Jamie shook his head. "Don't, Philip. Please. We never talk about what happened. Let them think you came back to spend time with us."

I laughed. "They'd never believe that. But I'll ask after Christmas if it'll make you feel better."

"It won't." He carried our plates to the dishwasher and shooed away Dilsey's inquisitive nose as he loaded them into it. When an alarm sounded on his phone, I muted it.

"Wow, Jamie. Up before your alarm."

He refilled our mugs. "My long-sleep days are over. Some nights I'm lucky to get any at all."

"Why?"

He snorted. "You're kidding, right?" When I only leaned back in my chair and sipped my coffee, he sighed. "Classes, studying, patients. Thinking about things. Emily Warner. But mostly I worry about what to do next. Even if I'm accepted into my first-choice residency program—which isn't a given—I'm not sure I should go."

"Why not?"

He settled into his chair and ran his finger around the rim of his mug. "What made you change your mind about going into animal law? When you decided to teach, how did you know it was the right thing?"

"I never *decided* to teach. It just happened." After the shooting, what I did for a living, or at all, no longer mattered. Why bother mapping your life if a stranger could waylay it in an instant. "I had to find something to do."

"How ambitious."

"We can't all be doctors."

"Tell me about it." His gaze appeared unfocused.

"You second-guessing your career choice?"

"I guess not. Wavering on my specialty, though."

"Which is?"

"Trauma surgery."

"Seriously? You?" I almost laughed.

Blood and guts made Jamie violently ill when he was a child. One summer when Jamie was eight or nine, Henry found a predator-ravaged rabbit near the house, and told Jamie he wanted to show him something. We heard precisely when Jamie saw it. So did our parents. They made Henry clean up Jamie's vomit and properly bury the bunny. Conquering his squeamishness enough to withstand med school, and to be considering five or six more years of residency and then a lifetime of digging his hands directly into blood and guts, was impressive.

How else had he changed? He hadn't been more than a boy with a boy's dreams the last time we dug deep. My choice. I'd needed to revise my expectations for my future, and I'd given him plenty of space to revise his. And he had. Trauma surgery. He'd contribute to his community in ways I never would. I was proud of him and disappointed in myself. My choice, though.

I pushed away the encroaching sadness. No, not sadness. Discomfort elicited by Jamie's quandary. I returned to the practical. "Being an MD doesn't commit you to practicing medicine. There's research. Or jobs with pharmaceutical companies. Or"—I tapped his wrist—"you could be one of those know-it-all media docs. Dr. Jamie telling us on Monday that eating beef will kill us and on Tuesday that eating it will extend our lives."

"I'm not doing any of that. It needs to be . . . I don't know. Meaningful, I guess." He gulped some coffee. Bracing again? "When Teddy and Dad and you got shot, I felt like I was swimming through mud. My arms and legs barely moved, and I couldn't hear anything. All I did was puke. I didn't help Henry and the caretaker guy tend to y'all. If I had, everything might have been different. I don't ever want to feel so helpless again. Or worse than helpless: *useless*."

I fidgeted at his frankness. "Jamie, you were fifteen years old. Anything you did or didn't do wouldn't have made any difference." I didn't even recall him being part of what happened that morning. That was how I remembered it; Jamie wasn't there at all. Our father, yes, and Vincent Gardner and vaguely Henry and another man who I presumed was the property caretaker. But not Jamie. Not Teddy either.

"I don't think I believe that," he said.

"You don't have to be noble. Let someone else be a trauma surgeon. You have plenty of other options. Finish your MD, go to law school, and practice medical law."

"I'm not practicing any kind of law."

"Find another profession, then. Anything. Don't make it so complicated."

"Everything's complicated." Elbow on the table, he pressed his chin into his hand and frowned. "You wouldn't be here if things weren't complicated. If they didn't matter."

I opened my mouth to argue and realized he was right. Everything was complicated. With our father's arrival and my mention of Emily, things were about to get more complicated.

We finished our coffee in silence.

CHAPTER 9

SHORTLY BEFORE TEN THIRTY, Henry borrowed Jamie's car to pick up the ham for Christmas Eve supper, run errands for the family, and meet a friend for lunch. At the same time, Jamie and my mother left in her Lincoln to fetch our father from the airport. I remained with Dilsey at the farm, assuring my mother I'd tackle her list of chores.

She didn't need to get our father. One of his security people could do it—they'd be around anyway. But even when we were kids—and before 9/11—when he was a regular guy returning home from a law conference or a meeting with distant clients or colleagues, our mother frequently made airport runs a family excursion. We'd pile into her SUV and get to Charlotte or Greenville early enough to watch through the huge windows inside the terminal and concourses, bodies pressed against the glass, as the planes arrived and departed.

Our father usually deplaned first, striding into the gate area, scanning the waiting crowd. He'd kiss our mother and hand me his rolling carry-on, but he never relinquished his briefcase. He'd nestle the youngest child—at first Jamie, then Teddy—in one arm. Perhaps he'd once carried me as well. How bizarre to contemplate that sort of response after all that had happened between us.

Today, after everyone left, I waited for a few moments with Dilsey and the unlit Christmas tree in the central hall, listening to the house. It wasn't silent, exactly. Like every house, it spoke its own language. But the language was unfamiliar now, so long unheard, so long unused. Or perhaps the language itself had transitioned to a dialect never intended to be understood by intruders.

I shook away the strangeness and studied the list of chores. If I hustled, I'd finish most of it in the nearly three hours I had to myself. I was happy to help, but I hoped staying busy didn't speed up the time before they returned.

I vacuumed the entire first floor and the staircase, mopped the kitchen, cleaned both of the half baths downstairs, added water to the Christmas tree, and spritzed the front-door wreaths. On the back porch steps, I brushed Dilsey. Afterward, she rolled on the soggy dead Bermuda grass, so I brushed her again.

Next, rag in hand, I dusted the house room by room. Nine months after the shooting, when I left the farm for what I expected would be the last time, generic period artifacts had already replaced the personal mementos marking the house as *our* house. Then, as now, it resembled any house of its era open for public gawking, showing how things were *back then*. But we weren't open to the public. And the impersonal decorations in no way reflected what had been hidden under the perfect surface.

After hesitating for the briefest of seconds when I reached my father's study, I slid aside the pocket door, surprised it wasn't locked. The room was as I remembered: book-laden built-ins; enormous oak desk, bare except for a blotter and phone; plush office chair; wall-mounted television; and in the left corner closest to the door, a wet bar. The air smelled of old books, leather, and bourbon. If I rifled through Dad's desk drawers now, when no one was there to know, would I find anything about the shooting? About Emily? Notes stuffed into a nook revealing information or an unexpected secret? Was a dark secret the reason, when I'd walked in on my parents a few months after the shooting, they'd abruptly silenced their tense, hushed voices?

I wouldn't intrude now, not even to dust. I didn't care about anything he might have hidden.

Or maybe I was afraid of what I'd find—or what I wouldn't find. Annoyed at myself for lacking the courage at the age of thirty to violate my father's space, I backed out and eased the door shut.

With Dilsey following, I climbed the stairs, dusting as I went, then I dusted the occasional tables in the second-floor hallway, glancing repeatedly at Teddy's closed door. I resisted the temptation to open it, questioning why I wanted to, knowing as my hand hovered over the knob that I would. What if the door opened? Would I find the room untouched? Did the colorful world map marked with Post-it flags of the places Teddy wanted to visit still hang on the wall? And what about his floor globe? The world had changed so much that it would be outdated now.

What if the door didn't open? Or what if it did but the room was empty or, even worse, empty of everything that made it Teddy's?

Guided by a compulsion beyond my control, my hand turned the knob side to side, jiggled it up and down. Locked. As it had been when I'd returned home from the hospital after he died. I wondered again who kept the key or whether, as with everything associated with Teddy, it too had been discarded.

Jamie's room was next door to Teddy's, and on impulse I cut through it to the shared balcony. Teddy's exterior French doors were locked, too—no surprise there—and their wide shutters tilted enough that nothing inside showed except slivers of oak floor.

Slightly disappointed—vastly relieved—I rolled my shoulders to release the tension, backtracked through Jamie's room, and crossed the hall into my own. Outside on the balcony, I propped myself against the balustrade. Dilsey joined me and poked her head through the pickets. Her twitching nose processed the aromas of the fields and the horses in the balmy, humid air that falsely suggested we might bypass winter altogether and slip directly into spring.

How different today was from my first days home after the shooting, days I'd never allowed myself to revisit. Overnight freezes and clear skies had yielded to light-jacket temperatures and bright sunshine, but my parents kept me bundled inside. Weak from two surgeries, pneumonia, and a systemic infection; bruised from innumerable IVs; woozy from more drugs than I'd taken in my entire life; and with my right arm immobilized against my chest, I was pretty much helpless. But after nearly six weeks of confinement, I longed for fresh air. My only time outside had been the Christmas Eve flight from Nashville and the drive from the Greenville airport to the farm. Those didn't count.

So, midafternoon two days after the Christmas we didn't celebrate, while Dad napped and Mom kept him company, while Jamie hid in his room and after Henry had fled to his parents' house in Maryland, I escaped unobserved from the house and wobbled to one of the golf carts stationed on the parking pad. I'd intended to visit Huckleberry and Sawyer first thing but, exhilarated by my sudden freedom, I instead navigated one-handed past the main barn and into the fields.

During any normal Christmas vacation, on a sunny day not unlike that one, the family would ride on horseback into the mountains, stopping midday to eat the lunches we'd packed, returning at dusk exhausted and invigorated by the brisk air, the stunning landscape, and each other's company. That year, Teddy would've accompanied us on his first non-pony, the horse Dad and I had selected for him the previous spring. Teddy named him Huckleberry, and they became inseparable.

Puttering along the paved path, I considered Huckleberry's future and almost immediately knew I'd take him when I moved Sawyer to wherever I lived after college, for no reason other than Teddy loved his horse and I loved Teddy. Huckleberry was young enough that my parents probably wouldn't want to feed him for the next twenty years. He'd be good company for Sawyer. He'd have to stay at the farm for only another eighteen months or so, same as Sawyer. My parents would be okay with that. Teddy would've been too.

Inspired by my plan, I meandered northwest among the pastures and toward the mouse-gray mountains, past where the paved path roughened into the corrugated dirt farm track and in the general direction of the pond and our tree house. Toward the cemetery, too, I realized with a suddenness that constricted my chest. Two centuries of family rested there. More importantly, Teddy was now there. My family could have, *should* have, waited to hold his funeral until the hospital released me. Why hadn't they? It couldn't make a difference to Teddy. I stopped the cart and squeezed the steering wheel. Burying him without me in attendance was so unfair. They had no right.

But I could visit him now.

In the pasture to my right, a few grazing horses flicked their ears without raising their heads. When I was eight, we'd buried a young mare in that pasture in a spot now indistinguishable from the rest of the field, as if she'd never existed. The mare had died in darkness, foaling three weeks before her due date. Ruptured uterus, Dad explained, but I didn't know then what the words meant. On that atypically sultry morning in early May, he and I had watched the brutal efficiency that marks farm-animal disposal. The grave dug by a green and yellow backhoe had been long and wide and deep enough for an elephant.

Dad's arm around my shoulders had pressed me to him. He wore a suit and was late for work.

The decomposing baby and its mother, her legs rope-bound against her body, buzzed. Insects, Dad said. That fact fascinated more than repulsed me.

The backhoe shoved her into the hole, and one of the workers tumbled the foal on top of her. The guys dusted the horses' bodies with lime, and the backhoe piled red clay soil over them, and that was it.

Dad's gentle play-by-play taught me all I needed to know about dying.

As I sat in the golf cart, an image of Teddy's grave replaced the memory of the mare. Someone would have put sod over it, but that couldn't disguise the recent excavation. My longing to visit the cemetery and the horses imploded, and I slumped, demoralized and exhausted by the barrage of emotions that had accosted me in the short time I'd been riding around the farm.

I turned back toward the house.

When I reached the barn, I stopped to allow a pickup towing a shiny silver two-horse trailer to maneuver close to the main door already wide open to the breeze. The driver hopped out to lower the ramp. Ross, the farm manager, emerged from the barn leading a small bay horse wearing a blanket and leg wraps for travel. Horses came and went all the time.

I gasped. The horse was Huckleberry. Teddy's horse.

I flung myself from the cart and tottered to the trailer as Huckleberry and Ross reached it. "Ross—"

"Philip! I don't think you're supposed to be out here."

"What're you doing?"

"Sending Huckleberry to his new home." He patted the horse's cheek. "He's a Christmas gift for a little girl."

The burst of adrenaline that propelled me from the cart to the trailer left me lightheaded and nauseated. "But *I'm* his new home. Or I will be when I leave. After graduation, I mean. Which isn't too far off. It's all planned. It's perfect. He can't go anywhere now." Panting, I tried to throw enough words at him to convince him that Huckleberry had to stay.

With my left hand, the only one I could use, I snatched at the lead rope. Ross released it and steadied me with a hand on my arm. The truck driver shook his head and retreated to the cab.

Maybe Ross thought he was helping. He'd worked there since before I was born and most likely made more farm decisions than my parents did.

"Do Mom and Dad know what you're doing?"

"They arranged it."

An icy hand squeezed the breath out of me. "That doesn't make sense." My parents and I hadn't discussed

Huckleberry yet. We hadn't even discussed Teddy. I swallowed hard and leaned against Huckleberry to keep myself upright. He tossed his head but didn't move otherwise.

Ross backed away and spoke quietly into his phone.

With the hand holding the lead rope, I stroked the horse's neck. Deep inside, I knew that keeping Huckleberry wasn't the issue. Wasn't what I was fighting against. The problem was that letting him go now, without enough distance time-wise and emotion-wise from Teddy's death, equated to letting Teddy go. And I sure as hell wasn't ready for that. How could any of us ever adjust to Teddy's absence? There would never be enough distance or time. As anguished as I was, I knew that making my case for keeping Huckleberry wouldn't make Teddy's absence hurt less. But, oh God, I wished something would. My heart was raw, and once again it was being flayed.

I sensed that I wasn't supposed to have seen Huckleberry leaving. By the time I'd learned he was gone, he'd have settled into his new home, and I wouldn't have been able to do a thing about it. Like when I learned Teddy had been buried without me there to say goodbye.

I'd been trying to say goodbye every moment since I'd learned that he was dead and buried. He hadn't died in darkness like the mare, but he'd been buried in the same red earth. And I couldn't bear to think of him there.

A golf cart approached at a speed for which I'd have been chastised, and pulled up beside Ross. Mom drove, Dad beside her on the bench seat. In a tone that dared me to argue, she said, "Go on back to the house. You shouldn't be out here."

I had to try. "Huckleberry can't leave. I'll keep him."

Dad clenched his fists. "You're in no position to do anything right now."

"I mean after—"

"Go to the house."

"But *why*? Teddy's only been gone five weeks."

"Would you feel better if we waited fifteen weeks?" His voice deepened with anger. "Fifty weeks?"

I didn't bother to reply.

"Go back to the house."

Mom laid a hand on his arm, then came to me and rubbed Huckleberry's forehead. "It'll be easier if there aren't so many reminders."

"Easier? *Easier?*" After a flash of anguished insight blazed through me, my gut clenched. Huckleberry wasn't the only reminder of Teddy to disappear. None of his ornaments hung on the Christmas tree. His photos on the staircase landing—not only my favorite with Huckleberry, but all the family photos that included him—had vanished. No one had even spoken his name in my presence since the day Mom and Dad told me he'd died. "This isn't about *easier*."

Mom pried the lead rope from my trembling fingers and let Ross lead Teddy's horse into the trailer. I stared after them, resisting Mom's attempt to guide me to her golf cart, pulling free and reaching the trailer at the same time Ross banged shut the tailgate and rammed home the slide bolts. The truck and trailer rumbled away from the barn. I followed for an unsteady few steps till they disappeared among the trees lining the farm's service drive. And just like that, Huckleberry was gone forever.

"All right, back to the house." Dad's voice wavered.

"Bennett, please. Give us a sec—"

"Let me handle this, Laurel," he said with uncharacteristic sharpness tinged with something else. Exhaustion? Anger?

She squeezed my arm and approached Dad. Their low argument excluded me, and when Mom drove away in my cart, Dad cleared his throat and slid across the bench seat. His skin was ashen, and he'd dropped considerable weight since the shooting.

"Listen to me, Philip. I can't fix this. I know you want me to, but I can't. Teddy's dead. It's a terrible thing, what happened to him. And to you. To all of us, in fact. But no one can undo it. So, now we put all of it behind us and focus on seeing you through the next few months of surgery and rehab and returning to normal."

I gaped at him in disbelief. In rage. "*Normal?*"

"I know it's hard. But you're resilient. And if you want grief counseling, we'll arrange it."

"Grief counseling?" Arrange my emotions until they fit perfectly into a preconceived configuration, like furniture in a room? "Hell no, I don't need that. What I need is to know how this possibly could have happened to us. *Why?*"

Dad gazed at me, expressionless. "These things happen all the time, though not usually in our world. One person's actions deeply and irrevocably create ripples in the lives of people they're not meant to touch, and change them forever. That's what happened, Philip. Nothing more, nothing less."

Without anything to brace myself against, I swayed, consumed by grief and despair and confusion and anger, grasping a truth that blazed through me for a terrifying instant before smoldering into an overwhelming numbness. Our perfect family was perfectly nothing. Mom and Dad didn't care about Teddy. They didn't love him. Not like parents are supposed to. They didn't want to grieve for him. They didn't want to *remember* him.

They were monsters.

No, monsters had feelings. They had nothing.

I'd taken for granted their love for him, for all of us. But if his death was nothing to them, if they wouldn't talk about him or display his ornaments or photos or honor the things he'd loved—like Huckleberry—what was the value of his life? And by extension, what was the value of Jamie's life and Henry's and mine—how did ours differ from Teddy's?

By not talking about him, by not letting memories of him see daylight, they were killing him all over again. Their own son.

My little brother.

A decade later, I lingered on the balcony of my childhood bedroom, transported by memories. I realized with a shock how quickly—how very quickly—the equivalent of Teddy's life span had vanished. When he died, he'd shared half my life, but now the percentage of his life in mine had decreased to a third. Year by year, our mutual existence would dwindle to almost nothing. If we'd honored him in some way, we'd have retained a sense of him in our lives. But we hadn't, and now it was too late.

How strange to think about Teddy so much. I hadn't dwelt on the shooting and its aftermath in a long time. Until Emily Warner contacted me, I'd had no reason to. I'd put those events behind me.

Dilsey bumped my leg, then reared and placed her forepaws on the balustrade. I fondled her ears before tapping her chest to back her off, concerned she might spot a deer or barn cat and launch herself from two tall stories up.

An instant after she tipped her ears forward, I also heard a car approach and pushed back from the balustrade to head downstairs. Time to see whether last night's dress rehearsal with my mother had prepared me for today's performance with my father.

CHAPTER 10

WHAT SURPRISED ME most was the silver in my father's thick hair, as though he'd dipped his comb in mercury and swiped it over his entire head. If he'd changed at all since I saw him nine years ago, he was more vibrant–his step springy as his left hand swung my mother's, his briefcase, as always, clutched in his right hand. His unknotted tie lolled around his neck like a silky striped snake. He'd brought no luggage from Washington. Everything he needed was already in the house.

I looped two fingers through Dilsey's collar and waited on the back porch for him to make the first move, offer the first words–though what we needed to say to each other was long past being sayable, and without that, there wasn't anything else. Or there hadn't been until my conversation with Emily. How and when I'd broach Emily's concerns, I hadn't yet decided. If she'd contacted him, perhaps he'd raise the issue first. More likely, he'd ignore her existence.

Without warning, Dilsey streaked from my grasp, arcing past my parents to Jamie, who bounced a tennis ball on the walkway behind them. Dilsey danced around him, and he teased her, juggling the ball from hand to hand before hurling it across the lawn.

Instead of returning the ball to Jamie, she sat in front of my father, bobbing her head and mouthing the ball, waiting to release it until he asked.

"Take it, Bennett," Mom said.

Without moving, he studied Dilsey. "Nice dog."

My mother disengaged her hand from his, took the ball from Dilsey–saving my father from the slimy thing–and tossed it across her body to the left. Dilsey dashed after it.

He could have at least thrown the ball. It's not like he couldn't wash his hands.

I descended the porch steps, and my father set down his briefcase and extended his hand, looking me in the eye. Relieved he didn't attempt a hug, I gripped his hand, keeping an arm's distance between us. Neither of us spoke, but before our silence became more torturous than awkward, my mother said, "Lunch in thirty minutes."

When they entered the house, Jamie sighed. "That went better than I expected."

"What did you expect?"

"Not sure." He heaved the ball again. "What did *you* expect?"

"I don't know."

Dilsey's long tongue flopped from the side of her mouth as we gathered for lunch at the kitchen table. In the archway between the kitchen and dining room, she stretched flat on her side, huffing. We complimented my mother on the curry chicken salad and homemade bread, then drifted from topic to topic through extended silences like four colleagues struggling to finish the dull agenda of a mandatory team-building business lunch. Henry would have livened things up, but undoubtedly he was enjoying a much more relaxing meal with his friend. To my amusement and relief, even the consummate politician didn't seem too inclined, or able, to talk about anything that might turn intimate.

He came close, though, when he said, "You'll ride while you're here?"

"Not planning to." Visiting the horses, even setting foot in the barn, would spark too many tough memories. Emily had already kindled enough of those.

"Say hello to Ross, at least. He asks about you."

To avoid an argument, I nodded and continued eating.

He tried another topic. "Tell us about the fire."

"What specifically?"

"Are you doing okay?"

Because I'd assumed he meant the fire's cause or its effect on end-of-semester activities and resolution of grades or even about plans to rebuild, his question caught me so off guard I gaped at him. "I'm fine."

"Because I'd understand that if any of your students died, you might need to come home here to—"

"I said I'm fine." He'd misread my expression or my hesitation. No surprise there.

For a few moments, we ate in silence except for the tinkling of forks on stoneware and the ice in glasses. I didn't want to discuss my students or the fire or how I felt—or, more accurately, how I *didn't* feel—about any of it.

My mother, after watching us deliberately not watch each other, said, "I'm sure the students appreciated you sharing Dilsey with them. It's so nice you're able to take her to school."

I lowered my fork. How did she know?

"We saw you on the news. Letting her mingle with the students, especially that one girl."

Emily had seen a news report too. And thinking about

Emily provided the impetus to ask about her right then. "Do you know anyone named Emily Warner?"

Jamie reared back against his chair. "Philip, don't."

Mom turned to him. "One of Henry's girlfriends?"

"She contacted me–" I cut my eyes to my brother, "and Jamie about the shooting."

"What shooting?" she asked before she softly said, "Oh."

"We're not discussing that." My father's voice was low and firm.

Of course we weren't.

"She's looking for information about Vincent Gardner, the guy who–"

"We know who he is."

"Did you know he had a daughter?"

His gaze didn't waver. "I did not."

Jamie glowered at me and stalked from the kitchen.

I wanted to believe my father, but he was always thorough, and I couldn't imagine, even if he hadn't known at the time of the shooting, that he hadn't eventually learned of Emily's existence. "But he did have a daughter. I spoke to her."

My mother gasped.

My father remained expressionless, but the change in his breathing betrayed emotion I couldn't identify.

"When?"

"Day before yesterday." Blindsiding him, a nearly impossible feat, produced such a rush of satisfaction that I added, "We met, in person, for about an hour."

"*In person?*"

"Even if you didn't know she was his daughter–she does have a different last name–you'd know her from the email she sent you last fall."

"I've received nothing from her."

My silent stare declared that I didn't believe him.

"Philip, I don't see most of my Senate email, which is the only address she'd have access to." His voice had forcibly calmed to the clipped businesslike tone he used with clients and reporters. "My staff handles email and flags anything important, which is almost nothing."

"They wouldn't consider the shooting, *our* shooting, important? Your staff protects you even from that?"

"Philip, don't–"

He stopped my mother with a hand on hers. "It's not a matter of them protecting me. It's a matter of thousands of emails and only twenty-four hours in a day."

"The shooting left her an orphan."

"That's unfortunate for her, but it has no bearing on us."

"She wants to find out why her father died and–"

"That should be obvious to her. To you as well."

"I doubt she'd have bothered me, *us*, if she'd found records of the police investigation. They don't seem to exist. Which makes her–and me–assume someone's hiding something, and I want to know what and why."

"No one's hiding anything. In Tennessee, *local* police investigations are public record after a case closes. But records from the Tennessee Bureau of Investigation stay sealed, even after a case is resolved."

"That's legal?"

"State statute. So, yeah, it's legal."

I continued to challenge him. "How do you know? You practiced law in South Carolina."

"It doesn't mean I'm not aware of laws in other states."

Was it that simple? Nothing about the investigation was special and neither he nor his political cronies were hiding anything? I twirled my knife, hopeful that one of Emily's main concerns had such a straightforward explanation. "Okay. But why would the state have investigated at all? It happened in one location on private property, no crossing of county or state lines or anything like that."

"The local sheriff contacts the DA for help and the DA asks the TBI to investigate."

"And that happened because of you?"

"Partly, I'm sure, but mostly because a major crime involving so many people was far larger than a two-person rural law enforcement office could handle."

I pictured the nondescript little town closest to the hunting property—a hilly, tree-shaded main street with a few stores and on-street parking with lines so faded, luck guided you between them. An old brick post office and a gas station with a small convenience store. A few houses. I didn't recall a police station or a fire station. A quiet little place where a major crime investigation should never have been needed.

"There's no way to get access to those records?"

He paused so long, I expected he'd give me step-by-step instructions. "Not without an act of Congress."

He was exaggerating, but I got his point. "So how—"

"That's enough, both of you." My mother's firm tone—and the hands she'd pressed into the kitchen table—prevented further discussion.

My remaining questions could wait. At least I'd opened the conversation, though I'd reneged on my promise to Jamie to wait until after Christmas.

She handed me our plates to take to the sink. "Let's enjoy the holiday, today with just us and tomorrow with everyone else."

"Everyone else?" I didn't like the sound of that.

She recited the names, twelve of them, all among my parents' oldest and closest friends. And she offered a quick update of what they were currently involved with.

Dad's law school pal and courtroom prosecutorial adversary, Adrian Wells, was now the head prosecutor for this region. College friends Dan and Irene Riggs owned a barbecue restaurant just over the line in North Carolina and had concocted what might be the world's best banana pudding. Audra and Norm Trent had introduced my parents and now published a regional monthly features magazine. The Trents' two daughters, around my age, and their husbands and a total of three young children.

I hadn't seen those people since the spring after Teddy died. Saying I wasn't at my best back then understated the truth. While I'd struggled through the rehab to regain basic function in my right shoulder and arm, they'd streamed endlessly in and out of this house and the Washington house, bearing food and cheery chatter and moral support I not only didn't want but resented. When anyone mentioned Teddy or the shooting in my presence, my parents extinguished those topics before I could.

The Christmas a year after Teddy died, right before my last undergraduate semester, when I'd recovered as much as I ever would and when our parents expected all of us to come home, I'd hunkered down in the apartment I shared with Henry and he'd gone without me. After that, I'd fabricated reasons to stay away until I was no longer factored into Christmas at the farm. I'd not only removed myself from family get-togethers, I'd taken myself out of the family.

Now, other than knowing they no longer exchanged gifts, I had no idea how–or if–my family even celebrated the holidays. Henry didn't volunteer the information, and I didn't ask. And, consequently, I never considered that this holiday visit wouldn't be just us.

My mother beamed. "Everyone will be *so* happy to see you."

The sentiment wasn't mutual.

CHAPTER 11

ON A RAINY Christmas so warm and humid that Mom had switched on the air conditioning, the first guests arrived at two o'clock as I skewered the third-to-last bacon strip into the last marinated scallop. A hearty chorus of *Merry Christmas* mingled with the "Deck the Halls" piping through the house's intercom system.

My mother folded her apron into a drawer. "Twelve minutes under the broiler. I preset the timer and temp. Punch On and don't let them overcook. When they're do—"

"I know, Mom. Arrange them on the platter and take them to the hall." My father and Jamie had arranged long tables by the Christmas tree where everyone would gather before gravitating into other rooms.

She flashed an okay sign and disappeared toward the back door.

Henry smirked. "In case you've forgotten how to do anything." At the sink, he peeled the last of a mountain of potatoes with which he'd make the beer-cheese and bacon mashed potatoes he claimed to have invented and which had apparently become a holiday staple. And not just for Christmas Day. He'd made them last night, too, to accompany the Christmas Eve ham.

I ignored him, slid the scallops under the broiler, and returned to the table, listening to the happy hubbub from the back porch. Everyone except formal company always parked around back where we parked and entered the house from the rear, as we did. When we were kids, anyone could drive up at any time. Now, Zack or one of his crew would funnel expected visitors through the front gate and turn away anyone else.

Jamie, today's bartender, stuck his head into the kitchen. "Last chance for a drink delivery."

"Killian's." Henry switched on the burner under the stockpot of water and potatoes.

"Nothing, thanks." A drink, or several, wasn't such a bad idea, but for the moment, I consoled myself with the two leftover bacon strips.

"You want something later, you know where to find me." Jamie disappeared.

Henry stirred salt into his potatoes. "Isn't this way more fun than microwaving a frozen dinner?"

"I'd be grilling a steak." I wiped my hands on a wad of damp paper towels and leaned back to await the chime of the oven timer.

By the time I'd plated the scallops, individual voices blended into a cheerful undertone. Hoping to avoid mindless small talk, I hustled through the group, intent on depositing the appetizer on the table and fading upstairs to keep Dilsey company. No one would miss me till dinner, at which point I'd come back down. Except, with everyone milling around in the main hall, slinking away unseen would prove difficult. Maybe I'd slip into the kitchen and babysit Henry's boiling potatoes while *he* socialized.

But, as if I'd emerged onto a stage, the conversational hum dissolved into silence when the guests saw me.

Audra Trent recovered first. "Laurel! This is your best-kept secret yet." She slithered toward me so smoothly, her wine barely rippled in its glass. "Philip. You decided to grace us with your presence."

I glanced uneasily around without making eye contact with anyone, searching for an escape option before Mrs. Trent reached me, but none existed. "Hey, everyone."

She selected a scallop and spun it on its toothpick. "Look at you, all grown up. I want to hear what you've been up to. Your mother doesn't tell me a thing." She nibbled on her scallop. "And I want to hear all about your new job. About that fire. Terrible thing, but a great news story. We wanted a local angle for a feature, like some local kid attending there. Then when Laurel reminded me you teach there, I had my people browse around online. Turns out you have quite the following, your own fandom. Or your dog does. Before you head back, I'll have a reporter and photographer meet with you."

"I'm not interested."

"*Your* interest is irrelevant, my dear. Our readers' interest is what matters."

Not to me it didn't. I edged toward the food table. She matched me step for step.

"We'll talk at dinner." She snagged another scallop with the hand that held her wine and squeezed my arm with the other. "Laurel," she called out. "Seat Philip beside me."

From the kitchen threshold, Henry raised his beer bottle in a silent toast.

The scallops never reached the table. I endured hand-shakes, kisses, and small talk with a grace I'd not known I possessed. At the one opportunity I found to shove the plate at someone and escape, my beaming mother materialized beside me and I was trapped.

"Enjoying yourself?" she asked.

I nodded and conceded defeat. I glided through the downstairs rooms, eventually relinquishing the empty plate for a rocks glass of something dark from Jamie. Jack and Coke, I discovered, easy on the Jack. He remembered.

As I fixed my own second drink at the bar in Dad's study, Mom entered with Mrs. Trent and the eldest Trent grandchild, Madison, who was about six.

"Does Dilsey like children?"

Dilsey was one of those dogs that inherently loved kids despite, or because of, her limited experience with them. "She does."

Madison clapped her hands. "Can your dog do tricks?"

"Lots of them." I smiled at her enthusiasm.

"Wonderful," Mom said. "Why don't you bring her down?"

Immediately, my remaining tension drained. Madison and her younger sister waited at the bottom of the staircase when I returned from my room with Dilsey carrying her ball. Dilsey sat in front of them, and they patted her head with the flat of their palms, in the way most dogs hate. Her tail wagged from side to side.

Dilsey demonstrated the simplest of her tricks, first with me, then with the girls. Sit, down, speak, spin to the right and to the left, beg, roll over, play dead, catch.

Madison asked to hold Dilsey's leash, and we paraded from room to room, outside onto the front porch and to the back and through all the rooms again, with the girls sharing my dog. I steered them away from the appetizers and other hazards and occasionally untangled the leash, but otherwise I didn't interfere in their fun.

For the first time since arriving, I was comfortable. The girls were sweet and appreciative, and they and I shared no history that made us wary of each other. And Dilsey, always happy, always gentle, eased whatever tensions still existed between the other adults and me.

We were making our last pass through the kitchen when I noticed my mother was setting filled dishes on the table for Henry and Jamie to carry into the dining room. My father was carving the roasts.

"Time to put Dilsey up, I assume," I said.

"Almost. Ten minutes till dinner."

Dilsey raised her head, sniffed, and released her ball.

"Watch this, girls," Dad said. He called Dilsey's name and tossed her a slice of prime rib from the end of the carving fork.

She caught it and wagged her thanks. Madison and her sister giggled.

"Don't feed her that."

"It fell." He winked at the children, and again they laughed. "It's *meat*, Philip."

"Loaded with seasonings she doesn't need."

He opened his mouth to respond, but Mom smacked him on the hip with the back of her hand, shot me a warning glance, and nudged Dilsey's ball to her with a foot. "Time for Dilsey to go back upstairs."

"Can I go with her?" Madison asked.

"No, sweetie. Go find your mother and wash your hands."

The children, Dilsey, and I ambled into the hall. Beside the Christmas tree, the Trent daughters chatted with their husbands and Mrs. Riggs. Adrian Wells's and Henry's voices drifted in from the open door to the back porch. Madison handed me the leash, and I looked down at Dilsey. Ball in her mouth, she stared at the tree.

Several things happened so rapidly in succession, they seemed simultaneous. Madison said, "Bye, Dilsey," and reached out to pet her head. Dilsey dropped her ball, drew her lips over her teeth into what anyone would consider a snarl, and snapped at Madison's hand. Stunned, I froze. Madison screamed. Her mother also screamed. Madison's father slung the child into his arms. Dilsey, mouth gaping, flung strings of thick saliva on everyone nearby, then collapsed on her side in a grand mal seizure.

I shifted into autopilot–glancing at my watch, dropping to my knees, repositioning Dilsey to keep her head on the carpet. Unfortunately for the carpet, the back half of her body and a widening dark spot of urine were already there. The seizure was short–only thirty-six seconds and without the violence that could hurl her around a room like a demon-possessed thing. I could handle this calmly, efficiently, confidently. I'd had lots of practice since her first seizure two years ago when horrified and utterly ignorant about what to do–and positive that she was dying–I'd left her in the kitchen of my LA bungalow and fled into the living room. Within a minute or two–I didn't time them then–she staggered to me, drooling, eyes dilated. After a few more minutes, she was back to normal, and I almost disbelieved what I'd seen.

Now Madison *and* her sister were sobbing. I understood that–Dilsey had terrified them. But I expected better from the shrieking adults. When the immediate shock faded into what should have been silence, one voice–Audra Trent's, shrill and breathless–pierced that silence.

"How can anyone keep an animal like that? Laurel, you should never have let him bring it here. It stinks, and it's ruined your beautiful Persian. Why'd you–"

"Audra, please shut up." My father's words overpowered my mother's calming murmurs.

Jamie plopped down beside me and dangled the red tote of emergency meds. "In case you need this."

I hoped I wouldn't.

From behind us, Henry said, "Geez, Philip. The seizure I saw was at night. You never told me she might have one during the day." He set Dilsey's damp ball between Jamie and me. "Can I help?"

"Paper towels and white vinegar or club soda." I looked up briefly and gestured to the carpet. "Sorry, Mom."

It wasn't until the items appeared that I remembered I should've also requested a trash bag. I lifted Dilsey's head and placed a wad of paper towels under it to absorb the mucus-striped blob darkening the intricate pattern of the rug. Jamie unfurled a portion of the roll and soaked up the urine at Dilsey's other end.

Typical for Dilsey, she was unconscious and breathing hard. Her lungs sounded clear, though, which was a relief.

"What's happening?" Jamie asked.

"She has a few atypical complications. This long unconsciousness is one of them." I didn't mention the others. I'd worry about them only if forced to. In that situation, I'd need the contents of the tote.

A white plastic bag floated between Jamie and me. "You'll need this," my mother said. "Philip, are you all right?"

"Fine, Mom."

"Why did this happen to poor Dilsey?"

"The blinking tree lights," Jamie said. "I bet they triggered it. Happens with people."

That hadn't occurred to me. He was probably right. And that meant her seizures *weren't* coming closer together.

I scooted her away from the wetness and drizzled club soda over the soiled carpet. Someone patted the top of my head, and I squelched the urge to swat the hand away.

"You okay?" Mrs. Riggs. She sounded like my mother.

"Yes. Fine. Don't worry about me. I'm good." I knew what to do here and didn't want or need any sympathy.

She didn't take the hint. "Such a shame. She seemed like a good dog."

"Seemed?"

"Years ago, we had a dog with epilepsy, at least that's what the vet guessed. After the second seizure, we put him to sleep and got another dog."

The heat inside me exploded to my face. Jamie whistled under his breath, either recognizing my anger or experiencing his own reaction to the woman's stupid words. I'd always liked Mrs. Riggs, but I didn't know they'd thrown away what was probably a wonderful animal. To keep from lashing out with a reaction I'd regret, I clenched my jaw until she moved away.

From the kitchen archway, my father said, "She's just worried about you."

"Don't defend her."

Jamie and I waited for Dilsey to awaken. In the background, my mother urged everyone to the table, and my father passed us carrying the roasts. Our eyes met, and I thought he'd say something, rebuke me for ruining Christmas. But instead he looked at Dilsey, shook his head, and continued into the dining room.

CHAPTER 12

DILSEY AWAKENED SLOWLY, groaning and paddling as she swam up from the depth of unconsciousness. She raised her head and rolled onto her chest, Sphinx-like, looking around, blinking, and then staggered up onto splayed legs.

"I'm taking her out," I told Jamie. "Go eat. I'll finish cleaning up in a few minutes."

"I'll take care of it."

I unclipped Dilsey's leash and rocked her until she organized her wobbly legs. The wide hall was empty, the voices from the dining room subdued. The only two I distinguished were Madison's whimper and her father's comforting murmur. Bracing Dilsey with one hand on her collar and the other against her side, I helped her to the back porch and down the steps. The drizzle had increased to a light rain. By the time we reached the bottom step, her coordination had improved. I released her, and she swayed into the grass.

I sensed she'd have only the one seizure this time, but even the one surprised me. She seized on a fairly regular schedule and at a fairly predictable hour. I didn't expect the next one till about January tenth. This one, so soon after the last, and at an odd time of day, concerned me. I hoped Jamie was right about the tree lights triggering it.

At least I wouldn't have to suffer through a meal beside Audra Trent. She'd have nothing to say to me now. Most likely she took Dilsey's seizure as a deliberate affront from me to embarrass or offend her.

Dilsey puttered around the grass, snuffling from place to place, doing her business.

Jamie jaunted down the steps under an umbrella and handed me a second one. "The mood inside is somber, but everyone's recovering nicely from their hysteria. Mom and Dad have it all under control."

"Madison?"

"She's good. I swear her mother scared her worse than Dilsey did."

"Dilsey didn't try to bite her. The snapping was involuntary."

"I know. And if it makes you feel any better, Mom explained that. She's got your back."

It did make me feel better. Despite the gulf between us, she had been supportive and kind the past few days, and I needed to thank her.

"Let's go in; they're holding dinner for you. Mom rearranged the seating so you can put Dilsey in the hall and monitor her from the table." He grinned. "The perfect excuse to save you from Audra."

I shook my head. "I'll stay out here." I'd seen my father's frown when he'd carried the roasts to the table.

"Suit yourself." He jogged up the steps and into the house.

I called Dilsey and strode toward the fields. Although she provided an excuse to skip dinner, the awkward mingling among the guests earlier confirmed that events, time, and distance had irrevocably separated me from people I'd known my entire life. And with that confirmation came relief and freedom from whatever sense of responsibility toward them had lingered. I was right to have stayed away, and despite Emily Warner's email, I should have remained away.

A whistle shrill and clear, like the first note of an emergency siren, stopped me. Had to be my father. We—and my mother, too—had often accused him of summoning us like dogs. But he detested shouting, and his whistle resounded throughout the farm. We never mistook it for anything but what it was: a call to *come to the house now*.

Dilsey threw up her head and wheeled around, prancing in place for a moment before dashing back. I called her, and when she ignored me, I reluctantly followed. She sat on the bottom step, peering over her shoulder at me.

"We're waiting dinner on you," he called from the porch.

"I told Jamie—"

"I know what you told him." He held open the door.

"It's just better if I—"

"Don't complicate things. Come on in."

I didn't argue further, and as Dilsey and I passed him, he said, "We'll discuss it later."

"There's nothing to discuss."

"Later."

I washed my hands and settled Dilsey in the hallway. She aimed her twitching nose toward the dining room, and only then did I notice the luxurious blended aroma of the roasts and side dishes so unsettlingly familiar from past holidays.

From my seat on the corner, Irene Riggs to my right and my father to my left at the head of the table, I could reach Dilsey quickly without disturbing anyone. The kids sat on the opposite side at the other end, as far from Dilsey and me as possible. My mother faced my father at the foot, and the food at her end of the table mirrored the food at his. No one had begun eating, but someone had filled the wine glasses. The only thing missing had been me.

"Sorry for holding things up," I said.

My mother asked, "How's Dilsey?"

"She's okay now, thanks."

Mrs. Riggs smiled. If she mentioned euthanasia again, I wouldn't let it go this time. She didn't, though. She looked from my father down the length of the table to my mother. "Never a dull moment with y'all. Who's saying the blessing?"

"That would be me," my father said, and everyone around the table offered their hands to their neighbors. Mrs. Riggs squeezed my right hand. I laid my left on the napkin on my lap and stared at the hand my father offered. His split-second glare acknowledged the broken link.

I bowed my head with everyone else for his words of thanksgiving recited by rote. Why bother when what we should have been thankful for no longer existed?

Immediately after *amen*, Adrian Wells called out from his place on my mother's end of the table. "Laurel, Bennett, please forgive my impropriety here, but I'd like to propose that Philip offer up a toast."

What? I barely had time to register his words before my surprise escalated to anxiety. I darted a glance down the table but the five people between Wells and me blocked him. Was he joking? Even with time to form a proper toast, what would I possibly say? "Shouldn't my father do the honors?"

He forced a smile. "Go on, son."

I leaned forward to scan the faces around the table, some slightly smiling, some, like my mother, peering expectantly at me. The significance of Henry's squint and Jamie's almost imperceptible head shake weren't clear. My father shifted in his seat and frowned.

I gripped my wine glass by the base, and it shook a little. What I wanted to say was *Thanks loads, Adrian.* But instead I said, "Thank you, Mr. Wells," and again swept my gaze through the expectant guests. Suddenly, I knew the only toast I could possibly offer. It might not elevate the gathering or gladden their hearts, but at least it would be sincere.

I raised the glass, my hand steady once again. "To Teddy."

In the instant of profound silence that followed, I alone sipped my wine. I sat, dismayed—though I shouldn't have been—that even one simple mention of Teddy was enough to draw a silent, cold response from people who should have appreciated it. Then Jamie lifted his glass. "To Teddy," he said, meeting my eyes. My parents, their friends, and Henry echoed the toast, and Madison's little sister whined, "Mommy, I'm hungry."

We ate then, passing our plates family style to either end of the table for the prime rib and from person to person for everything else. Despite the tension, I found unexpected comfort in the same routine that had played out in my childhood. How surprising that, unlike so much else about our lives, it remained intact.

The children behaved. The adults did as well. They praised my parents' cooking, argued the seasons of their alma maters' football teams, and extolled the virtues of a local artist whose work had been displayed by an Atlanta museum. They reminisced about the year's celebrity deaths and the terrorist attacks in Paris and most recently California. The conversation flowed easily among friends who had shared their lives for decades.

I listened, avoiding eye contact with anyone, responding when spoken to but offering nothing. Even after all these years, or because of them, I had nothing to say. No one asked me anything of substance, and I guessed that they were reluctant to engage me, or that my parents had instructed them not to. My father glanced my way a few times but talked around me to others. No one mentioned Dilsey or acknowledged the delay to the meal. For people who knew as much about us as we knew about ourselves, they acted as if nothing out of the ordinary had happened. That didn't surprise me.

When we finished, Jamie, Henry, and I rose unbidden to clear the table, an ingrained holiday tradition I resumed automatically. Dilsey followed me and curled up under the kitchen table while we set the first round of plates on the counter. She remained there while we traipsed back and forth, with me rinsing dishes and loading the dishwasher, Henry filling coffee cups and carafes, and Jamie taking dessert orders. Jamie made a show out of scooping out the banana pudding and slicing the apple and sweet potato pie with surgical precision. He also got away with filching bites of everything and licking the utensils before he dropped them into the sink. During dessert at the dining room table and after-dinner drinks in the living room, Dilsey placed herself back in the hallway, watching for someone to drop food to the floor the whole time. Afterward, she trailed me from room to room.

I longed for Christmas to end.

At nine o'clock, when I accompanied my family into the drizzle with our departing guests, the day's heavy weight finally lifted. Each of the three sleepy children sprawled over a parent's shoulder.

In the parking area, Mr. Riggs pumped my hand. "Come visit us at the restaurant before you head back."

Mrs. Riggs kissed my cheek. "It was fabulous seeing you." She nodded to Dilsey. "You're too young to worry about a sick dog. Save it for when you have no choice, like when you have children." She squeezed my hands and settled into her passenger seat.

I clung to enough composure that I didn't slam her door. "Mind your own damn business," I muttered before noticing the several inches of open window. Maybe she hadn't heard me. Maybe I didn't care if she had.

Together in the drizzle, the five of us watched the line of taillights wind down the drive and disappear among the trees. I blew out a sigh of relief.

Henry laughed. "It wasn't *that* bad."

When I didn't respond, my mother said, "Don't think twice about Dilsey's seizure. I invited her downstairs. And Madison understands that Dilsey's sick and didn't mean to snap at her. She's fine." Her voice softened. "But are *you*?"

"I'm used to it. It's no big deal."

We filed along the walkway and up the steps onto the porch. My father opened the door for us, and waved Jamie and Henry through. To me, he said, "Wait."

My mother about-faced so abruptly, Jamie collided with her. "Not now, Bennett."

"It's all right. We'll be right in."

"*Bennett.*"

"Five minutes."

Her mouth tightened, and she disappeared into the house.

He shut the door.

I backed all the way to the railing. I'd known it was coming, whatever advice he thought he had the right to give. In the one day we'd been together, signs of his disapproval had been impossible to ignore. But I hadn't expected a lecture on Christmas night.

Dilsey frolicked around me, danced in front of Dad, and raced down the steps.

Arms crossed, Dad leaned against the door, blocking anyone from interrupting and me from escaping inside. "They're right, Irene and your mother. Even though Dilsey's good company, her epilepsy is taking an obvious toll on you."

I was incredulous, but remained calm. "It's not."

"If your mother hadn't allowed Dilsey in the house, you wouldn't be here. And isn't your real reason for taking her to school to keep an eye on her? Also," he said as he tilted his head, "how many thirty-year-old men haul around a dog crate fitted with crib bumpers?"

"All minor concessions."

"Those are three *minor* concessions I picked up while spending fewer than thirty-six hours with you. How many would Henry tell me about if I asked him?"

"None." I kept the extent of Dilsey's seizures to myself, of course. During the four months I'd shared Henry's house, he'd slept through all but one seizure and he accepted my explanation that insomnia caused my periodic bouts of exhaustion. He didn't need more information than that. No one did. I didn't need anyone's criticism or pity or ignorant advice. Dilsey's welfare was a matter solely between my vet and me.

His shoulders sagged. "Maybe you're allowing your concern for her to isolate you. From everything. From everyone. Is that healthy?"

"I assure you that I'm not isolating myself. I teach my students, mingle with faculty, fix my house—"

"And yet, after her seizure this afternoon, you wanted to skip dinner."

I shrugged.

"And here's something else: have you considered your liability if she bites someone?"

I pushed away from the railing. "Dilsey wouldn't ever hurt anyone." The truth was, until today, the possibility she might bite during a seizure hadn't occurred to me. But he didn't need to know that. Not having thought it through would be another strike against me.

"Intentionality on her part is irrelevant. Prior knowledge on yours is not."

I jammed my fists into my pockets. "I assure you that she is not going to bite anyone."

"Just look at the whole picture–legal, financial, and practical. Emotional. All quality-of-life issues."

"Her quality of life is excellent." I was furious.

"I'm not referring to *her* quality of life."

I turned my back on him. In the lamplight along the walkway, Dilsey trailed something elusive to me. Beyond her, the farm rested dark and quiet, the only sounds her panting and the drip-drip-drip of water from the eaves. "My quality of life is perfect," I said to the yard. "Frankly, though, it's none of your concern."

From directly behind me, he said quietly, "You're my son. Your life will always be my concern."

I whirled, yanking my hands from my pockets. He stood so close to me, I could have punched him easily. "Drop the fatherly pretense. You forfeited the right to be involved in my life long ago."

His tone was measured and maddeningly reasonable as he responded. "You could consider euthanasia, you know, before she–and you–suffer any more. Our farm vet can do it . . ."

Dilsey bounded onto the porch and retrieved her towel from the rocker. I edged away from my father and tugged it from her, hands shaking, blood pounding in my ears. "How convenient. When I get home, all I'd have to do is donate her stuff to a rescue and trash her meds. Like she never existed." Just like Teddy.

"That's not what I—"

Furious, I pushed inside and went upstairs, past the landing devoid of photographic evidence that we ever were a family, past Teddy's locked door, to my room at the end of the hall. When Dilsey's tail cleared the threshold, I slammed the door so hard, the balcony and bathroom and closet doors rattled. The clamor didn't resound like the co-ordinated midnight slams Henry once orchestrated, but it was the best I could do alone.

CHAPTER 13

I DIDN'T CONSCIOUSLY decide to leave the farm, but when I woke earlier than usual the next morning—exhausted, throat dry, eyes gritty—I knew I would. If I went before anyone else woke up, it would be as if I hadn't been there at all, as it had been for years and as it should have remained. The son who died and the son who might as well have, both without a place in the family. Most likely, my early departure would annoy Henry, but he had other transportation options. No reason to ask him if he wanted to leave this soon. He wouldn't.

I tossed my suitcase onto the bed and threw clothes into it, not packing so much as emptying the dresser drawers and closet. From her cushion, Dilsey tracked my every move, ears so alert that they wrinkled her forehead, knowing we were leaving and accepting the plan with no need to understand why. Dogs were so easy.

In the hallway lit by a single nightlight across from the stairs, I eased along the creaky oak planks of the old house, carrying my rolling bag in my left hand and holding Dilsey's collar with my right. At Teddy's door, I hesitated, fighting an urgent desire to kick it in and learn once and for all whether his room was untouched or empty or something in between.

But I moved on.

Downstairs, I flipped on the back porch light. The rain had stopped. Not that I minded it. Like the darkness, it soothed me even when I had to drive in it. Especially then.

Dilsey trotted away to take care of her business. I loaded my suitcase into the Expedition and wheeled the empty cooler to the house. In the kitchen, I switched on the coffee pot, then loaded the cooler with Dilsey's food and set her meds bag on top of it. She needed to eat soon, but I'd stop to feed her. I tore a sheet from the notepad by the phone and left my message by the coffee pot, weighted with the pen: *Thanks for your hospitality. —P.*

Dilsey waited on the porch. I snagged her damp towels from the rocker, remembering the one she'd cheerfully brought to me while Dad and I argued about her the previous night, and loaded everything into the SUV, including her. One more trip upstairs, and I'd be on my way.

I opened the back door and bumped into Jamie. As he had Christmas Eve morning, he wore shorts and a T-shirt, but today he was barefoot. He clutched a piece of paper that looked suspiciously like my note.

"Go back to bed," I said, startled. I'd been so quiet.

He scowled. "What're you doing?"

"Exactly what it looks like. Heading home." I stated it matter-of-factly, feeling neither embarrassed at getting caught nor defensive for deciding to go.

He thrust the note in my face. "This is so rude." He crumpled it and dropped it between us.

"Better than nothing." I flattened my hand on his chest and pushed him into the house, kicking the balled-up note aside.

"*Worse* than nothing." He balanced himself and picked it up. "You weren't going to say goodbye even to me."

"I didn't want to wake you."

"Bullshit."

"Call it whatever you want."

"And you're stranding Henry."

"He can ride back with you. Or rent a car. Or fly." I pushed past him to the staircase, and when I reached the landing, he called out, "You're just pissed about last night."

"Shh." The last thing I needed was our parents appearing. "I'm not." Validated. Determined. But no longer angry.

I expected him to follow me, but he didn't. When I descended the stairs with Dilsey's cushion and water bowl and the sheets from my bed, he was standing by the dark Christmas tree holding my crumpled note by a corner, eying me. He opened his mouth but said nothing.

After dropping Dilsey's things and the sheets by the door, I returned to the kitchen to rewrite my note and pour my coffee. When I turned around, Jamie leaned on the doorframe.

"Dad told Mom what he said to you."

"Of course he did. He tells her everything."

"She was furious with him. Told him you'd be gone when we got up this morning. Told him he needs to learn, and I quote, 'when to keep your damned mouth shut.'"

I blinked in disbelief. She never spoke that way to him—nor he to her—at least not within earshot of me. "She did not."

"She did. He shouldn't have talked about Dilsey the way he did—I get it. But the big point you're missing is that they're worried about you."

"They don't care enough to worry. They're meddling."

He juggled my note from hand to hand. "You don't know how it's been, because you took off right after your rehab. As though you blamed everything on them. The shooting. Teddy's death. Your injuries. Don't forget Dad almost died too."

"I don't blame them. I—"

"And you cut *me* out, and I don't know why. What was so damn hard about sticking around? I *needed* you. Did that ever occur to you, you selfish bastard?"

"Jamie—"

"Yeah, you intentionally cut me out of your life, and I resent the hell out of it."

As I sipped my blistering coffee to give myself time to prepare a response, he took one long stride toward me, his face tight, his hands balled into fists. "You should've come here to apologize for disappearing, but you showed up only because you wanted something. How inconsiderate and selfish. And now you've got yourself all worked up, and you're not even staying long enough to ask what you came for."

"I learned what I came for. Part of it anyway." After last night, even if I stayed, my father and I couldn't have a civil discussion about anything, much less a topic as volatile as Emily Warner. Meaning no talk about the shooting and nothing about Teddy.

She'd made such a mess of my life.

I left the kitchen through the door into the dining room. When I emerged into the hall, Henry was perched on the bottom step—like Jamie, barefoot. I gestured at my sheets. "Toss those into the washer, okay?"

"You can't leave." His gaze bounced from me to the sheets to Jamie, who'd followed me.

"You can ride back with Jamie."

"What? No. I don't care about that. Can't you apologize and stay? We still have another week. We—"

"Henry, I'm not apologizing. I'm leaving. I tried, but it's too complicated."

Jamie snorted. "You haven't tried at all."

With Dilsey's bed and bowl wedged under my arm, and carrying my coffee, I returned to my truck and Dilsey. I sat there unmoving, gripping the wheel, staring through the rain-speckled windshield. Jamie was wrong; I did try, but my father had proven the pointlessness of any attempt to reconnect. In the past two weeks, I'd thought more about the shooting and Teddy and the distance between us than I had in years. Stewing about all that stuff was part of trying. I thought I'd moved past the shooting, but if questions from a girl about as old as Teddy would be now affected me so deeply, could I have really moved on?

In light of my disastrous visit, I couldn't imagine ever returning. I'd finish remodeling my house and pass the years teaching students to read analytically and to write. Meanwhile, despite his doubts, Jamie would become an excellent surgeon. Henry would shuffle real estate documents from one corner of his desk to another. Both of them would eventually raise families. My father would continue manipulating people and policy, and my mother would oversee all of them and the farm too. Henry would update me. He'd always be around, would always know what was happening with my family. Teddy would remain dead. And the same questions would remain unanswered because no one ever looked back long enough to answer them.

Even Emily would move on.

In a couple of hours, my parents would find my note— it and the pile of sheets the only evidence I'd been there. With a pang of regret so strong it surprised me, I realized I hadn't thanked my mother for allowing Dilsey to stay in the house. I should have done that first thing. I should add it to my note, right now, before I reconsidered. I opened my door and, in the unrelenting drizzle, returned to the house.

The sheets lay where I'd dropped them. Henry was gone. Jamie slouched on the third step, elbows on knees, head in his hands, a shift in position his only acknowledgment of me.

In the kitchen, I reread my note and sighed. It *was* inadequate and—Jamie was right—it was rude. Worse than no note at all. A quick thanks about Dilsey wouldn't remedy that.

Not knowing what else to say and unwilling to wait long enough to figure it out, I tore the note in half and then in half again twice more and floated the pieces like confetti into the trash can.

CHAPTER 14

THE DAY AFTER New Year's, Henry's Mercedes vanished from my driveway while Dilsey and I hiked around a Grainger eerily quiet without the students. Henry had the gate code, so he didn't need me there to let him in. But he hadn't warned me he was coming. Neither he nor Jamie had contacted me since I left the farm—unlike Emily Warner, who'd emailed me at least once every day. I'd deleted every email without responding.

I leaned back in the recliner in my study. Henry had come and gone without leaving a note, so I didn't know whether our plans for my house repairs over the next few weekends were still on. It wasn't like him to leave me hanging, but after he and the others rehashed our conversations and my abrupt departure, he was probably pissed. Twice I'd started a text to him, then deleted it. If he intended to come, he'd contact me or show up. Not that I *needed* him there to finish the house. All that remained was a bit more painting and dealing with leaky plumbing under the kitchen sink. Henry could fix nearly anything, and what he couldn't fix, he could patch or conceal. Until he got over being pissed, what I couldn't handle myself I'd have to hire someone to do.

The real problem was that without him around, I wasn't motivated. Instead, I immersed myself in second semester prep, which now included reading garbage that had no bearing on writing or literature, including didactic and repetitive psychology articles about *managing* people involved in—new favorite term of the administration—*mass disasters*. In addition, the university urged all faculty and staff members to avail themselves of the counselors hired for the students. Grainger University needed to acknowledge that, yes, we'd survived a tragic event and should recognize the event with a small token—a moment of silence or a memorial tree—but should then proceed with providing a top-notch education to the students.

It's not that simple, something inside of me warned, but I pushed away the thought. Life was all about moving forward and marching on. I considered whether telling Emily Warner about the statute regarding TBI investigations would enable her to move forward, but mostly I wondered whether it would stop her from pestering me. Although, like me, she still wouldn't know why her father had attacked us, that minor piece of information should assure her no one had concealed relevant details. My father seemed to have no qualms about telling me, and telling Emily was the least I could do.

I suddenly questioned whether he had told me the truth. Using a few keywords, I found what I needed. Records of criminal investigations of the Tennessee Bureau of Investigation *were* confidential. I ran my hand through my hair. So why hadn't Emily found that information?

Cut her a break, I scolded myself. Even after she said the records didn't exist, I had never considered researching that possibility because I'd assumed a political or other ulterior motive for their unavailability or some wheeling-and-dealing on my father's part to keep them secret.

Still, I wavered about emailing her.

But my role in her life–killing her father, leaving her an orphan–unintentional as it was, began to nag at me. I owed her the simple explanation, and sharing it should satisfy her enough to stop her from harassing me. On the other hand, she'd been persistent enough that any communication from me had the potential to encourage her to continue to hound me.

I needed to think more about contacting her. Or not.

The day before classes resumed, I conceded to my conscience and emailed her: *By law, the police investigation records of the shooting aren't available. Takes an "act of Congress" to get them. Simple as that.*

That simple explanation should eliminate any need Emily had to contact me further.

CHAPTER 15

MY FIRST CLASS of the delayed semester began two weeks after the New Year. After obsessing about whether to arrive early to "be there" for the students or to trail the stragglers and give everyone time to talk before I disrupted them, I ultimately split the difference. Not because of indecision but because that was when I arrived. I'd been up nearly the entire night with a seizing Dilsey and delivered her well before daylight to my vet because I couldn't leave her at home alone or in my office in her condition. Then I raced around campus in search of one of Grainger's coveted parking spaces and stopped by my office to deposit my jacket and laptop and print out my roster and notes.

Scottie Marston hopped off the bench outside my office when I approached.

"Hi, Scottie." I unlocked the door.

She followed me into the office and eyed me for longer than seemed necessary. "You all right?"

"Fine."

"Because you look..." She cocked her head. "...disheveled."

"Do you need something? I have class in a minute." I revved up my laptop.

"Seventeen minutes. This'll take three. You remember Nicole, the girl that Dilsey—"

"I remember."

"She's in your first class. Trish wondered if you'd bring Dilsey to class to kind of ease Nicole back into things. You know, like a therapy dog."

I called up my roster, and my printer hummed to life. Even though Dilsey accompanied me to school nearly every day, bringing her into the classroom had never occurred to me. Our department chair's suggestion surprised me.

"Not a good idea; Dilsey will distract everyone. What if someone's allergic to her?" *What if she seizes? Snaps? Bites someone?*

Scottie handed me the page from the printer. "Speaking of, where is she?"

"Not here today. She wasn't feeling well."

"Aww." She leaned against the doorframe. "So, I can tell Trish yes?"

I considered the idea while the printer spit out my notes. Having Dilsey's gentle, calming presence in class intrigued me. Besides, bringing her to class would be my concession to the counseling the administration was pushing. If she were with me today, I'd do it. Probably. "Tell her I'll think about it."

"Better than no, I guess."

We parted ways on the second floor. I dragged myself into the classroom at seven fifty, wanting only to cross my arms on my desk, rest my head on them, and sleep.

Six or seven students had circled their desks in the center of the room, facing in, Diet Cokes and napkins scattered among them. Despite the early hour, they appeared to have been there a while. A large Rubbermaid container topped by a roll of paper towels sat on an empty desk.

My arrival killed their chatter. They assessed me without even pretending to be covert about it. Feeling and looking like road kill was not how I'd planned to greet the semester.

"Um, happy New Year."

"Hey, Dr. Rutledge." The greeting was from Kate, the girl I'd stumbled upon in the stairwell the day of the fire. "Happy New Year to you too. Want a muffin? We're celebrating surviving last semester."

"Literally," another one said, and they all laughed.

That wasn't what I expected. I'd envisioned them staring at me teary-eyed, awaiting consolation, which I had neither the inclination nor the ability to provide. Maybe humor in the face of sadness buoyed them, and I wouldn't have to struggle through class with devastated kids, because they weren't actually devastated.

"He doesn't need a muffin." A guy I didn't know interrupted my thoughts. "He needs coffee. By IV."

More laughter. Not laughter—snickers. I must have looked like shit.

Not sure what else to do, I moved to the tub and lifted the lid. I selected a blueberry muffin, tore off a paper towel, and sat behind my desk. My presence had stifled the banter, and the students seemed to be waiting for me to say something.

"Don't mind me. We still have a few minutes before class begins." I tossed out a smile and picked at the muffin. They resumed murmuring among themselves. A few more students joined the group. One was Nicole.

Right away she asked, "Where's your dog?"

"Not here today."

"Can you bring her?"

I suspected she'd planted the idea with Trish, not vice versa. Wasn't Nicole afraid of dogs? *Dilsey's special,* Scottie had said.

Kate smiled. "I told everyone at home how awesome she is. Showed off her viral videos and photos."

"Ugh." I didn't mean to comment aloud.

"I did too," Nicole added. "Please let her hang out with us."

"I'm considering it," I said as the library bell sounded eight o'clock. I shut the door and counted heads.

Ninety-five minutes later, finished with class, I reached my office. Overall, the class had gone much better than I'd expected. Fire notwithstanding, the kids would be fine.

The relief energized me. In the twenty-five minutes before my second and final class of the day, if I hustled I'd have time to call Dr. Emerson to check on Dilsey, shower, and get back to campus only a few minutes late.

I dropped my folder of notes on my desk. My office phone blinked with a message I didn't have time to listen to, but I listened anyway in case it was Dr. Emerson.

"I get that you're busy with classes, but *please* call me back." Emily Warner.

My inclination was to grab my phone, remind her that yesterday's email about the investigation records more than met any obligation I had to her, and reiterate *leave me alone.* But I didn't. Nor did I go home or call Dr. Emerson. Instead, I slumped into my chair and stared out the window through half-closed eyes, thinking about everything and nothing until an urgent sense of passing time prompted me to glance at my watch and hustle, five minutes late and unprepared, to my ten o'clock class.

Afterward, I stopped by the vet. Even though Dilsey loved Dr. Emerson and used each clinic visit as a prime friend-finding opportunity, I worried about her. The staff could handle her seizures and post-seizure behavior, of course, but not the way I did. I couldn't imagine Dilsey was anything more than just another patient to them.

The receptionist scrutinized me and pointed toward the row of molded plastic chairs sitting against the wall, then disappeared. A moment later, she returned to her station. Dr. Emerson entered the lobby from one of the exam rooms, and I rose to greet her.

"Dilsey's fine," she said. "Woozy, but no more seizures."

"Great. Can she go home?"

"I'm keeping her till we close. Not for her sake—for yours. Get some sleep and don't worry about her."

"I'm good," I said, eager to settle her in at home.

"Have you *looked* at yourself?"

I smiled. I liked Dr. Emerson. How she'd landed in an out-of-the-way college town like Grainger was a mystery to me but a miracle for Dilsey. "I've gotten that a lot today."

"Not the best start to the semester for you, huh?"

"It is what it is."

"I swear I don't know anyone else who'd go through what you do for Dilsey. Her amazing quality of life is a testament to your dedication."

"Thanks, but it's what anyone would do." Except Irene and Dan Riggs. Except my father.

"We'd like to think so, but it's not." She pulled on my arm and physically turned me toward the door. "We love having Dilsey, though we don't love the reason she's here. She's such a happy, good-natured soul. Even as we speak, she's keeping a couple of techs company in the break room during lunch."

"They won't feed—"

"Philip, go home. We close at six."

I left, but my house was empty without Dilsey. Everywhere I went, she went, shadowing me from room to room, including the bathroom. Eventually, I'd convinced her I preferred to shower alone, but still, every time I shooed her out, she softened her dark eyes, flattened her ears, and drooped her soft lips. I missed her today.

After I showered and shaved, I considered crawling into bed and pulling the covers over my head to make all of it—Dilsey's seizures, the fire, my classes, Emily Warner—vanish. But it wouldn't vanish, and so I dressed instead.

Simultaneously exhausted and wired, I entered my downstairs study and switched on the floor lamp beside my recliner. As it always did since I placed it there just after Christmas, the framed photo on my bookcase drew my attention. Ross, our farm manager, had taken it—Teddy and me astride Huckleberry and Sawyer on our last ride before I returned to college my junior year. After Teddy died, after he no longer mattered, I boxed up the photo. But memories of Teddy evoked by contact with Emily kindled a need to see that photo.

I brushed dust from it and settled into the recliner with a sandwich and my laptop, intending to reread my class notes, review the syllabus I'd reviewed a hundred times already, and check email for questions from students or directives from the administration.

Why couldn't I just ignore Emily's message? I'd already told her what I knew; that should have ended it. What else did she want from me? I sighed. The only way to find out was to call her. While I was at it, I'd reiterate that I didn't know anything else and hope that the admission would convince her to leave me alone. I called her from the kitchen where my phone was charging.

She answered on the first ring.

"How'd you find out about that law?"

"From my father."

"You believe him?"

Embarrassed to admit I'd not trusted him enough to take his word for it, I squirmed, glad she couldn't see me. "I looked it up."

"So how do I go about getting the act of Congress you mentioned?"

I should have figured she'd ask. "Ha. It's impossible."

"Nothing's impossible, not if you want it bad enough."

"I don't know. Hire a lawyer."

"Your father's a lawyer. Ask him."

I should've seen that coming too. "Look, Ms. Warner–"

"Emily. I *have* to see those police records. They must contain some clue about why my father attacked y'all. Please."

I wound the charger cord around my fingers. "So, I find out for you, if that's even possible, and then what? You'll want something else from me and something else after that."

She laughed a little. "Yeah, you're probably right. It's that important."

I unwound the cord. I wanted to tell her it wasn't important, not any longer. But if that were the case, I wouldn't have gone to the farm or asked my father about the investigation records. I wouldn't have emailed Emily about them and now returned her call, not even because of my guilt, justified or not, for leaving her parentless. Or was it more than that? And if it was more, what did that *more* entail?

And what if I did help her? What an unwelcome thought. My own life wouldn't change in any appreciable way. Helping her wouldn't affect my job, my house, my dog. What I'd learned from the shooting and its aftermath wouldn't change. I'd still have only one brother.

Helping her would waste my time and cost a few awkward conversations with Henry and possibly with my father, which would piss him off—actually a benefit, under the circumstances.

Ultimately, we'd learn little or nothing. Then I'd walk away, and she'd be gone. She'd have found nothing, but she'd have tried. Ten years too late, she'd move on with her life. More importantly, I'd move on with mine. Again.

I should have said no, but saying yes would end it for both of us.

"All right," I said. She now had my cell number in her call log, and I gave her my personal email. "Let me see what I can find out. I'll call you."

CHAPTER 16

ON SATURDAY AFTERNOON, I set the baby monitor on the kitchen counter and gated Dilsey in with a new bone before carrying primer, tray, and rollers upstairs to the last unpainted bedroom. Shortly before Thanksgiving, Henry had smoothed over the nicks and scars in the old plaster there and in the dining room so we could finish before Christmas. When he got busy with work and the fire happened, the patched walls remained unpainted. Now, I resigned myself to finishing alone. Not a big deal. I'd prime and paint as much as I could, then hire someone to take care of the spots I didn't have the maneuverability in my right arm to reach or the ambidexterity in my left to manage without creating a mess. Dining room now, and then, after supper, the bedroom. Alone with the blank walls and the chilly breeze flowing through the open windows, and despite the smooth jazz from a radio, I surrendered to thoughts of Emily and her father, and mine.

Since I'd spoken with her two days earlier, I'd wrestled with how to get access to TBI records without asking Dad. Henry might know, but apparently he was still miffed about me leaving the farm; I hadn't heard from him. Another option was Adrian Wells—I'd known and respected him my entire life. But he'd tell my father, which would lead to another heated discussion between us that I could avoid by asking him directly. Or I could hire an attorney I didn't know, but that option presented its own set of problems.

Hands on autopilot, my thoughts circled back to Henry. I might have left the farm without him, but I hadn't stranded him there. He was being a jerk about not getting in touch. If I were to get this thing with Emily done, I had to move past our differences. I hoped he would as well.

The work went smoothly, and after supper, I left a message for Henry, not expecting an immediate response since, as was typical on the weekends, he probably had a date with one girl or another. "We need to talk about the girl who contacted me about the shooting. Call me tomorrow."

In about ninety seconds, my phone pinged with a one-word text. *No.*

Did that mean *No, we don't need to talk about her* or *No, I won't call you tomorrow*? I texted back *No, what?* No response.

I left another voicemail. "I'm sorry about leaving without you at Christmas, but I had to go. I assume you're tied up tonight, but please call me in the morning. I have questions for you."

When a few minutes later my phone pinged again, I snatched it up. Maybe he didn't want to postpone the discussion till tomorrow.

But Emily had sent the latest text.

Thx again! Looking forward 2 hearing from u.

I hoped I didn't regret involving myself in her search for information.

Henry didn't call that night, but he also didn't call the next morning, nor did he acknowledge either of the two additional voicemails I left him. I wanted to believe his social life distracted him, but I wasn't sure it did. The worst part was, unless I continued to wait for him, I saw no other option but to call my father instead.

I'd last phoned my father during my senior year of college. Since then, Henry delivered the few messages we exchanged. As strange as it was, I didn't have my father's cell number. I didn't know whether my parents were at the farm or in Washington, so when I was sure they'd be home from church regardless of where they were, I sat on the back porch steps, back hunched against the wind while Dilsey explored a yard crisscrossed with sunshine and the shadows of naked tree branches, and called my mother's cell to ask her for his number.

"Philip. To what do we owe this pleasant surprise?"

My father's cheerful–arguably snarky–greeting dismayed me, and my mouth went dry. I'd never considered he might answer Mom's phone, and I wasn't prepared to talk with him. Certainly not now. I'd planned to enter his number into my phone, throw the ball for Dilsey, bathe her, and vacuum the house from top to bottom while mentally outlining what I'd ask and how I'd ask it. Procrastination? No, not really. Well, maybe. Moot now, though, because here we were, the two of us, and I couldn't think of a thing to say except, "Where are you?"

"Washington."

"Oh. Okay."

Something clanked in the background. He must be emptying the dishwasher. "Your classes have started?"

"As of Thursday."

"And your students?"

"All freshmen, as before."

"I mean, how're they handling being back?"

I didn't want to discuss my students. "Fine."

He waited a beat, I suspected for me to elaborate, then asked, "What's up with your house? Your mother and I would love to see it."

I couldn't imagine inviting my parents to Grainger—hated the idea. They didn't belong here. "Uh, it won't be finished for a while." I hope Henry hadn't mentioned how little work remained.

It was a long moment before he said, "And Dilsey? How's she doing?"

"She's fine." No way would I talk to him about her, not after our last discussion.

"I tried. I give up." His words were distant; he'd moved the phone away from his mouth. His sigh and the words that followed, however, came through loud and clear. "Since your mother's up to her elbows in flour, what message can I relay? I hope it's an apology for leaving so abruptly after Christmas."

In the background, Mom said, "Bennett, leave him alone."

I swallowed hard, recognizing I *did* owe her an apology. "I called to get your number."

His laugh contained no humor. "That's interesting, since you don't seem to have much to say to me."

I didn't know how to respond, so I remained quiet.

"I'll text it to you. But you've got me here and now, so what's up?"

I rose and paced the backyard, scuffing twigs and acorns. "I need to talk to you about the shooting investigation records. And Emily Warner."

"The hell you do."

"I'm helping her figure out how to get those records, and I—" I *loathed* saying it. "I need procedural advice from you. I asked

Henry first so I wouldn't have to bother you"—*so I wouldn't have to deal with you at all*—"but he's not returning my calls."

The shift in ambient sound told me he'd moved to another room, probably out of earshot of my mother. "Please tell me why you need to involve yourself in this."

Before the shooting, I could've been honest with him about what drove me: my need for answers, guilt for killing Gardner, admiration for Emily's resolve. But we had barely spoken since then, and our conversations had been terse and contentious. So, all I told him now was that helping her was the easiest way to get rid of her. It wasn't untrue.

"If you let it go," he said, "she'll disappear on her own."

"She won't. She hasn't yet. Besides, I can't let it go either. Not this time. What her father did was inconsistent with everything she believes about him. I get that she was young then, but"—I remembered what Emily had asked—"what if *you* did something contrary to what we knew of you? Wouldn't you want us to learn the truth, maybe even clear your name?"

"There's no clearing his name."

"Can't you understand why she—and why I—need to know why he came after us?"

"He came after *me*," Dad said quietly. "The rest of you were collateral damage."

No one had ever confirmed this, and now I recalled Emily's list of reasons her father would have attacked us, or at least Dad. "How do you know?"

"Someone is always threatening me. I've pissed off a lot of people over the years." He stated it matter-of-factly, bravely. "Even colleagues. Every threat was investigated. Occasionally, someone was arrested. I did have security measures in place, yet the weekend of our hunting trip, I made the mistake of abandoning those. Hell, the property is in the middle of nowhere. I wanted time alone with you boys. That's why I insisted Zack stay home."

"Had Gardner threatened you before?" My stomach roiled. Was involving his family in a threat he'd ignored additional evidence that we meant nothing to Dad?

"No. I wouldn't have endangered all of you by discounting him."

We were both quiet. Despite the security around him, private and otherwise, for nearly two decades and the news reports of threats and worse against other public figures, I'd never considered his job might be dangerous. He'd never discussed possible dangers with us. But knowing now about those dangers didn't change the questions I had and the answers I needed.

Dilsey delivered a gooey, muddy tennis ball. I petted her and scratched under her chin before throwing the ball and wiping my hand on my jeans. "When Emily finds what she's looking for or we reach a dead end, she'll disappear. I see no reason not to help her. I'm not asking you to actually do anything. Just tell me how to get the Tennessee records released or give me the name of someone who'd know. I can take it from there."

"Philip, please, leave this alone. Concentrate on your teaching and your house instead. And your dog."

Please? If I didn't know him so well, I'd think he was pleading. But pleading wasn't his style. Suggesting strongly, demanding–that was how Bennett Rutledge operated. Nothing about his response seemed right, and I wasn't sure why. "I'll think about it."

"I don't believe you will. Why can't you drop this?"

"You mean drop it *again*. Not this time." I was finished with the conversation. "You'll text me your number?"

"Yes," he said, and we disconnected.

I called Dilsey inside and settled into the recliner in my study with a Killian's, a legal pad, and laptop on my outstretched legs. Dilsey lay on the rug by the unlit fireplace, her head elevated on the cold brick.

My father hadn't answered my question, but our talk wasn't entirely unproductive. The biggest advance was the relative civility of our conversation—a surprising and considerable plus if I needed to call him again for the specifics that hadn't been forthcoming today.

I alternated chewing the end of my pen and tapping it on the pad, which remained blank. Now that I had to actively think about the shooting—not dismiss it as I had for most of the past decade—my mind was blank.

Emily claimed to know her father, but how could the man she remembered be the same man who attacked us? The same man who abandoned her? He had to have known that even if he survived—and I guessed he expected to survive, or at least hoped to—he'd spend years in prison. Dead or alive, he'd be abandoning his daughter. If Gardner *had* planned the shooting, why was my father's death worth a lifetime separate from the child he supposedly loved? Maybe Gardner had snapped. I included the possibility, but I didn't believe it. Even as a child, Emily would have noticed signs of problems, and she'd have mentioned those when we met. Or maybe she wouldn't have been *that* honest.

Time for some research.

With a bit of digging, I found the actual statute, which stated the two ways TBI records would be released: by court order or subpoena. That sounded like we needed an attorney. That was all right; I hadn't necessarily expected the search to be easy. If my father wouldn't find an attorney for us or tell me how to request those records myself, I'd figure something out.

I browsed for anything related to Vincent Gardner or the shooting but found nothing more than Emily had in her notebook. The nagging feeling that the search and pushing through all the red tape might be more complicated and take longer than I'd expected overwhelmed me. I'd been ignorant of the details for over ten years already. What was a little more time?

Mentally exhausted, I set aside everything Emily-related and worked on class prep until suppertime. As I contemplated the contents of the refrigerator, Dilsey dashed from the kitchen to the front door, and even before her excited whining escalated, I knew Henry had arrived. No one else could get in. Maybe he'd brought dinner.

He entered the kitchen, and I gave him the once-over.

"You couldn't just return my call?" But I was glad to see him.

Dilsey danced around him. "You're lookin' good, Miss D." He play-grabbed her muzzle. "I'm here to talk some sense into your owner."

"About what?"

"What's for dinner?"

"Leftover meatloaf?"

"That works."

I handed him a beer, and he settled at the table, Dilsey at his feet thumping her tail against the legs of his chair. "About Christmas."

"Don't start, Henry. You know why I left. I don't want a bunch of drama over it."

"I didn't cause any drama." He drew circles on the table with his beer, smeared the condensation with his sleeve, and set the bottle on a napkin. "But that's not why I'm here. Since your call last night, I've been thinking about that girl. If she contacts you again—"

"That horse already left the barn. I'm helping her." An unexpected wave of satisfaction at defying him, and my father, washed over me. I prepped the meatloaf for the oven, waiting for his reaction.

When I faced him again, he'd leaned back in his chair and crossed his arms. His argument pose.

"She threatened you, didn't she?"

"Not at all."

"Then I don't get it."

"She's asking me what I asked my parents ten years ago, questions they never answered. How could this guy pull off the shooting? How'd he track us down in the middle of absolute nowhere? Why would he even want to?"

"He was nuts. And crazy people do things that make no sense to normal people. Drop it. This'll become a big mess that someone else will have to clean up. Your dad can't get involved because of his position, so that leaves me, and I don't want any part of it."

I shoved the meatloaf into the oven. "It won't get messy. All we need is a little help with getting a subpoena or a court order to release the TBI records."

"You help her with this, and next she'll want money and God only knows what else."

He's probably right. "*It's that important,*" Emily had said.

"She won't." I made sure he was looking at me when I added, "That's not what she's after."

He sipped his beer and rubbed Dilsey with one foot. I stuck yesterday's mashed potatoes in the microwave and chopped a cucumber and a tomato for a salad before he spoke again.

"Fine. I'll advise you, maybe give you some contacts." He pointed his beer bottle at me. "Nothing hands-on, but only to keep you out of trouble. I'm telling you, though, that getting involved with her is a bad idea. I've realized, though, that she and her quest are what nudged you to go home. Even though that visit turned to shit, it was a start. If Vincent Gardner's daughter is what it takes to push you closer to your family, the least I can do is offer a little help. But there's one catch."

"Of course there is." But I was relieved and pleased at his offer of advisement. Our plans had just taken a great leap forward.

"I get to meet her first. But if she's conning you or causing you—any of you—more pain than you've already suffered, I'll do my damnedest to make sure that she never bothers any of us again. Got it?"

"Got it." He was going to help, and the price was a meeting with Emily. Easy.

"You arrange the time and place for us to meet, and I'll be there." Leaving his empty bottle on the table, he disappeared into the dining room and rummaged noisily around in the wine fridge. When he reentered the kitchen with a bottle of cab, he nodded back toward the dining room. "You painted without me? You thought I wouldn't help you finish?"

"I didn't know."

He frowned and poured a glass for each of us. "To finishing together what we start together."

I clinked my glass against his, grateful for his friendship, and looking forward to him helping me get rid of Emily once and for all.

CHAPTER 17

I EXPECTED HENRY'S assistance regardless of what he thought about Emily because he seemed as anxious to get rid of her as I was. His help would bolster our ability to get this project over with, if not as quickly as I'd like, at least efficiently. Emily would be pleased.

But her tone when I phoned her the next afternoon to arrange a meeting held an edge that suggested wariness. "Why now? He could've saved me a lot of time and trouble answering the email I sent him last fall."

So she *had* contacted him. "Those connections you think I have? He's the main one, the only one. He knows people and processes and can get us on the right track. But he wants to meet you in person, as he would any client."

"Client?" Now she sounded amused. "I hope I can afford him."

"You can."

We agreed to meet the following Saturday in Grainger's fifties diner, Cast Party. For the five days before that, I'd relegate Emily and the shooting to a back burner and focus on my students.

My Monday morning university email contained another plea from the administration for faculty members to avail themselves of the counselors to deal with their own fire-associated emotions to better "manage our students during this difficult time." I deleted the email as soon as I scanned it. We didn't need to "manage" anyone.

My concession to helping the students was to allow Dilsey to attend class. She'd recovered from the previous week's seizures, and I didn't expect any repeat of the Christmas disaster, at least not this week, but keeping a close eye on her wouldn't hurt.

In each class, Dilsey trotted among the kids, tail waving up and down and side to side, greeting everyone before settling by me. Occasionally, and without any reason I detected, she gravitated to one student or another, leaning on a leg or flopping down by a desk. First period Tuesday, she spent the entire class under Nicole's feet.

During that first full week of the semester, my students settled into a routine, enthusiastically greeting Dilsey at the start of each class, trailing their hands along her back as she trotted up and down the aisles, petting her as they exited the room at the end of class. As the week progressed, Dilsey increasingly stayed more often beside me than among them, proving to me that they didn't need to be comforted. By Friday morning—the only time all week Emily contacted me, and only to confirm we were still on for the following day—Dilsey scarcely left me at all.

At one o'clock on Saturday, Henry and I pulled into Cast Party's parking lot one after the other and found Emily huddled in her running Focus. She'd backed into her space to, I presumed, make a quick getaway. I knocked on her window, and when she emerged along with a blast of heat into the frigid sunshine, I introduced her to Henry. She offered her hand, and he clasped it a beat too long. The slight downturn of her mouth indicated she noticed too. My confidence in his assistance wavered at his power play.

Inside, the soda fountain counter from the diner's original life as a drug store remained, but otherwise Cast Party was a big open room with vinyl aqua booths along the walls and down the middle, and pink chairs and chrome-legged Formica-topped tables everywhere else. The atmosphere and prices resonated with the students and with my colleagues as well. An old jukebox in one corner played nothing but Broadway show tunes.

A booth was too cozy for our purposes, so I requested a table. Henry sat to my left, and Emily sat across from me. He wore a sport coat over a dress shirt, a contrast to my more casual attire. Emily had dressed up too: business casual and makeup, with her hair styled instead of pulled into a ponytail. She looked older and more serious than she had either of the two times I'd seen her. I realized how meaningful they both considered the meeting–how desperately she wanted to impress him, how determined he was to intimidate her–and my momentary bemusement dissolved into concern.

After we ordered, Henry opened the teal notebook Emily had placed in front of him. At first, he flipped nonchalantly through the pages, but then he slowed until he handled each page almost tenderly, scanning the words before advancing to the next page. The deeper he delved into the notebook, the more slowly he read–and the more he clenched and unclenched his hands. I remembered my first reaction and sympathized with him. He said nothing, and neither Emily nor I interrupted him. The waitress arrived with our beverages and, without glancing up, Henry edged the binder closer to himself.

When he reached the last page, he sat quietly, hands flat on each side of the open notebook, holding it down, staring at it. When he lifted his head, to my astonishment, his eyes glistened.

He shoved the binder toward Emily, stood, and cleared his throat. "Forgot something. Be right back."

To give him privacy, I didn't turn around, but Emily tracked him, bouncing her straw in her Diet Coke. When she lowered her eyes and sucked on her drink, I figured he'd left the diner.

"He's out there slashing my tires, isn't he?"

I shook my head. "Not his style. More likely he's calling a tow truck."

Her mouth curled up a bit, but she didn't follow through with a smile. From the Mason jar wedged between the condiments in the center of the table, she helped herself to a fat dill pickle, cut it into quarters, and ate it with a fork. Henry still hadn't returned by the time she'd finished, so she speared a second one. The jukebox started with "The Point of No Return," and I couldn't help but grin. Emily didn't seem to notice.

I leaned back, tasted my iced tea, and nudged away the possibility Henry might head back to Richmond without finishing the meeting or the last of the painting we'd planned for the rest of the weekend. The notebook seemed to have rattled him as much as it had me.

Emily had sliced pickle number four when a composed Henry returned. He dragged the binder toward himself again, snapped it shut, and folded his hands on top. "Impressive compilation. You're pretty good at surfing the Web and printing."

Emily sat motionless, midchew, at his blatant insult, then swallowed. "I . . . thanks."

"Ever dug any deeper?"

"I've tried. I can't find anything, not even exactly where the shooting happened. That's why I need help."

"And what in particular do you need help with? What are you hoping to learn?"

She looked at me.

I'd told him, but he had to hear it from her. "Explain one more time," I said lightly, hoping to put her at ease.

It didn't work; she clenched her jaw. "Why my father risked *everything* to try to kill Philip's father. How they even knew each other."

"They didn't," Henry said flatly.

"Prove it."

"You can't prove a negative."

"For Daddy to have been involved in something like that shooting, he and Senator Rutledge had to have known each other. That was not something he'd do for no reason."

"Oh? But he'd do it if he had a reason?"

Emily pursed her lips. "You know what I mean."

"So, hire a private investigator or an attorney."

She lowered her eyes. "I can't afford to. That's where I hope you come in. Even if you'd just tell me where everything happened or"–she glanced at me–"go there with me . . ."

"No." My voice came out louder, more emphatic, than I intended, but I needed to dispel that fantasy immediately. "I'm never going back there."

She traced her finger vertically through the condensation on her glass, creating a path from top to bottom, but said nothing.

Henry jumped in. "What if after spending all your time and wasting Philip's and mine–and since you claim limited resources, spending our money—what if, after all that, you learn nothing? Which, you need to understand, is far more likely than not."

"I don't believe I won't find anything."

"But if you don't?"

"I owe it to him to at least try. *And* I owe that to myself." Elbows on the table, she leaned toward Henry. "Yes, I need to know—anything and everything that I can discover. But I also need to be a daughter, to do for him what he didn't do for me."

I thought she was going to cry, but she reached out and dragged the notebook to her, pushing aside a ketchup bottle and the pickle jar.

"He didn't act like a father in his final hours, but he had before then. I don't know why he did what he did, but I'm not going to give up the way he gave up on me. I can't." She clutched the notebook to her chest. "I won't."

This girl had guts. Henry was not the easiest person to stand up to.

Henry sat back, crossed his arms, and studied her. To her credit, she didn't blink or look away. Not even when someone at the far side of the diner dropped a tub of dishes.

"What do you plan to do with whatever you learn?"

"Do with it?" She sounded surprised. "Nothing."

"*Nothing?* You expect me to believe that?"

"You don't have to believe it. But having some answers would be enough."

Henry's eye roll was so theatrically exaggerated, I chewed the inside of my cheek to keep from laughing.

"Philip tells me you were adopted. What do your parents think about this little scheme of yours?"

Good question, which I'd never thought to ask. How *did* the Warners play into this scheme?

Emily leaned back in her chair and cocked her head. "That, Mr. Linden, is none of your business."

Henry opened his mouth, then apparently changed his mind about voicing his thoughts. He unwrapped his straw and jabbed it into his tea. "All right. What other relatives do you have? Why can't they help you figure things out?"

"I don't have other relatives. Daddy had a brother, but I didn't know him, and anyway, he died."

"How old are you?"

"Almost twenty-two."

"What's your birth date?"

Her face reddened. "I *said* I'm almost twenty-two."

Henry's career as a commercial real estate attorney wasted his ability to cross-examine an opponent. I suspected he knew the answer and was testing her. Still, he didn't need to treat her rudely.

She narrowed her eyes. "Why do you need to know?"

Good question. He continued to wait, and she relented.

"February 27, 1994."

"And you live where?"

"Just outside Greenville, South Carolina."

Greenville was a five-hour drive from Grainger. Emily's trips between the cities would have been neither convenient nor inexpensive, especially if she'd stayed overnight.

"You're from there or you just live there?"

"I've lived in the area my whole life."

Meaning she'd always lived within an hour's drive of Mom and Dad's farm. Did that mean anything?

"And job-wise, you do what?"

"I drive for Uber."

Henry smirked. "And when you get a real job, one that'll actually support you, what'll you do?"

Emily rose so abruptly, her chair toppled. "I don't have to take shit from you." Her voice was furiously quiet. "I've been a good sport, but I'm over you." She snatched the notebook and leaned down to retrieve her coat and purse from under the fallen chair.

"Don't leave." I moved around the table, righted her chair, straightened her coat, and reattached her purse. "He's—"

A waitress, not ours, touched Emily's arm. "Everything okay?"

The nearby diners gawked at us, or tried less-than-sur-reptitiously not to. Embarrassed, I avoided eye contact with any of them.

Emily smiled slightly at the waitress. "We're good. Thanks for checking."

As the waitress moved on, staring not entirely benevolently at us over her shoulder, Henry leaned back, fingers laced behind his head. "I'm trying to figure out your deal. Your ulterior motives. Your . . ."

Her glare must have skewered him because he looked away. To me, she said, "I'll do this with or without you. Call me when you decide if you're in or out."

I realized then that although Henry had almost assured me he'd help us, his intent today was to separate Emily and me. He neither believed her story nor trusted her motives. He'd decided about her before we'd ever arrived. But I'd decided as well.

"I don't need to call you. I already told you I'm in." I patted the back of her chair. "Let's finish. I promise he'll stick to pertinent subjects. Won't you, Henry?" I glided her chair under her and returned to my own.

He sipped his tea, his eyes flicking from Emily to me, and back to Emily. "You want pertinent? Okay. Tell me about your father."

"What specifically?"

"How about you start with his criminal record?"

Emily slammed her hand to the table. "My father was no criminal!"

Henry raised his eyebrows.

"Well, I mean before . . ." Her defiance deflated quickly.

From the inside breast pocket of his coat, Henry extracted and unfolded a sheet of paper. "April 3, 1987: open container of beer or wine in motor vehicle—pleaded guilty. December 23, 1987: speeding, more than ten but less than fifteen miles per hour over the speed limit—pleaded no contest. March 4, 1989: seat belt violation. Oh wait, that's a noncriminal offense. Ah, here we go. July 21, 1989: another open container violation—pleaded guilty. May 12, 1990: petit or simple larceny—pleaded guilty."

Emily turned the notebook on one end, shielding herself from his words. "Stop."

"Henry." I got his point, but he didn't need to assault Emily with his snarky attitude.

"But I'm finally getting to the good stuff. And this is from only one county." He extended the sheet of paper to her. When she didn't move, he shook it. She stared at him but still didn't take it.

So I did. He'd printed a spreadsheet of dates, court case numbers, crimes, dispositions, and penalties, none suggesting a propensity for violence. Why hadn't he mentioned Gardner's impressive résumé of misdemeanors to me? After Emily's birth, the only two items were a public disturbance charge in April 1996, for which he paid a hundred-dollar fine, and a first-degree harassment charge in late January 1998 that was dropped.

"Henry," I said, "these are hardly violent crimes. And almost all of them happened before Emily was born."

"A criminal's got to start somewhere."

Emily picked at a nick in the table's Formica. I felt sorry for her. She was so young when her father died, she couldn't have known about those early transgressions that he most likely—and appropriately—never intended her to know about. I slid the spreadsheet facedown to her.

Without touching it, she said to Henry, "Did you do the same search for Bennett Rutledge?"

His head snapped back. "Of course not."

My stomach flipped. Searching such records for my father had never occurred to me, and I understood instantly how Emily might never have considered that her father had a criminal record. If I couldn't imagine one for the man I knew, how could I blame Emily for thinking the same about the man she knew, even despite his one horrendous crime? But surely my father's thriving law practice and his seamless transition into a very public life proved he had no record.

I thought of something else. "Henry, did my father ever defend Gardner?"

He shook his head. "Not as far as I know. Mostly for what he was charged with, Gardner wouldn't have bothered with legal representation. He'd pay his fine or spend his few days in jail and move on. Besides, he wasn't exactly the *class* of guy your dad defended."

I knew what he meant: Gardner wouldn't have earned my father a large enough paycheck.

Without even scanning the spreadsheet, Emily slipped it into her notebook. "How'd you find this?"

"A publicly available database of court case records." He recited the URL.

Her next search, I knew, would be for my father in that database. Mine would be, as well, to prove to her and confirm to myself that I was as serious as she was about uncovering the facts. I'd checked behind my father on the Tennessee statute. This wasn't much different.

"What else aren't you telling us?"

"A lot, but only because I don't *know* anything." She tapped the edge of Henry's printout. "*This*, for example. I keep telling you that's why I need the police records. That's why I need your help."

The waitress arrived with our food. Emily moved the notebook to the empty spot between us and dumped ketchup on her burger, fries, and even her pickle spear.

Before any of us took the first bite, a familiar voice interrupted.

"Hey there, Philip. I never expected to see *you* here." An instant later, Scottie Marston stood behind the empty chair, her hands resting on its back.

Henry and I pushed away from the table. "Hey, Scottie," I said, still distracted by the intensity of the conversation.

"You guys are so polite. No need to stand on my account."

Henry raised an eyebrow. "Scottie? Like the dog?"

She grinned. "Exactly."

I introduced them—Henry as my longtime friend and then Emily. When I stumbled over our relationship, Henry offered, "Emily and Philip are collaborating on a family project."

"Genealogy?"

"Something like that," Emily said.

"Nice to meet you both." Scottie looked toward the door.

"Old folks are about to overrun this place. Fourth Saturday of each month, residents from the senior center where I volunteer come here for a late lunch. Cast Party's not so busy then, so no one feels rushed."

"Grainger has a senior center?" I asked.

"Serves the entire county." She patted my arm. "Old professors need somewhere to go between retirement and death."

Henry laughed.

She turned to leave, then spun around. "Oh! I have a brilliant idea. Why don't you bring Dilsey to the center one of these days? Your students rave about having her in class, and she'd be a hit with the seniors."

My students had the motor skills and cognitive wherewithal to get out of her way if she seized. At least, I hoped they did. Elderly people might not. "I don't know . . ."

"Think about it. We'll talk later." She breezed away and again returned. "Don't forget you promised me a tour when you finish your house." Then she really left.

"Cute." Henry sat. "What about a tour?"

"Nothing," I said curtly.

We ate in silence until Emily got us back on track. "We were discussing how to get the investigation records."

"Right," I said. "Takes a subpoena or court order."

She frowned. "How do we do that?"

We both looked at Henry. He bit into his sandwich and chewed slowly, swallowed. "There's a straightforward process for each."

"You'll do that for us?" I asked.

"I won't *do* it, but I'll tell you how."

"We can do it without an attorney?"

"You have one for what you need, which is to advise you." He tapped the end of the spreadsheet peeking from the notebook. "Starting with this advice. Check out other court databases. See what kind of a guy you're really dealing with."

Emily's knuckles whitened. "Okay."

He laid his business card on the table beside her plate. "I talk with Philip regularly, but I expect to hear directly from you too. I can't advise you if I don't know what's happening, what you've done and what you need to do, and what you find."

Emily blew out air, apparently as relieved as I was to have his buy-in after all.

Our waitress appeared between Henry and me. "How many checks?"

Henry raised one finger. "Give it to me."

"I'm separate," Emily said.

"One," Henry said, and the waitress left, muttering something unintelligible.

After Henry paid, we walked Emily to her car. She circled it, eying the tires, and I turned away to hide my smile. If Henry noticed, he didn't let on, just waited with his hand on Emily's door till she clicked the locks and then opened it for her. She pitched her purse onto the floor and laid the teal binder on the passenger seat. Her scowl suggested she might bite off his gentlemanly head, but instead she said, "I'll be in touch."

I admired her restraint.

As he closed the door, I rolled my tight shoulders, relieved the meeting was over. Emily practically raced from her space and out of Cast Party's parking lot.

"You didn't have to be so hard on her, Henry. She's just a kid."

"I wasn't hard on her. I'm trying to keep *you* out of trouble."

"What's that supposed to mean?"

"I needed to figure out if she's who she says she is, and is doing what she says she's doing, with no ulterior motive." He kicked a pebble. "Her dad's not the only person in that family I searched in the database. But she's clean, and after talking with her, I'm willing to go along with this *for now*. Not that I have much choice."

"You always have a choice."

He eyed me for a moment, then shook his head.

"What?"

"Nothing," he said. "Meet you back at the house."

I followed him out of the parking lot. Good ol' reliable Henry. He helped me out despite his reluctance to have any part of Emily. I should be as good a friend to him as he was to me, and as soon as we finished with this Emily business, I'd work on that.

I turned Dilsey loose in the yard to run in the midafternoon frigid temps she loved. I settled at the kitchen table with my laptop while Henry changed into painting-appropriate clothing. Despite my differences with my father, researching him in the South Carolina court system database felt sneaky. Not unjustified, however.

As far back as the records went, I searched for him with and without his middle initial, in the county where the farm was located, in the surrounding counties, and in a few more at random, and found nothing. For diligence's sake, I searched the same databases for my mother under her maiden and married names. No hits, not even a minor traffic violation. Relieved, I leaned back in my chair. I hadn't expected to find anything, but Emily hadn't expected any criminal activity from her father either.

On the table, my phone vibrated.

"Your friend Henry isn't a very nice person," Emily said by way of greeting.

Given his interrogation of her, I wasn't inclined to defend him. "Does it matter?"

"He's protecting you, isn't he?"

"What on earth would he protect me from?"

"Me."

The thought of needing protection from Emily was laughable. "You heard him. He's advising us, and that's all you should care about."

"Do you trust him?"

"Absolutely. I trust him absolutely. We've been friends most of our lives. We've been through a lot together. *A lot*."

"Like the shooting."

"Yeah, like that."

"Because I'm not so sure . . ."

"What option do we have?"

"I guess you're right."

"I am right. So, let's start with the court databases. As soon as I find out about the paperwork for the TBI records, I'll call you. Next day or so, okay?"

We signed off, and I joined Dilsey outside to play ball, content to finally have the start of a plan.

CHAPTER 18

DURING THE NEXT week, Emily and I talked almost every day. I had to give her credit—she took Vincent Gardner's misdemeanors seriously and scoured the court databases for all of South Carolina's forty-six counties and for the bordering counties of North Carolina and Georgia from his eighteenth birthday until his death nineteen years later. She uncovered a few additional minor offenses but nothing suggesting a propensity for violence and nothing at all after her birth except the public disturbance and dropped harassment charges Henry had found. When she relayed all that, she sounded relieved. Since I hadn't known what to expect, I didn't know whether to be disappointed or discouraged.

In all the databases in which Emily searched for her father, she made sure to tell me that she'd scrutinized them for mentions of my father as well. In addition, she browsed DC's records and those of the nearby counties in Virginia and Maryland. As I expected, she found nothing. When I reminded her Dad's political adversaries would long ago have unearthed and broadcast any wrongdoing or perceived wrongdoing, she said only, "You never know."

As I cleaned up after supper on Friday night nearly a week after our meeting at Cast Party, she called, clearly frustrated.

"I emailed Henry yesterday to fill him in. He sent back a snarky reply advising me to check the databases of all fifty states. That's over three thousand counties plus the big cities that have their own systems."

I choked back a laugh. "He's messing with you, Emily."

"Really? He sounded serious." She drummed something like a pen against her phone. "I don't need to do it, do I?"

"Hell no. You might spot-check Tennessee and look at DC, and surrounding counties—as you did for my father—but nothing else."

I updated her on my lack of progress. Aggravated with Henry's nonresponse—too busy to deal with it this week, he'd said twice, though he'd made time for Emily—I sifted through Tennessee government websites until I found a subpoena form. There was no information about filing for a court order, so I forwarded the form to Henry to confirm it was correct for our purposes. Finally, late in the afternoon just today, his paralegal emailed me back: *Looks okay.*

"What kind of an answer is that?" Emily asked.

"Not much of one. I'll fill it out over the weekend and overnight it to the county courthouse." The more I talked, the more uncertain the process felt. "It requires the signature of"—I scanned the document—"a county clerk. Or maybe that's *the* county clerk. I guess he or she will sign it when they get it. Needs a case number too. I assume they'll assign one."

"That all sounds kind of iffy."

"Yeah." I'd been thinking the same thing. I considered that I might need to show up at Henry's house over the weekend and confront him, demand some practical help.

"Once they have the form, how long till they release the records?"

I'd neglected to ask, and the document didn't mention a time frame. "I'll get back to you."

"They *will* release them, right?"

"If we jump through the right hoops, why wouldn't they?"

She sighed. "This all feels so unnecessarily difficult. But okay, I'll keep looking for Daddy and your father in the various databases, and you'll wait on the court stuff. What else can we do?"

"Have any names recurred in the records? For example, in the plaintiff or arresting officer or attorney fields? We could track down those people, maybe interview them."

"No, nothing like that."

"Let me think a sec." I closed the dishwasher and squeezed dish soap into Dilsey's stainless bowl. "Why not drive by your old neighborhood, the one where you lived with your father? Talk with the neighbors, see if they remember anything that might be pertinent."

"It's been ten years. People forget things, move away, die."

"Not all of them." I had no idea what kind of place Emily had lived in with Gardner, hadn't even considered it. Had they lived in a transient area, like an apartment complex? A suburban subdivision? A cozy country cottage on acreage?

Her silence stretched on. "Emily?"

"I haven't been back since . . . I don't know what it's like now."

I scrubbed the bowl. "Take a friend. Just get in the car and go. It's no big deal."

"Like it's no big deal for you to go back to that place in Tennessee?"

"I won't go there because it's private property." I swallowed the lump in my throat.

"You go right on believing that."

My body tingled with the memory of the narrow road leading to the even narrower gravel drive snaking through dense hardwoods and pines to the cabin. The side porch steps Dad and I descended in the deep purple twilight of that Sunday morning. The frosty breeze. The kennel. I breathed in and out, in and out, in and out until I could talk again. "It's not the same."

"It's exactly the same." She exhaled audibly. "I'll only go if you come with me."

"Take one of your friends."

"If I find someone to ask about Daddy, about what they might have known or even guessed, you'll ask better questions than me." She crunched something. Ice? "Because I might freak out."

"Emily, you hunted me down and stopped me—a perfect stranger—on the street and coerced me into meeting with you and convinced me to do something crazy. Then you held your ground with Henry. You won't freak out."

"This is different. If we went tomorrow, we'd get it over with. *Please.*"

Other than the inconveniently long drive, I had no legitimate reason to refuse. Plus, I had to admit that Vince Gardner's turf piqued my curiosity. And then there was that debt I owed Emily; I was responsible for her father's death. What the hell—I agreed. She texted me later with a meeting place, and I offered to drive both of us to her old neighborhood. I considered spending Saturday night at the farm but quickly opted to drive round trip in one day. After the debacle of my Christmas visit and without Henry and Jamie as buffers, I'd be not a guest but an intruder.

CHAPTER 19

AT ONE O'CLOCK the next afternoon, Emily and I met in the outer parking lot of a Walmart a few miles from our destination. She hoisted herself into my Expedition, and Dilsey welcomed her by snorting and thumping her tail against the crib bumpers in her crate.

"I thought I was okay." Emily buckled her seat belt and fiddled with her ponytail. "Now I'm . . . If you hadn't driven all this way . . ."

"Don't worry. If you don't want to go, we won't go. Or I could go without you." Snoop a bit, get a feel for the place. If someone happened to be around, ask about Gardner. Not sure how smart that would be, but I could try.

She quit with her ponytail. "You'd do that?"

"I told you: I'm all in."

She squared her shoulders. "Let's go."

We rode in silence for the six minutes from when I input the address into my GPS until we left the highway. The string of abandoned businesses with trash-littered parking lots, plus a Kroger, Home Depot, and Pizza Hut bustling with cars and shoppers, suggested an area in transition. The direction of transition, however, was unclear, and Emily's blank expression and drumming fingers as she swiveled her head provided no answer.

From the highway, I turned left onto a narrow cracked-asphalt street. Leafless old oaks and maples and precariously tall thin pines almost obstructed our view of the early 1960s brick ranches with mostly well-maintained yards. Though not fancy, the neighborhood suggested coziness and comfort, a great place for a single dad to raise his little girl.

But did the fact that no one was outside, despite the fifty-degree temperatures and the sparkling sunshine of a spectacular winter day—a Saturday—mean anything?

"Here we are." The carport of the single-story white frame house and the street in front were empty.

Emily leaned across the console to peer out my window. "That's not it."

"The number on the mailbox matches the address in the GPS."

She shaded the glare on the GPS, then hopped out and crossed to the apron of the narrow driveway, hands on hips, taking everything in.

I lowered my window. "Maybe the house was remodeled."

"Who'd remodel a brick house into one with siding? Besides, the windows look different than I remember."

"You can add or subtract windows." Or possibly she remembered wrong.

Without a word, she strode to the front stoop and rang the bell. When no one responded, she rang it three more times.

"I'm going around back," she called. "In case they're outside."

I doubted they were, but just in case, I didn't want her going alone. I parked, locked Dilsey in, and followed Emily through the crunchy brown grass. The lot totaled roughly half an acre, most of its length behind the house. The only tree, a white oak, would shade half the backyard in summer. I spotted a tree house through the dried leaves clinging to its supporting branches.

Side by side, Emily and I examined it. When she spoke, her voice trembled. "He built that for me."

It was more tree deck than tree house. It rested on the lowest branch, and a simple fence with the pickets closely spaced would prevent a distracted child from tumbling off. Some pickets and floorboards were missing, and the entire structure needed staining, but from below, the supports anchoring the tree house to the branch and trunk appeared intact.

Emily pointed to a gap. "Daddy built a ladder up to a gate that latched. He made me promise to keep the gate closed when I was up there."

"How old were you when he built it?"

"Six? He built it right after we moved here. Till I was eight or nine, he wouldn't let me climb up without him." She flicked something from her right eye. "Sometimes we'd have picnics up there. Sometimes overnight campouts."

There was something elegantly beautiful in the tree house's simplicity, in the gift he'd handcrafted for his young daughter when their lives together were normal. How strange to consider that the same man had killed a child. Killed Teddy.

If he hadn't shown up in Tennessee that day, I wouldn't have shot him and, at that moment, he might be standing here with Emily sharing memories of her childhood.

I shifted uncomfortably, but Emily didn't notice. She circled the tree, examining the tree house from all angles. "Did your father ever build you one?"

"No." Still unsettled, I didn't mention that my great-grandfather and his brothers had, though not specifically for me. As teenagers, they'd constructed a fort in the largest oak on the farm, the one between the pond and the cemetery. It had a solid floor and walls on two sides, about three feet high. At intervals along the walls they'd drilled holes sized perfectly for the muzzle of a shotgun, or a stick pretending to be a shotgun, for defending the fort. The third wall was the tree itself. The open fourth side faced northwest toward the mountains.

Teddy, Jamie, Henry, and I had loved the tree fort. When we knelt on its floor and leaned just the right way around the oak, we could see the main barn and an edge of the house. From early spring through late fall, the foliage hid anyone in the fort, and through the leaves, the birds, the stream feeding into the pond, and other natural sounds, we'd pretend not to hear Dad whistle us in for dinner or for chores. Up there, the only world that existed was the world we invented.

Even after the fort lost its appeal for Jamie and Henry, I always went to it to think. It was where I taught Teddy to read the summer he was five. Through the years, he and I spent time there whenever I returned home from school. On our last visit, three months before he died, we read aloud, taking alternating chapters from *The Call of the Wild*. I'd leaned against a wall, legs outstretched. Teddy lay on his back, arms straight up holding the book, his voice floating through the oak's canopy. The green leaves were at their darkest, gripping the last of the summer as they prepared to turn gold and drift away forever.

I jumped when Emily touched my arm. "Sorry. I was thinking."

"About what?"

How could I share with a virtual stranger, with whom I had nothing in common except her criminal father, that her memories kept triggering my own not so dissimilar ones? "Nothing important."

My gaze followed hers for a final look at her tree house before we returned to the front yard.

"I guess now we knock on some doors?" she said.

From the house across the street, a woman peered at us through the glass storm door.

"She look familiar?" I asked.

"Not sure, and I don't want to stare." Emily wrinkled her nose. "Weird people lived there. The Browns. They yelled at kids who went into their yard. Not me, but most kids. Daddy went over there, and sometimes I went with him, so I guess that was why they left me alone. They had a son in his twenties or forties or something who was more like a monster than a person." She shuddered. "So scary."

"Want to see if that's her, talk with her? Or with whomever answers?"

"Only as a last resort."

We walked up the street. Like many of these old neighborhoods, this one had no sidewalks, so we wandered down the center of the road. About nine houses up, a kid, twelve or so, bounced a basketball in a driveway, alternately making one-handed tosses to the hoop on the front of the carport and glancing at the phone in his other hand. We stopped and waited for him to notice us.

"Whassup?" He balanced the ball on the palm of his throwing hand.

"Are your parents home?" Emily asked. "We'd like to . . ."

He turned tail and escaped through the carport door into the house.

Emily and I looked at each other. "Lesson number one," I said with enough of a grin to assure her I wasn't criticizing her; I'd probably have asked the boy the same question. "Never ask whether the parents are home. Because, you know, we might be kidnappers."

"Ha-ha!" She scanned the empty yards nearby. "Looks like no one else is out." Without another word, she turned abruptly and marched back to the Expedition.

I followed, surprised how quickly our unsuccessful encounter with the kid discouraged her. "Now what?"

She leaned against the front grill, arms crossed, frowning at the asphalt.

Despite my temptation to suggest we leave, I refused to let her give up so easily. She'd regret it, and I'd probably have to drive back down here to finish what we should deal with now. "How about you start with the houses on either side of yours and ring doorbells? Ask if they remember anything about your father. I'll keep an eye on you from here."

When she didn't acknowledge my suggestion, I popped the back hatch with my remote. "You figure it out, and I'll walk Dilsey."

But Dilsey had other ideas. She dragged me around the truck and bounced up to lick Emily's face. Unbalanced, Emily staggered a step and wrapped her arms around Dilsey to steady herself. Dilsey snorted happily against her cheek.

I apologized, but Emily shook her head.

"She's so sweet, and she gave me an idea. Let's take her with us. How threatening can two people with a Lab be?"

She had a point. So, accompanied by Dilsey, we started in the opposite direction. At the house across the street, the storm door opened, and a woman emerged, mid-sixties at least, wearing a shapeless sweatshirt and faded jeans.

"An opportunity presents itself." I sidestepped Emily's restraining hand and, determined to get this over with, strode up the driveway with Dilsey.

"Can I help you?" The voice was hostile.

From behind me, Emily said, "Mrs. Brown?"

"Who's asking?"

"Um . . . we're sorry to bother you, ma'am. I'm Emily War–Emily Gardner." She joined me. "My father–his name was Vince Gardner–and, well, we used to live there." She pointed across the street. "But it didn't look like that when we lived there."

The woman's glower dissolved into a simple stare. "Emily Gardner? Oh dear Lord, what are you doing here? I never thought I'd see you again." She opened her arms to hug Emily, but when Emily froze, she lowered them. "Please, come in."

I placed my hand on Emily's tense back and pressed her forward. "Go on. It's okay. I'll wait right out here."

The woman held the door open for us. "Please, you come in too. Bring the dog."

We entered directly into the living room. Mrs. Brown's house didn't appear to have been remodeled since its construction, but it was comfortably worn and clean and smelled like musty vanilla. Numerous knickknacks and a few trade paperbacks cluttered the built-ins beside the fireplace. She layered our coats over the back of a well-worn armchair and indicated the couch with her hand. We declined her offer of coffee or tea, and she dropped into a shiny leather recliner across from us. Dilsey settled at my feet.

Still apparently disbelieving, Mrs. Brown said, "Emily?"

Emily smiled. "It's really me, Mrs. Brown. How've you been?"

"Better'n I deserve."

"And Mr. Brown? And Cliff?"

"Sam's good. He's volunteering at the church today." She lowered her eyes. "Cliff passed a few years ago."

"I'm so sorry."

"He was thirty-seven, you know, and Sam and me, we worried what would happen to him after we were gone." She smiled feebly. "The good Lord took him in his sleep. It's all good."

"Yes, ma'am," Emily said.

I suspected the ensuing silence felt as awkward to Emily and Mrs. Brown as it did to me. But now that Mrs. Brown seemed amenable to talking, Emily didn't need me to bail her out and could take the lead herself. I focused on a stack of *Southern Living* magazines in the basket on the floor beside Mrs. Brown's chair and willed Emily to speak.

Finally, she asked, "What happened to our house? It was brick, wasn't it?"

"You're right, hon. The bank claimed it. No one took care of it, so Sam mowed the yard every few weeks. It was the least we could do for Vince. Then one New Year's Eve, some kids set off fireworks inside—it was freezing, and they were stupid—and they burned it. Outside charred, inside gutted, Sam said."

Emily's eyes teared, and she sagged back onto the couch. "Daddy loved that house. Me too."

"A real shame, hon. Took most of another year for the county or bank or someone to tear it down."

"When was the new house built?" I asked.

She shrugged. "Five, six years ago."

"No one's there now?"

"A man. He travels a lot. Unlike your daddy. Vince was always around with you, always helping Sam fix something, checking on me and Cliff if Sam was gone. He'd bring you over, and you'd hide in a closet. Or sit on the back porch alone."

"I remember."

"We eventually figured out you were afraid of Cliff. Vince tried to make you play with him, but after a while, I told him to leave you alone."

Emily blinked rapidly. "I *was* afraid of him," she whispered. "I'm sorry."

"It's okay, hon. You were a little girl. It's normal to be afraid of things you don't understand. At least you were never mean to him. More'n I can say for other folks, even the grown-ups. Sam and I protected him as best we could. If that meant chasing kids away or screaming at their parents, so be it. But they're mostly gone now, moved away, parents and kids both. When you have your own children, you'll realize that you'll do anything to protect them, no matter how it looks to anyone."

"Yes, ma'am."

Not anything, I thought with an unexpected surge of anger. Not staying home with your daughter instead of running off to another state to kill a man.

Mrs. Brown looked down at her hands. "Sometimes I was afraid of Cliff too. He never got older than five years old, even when he was thirty-seven. Sometimes, when he got"—she struggled for the words—"hard to handle, Vince would help Sam settle him."

Apparently sharing my surprise, Emily leaned forward. "Daddy did that?"

"Cliff loved him. One time, Vince talked us into letting him take Cliff bowling with him to that warehouse place—"

"Bowled Over. I still go there."

"Uh-huh, that's it. But it was too much stimulation for Cliff, and he got, um, excited. It didn't go so well." She smiled, a private little smile at the memory. "But his behavior didn't faze Vince. He set things right with his friend, the guy who owned it then, and by the time they got home, Cliff was calm and happy and sticky with ice cream."

Emily elbowed me. "I told you Daddy was a good man."

"He was," Mrs. Brown said. "Rough around the edges, but good to us and you."

I struggled to reconcile the Vince Gardner from the shooting with Mrs. Brown's characterization. Her words affirmed Emily's core belief about him, and Emily needed that. Deserved it. But those same words confused me further. How could the man they portrayed have resorted to violence toward my family?

Emily offered the older woman a half smile. "I was only eleven when he died, and now I'm getting to know him all over again. Thank you, Mrs. Brown. What else can you tell me?"

She smiled again, this time at us. "Vince was in a bit of trouble when he was young–he told us that–but he got himself together. He did the best he could. His brother dying broke his heart. Told us he was alone in the world after Mel was gone, other than you. Then he shot the senator and got himself killed. It made no sense."

"None," Emily agreed.

"After he died, I never saw you again. When the police talked to me about Vince, I asked about you, but"–she slowly shook her head–"they wouldn't say. Maybe they didn't know and were too busy to find out. They were all over your house like fire ants on a honey bun."

"What happened to all our things?"

"The police hauled a lot of it away. Right after they left, when I thought no one would notice, I snuck over there. Stuff was everywhere, dumped out of drawers and closets. I took a few things. Stole them, truth be told. Nothing big. Something to remember you by. A week or so after the cops left, the house got broken into. I was afraid to go in after that, you know?"

"Yes, ma'am."

"What happened to you? Where did you go?"

Emily sat back, folded her hands on her lap, and sucked in her lower lip. About the time I decided she'd refuse to answer, she said, "Everything changed."

"If you don't want to talk about it, hon . . ."

"I stayed with friends while Daddy was on a 'business trip.'" She air quoted the last two words. "On the Monday night before Thanksgiving, a social worker appeared at their door to pick me up. She told me Daddy had died in a hunting accident."

"Vince didn't hunt." Mrs. Brown's declaration left no room for doubt.

"I know. Then she drove me here, home, and gave me ten minutes to get everything I needed—clothes and shoes, 'necessities' she called them, whatever would fit into my suitcase and the shopping bag she'd brought. The house looked like it had been vandalized, stuff thrown everywhere. Some things seemed to be missing, but I didn't know exactly what. At first, we couldn't even find a suitcase, so she pulled out black trash bags to use instead. Trash bags. We finally found a suitcase in the spare bedroom under a pile of papers and clothes."

My gut tightened. I pictured her in a house similar to Mrs. Brown's, a little girl bewildered and frightened, her few necessities but nothing she loved, none of the tokens that symbolized her life and her relationship with her father, tossed into the messy trunk of a stranger's car. She'd held onto the memories and the feelings they conjured all these years because despite everything else that had happened, no one had told her they didn't matter.

She hunched her shoulders and picked at a nail. I reached over and patted her back. Dilsey sat up and pressed against Emily's legs, and Emily reached out a hand to pat her. Across from us, Mrs. Brown leaned forward, gripping the armrests of her recliner, her mouth set in a straight line.

"But I just stared at the suitcase and shopping bag. The lady went through my drawers and closet and the clothes on the floor and tossed stuff in, whatever she laid her hands on. The policeman guarding the house rifled through them like he thought I was stealing something, even though I was leaving not just stuff valuable to me, but everything. All our photo albums. The coloring books Daddy and I worked on together. My model horses. CDs. The silver locket he gave me for my tenth birthday.

"I had to talk to the police, but I didn't know anything. After that, I asked the lady what would happen to me, to my things and Daddy's, if I could go to his funeral, where I'd live. She said not to worry, everything would be taken care of. And everything was, I guess, in a way."

"You poor thing," Mrs. Brown murmured, palming tears from her cheeks.

"For a few years, I lived in different foster homes. They were all okay. When I was thirteen, a teacher at school sort of rescued me from kids who were picking on me. One thing led to another, and he and his wife ended up fostering and then adopting me. He teaches phys ed and coaches some sports teams, and she teaches art. They're awesome."

"But they're not your daddy, are they, hon?"

Emily shook her head. "I miss him so much. Why did he leave me?"

I marveled at the strength of a little girl surviving an unimaginable hurt, even more determined now to find out why she'd had to. The answer seemed no closer than it had that morning or a decade ago, but for Emily's sake, I was glad we'd come.

"I don't know, hon. But no matter what, he loved you." She gazed at us, taking us both in, then stood. "Wait here."

Mrs. Brown rummaged noisily around in another room before returning with a large box she carried without effort and set on Emily's lap. "I found these on the floor of your closet."

Emily peered inside. Immediately, the tears flowed, silent and plentiful, and she hiccupped a repressed sob.

Mrs. Brown's mouth drooped, and she backed away to her chair. "I'm so sorry. I thought—"

Setting the box on the floor, Emily rushed to the older woman and threw her arms around her. "Thank you so much," she whispered. "Thank you."

I averted my eyes and pulled aside the flap. Inside the box, in a jumble of legs, heads, and tails, were molded plastic horses. Nice ones. Breyers. I lifted out a buckskin quarter horse mare with a chip in her tail but in otherwise perfect condition. Dilsey grabbed her from me and took her to Emily.

One after another, I examined each of the nine other models and set them on the floor until a herd of Breyers circled the box. Mrs. Brown's actions—not only presenting the model horses to Emily but her brave act of rescuing them in the first place—overwhelmed me, and if either of them had spoken to me, I wouldn't have been able to respond. This woman was not the Mrs. Brown that Emily had described, or the one who'd glared at us when we approached her house. Today, nothing was as it seemed.

The remaining item was flat and wrapped in brittle yellowed newspaper: a glassless framed eight-by-ten photo of a man and a school age girl. Vince and Emily Gardner, both of them blond, smiling, and relaxed in shorts and matching teal T-shirts on a sunny day. Emily stood three rungs up on the tree house ladder—in that position she was as tall as he was—her arm around his shoulders. The only other photos I'd seen of him were the frowning, serious one from the news articles and the one Emily had used to ID herself to me on the street in Grainger.

"Emily." I angled the photo toward her when she turned away from Mrs. Brown.

Her eyes teared. "The only picture I had was a crumpled, torn-up piece of one that must have been under a pile of my clothes and somehow ended up in the suitcase."

I hadn't thought to ask where she'd gotten that photo or why it was in such poor condition.

Mrs. Brown squeezed her. "Vince would be so proud of how you've grown up. Don't ever let anyone tell you he wasn't a good man. Even with what he did."

"I won't." She wiped her face, and with both hands damp, she took the photo from me. "Thank you so much. Can I visit you again sometime?"

Mrs. Brown's smile radiated through the room. "I'd love that."

I nestled the Breyer horses back into their box, and we collected our jackets and emerged into the brisk sunshine. At the top of Mrs. Brown's driveway, we turned. She'd shut the door, rendering her house as foreboding and nondescript as when we'd approached it.

When we reached the Expedition, I raised the hatch and set the box beside Dilsey's crate. I opened the door for her to hop in, but she instead curled around Emily's legs. Emily knelt and hugged her.

Once we'd settled in our seats, Emily clutched the photo on her lap.

I started the truck. "What next?"

"I want to go home." Her voice was quiet, exhausted.

"You don't want to talk to other neighbors? Since we're here?"

"No."

We retraced our route to the Walmart.

Emily shook her head. "The Browns . . . I'd always believed they were weird and hateful, but they were only protecting Cliff. Why didn't I know they and Daddy looked out for each other, for Cliff and me?"

"You were a little kid. Kids don't pay attention to that kind of thing."

My parents never said anything about their friends Audra and Norm Trent either, but their ubiquitous presence shadowed my childhood. I suddenly realized with horror that the Trents most likely would have assumed legal guardianship of us if Mom and Dad had died. Unlike Emily, we'd have ended up not adopted by a family that wanted us but with well-connected friends of my parents who I'd never thought cared much for my brothers and me. How different our lives would have been.

"Nothing's like I thought it was," she said, and I was beginning to agree.

After hearing her story and Mrs. Brown's, I owed her that bit of comfort. "Your father was—I mean that he was what you thought he was. You assured me from the start that he was a good father, and what Mrs. Brown said confirmed it."

She blinked. "Thank you."

"Which makes what he did to us, to my family and to you, all the more absurd." I parked beside her car and popped the locks, but she made no move to leave. Maybe she was waiting for me to suggest our next step.

"I'll FedEx the subpoena form on Monday, and you'll finish with the databases. If you remember specifically where your father worked, we can interview his old boss or co-workers. Or visit the Greenville and Spartanburg courthouses. Someone there might remember him." He'd been there often enough early on, but I resisted mentioning that. "I'll ask Henry for more ideas."

She nodded and opened her door. As I lifted the box of horses from the back, she stroked Dilsey's face through the wire of her crate. She put the horses in the trunk, but took the photo into the Focus with her. After she exited the parking lot, I aimed my Expedition not for Grainger, as I'd planned, but inspired by our talk with Mrs. Brown, for the farm. It was the closest thing I had to an old neighborhood.

CHAPTER 20

I DROVE THE back roads north through the rolling countryside of naked hardwoods and evergreen pines, still flabbergasted by Mrs. Brown's portrayal of Vince Gardner. Even Emily had underestimated his generosity of time and spirit, and what could only be a God-given capacity to so kindly and deftly cope with Cliff. On the other hand, none of that explained what had propelled him to violence at my family's getaway. None of it explained anything we'd driven there to find.

I mulled over what Mrs. Brown had told us about him and then the facts Emily had relayed during our various conversations. *He managed local construction projects,* she'd said when we met at McDonald's.

At the farm, the staff had always handled the considerable routine maintenance of the house and the barns, the other outbuildings, and the fencing plus minor construction projects like run-in sheds. However, my parents—or more accurately, Ross, their farm manager for the past thirty-five years—contracted out major repairs and new construction. Had Ross hired Vince outright or contracted with a company Vince worked for? If so, had something happened at the farm that had angered Vince to the point of violence?

Or had he perhaps visited our farm in some capacity other than work? He was a lifelong resident of the region, and my father was well known even before he entered politics, so surely Vince knew where we lived. Perhaps they had fallen out over something. Yet, for the nearly seven years between my father's swearing-in as governor in early 1999 and the shooting in late 2005, my parents had lived mostly in Columbia or Washington. Had something happened between my father and Vince before that, as early as when Vince was a teenager and committing petty crimes? Could he have been a stalker, obsessed with a political celebrity or—I shuddered—with my mother? Maybe he simply mistook my father for someone else. Yet, no matter if Vince knew him or not, none of those possibilities fit with Mrs. Brown's portrayal of the man.

I didn't doubt Ross would remember any interaction with Vince, but would he tell me if he did? Debatable. Still, a quick chat with him was likely to reveal everything Emily and I needed to learn and put an immediate end to all this. Or he might confuse us further. At the very least, I'd check off another box.

I didn't have the code to the main gate, and calling Henry or Jamie for it—or worse, my parents—could deteriorate into a discussion I didn't want right now. Most likely, someone would report my presence to my parents, but I couldn't do anything about that, and I'd be long gone by then. In case I was wrong and someone in my family phoned to ask why I was at the farm, I muted my phone, tossed it into the console, and turned onto our road.

I entered the first drive, the wide service entrance for employees, horse trailers, and trucks delivering feed and other supplies. As teenagers, Henry and I had, more often than we admitted, used it as a shortcut to the house when sneaking in after curfew. No fence or human had guarded the farm then.

An unfamiliar man emerged from the guard shack. He wore a holstered handgun and carried a clipboard.

I lowered my window. "I'm Philip Rutledge."

He squinted at his clipboard, but I'm sure he didn't expect to find my name there. "Then you should know this is the service entrance."

"I do know that, but I'm not going to the house." My ignorance of the gate code was none of his business.

"ID?" He extended his hand.

I rolled my eyes but handed over my license. Even though we'd never met, he knew I was who I claimed to be. He was stalling, buying himself time to report to his boss or to Ross. He wasn't high enough up the food chain to call my parents himself. When he carried my license into the shack and shut the door, I put the Expedition in park and drummed my fingers on the steering wheel. This might take a while.

I first learned about the farm's new security measures the February after the shooting, almost exactly ten years ago. After the New Year and five weeks past the first of two surgeries I'd undergo to repair my shoulder, I'd involuntarily accompanied my parents to Washington. I'd existed in a guest bedroom at their house there, joining them downstairs for meals only after losing multiple skirmishes about my attitude.

The truth was, I didn't have an attitude. I just didn't care. Not about what they called my "recovery." Not about acknowledging or returning the phone calls from Jamie, Henry, my then-girlfriend, and my other college friends.

Not about the pain that stole my energy, appetite, and concentration, and for which I refused to take the prescribed oxycodone or anything else stronger than ibuprofen. Not about the rants from the physical therapist who, after I quit the second time, promised or threatened—I couldn't tell which—I'd have no significant use of my shoulder and arm ever if I didn't follow the pain management protocol that enabled me to tolerate her maneuvering me. I didn't care about anything.

My mother was probably the one who concocted the idea to drive me back to the farm. Fresh air. Familiar surroundings. The horses, barn dogs, and cats. My own bed. Plus a surprise she wouldn't explain. It would all cheer me up, she promised. I hated surprises and should have protested, but I didn't care enough even to protest and instead let her think whatever she wanted to think. A different setting and a surprise couldn't change anything.

Tailed by one of my father's security guys, we left Washington early on a frigid Friday in mid-February for the eight-hour trip. I was relieved we didn't fly. I'd always preferred the mental purge of a long and solitary drive to the frantic crush of airport security, boarding, and seating. My parents knew that. My mother drove, and to avoid the pressure of the seat belt on my right shoulder and right side of my chest, I rode in the passenger seat behind her. During most of the trip, I slouched against the door, eyes shut against the snow-threatening sky that occasionally spit sleet. We stopped every two hours for a break. For herself, she said, but mostly she hovered over me. One stop was one too many. If we had to take the trip, I wanted it over.

Eventually, we entered the service drive. "We're here," she announced with too much gusto for having driven all day.

When she braked, I straightened and peered out. A new guard shack stood in a previously nonexistent clearing. A tall picketed iron fence, also previously nonexistent, edged from the trees and across the drive, as if protecting us from random disasters was possible or even worthwhile after all that had happened.

The security guard waved but didn't leave the warmth of his shack. The gate slid open, and we drove into the compound that had once been just a horse farm. At the main barn at the end of the winding drive, she stopped, tapped the car horn, and opened her door. "Thought you'd want to say hello to Sawyer first thing."

The cold air slapped me as I struggled from the car and faced the open double doors of the barn and the wide aisle between the rows of box stalls. At the threshold, Ross appeared with a horse.

My horse. Bright-eyed, prick-eared, snorting smoky puffs into the cold air when my scent reached him. A chunky chestnut Morgan my parents had given me on my fourteenth birthday. He'd been three then, barely old enough to train under saddle. Henry with his sleek hunter-type horse and even Jamie mocked him, but his sturdiness and uncomplicated temperament captured my heart.

My chest tightened with longing as I inhaled the comforting sweet aroma of clean horses, hay, and the tang of the pine shavings we used for stall bedding. I eased forward, and Sawyer flicked his ears, bobbed his head happily. When I reached out to him, he rested his warm, whiskery chin in my cupped left hand. He tried to push his head against me, but Ross restrained him. I squeezed my eyes shut, and for one tranquil moment, the nightmare of the past few months receded.

And then, despite Ross's firm hold, Sawyer butted me in the chest, and a bayonet of pain went through my torso, shoulder, and arm. Nauseated, headachy, and shivering, exhausted from the drive and the relentless, inescapable physical torment, I jerked away. Sawyer threw up his head in surprise.

I'd never linked Sawyer with Teddy in my mind, but now a barrage of memories of them together assaulted me. Teaching Teddy to groom and ride on reliable, confidence-instilling Sawyer. Our early short excursions around the farm. Later, when Teddy had Huckleberry the summer before he died, our mounted exploration of the meandering trails among the shady foothills. At that moment, Sawyer's presence reflected Teddy's absence like an empty mirror.

I about-faced and wobbled toward the car, shaking, barely able to push out the words. "Get rid of him. Like you did with Huckleberry."

"*Philip!*" my mother gasped.

"He doesn't mean it," Ross said quietly over the clip-clop of Sawyer's hooves on the drive as they followed me. "Philip, come back down here tomorrow morning after you've—"

"I do mean it, Ross."

In a flash, my mother inserted herself between me and the car, blocking me from opening the door. Her chin trembled, and she seemed to search for words before she shook her head slowly, disbelievingly, and stepped aside to allow me to yank open the door and sink into my seat. When I slammed the door, she stared at me through the glass, then strode away to talk with Ross.

She returned and started the car. "You'll change your mind when you feel better."

"I won't." Ever change my mind. Ever feel better.

More to herself than to me, she murmured, "I don't understand you anymore."

I didn't fasten my seat belt for the short drive to the house or thank my mother for trying to cheer me up. I didn't acknowledge the throng of my college friends who, incited by Henry, yelled *surprise* as I followed Mom into the entrance hall blazing with bright helium balloons tied to every solid object within view. I lowered my head and trudged upstairs, past the closed and probably still locked door of Teddy's bedroom to my own, kicked off my shoes, and dropped, fully clothed, into bed.

Later, but before the edges of daylight peeking around the shuttered balcony doors had dissolved into night, Henry and Mom entered without knocking. I lay on my back under the comforter, staring at the ceiling.

"Come on downstairs," Mom said gently. "Your friends cut class and came all this way to see you."

I shook my head.

"Then everyone's coming up here." Henry bounced on his toes like an excited child, the balloon in his right hand bobbing. "We're here this whole weekend to party. If the party's in your room, we're good with that."

"No, don't." Since the shooting, my family had made every decision for me, from my surgeon to my meals, running my entire life. I'd lost my independence. Now they couldn't even honor my wish for privacy.

"C'mon. Everyone misses you."

"I said no."

Henry yanked the balloon from the air and picked at the knot. "No's not an option. Ten minutes, and we invade." He left, leaving the door open, the balloon at the end of its tether again trailing him.

My mother sat on the edge of the bed and trapped my hand under hers. "Henry's worried about you. If nothing else, humor him and come on down. He worked hard to put this together."

"I didn't ask him to."

She inhaled so deeply, she might have sucked all the oxygen from the room. "What can we do for you, Philip?"

"Can you turn back time?"

Next best thing might be to honor Teddy in some obvious way, like return his photos to the wall or Huckleberry to his stall. Or talk about him. Even that. Or at least tell me why she and my father had banished him from our lives. Now might be the time to ask her. She wasn't *always* a mind reader. But then, I remembered how she'd abandoned me when she could have sided with me about Huckleberry. Immediately after he was taken away, she drove off in the golf cart to let my father explain their position: forget about Teddy and move on. What was the use of pressing her for answers to questions she wouldn't even try to understand?

She squeezed my hand. "No one can fix what's happened. You know that."

"Then why ask? Why pretend you want to do anything?"

She didn't answer. She might have stopped breathing.

"Teddy—" I started.

She picked up my hand with both of her warm ones, steady now. "Dad and I can't bring him back, and dwelling on the past isn't healthy. *You're* our focus now. You—and Jamie and Henry—will get through this. I promise things will get better. They always do, even when it seems impossible. But for that to happen, you have to participate."

"*Participate?*" So life now was a game, and my parents were the referees ensuring we followed the arbitrary rules they'd set, including avoiding any mention of Teddy, if her cutting off my question was any indication.

I tried to pull my hand away, but she held tight. "A good start would be getting up and visiting with your friends. Then, when we get back to Washington, cooperating with your PT. Dad and I want you out of our house and back to your life as quickly as possible."

She let me go when I pulled away again. I scooted to a sitting position against my pillows and looked around the room as if seeing it for the first time. If I'd had any doubts I'd been wrong after my altercation with my father five weeks earlier at the horse trailer that waited to take Huckleberry away, my mother had just erased them. Teddy was gone. Now she wanted me gone too. Jamie and Henry as well, I assumed. The sooner I left, the better, even if I first had to face another surgery and months of rehab. Leaving was as good a goal as any.

She gazed at me unblinking, waiting for me to say something. So, I gave her what she requested, the only thing that would make the entire ordeal end. "All right."

I visited with Henry and our friends. I tolerated their chatter about exams, professors, parties, plans for spring break and the summer, and their careers and other matters I cared nothing about. I responded politely and pretended to be interested, to be normal.

When my mother and I returned to Washington, I endured the physical therapy and the next surgery and more PT. I still refused the prescription painkillers, but otherwise, I cooperated. The next school year, I studied hard and applied to graduate school. I graduated, moved away—with Henry in tow—and studied more until I left that place and those people and created a life for myself that excluded most of them.

In retrospect a decade later, I wouldn't change any of it. But because of my decision to move to Grainger, which seemed sound when I made it, I was at the farm for the second time in five weeks. Emily had shown me that I quit asking the hardest questions too soon and too easily, as if I hadn't truly wanted answers.

I started when the security guard tapped my window. He held my license between his thumb and forefinger. As soon as I lowered my window and took it, he activated the gate from the remote in his other hand.

It was nearly four fifteen and, even on a Saturday, I expected Ross to be there to oversee the horses' late afternoon feeding. He'd always been hands-on with everything to do with the horses and, with my parents' blessing, with us kids too. Even Henry respected him as the benevolent dictator of the working aspects of the farm.

At the barn, I leaned against the truck's hood, hands in pockets, pulse slow and steady as I gazed inside. Even thoughts of Huckleberry leaving and my rejection of Sawyer never entirely dispelled the childhood joy of being around the horses, and I regretted not visiting them at Christmas. Whatever anxiety I might have at facing Ross dissolved as I breathed in the tranquility of the barn.

I'd forgotten how bright the barn was. Even late on a winter afternoon, with the double doors at each end flung open and light filtering through the windows in each stall, no one had needed to flip on the overhead lights. The pebbled concrete of the center aisle was swept clean and deserted except for two feed carts and two people scooping supper for the horses that whinnied and stomped. Several big dogs of indeterminate breeds lolled in the aisle.

To keep from disturbing them, I entered the farm office to the side and closed the door. The room was tidy, warm, and deserted except for a fluffy orange tabby curled on a guest chair. When I scratched his head, he squinted and purred.

I turned when the door opened again.

"I heard you were around," Ross said.

So, I was right about the security guy calling Ross. But there wasn't any reason I shouldn't be there. About Emily, my father had said, "Leave this alone." But he knew I wouldn't and acknowledged as much. Even if someone told him I was at the farm, he had no way to know it was because of Emily. And if he did, so what?

"Hey, Ross. How're things? How's the family?" I suddenly realized that other than my directive to him to get rid of Sawyer ten years ago, we hadn't spoken since I'd blocked the trailer into which he was loading Huckleberry. Did he remember that? Was he still married? Widowed now? When did I last hear anything about his family? Ross had always been a major part of life at the farm, but I'd been so wrapped up in disappearing, I hadn't even thought about him, much less inquired since then. I shifted uneasily.

"Everyone's fine. Thought you might drop by when you were here at Christmas. Even if just to see the horses."

Buying time for an excuse, I scratched the cat's head. "I wasn't here long."

"Mm-hmm." He let the silence build. "What can I do for you?"

"I'm tracking down information about the man who shot us."

"Your father knows you're asking?"

I squirmed, but only a little. "We've discussed it."

His eyes bored into me for a moment. "All right."

"The guy's name was Vince Gardner. Did he ever work here, maybe as a direct hire or part of a construction crew?"

"No."

"You're sure?"

"Positive."

"Was he ever here for any reason? Like to shoe a horse? Deliver feed?"

He shook his head. Slowly. Definitively.

"Stalking then, creeping around? Anything like that? Anything at all?"

"No, Philip. He was never here for any reason. The FBI asked me those same questions. So did your father. I told them the same thing."

Deflated after convincing myself he'd have answers, I said, "Okay. Thanks." Ross wouldn't lie, certainly not to the authorities or Dad and probably not to me. Another Vince Gardner dead end.

Ross extended his hand. "Have to get back to work. Good to see you here."

The instant he left through the interior door into the barn, I found I urgently needed the answer to one more question. "Ross?"

He stuck his head into the office.

"What happened to Sawyer? My horse?"

He peered at me, his mouth a straight line, and when I expected he'd turn away without responding, let me believe, true or not, that something dreadful had befallen Sawyer, he came fully into the room and closed the gap between us to a few feet. "I wondered if you'd ever ask. Your parents kept him for over six years, waiting for you to return or to ask us to send him to you. Your mother and my grandkids kept him busy. But after a while, she figured you really wouldn't ever want him and asked me to find him a good home."

Six years was a long time to feed, pay vet bills, and otherwise care for an unwanted horse. I mentally replayed Huckleberry's departure, only this time the horse Ross loaded into the trailer was Sawyer and I wasn't around to block the ramp and stop him. The guilty regret that tightened my throat made any question of Sawyer's departure moot.

Ross pursed his lips. "You should have come back for him. It would've made all the difference."

"To whom, Ross?" I gripped the orange cat's chair so hard, it tilted. The cat jumped off and shot me a narrow-eyed reprimand.

"To the horse. Your parents. All of us." Without another word, he disappeared into the barn, leaving the door open. The cat followed me to the exterior door and meowed when I shut it.

Fuming, I hoisted myself into the Expedition and slammed the door. Even without a direct confrontation with my family, returning to the farm had yet again proven to be a mistake. Always would.

Dilsey whined and banged around in her crate. As much as I wanted to leave, I owed her a run. A walk might help me vent frustration as well. I jammed the key into the ignition and bumped along the narrow paved path that bisected the pastures. When the pavement ended, I parked, freed Dilsey, and started walking.

But instead of bounding away, Dilsey hung with me, alternately batting my hand with her muzzle and grabbing it in her soft mouth. I shooed her away, and she zoomed around for a moment, then returned to lean against my leg and play-bite my hand. Had I considered she wouldn't run on her own, I'd have brought her ball.

Although dusk was an hour away, the sun had dropped behind the mountains, inviting the evening's chill to replace it. I cooled down as Dilsey and I ambled through the fields. I should never have asked Ross about Sawyer. Till then, our conversation had been cordial. How contradictory to civilly discuss a murderer yet heatedly discuss a gentle horse.

When Dilsey and I reached the pond, we veered into the cluster of trees where the centerpiece was the oldest oak on the farm. The tree fort I had thought about earlier was visible about fifteen feet up among the leafless branches. It appeared solid still, but the ladder was gone.

If I had full use of both arms or was more athletic, I might have climbed the tree without the ladder. Instead, I studied if for a moment before backing away and circling the tree. What Vince Gardner could have built for Emily here! He might have imagined a castle large enough for an overnight camp out for the two of them *and* for a picnic with all three Browns.

But to Emily, I suspected that the scope or grandeur of the tree house mattered little if at all. What counted, and was so clear a few hours ago, were the memories she'd made with her father. Happy memories I'd have doubted the truth of if Mrs. Brown hadn't confirmed it. I'd made happy memories at our tree fort too.

Wondering about what I knew of my family before the shooting versus what I realized after it, but too tired to think anymore, I zipped my jacket and called Dilsey for the trek to my SUV and the long drive home.

CHAPTER 21

THE NEXT DAY, dragging from having arrived home at midnight and cramming one day with a weekend's worth of class prep and house chores, I only got around to calling Emily after supper. I'd update her on what I'd learned about her father from Ross–which was nothing–and we'd plan our next steps.

But she didn't respond to my call or my subsequent text. Curious, considering how hell-bent she was to get to the bottom of what happened. On the other hand, she had a life outside the project and me. Before going to bed, I left another voicemail. Now that I'd invested myself in our search for information, I was anxious to finish, forget about her and her father, the shooting, and the rest of it, and resume my uncomplicated life.

I completed as much of the subpoena request form as I could. It contained no specific instructions about how to submit it, so I contemplated calling on Monday to ask but decided to overnight the thing to the court clerk in the county where the shooting occurred.

On Monday, I lectured, with Dilsey in class with me doing her thing and being rewarded with a random pat on the head, an ear scratch, a hug. I also attended two faculty meetings and held office hours, but I did overnight the subpoena request. And I left another voicemail and text message for Emily. Maybe she'd discovered something about her father she didn't want to admit. Or, like me, hopeful we'd finish this sooner than later, maybe she was busy ticking off her own boxes.

On Wednesday evening, Henry called while I cleaned up after supper. "Tell me you weren't with Emily at the farm this weekend." His tone echoed the one my father used when we were teenagers. *Tell me you didn't let so-and-so drive your car.* It irked me even more coming from Henry.

"If you know I was there, you know I was alone." Ross must've told my parents I'd visited and what I'd asked. No surprise there. But why would they have mentioned that to Henry? Maybe they talked more regularly than I thought they did. I drummed my fingers on the kitchen counter as I wondered if they'd contacted him purposefully about my visit. If they had, why would they? Probably out of surprise he hadn't accompanied me. Not that my visit was a secret. I'd have told him at some point anyway, probably in the same conversation after Emily told him we'd visited her old neighborhood.

"Don't let that girl drag you into things to satisfy her own curiosity."

"What *things*? Asking Ross for his perspective is perfectly reasonable. Besides, I thought you were helping us."

"Watch yourself around her. And—"

"Oh, come on, Henry."

"And tell her to call me. I haven't heard from her since last week."

"Neither have I."

"*That's* encouraging. Maybe finding her father's criminal record was more than she bargained for and she's quitting. And you can do the same."

"I'm not quitting."

"Don't be stupid."

I don't want any part of it. That was what he'd said the weekend before we met Emily at Cast Party. He'd made his stance clear. I'd dragged him into this as reluctantly as Emily had dragged me in. But he *had* agreed to help us, and if he'd changed his mind since then, he needed to say so. "You're backing out, aren't you? After promising to help us."

"I said I'd *advise* you. I'm advising you to drop this nonsense. I can't back out unless I take you out too."

"What does that mean?"

He sucked in a loud breath. "Nothing. Never mind. Just don't trust her." Before I responded, he added, "Talk later," and disconnected.

I called him back immediately and later, but he didn't answer.

By the next Monday, nine days after visiting Emily's neighborhood, nine days overloaded with grading papers and meeting with students, when I still hadn't heard from her, I allowed her silence to annoy me. And worry me. I texted her again. "Did Greenville fall into a sinkhole?" Nothing.

Two days later, while I was preparing to leave the office, she finally called.

"Don't be mad. I'm sorry. I've been so depressed. Seeing my old tree house, talking to Mrs. Brown, getting my model horses. And all that on top of finding Daddy's record. All the years of waiting, and then in one week I learn so much, good and bad, and it got to me." Her voice caught. "I just couldn't deal with it. So I Ubered all week, talked to riders about nothing. Tried to process what I'd learned and what I might learn and thought about what I wanted to do next. I needed space to think, you know?"

A veil of disappointment settled over me as I realized the space she needed was to help her make a decision. How could anyone as resolute as Emily walk away? "You're quitting, aren't you?"

"I thought about it. Imagined letting go." She sighed. "But I can't. I need a few more days, though. Do you understand? I'll call you over the weekend."

I shouldered my backpack and switched off the desk lamp, heartened that Emily was okay and wasn't giving up. When I picked up Dilsey's leash, she charged out the partially open door, woofing excitedly.

Scottie stood in the otherwise empty hallway, arms wrapped around an upright Dilsey, who licked her cheek. "Hey, girl. Happy to see you, too."

I pulled Dilsey off, and Scottie brushed dog hair from her clingy sweater. "Wanted to catch you before you left."

"Sorry about the dog hair."

She waved away my apology. "First, I'm still waiting for my invitation to tour your house. Word on the street is it's finished."

"Word on the street?" How could anyone possibly know the status of my house?

"Second, we need to talk about bringing Dilsey to the senior center. And third, I have a recipe I need to try out on an unsuspecting victim. So, I'm propositioning you to combine all three: tour, discussion, dinner."

Propositioning? I blinked at her, caught so off guard I was unable to summon one of the excuses I kept ready for times when a simple "no" seemed too rude. She'd asked before Christmas to see the finished house, mentioned it when she ran into Henry, Emily, and me at Cast Party, but I never expected her to follow up, and I'd never have offered.

"Good," she said, arms crossed. "Clearly, you have no plans and can't even conjure up a flimsy excuse. Friday, five thirty, early enough for a quick outside tour while there's still daylight."

In her mind was this a *date*? She was attractive and nice, and I didn't want to hurt her feelings, but . . . "Scottie, I have a personal policy to not . . ." Not what? Socialize with? Visit? Hang out with? "Um . . . *fraternize* with people I work with. I—"

"Philip." She cocked her head, and the corners of her mouth twitched. "Relax. It's not like it's a date."

Embarrassment blazed from the back of my neck into my cheeks. I stared at the floor, unable to respond.

"How about this?" Her voice betrayed her attempt not to laugh. "Ask some of your other friends. I'm not the only one dying to see your house. I can cook for eight as easily as for two. We'll have a big ol' dinner party. You won't have to worry about *anything*. It'll be fun."

I winced. The only thing worse than dinner with Scottie at my house was dinner with a mass invasion at my house. I *had* unwittingly promised her a tour, but I hadn't promised anyone else. "No group. Let's keep it to just us. Shall I make dessert?"

"Nope. Leave it all to me." She patted Dilsey and bustled down the hall and around the corner.

Why could I never say no to Scottie? I turned the key in my office door with more force than was necessary. Since I'd moved to Grainger, she'd been nothing but helpful and considerate to both Dilsey and to me. And she brought Christmas cookies. Fine. I'd let her cook one dinner, show her around, and be done with the commitment. Simple.

CHAPTER 22

IN PREPARATION FOR Scottie's visit, I canceled my Friday afternoon office hours to make time for all the household chores I normally saved for Saturday. First, though, because Friday marked day ten since the court clerk had received my subpoena request form and day ten of hearing nothing, I called for a status report.

"Yes, sir, we have your form right here. There are issues with it. We'd planned to mail you a letter to that effect next week."

"What do you mean, 'issues'?"

"Hold please."

The line went silent. She couldn't simply relay the *issues*?

"You still there, sir?"

"Yes."

"So, it looks like you're not a Tennessee resident."

"That's correct."

"You need to be one to request public records from this state."

I rolled my eyes. "And I'd have known that how?"

"It's probably online somewhere. Or you could've called to ask."

Could have if the issue of residency had occurred to me. Damn, Henry should have known or at least suspected that.

He didn't practice in Tennessee, but neither did my father, and he'd known about the confidentiality of the investigation records. "You couldn't have called to tell me that the day you opened the envelope?"

Her noncommittal tone turned icy. "We're busy. *Sir.*"

It was a tiny rural county; how busy could they be? But venting at her would get me closer to nowhere than I was now. "And so?"

"We're rejecting your request."

"I figured. Can I appeal?"

"You're not a resident, so no. If you want to resubmit, you need to have a Tennessee resident make the request for you." She paused. "But you do know the records you requested aren't publicly available?"

"That's the whole point of filing for a subpoena."

"Yes, sir. Well, okay, as long as you know. If there's anything else I can do for you, don't hesitate to call back."

I politely ended our conversation and impolitely cursed her ineptitude under my breath. Totally her fault for not contacting me sooner, but not her fault about the residency law. Or that Henry misadvised me. Or that I believed what he'd told me in the first place. I resisted the impulse to call and confront him, and instead tackled my chores.

You need to have a Tennessee resident make the request. I'd attended college in Tennessee and most likely still had friends there. *Former* friends who'd not heard from me in years. If I located any of them, I couldn't be sure that one would even agree to submit the form on my behalf.

Henry probably knew someone there who'd help. He had friends everywhere, but would he ask?

I emailed an update to Emily and told her I'd call after I spoke with Henry. I didn't have time to think about some red-tape procedure now. I needed to concentrate on dinner with Scottie. Tomorrow I'd give Henry a piece of my mind, then persuade him to solicit help from one of his contacts.

What overwhelmed me most wasn't the heft of the baking dish I carried into the house, or the loaf of homemade bread Scottie stacked on top of it, or the enormous and warm aluminum-covered dessert I carried in during our second trip from her Soul, or even the tin of homemade dog treats for Dilsey. What stunned me was the squat oval vase packed with cut daffodils Scottie lifted from the floor behind the driver's seat.

I must have looked surprised, because she asked, "What?"

"No one's ever brought me flowers." Not even in the hospital.

She smirked. "You think there's something wrong with guys receiving flowers?"

"It's not that. It's . . ." Just that Scottie had thought of flowers when no one else ever had. "Unusual." An understatement. "At least for me. Thank you." I didn't know why, but the gesture rattled me.

As soon as she placed the daffodils on the kitchen table, I couldn't imagine them never being there. Brightening the room with flowers had never occurred to me.

"A little color can transform everything," Scottie stepped back, hands on hips. "Perfect. Now, are there any tricks to your oven?"

Following her instructions, I set it to 350 and leaned against the doorframe of the mudroom, arms crossed, while she rearranged my refrigerator to accommodate the salad, rummaged through my drawers for utensils, and otherwise appropriated my kitchen. Whether her presumptuousness annoyed, impressed, or amused me, I couldn't decide. Maybe all three.

She slid the baking dish into the preheated oven, washed her hands, and dried them on a paper towel she snagged from the roll hanging from the cabinet closest to the sink. "Where's your trash?"

"You can't find it on your own?"

"Smartass." She opened the cabinet under the sink and dropped the damp towel into the trash can there. "The chicken has to bake for fifty minutes. Why don't you show me what you've done outside while there's still a little daylight? When we come back in, we'll set the table, toss dressing on the salad, and cut the bread."

"Your Christmas trip," I said testily. "Was the cruise director on vacation?"

She was quick. "Nah, but he was busy implementing all my suggestions."

Her good humor instantly shifted my mood, and I grinned. The house might be mine, but she'd placed herself in charge of the evening. All I had to do was go along. No decisions to make. In a few hours, I'd have met my obligation. I'd thank her, send her on her way, and figure out why Henry had, at best, accidentally misinformed me or, at worst, misled me about the subpoena. I relinquished control of the evening to Scottie, and my frustration and the resulting tension in my neck and shoulders dissolved.

In the yard, bundled against the subfreezing temperature, we strolled the interior perimeter of the fence, taking turns throwing Dilsey's ball.

"Nothing out here you haven't already seen," I said, gesturing. "The house itself took priority. New roof, painted trim, pressure-washed brick. An arborist comes out next month, and I'll overseed the grass, but otherwise I have no plans for the yard."

"I noticed at Christmas that you pulled up all the bushes around the foundation."

A flash of a morning twilight that mirrored tonight's, in which a human silhouette emerged from the overgrown privet around an otherwise well-tended cabin in Tennessee, passed so quickly through my mind, I'd have disbelieved seeing it if my hands hadn't gone clammy. I stuffed them into my jacket pockets and squeezed the lining. "It was privet. Inappropriate for around a foundation."

"What'll you replace them with?"

"Still researching." *Nothing.*

I hustled her and Dilsey into the house and upstairs, through the two furnished guest bedrooms and connecting bath, the empty bedroom, and the hallway bath. We zipped through the master suite I'd converted from two bedrooms and a small bath.

"Nice," Scottie said as we walked toward the stairs "Now you get to decorate. What are you planning to hang on the walls?"

"The walls?" I hadn't thought about the walls. "Nothing."

"Nothing? How dull. If you want some ideas—"

I shook my head. "Thanks anyway."

Back downstairs, I showed her through the living room, the dining room—where the only furniture was a wine fridge—the half bath, and the pine-green kitchen with its oak cabinets.

The last room on the tour was my study, a room separated from the entrance hall by glass-paned pocket doors. I slid them open, flipped the wall switch, and waved Scottie in. She scanned the room, tipped her head toward the ceiling fan and down to the carpet. On what would've been her second pass, when her gaze lingered on the bookcase, I tapped her arm to draw her attention away from the single photo I displayed in the entire house.

But instead of being distracted, in three strides she reached the bookcase and lifted the photo of Teddy and me on our horses. She studied it, then me, then the photo again. Gently, she set it back in its place and, to my relief, left the room without a word.

I switched off the lamp and slid the doors shut. When Dilsey and I joined Scottie in the kitchen, she'd taken the salad from the fridge.

"I can't even imagine," she said quietly.

My stomach clenched. No way could she have guessed about Teddy, so she knew about my past. If she asked for specifics or even tried to build a conversation around Teddy's death, I'd politely shift subjects. Or not-so-politely cut her off. Whatever it took. "Red wine's all I have."

"What?"

"With dinner. Cabernet okay?" I hadn't planned to serve wine, but it seemed a fair exchange for the daffodils. Besides, I suddenly needed a drink.

"Perfect."

Scottie pulled the baking dish from the oven as I returned with a bottle of cab from the wine refrigerator in the dining room. Dilsey sat at attention, drooling, eyes begging for a morsel, and when Scottie looked inquiringly at me, I shook my head.

I couldn't blame Dilsey for trying. My mouth watered while I set the table with my stoneware and utensils, tumblers with ice and water, and stemless wine glasses. We settled in, and I poured the wine. When I didn't offer a toast, she tapped my glass.

"To fixing what's broken—your house and hopefully Carter Hall."

I raised my glass. "To fixing things."

The food was fabulous. She'd cooked the chicken, along with scallions, mushrooms, and water chestnuts, in a creamy vermouth sauce over brown rice. The homemade bread and salad were perfect. I hadn't realized how hungry I was.

Scottie shepherded our conversation from one safe topic to the next. The status of students affected by the fire. The busy counselors. Uncertainty about the future of the burned-out residence hall. Odds and ends about Grainger and its faculty and staff—but nothing gossipy or inappropriate. Or personal.

Dilsey chewed a bone on her bed, occasionally regarding us with her soft gaze. Despite myself, or perhaps because of the wine, I relaxed and succumbed to a rhythm of answering Scottie's questions or responding without having to offer, or refuse to answer, anything outside my comfort zone.

Until she mentioned her volunteer work at Grainger's senior center and the role she envisioned there for Dilsey.

"She's not a real therapy dog, Scottie."

"Doesn't matter, not for this place. As long as she's well-behaved and clean and passes a vet check, she's good."

Would Dilsey pass a vet check? Epilepsy wasn't infectious, but still.

My expression must have betrayed my concern because Scottie said, "Look how much she benefits your students. They're more settled than most other freshmen, less stressed. Getting better grades too."

"How do you know?"

"Trish mentioned it. Other professors, too, and not only ones from the English department. And the students themselves say how much they love having her in class."

"I'm glad. They've never told me. Actually, after the first few class sessions, they stopped talking about anything not directly related to their assignments."

She twirled her wine glass. "You're probably not the easiest person to talk with."

I ignored the observation and split the last of the wine between us. "How'd you end up working at the university?"

"My dad was a military officer, Air Force, and by the time I finished my junior year here, I'd lived in Grainger longer than I'd lived anywhere. When I graduated, I couldn't bear to leave and applied for the first job I was even remotely qualified for."

I finished my wine. "Where's your family now?" As soon as I'd asked, I regretted it. If I inquired about her family, she could reciprocate, and I didn't want to discuss mine.

"Northern Virginia. Dad's a defense contractor at the Pentagon. Mom's an accountant. I have two younger brothers. One's an IT geek in Cincinnati. The other's a lieutenant in the Navy and stationed in San Diego."

I nodded and attempted to end the discussion by carrying our plates to the sink without commenting. As I rinsed them and opened the dishwasher, Scottie appeared by my side with our glasses and the empty breadbasket. "Tell me about your family."

I knew that was coming; I should never have let the conversation drift in that direction. "Nothing much to tell. Parents, one younger brother."

"Must have been fascinating growing up in a political family."

"Not really."

She took the hint. "Your brother does what?"

"He's a med student in Charlottesville." I dried my hands, trying to signal her to stop asking.

"Charlottesville's practically right up the road. It's wonderful you guys get to visit. My brothers are so far away."

I hadn't spoken with Jamie since the morning I left the farm. Not for any particular reason. I hadn't cut him out of my life, as he'd accused me. I'd just gotten used to living without him. *I should call him, though. I really should.*

I'd been enjoying myself until this conversation. Despite being a bit intrusive, Scottie was easy to talk with, but our conversation epitomized my aversion to socializing with anyone. I didn't want to talk about my family or my life outside the university, but common rules of social engagement dictated that people couldn't get acquainted without poking into each other's histories. "What's for dessert?"

"Coconut bread pudding." She opened drawers till she found the knife and spatula she wanted.

I clenched my jaw and flipped on the coffee brewer. If she noticed my shift in mood, she chose to ignore it and continued talking.

"Your dad's always on the news." She found dessert plates in the upper cabinets and set them on the counter.

I'd tolerated enough of her searching through my kitchen. "You can't just ask me for what you need?"

"More efficient to look myself. But if it bugs you, yeah, I'll ask." She shrugged. "So anyway, the university HR checks social media for all new hires."

"I don't do social media. And what does HR checking have to do with you?"

"I research everyone new to the English department. Usually only grad students, because we rarely hire new faculty. You have zero social media presence, at least until the fire, but . . ."

"But I have a news presence."

"Yes. I heard about the shooting when it happened—it made national headlines—but I'd forgotten about it. It was just one of those horrible things you read about. But I rediscovered it when I looked you up. So, I know what happened to you. To your father. To your little brother."

I reached into the refrigerator for the cream. No matter where I lived or how low-profile I was or how many years passed, anyone who had even a modicum of interest in me could learn about the shooting and connect me to it. Anyone researching my father for any reason, or randomly googling attempted assassinations of politicians would find me. Anyone hearing a news story of a tragedy involving college-age kids would find me. My life would never be private. Worst of all, to Scottie and Trish, to Emily, perhaps to the other teachers, my students, and Dilsey's vet, to *everyone* who'd known me since the shooting and who would ever know me, one brief event that I neither initiated nor controlled defined me. People viewed me not as a colleague, friend, or client, not even as the son of a US senator or the caretaker of an old house and young Labrador retriever. No. I was the poor guy who barely survived the tragedy that killed his little brother, who deserved, *needed*, their compassion and their kind words.

I resented the hell out of all of it.

Only when Dilsey tried to press her slimy bone into my hand did I realize I'd clenched my fists. I patted her and thought of an upside to Scottie's knowledge. If she already knew the facts that defined me—and, by extension, which defined my family—we didn't need to discuss any of it. So, I didn't bother asking to change the subject. I just did. "The other day, what did you mean by 'word on the street' was I'd finished remodeling the house?"

Then my phone rang. Scottie handed it to me, surprisingly without looking at it.

Henry. Perfect timing. "Gotta take it. Sorry." I had to add more distance between my family and the next topic. I scooted into the entrance hall and answered before the call could roll to voicemail. "What?"

"I was beginning to wonder. It's Friday night, so I expected you to be reading or doing laundry or whatever."

"Very funny."

"I'm coming by tomorrow morning. Early, because I have a date later. I've got something to give you."

"I've got something for you, too, and you're not going to like it."

He paused. "All right. Seven o'clock. Let's get breakfast out."

Scottie waved off my apology when I returned to the kitchen.

"To answer your question," she said, "the folks at the hardware store say they hardly see you now. The UPS girl we see all the time mentioned she hadn't delivered anything to"—she air quoted—"'that creepy house' in ages. Things like that. It all added up to your house being done."

It all added up, I mused, stirring cream into our coffee, to my misconception about living a secluded life in Grainger.

CHAPTER 23

WE ATE DESSERT in the living room, angled toward each other on the sofa, separated by the middle cushions, plates in our hands, mugs on coasters on the coffee table. Dilsey entertained us, shaking the floppy elephant she loved as much as her ball. Each time one end or the other smacked against her head, the toy emitted a tinny trumpet that enticed her to shake it harder. If she weren't so fond of the damn thing, I'd have pitched it long ago.

The first taste of bread pudding left me speechless. It was marshmallow soft and melted away my agitation from the conversation we'd just had. I shut my eyes and allowed the first bite to linger. Sometimes the little things made all the difference.

"What's wrong?" Scottie asked.

I swallowed. "Nothing other than you've blasted my formerly favorite dessert out of the galaxy."

She smiled. "Thank you."

Only the clink of stainless on stoneware and Dilsey's playing broke our easy silence. I licked my fork one final time. "Uh, excuse my manners."

"There's plenty more." She licked her own fork.

"No way. I'm stuffed."

"I'll leave the leftovers with you."

"How can I say no?"

"Thanks so much for showing me your wonderful house. Even though you didn't want to."

I regretted that my reluctance had been so obvious. Scottie was personable, if pushy and talkative. Her dinner was more than a fair trade for the tour. It outdid anything I'd have cooked for myself. "It's not personal. I . . . No, no, no!"

Immobile in the archway at the entrance to the living room, legs braced, Dilsey stared with wide and dark unseeing eyes. She'd dropped her elephant, and strands of saliva shimmered like tinsel from her lower jaw. Before I could move, her legs flipped out from under her, and she thudded onto her side.

My plate banged to the coffee table when I jumped up.

"Oh my God!" Scottie sprang from the couch. "What's happening?"

I yanked my sweater over my head, checked my watch, and knelt beside Dilsey. Placing the wadded-up sweater between her thrashing head and the floor equated to waltzing with a partner doing the twist. But I knew all the moves.

The seizure's violence threatened to pummel Dilsey against the brick hearth, so I slung her by her tail into the middle of the room. Her head twisted from side to side, her jaws clamping and releasing, clamping and releasing, with the decisive snap of an alligator's.

After two minutes and three seconds, she stopped thrashing and lay still.

Long, very long, but not record setting. Twenty-nine days after the last cluster on January 14. About right. The potential for Dilsey to seize this weekend should have prompted me to refuse or at least delay tonight's dinner, but Scottie's self-invitation had blindsided me, and I hadn't even considered that Dilsey might seize.

I gripped the loose skin over Dilsey's withers and rump and slid her away from a puddle of urine but succeeded only in spreading it. Her raspy heaving signaled the fluid pooling in her lungs. This would be one of *those* long, exhausting nights.

My heartbeat slowed, and I remembered Scottie. She stood by the coffee table, wringing the sweater I'd lost track of, not bothering to hide her tears.

Our eyes met. She wiped her cheeks with the back of her hand, folded my sweater, and tossed it to me. I raised Dilsey's head and arranged the sweater under it. When I looked up again, Scottie was gone. I didn't blame her.

"Scottie?"

From the hallway, she sniffled. "I'm right here."

"Before you go, can you bring me the little red tote bag in the upper cabinet beside the fridge? Her name's on it."

"Okay. I saw it earlier."

All that rummaging through my kitchen had paid off.

The tote dropped on the floor beside me, and Dilsey seized again. This one was much shorter, less violent. Afterward, with Dilsey stretched flat on the floor, only the rise and fall of her wheezing ribcage confirmed she was alive.

From behind me, Scottie asked, "Is she okay?"

"She's unconscious. Her body's re-circuiting itself."

Scottie plopped down to my left, behind Dilsey's head. She wore a dishtowel around her neck, and between us she set a roll of paper towels, a spray bottle of Simple Green, a plastic trash bag, and a box of tissues.

"Thanks," I said, wondering how she anticipated what I'd need. I tore off a few sheets of paper towel, leaned across Dilsey to sop up the urine, and dropped the paper into the bag Scottie held open. From the tote, I removed a syringe without a needle, lifted Dilsey's tail with one hand, and administered its contents into her rectum with the other. "Valium."

"In her rear end?"

She sounded upset. In the instant I decided to explain how Dilsey and I coped, I discovered I needed to hear the explanation, too, to convince myself Dilsey's epilepsy wasn't so bad.

"It's the fastest way—other than IV, which I can't do—to get it into her system to try to prevent a big cluster." I tossed the syringe into the trash bag and picked up another, one with a needle. "Lasix, a diuretic." I tented the skin over Dilsey's withers and injected her. "Her pulmonary edema—the wheezing you hear, her lungs filling with fluid—is an unusual complication. Goes along with the severity of her epilepsy." I capped and broke the needle, then set it on the floor between us and extracted a bottle of pills from the tote. "Once she's conscious enough to swallow, she also gets an extra dose of one of her regular meds. Or several extra doses, depending on how tonight goes."

"You said *cluster*. How many seizures is a cluster?"

"Maybe only the two." I considered how much I should tell her. "The worst was twenty-three seizures in sixteen hours. Last summer, right after I moved here."

She scooted closer and, leaning over the paper towel and Simple Green, pulled me into a one-armed hug I didn't expect. "How awful."

I froze, embarrassed. "Yeah."

In our motel room, before I moved in with Henry, Dilsey had begun seizing just after one o'clock in the morning.

After the ninth seizure, virtually indistinguishable from the eighth, I called her new vet, rolled Dilsey into a blanket, and dragged her to the Expedition. Lifting an unconscious, dead weight seventy-three pound Labrador retriever into the back of an SUV was no small feat. She seized again en route. And even with Dr. Emerson working her magic, Dilsey had thirteen more seizures before the cluster broke. That precipitated a week of a dog so physically and mentally damaged, I didn't see how we'd survive, regardless of what I did or how desperately I hoped. But we did.

"How can she have so many?"

"You know what kindling is?"

"Like for starting a fire?"

"Exactly. Kindling's a metaphor. Each little seizure is a twig that feeds the next one, which feeds the next one, until they produce the bonfire known as epilepsy. Or to put it another way, the more Dilsey *practices* having a seizure, the better she becomes at it."

"I had no idea." Scottie threw her tissue into the trash bag and pulled out another one. "When will you know if she'll have more tonight?"

"When she does or doesn't."

"And there's nothing you can do? Find the cause? A cure?"

"I tried. Blood tests, MRIs, EEGs. Idiopathic epilepsy, they call it. Epilepsy of unknown cause. Maybe a genetic component, maybe not. There's no cure, so control is the best I can hope for. She's on a cocktail of drugs several times daily. A homemade diet. I use few chemicals around here. She also gets acupuncture, which does little more than decrease the side effects of her medication, which is something. But her epilepsy is severe and complicated and resistant to everything." I slumped a little with the enormity of it all.

"Oh, wow," she said softly. "No wonder you keep her with you all the time. You must really love her."

Love? Without question, I was committed to her and, without resentment, I accepted the limitations her epilepsy placed on my life. I didn't mind the teasing about the crib bumpers or her constant presence wherever I went. I did the best I knew how to do for her. Did that define love?

"I'm responsible for her, is all."

"Uh-huh." Scottie slid away from me and back to her original spot.

Dilsey convulsed again, one violent motion that flung pink saliva and mucus on both Scottie and me. That time, she expelled three hard lumps of feces. I apologized, but Scottie said, "Don't," before spraying the floor with Simple Green and handing me a wad of paper towels.

Dilsey remained unconscious and drooling, her head resting in a puddle of goo in my sweater. Scottie pulled the dishtowel from around her neck and leaned toward her.

I grabbed her hand. "*Don't touch her.*"

She snatched her hand away. "I'm not an idiot. I wanted to wipe off her face." She sounded offended, dropped the towel, and scooted behind me to sit cross-legged on my right.

"Sorry. I'm sorry." I squeezed my eyes shut, seeing the near miss with little Madison. "At Christmas, at my parents' house, she had a seizure and almost bit a six-year-old. It scared the hell out of me. And the kid." I sighed. "*And* the adults."

"That's why you don't want her at the senior center, isn't it?"

"Yes."

She wiped her eyes and blew her nose again. "Sorry. Since the fire, every little thing's impossibly hard."

We sat for a few minutes without talking. With the note-pad and pen from the tote, I wrote the date, the beginning and ending times of each seizure, and the drugs I'd administered, setting it aside when Dilsey's back arched and she kicked her hind legs out behind her.

"Here we go again."

By any standard, that seizure, thankfully, was short. And five minutes after it ended, Dilsey rose unsteadily, wheezing, then went down again, this time on her chest, and coughed pink froth onto my sweater. I wiped her mouth with a paper towel and poked an anticonvulsant down her slimy throat.

Scottie's finger doodled on Dilsey's hip. "How often do you go through this?"

"Forty-three days is our longest seizure-free interval. And usually they occur in the middle of the night."

"You keep track?"

"In a log, yeah. What I wrote on that notepad will go into the log as soon as the cluster ends."

Scottie glanced sideways at me.

"What?"

"Nothing."

"I know what you're thinking. Same as everyone thinks."

"You have no clue what I'm thinking."

"You're wondering why I don't put her to sleep and get another dog."

She shook her head emphatically. "I'd never think that. I've finally figured out why sometimes you show up in your morning classes barely functional and looking like hell." She smiled slightly. "Or, as your students describe it, looking hungover."

"*What?* I'm always functional. Never hungover!"

"The kids worry about you, and they talk. Trish worries about you. So do I."

I didn't know whether to be grateful or angry. No matter how rough a night I'd had with Dilsey, I never missed class, never slighted my students. "No one needs to ever worry about me."

"Yeah, okay." Scottie crumpled her tissue. "Since you brought it up, why don't you put her to sleep and get another dog?"

I scratched Dilsey's neck, oddly unperturbed that Scottie had asked. "You've seen her quality of life firsthand. If you hadn't been here tonight, you'd have never known anything was wrong."

"You didn't answer my question."

"How could I?" I twirled Dilsey's soft ear around my finger. "Her seizures don't define her, they're a medical condition. What defines her is her gentleness and good humor, her zest for life. She was the perfect puppy, you know? Fun, active, healthy. I had no reason to think she wouldn't stay that way for her entire life. The seizures started out of nowhere. Even so, even after over two years of dealing with them, when she chases squirrels or interacts with my students or snores beside my recliner with her ball or her elephant nestled under her chin, I sometimes almost doubt her epilepsy is real. But all the little reminders—her meds and the crib bumpers—and the big reminders—the clusters—remind me our lives are and always will be affected by these, and—" I stopped, taken aback at my openness and worse, the wistfulness in my voice, as if saying the words aloud could fix anything. "Sorry. You didn't need to hear that."

Scottie wiped her eyes again. "Thank you for telling me."

Dilsey heaved herself up on shaky legs and immediately squatted. Scottie leaned across me for the paper towels.

I motioned toward the puddle. "A negative side effect of the Lasix is she'll pee about every fifteen minutes for hours."

We rose, and I guided Dilsey by the collar through the kitchen, mudroom, and screened porch and out into the yard. She peed again at the base of the steps and drifted around, sniffing, tripping over roots. I sat on the frigid top step in the semidarkness of a waxing crescent moon as she wandered.

The back floodlights suddenly illuminated the yard, and my jacket dropped across my shoulders. Scottie sat beside me and wiggled into her own coat. "Put that on. It's freezing."

Other than Dilsey crunching through the dry leaves and an occasional distant bark carried on the cold air, the night was silent. After a while Scottie said, "Have you ever known anyone with epilepsy? A person?"

"No. You?"

"One, in high school. Kids were so mean to her. One day, she had a seizure on the bus. The buzz was that she was possessed. I realized much later that we were terrified. Not of the girl herself, I don't think, but the condition she had that none of us understood and that she couldn't control."

"For such an ugly disease to have such a mystical aura amazes me. Some cultures consider people with epilepsy to be spiritually gifted."

Across the yard, Dilsey watched us, or at least gazed in our direction.

Scottie said, "You've put a lot of time into studying this, haven't you?"

"I'm trying to understand it. I never will."

"Have you ever considered that *Dilsey* is gifted? Maybe her deep intuitiveness is the flip side of her epilepsy."

"She's just a big, goofy, affectionate Lab."

"You don't recognize how extraordinary she is, do you? Don't understand her ability to connect with the people who most need that connection. Remember the day after the fire, how she was with Nicole—who's terrified of dogs, but not of Dilsey? How special is that? What she's done for your students, for all of us? How deeply *you* are connected with her?"

"She's friendly with everyone, Scottie."

"That's not what I'm talking about. This is different."

I didn't see it. Dilsey liked everyone, and of course she'd connected with me. I fed her, walked her, tended her every need. She was stuck with me.

Dilsey meandered toward us. I didn't like the purposelessness of her gait, and just as I stood, she collided with a tree and dropped into another seizure. I tugged her by the tail away from the tree, knelt beside her, and let the short seizure run its course.

She was so wobbly when she rose that I cradled her in my arms and carried her inside. Scottie held the door for us and followed with the jacket I'd dropped. As soon as I laid Dilsey on the kitchen floor, she seized again. I snatched my phone from the counter. Time to call the vet and take Dilsey in for IV Valium and whatever else the doctor thought necessary.

Dr. Emerson had given me her cell number and assured me emergency calls were part of the job and I should never hesitate to contact her, regardless of the hour. I always worried about bothering her, though.

"Philip." She sounded wide awake. "I'm in Seattle at a conference. How bad?"

I explained.

"You should have enough meds to get her through tonight. You know what to do. But just in case—" She gave me the numbers of the two closest emergency clinics: one sixty miles northwest of Grainger, the other in Richmond, sixty miles northeast. Too far, she and I both knew, and Grainger's one other veterinarian had underwhelmed me when I interviewed him last summer. Dilsey was better off with just me. "Call me again if you need to. I'll do what I can from here." We disconnected.

"My vet's away; we're on our own." Worry trickled through my voice. Dilsey lay flat on the cold tile, her mouth gaping. "Scottie, can you . . ."

She read my mind and tossed me a towel. I pillowed Dilsey's head on it.

"Philip, will you get upset if I ask you something?"

I straightened and squared my shoulders. She was about to ask the same question I asked myself every time Dilsey clustered. I asked it first. "Could she die?"

"Yes."

"During a single seizure, supposedly not. But if a cluster progresses to status epilepticus—a very long seizure or multiple seizures she doesn't regain consciousness between—a life-threatening emergency . . ." I inhaled deeply. "If that happens, then yeah, she could die."

Dilsey's breathing evened out. I slid her away from her newest puddles of drool and urine and stood to remove Scottie's purse from the coat rack in the mudroom. She still wore her coat from our trip outside.

"You might as well go on home; this could go on all night. I'm so sorry we ruined your great dinner. Thanks for that and for your help."

She accepted her purse and immediately dropped it on the counter behind her. "I'm not leaving you."

"Thanks, but I can handle everything."

"Philip, your dog's a mess. Your living room's a mess. I can clean up while you take care of Dilsey. And you, you're a mess too." She regarded my button-down Oxford spattered with Dilsey's body fluids and hair and dirt.

"Scottie—"

She slipped from her coat and slung it over the back of a chair, then faced me, hands on hips. "Is it so hard for you to accept that anyone might care enough about you and Dilsey to want to help? Of course you *can* handle all her seizures by yourself. You've proven that—not that anyone would have known, since you kept it all so secret. But tonight, there's no reason you should have to. And I won't let you." She stared a hole through me. "After everything that's happened to you, do you really want to go through this alone?"

I cringed. She'd practically forced her way into my house, invaded my space, pried into my family. Now, without naming it, she threw the shooting at me and refused to go. Her persistence could have pissed me off, but it didn't. Her earnest expression and sincere tone, her unsolicited help during the grossest parts of the past two hours, and her acceptance of the path I'd chosen for Dilsey softened her words. I *did* appreciate her help. More than that, I suddenly needed her calm and comforting presence.

I'd isolated myself in reaction to my family's response to Teddy's death. My choice. But my father's Christmas night accusation was true: Dilsey's seizures had isolated me in ways I neither intended nor desired. Like kindling, one twig had ignited another until my isolation became a bonfire. Was that one reason I'd been vulnerable to Emily's request for help? The shooting had isolated her too. Emily and me, strangers isolated and united by one moment in time. Perhaps her plea had touched me as much for the support I needed as for the support she needed.

Scottie hadn't moved. Her gaze dared me to deny her the opportunity to help Dilsey and me. All her tears and the tissues she'd used to wipe them away had smeared what little remained of her eye makeup. A glob of something plastered a tendril of hair to her right ear. Like my shirt, her silky cobalt blouse bore evidence of Dilsey's ordeal. She seemed oblivious to her appearance, though. Her focus was on Dilsey and me, and her offer seemed to have no strings attached.

"Thank you, Scottie."

I would accept the gift of help so generously—no, so *genuinely*—offered.

CHAPTER 24

AFTER FOUR MORE grand mal seizures, a few focal seizures during which Dilsey twitched, clamped her jaws, and foamed but didn't convulse, and more drugs, the cluster ended at just after three o'clock. I knew that only in retrospect, though, when a while later I dragged myself from sleep to the aroma of coffee.

Dilsey lay sprawled on her cushion, head dangling from one end, tail from the other. Her raspy breathing had quieted. I sat where I'd been beside her for hours, on the cold tile of the kitchen floor, braced upright against the hard cabinets, wearing the jeans and flannel shirt I'd changed into on my one trip upstairs. Satisfied she was comfortable, I stretched and pulled the blanket to my chin, relishing its warmth. I'd get up in a minute.

Blanket?

My eyes popped open. Scottie, lying on her stomach on the floor a few feet away, put down her phone.

"You're still here," I said, surprised.

"Of course." She rolled over and sat up. Stretched both arms over her head. "You fell asleep. I suspected you didn't mean to, but you had your hand on Dilsey, so I figured you'd know if she seized. You looked cold. I gave up on your thermostat, but I found a blanket in a guest room closet."

"I fell asleep? What time is it?"

"About seven." She wore the faded old college sweat-shirt I'd loaned her to replace her splattered blouse. She'd washed all the makeup off her face, and she looked amaz-ing, not like she'd been awake all night.

I'd offered her one of the guest rooms—no sense in both of us being sleep-deprived—but she refused, even when I promised I'd wake her if I needed her. I half re-membered her toting a full trash bag and an armload of towels through the kitchen and into the mudroom, which probably meant the living room was as pristine as when she arrived fourteen hours ago. As if the cluster never even happened.

Except it had, and I'd fallen asleep, and she'd covered me with a blanket. Sleeping in the presence of another person was the most intimate of acts—more intimate, even, than sex—and spoke to a level of comfort, and per-haps trust, with Scottie that I hadn't shared with anyone in a very long time. The weirdest thing was Scottie's pres-ence felt . . . natural.

She held a mug in both hands and peered over the top. I struggled to maintain eye contact with her and lost. An-other cup of coffee steamed on the floor beside me. She must have just set it there. The amount of cream she'd added was perfect.

"Everything will seem better once it's daylight," she said.

"I guess." Everything already was better, and not be-cause of daylight.

"Go back to sleep," she said, misinterpreting. "To bed. I'll hang out with Dilsey."

"No, that's okay. Once I'm awake, I'm awake."

She sipped her coffee. "Now what happens?"

"I'll try to convince Dilsey to eat. Update her seizure log. Bathe her as soon as she can stand long enough." She was sticky with urine and the blood-tinged saliva she'd thrashed into. "Clean up. Wash laundry. That sort of thing."

"Maybe take care of yourself too? Eat something? *Try* to take another nap?" She yawned. "I certainly see one in *my* not-too-distant future."

"Sorry for taking over your whole night." Despite my own exhaustion, I understood that she'd probably stayed for no reason other than she was too nice not to. She'd tackled the unpleasant task of cleaning up after Dilsey. She'd spent the rest of the night watching over us and then made coffee. She'd attended to every detail.

She stretched across the floor and patted Dilsey. "I didn't mean it that way. I'm glad I stayed. You didn't need to deal with her seizures by yourself, this time or ever." She raised a hand, keeping me from protesting. "And I learned a lot about, well, about a lot of things." She yawned again and stood. "I'm making us breakfast."

"Thanks, but no need."

"Dinner was a long time ago. Besides, cooking always makes me feel better." She flipped on the overhead light and pulled out my largest skillet from the drawer under the oven. To my surprise, I no longer minded her searching for what she needed. After last night, I had nothing to hide.

"Got any bacon?"

"In the freezer. But, Scottie . . ."

"Shush." She found the bacon, wrested it from its wrapper, and put it into the microwave. "Thaw cycle," she murmured to the microwave or maybe to the bacon.

The front door opened and shut.

"Whose blue car?" Henry called from the front entrance. A moment later, at the kitchen threshold, his gaze roved from me to Scottie in my sweatshirt to Dilsey on her bed and to all of us again before settling on the daffodils. Without raising her head, Dilsey acknowledged him with two half-hearted wags.

I knew what he was thinking, and in a different situation, I'd have been annoyed at his presumption.

He frowned, and then a grin played at the corners of his mouth. "Well, well. Isn't this cozy."

"I forgot you were coming."

"Clearly." Shrugging off his jacket, he said to Scottie, "I gotta say, as far as I know, it's been a long time since anyone spent the night with Philip."

She closed the distance between them in a few huge strides and poked him in the chest. "I don't think I'd be joking about last night if I were you. Nothing happened. Not *that,* anyway. Have *you* ever seen what he and Dilsey go through?"

"Yeah, I've seen a seizure. Two actually." He backed away from her. "You're the girl with the dog name."

"That's me. And you're Henry." She barely gave him time to nod before pointing toward the mudroom. "Make yourself useful and move the stuff in the washer into the dryer. I'll fix breakfast, and then I'll leave you two to whatever plans you had."

"No need to leave. Henry's just delivering something." *Move the stuff in the washer into the dryer?* "You already washed stuff?"

"Dilsey's towels is all. They weren't making the place smell any better. Oh, and your sweater is soaking in the laundry tub."

Henry shot me an I-don't-believe-this expression as he passed by Dilsey and me and rustled around in the mud-room. I ducked my head to hide my grin when the dryer rumbled.

He reentered the kitchen and peered over Scottie's shoulder, watching her crack egg after egg, one-handed, into the bowl, and toss the shells into the garbage disposal. The microwave dinged, and he set the thawed bacon on the counter.

"Out of my way." Scottie elbowed him, and he retreated to the table. She found an apron in the lowest drawer, which contained the miscellaneous kitchen stuff I rarely used. It was red with yellow flames and lettering that read "Hot and Spicy." A gag gift from Henry. Ugh. Scottie and Henry both smirked. She tied it around her waist before cramming the bacon into the skillet and covering it.

Dilsey sniffed the sizzling bacon and eased into a tenuously balanced sit. She must have felt better. I knew I did. I tossed the blanket aside, stood, and bent down to pick up my coffee. "I'm taking her out."

Henry followed us and, jacketless, we shivered in the clear, frigid morning. Dilsey peed and peered around the yard as if she'd not seen it before. I called her name to orient her. She shook, staggered a few steps, and then tottered around like an old arthritic dog, alternately sniffing, tripping over tree roots, and gazing into the distance. For a few days, she'd be body-sore and medication-woozy, but ultimately she'd be fine.

Beside me, Henry watched her. "Bad, huh?"

"It's been worse."

"But you needed help last night? You should've called me. I know it's a drive—"

"Thanks, but Scottie was already here."

"How come you haven't mentioned her?"

"Because there's nothing to mention. I was just showing her the house. *Only* because she kept asking."

"You don't have to explain." When I didn't respond, he continued. "She was a big help."

"Yeah."

After a few more minutes, Henry hugged himself. "Geez, it's freezing out here. I'll bring your surprise in from the car and meet you back inside."

It *was* cold, low twenties probably, testing the house's new HVAC system. Perhaps the cold would restore Dilsey to herself quickly. It sure dispelled *my* drowsiness. By the time she collapsed into a nest of leaves, I was wide awake.

I helped her up and, back inside, offered her water and settled her on her bed. As soon as she lowered her head, she was asleep.

Scottie had set my round oak table with everything except plates. A bowl of sliced cantaloupe sat on one side of the daffodils, a plate of buttered toast on the other. At the counter, she filled the plates with eggs and bacon, handed two to Henry, and followed him to the table with the third, which turned out to be mine.

Henry poked his fork into the eggs. "What's the brown stuff?"

"Cinnamon."

The eggs tasted so much like French toast that Henry joked about needing maple syrup—which I didn't have— and I remembered Emily dumping it over her eggs at McDonald's. That morning seven weeks ago now seemed like ancient history.

"I appreciate the breakfast, but you shouldn't have gone out of your way."

"I didn't." She nibbled a strip of bacon. "Cooking is never going out of my way. It's meditative, sensory. Creative even. Nurturing. And healing. It's been a tough few months. Chopping, whisking, stirring are my therapy. Plus, people enjoy eating, so it works out well for everyone." She pointed a piece of bacon at Henry. "Speaking of work, what do you do?"

As she had with me the previous evening, Scottie led Henry from topic to topic. Unlike me, he responded affably and countered with questions of his own. Their easy conversation and my full stomach lulled me into sleepy contentment.

We'd almost finished when Scottie said, "So, tell me about the genealogy project you're doing."

My head jerked in her direction. "What genealogy project?"

Henry grinned and failed to bail me out. Instead, he stirred the pot. "The one Emily said the two of you were working on that day at Cast Party."

"Right," she said. "That one."

I forked the last of the cantaloupe into my mouth and chewed to buy time to think of a response. Henry gazed steadily at me, daring me to lie to Scottie. *I told you not to deal with Emily*, I heard him thinking. *Get out of this on your own.*

I didn't want to discuss what Emily and I were doing, not with Scottie, not with anyone who didn't yet know about it. But I also didn't want to offend her. During the past few hours, she'd proven she could handle candor, and I owed her an explanation. "The project's a bit more complicated than genealogy, and I'm not comfortable talking about it right now."

Henry rolled his eyes, but Scottie reacted as I expected.

"Okay," she said before she gathered our plates and carried them to the sink. I threw her a smile of gratitude.

With three of us, cleanup took no time, and when we finished, Scottie collected her coat from the mudroom.

Henry's gaze followed her movements. "What, leaving so soon? Hang out another few minutes for the big surprise. It's the whole reason I'm here."

Scottie raised her eyebrows at me. I raised my palms in an I-have-no-idea gesture.

She laid her coat over a chair, and Henry herded us through the hall and into my study. A rectangular bubble-wrapped item, about six feet long and four high, its corners protected by foam corner protectors, leaned at an angle against my desk and file cabinet.

"I've been searching for a housewarming gift ever since you chose paint colors." Henry beamed. "It's an original oil by an artist from western Virginia. You'll love it."

Scottie laughed and touched my arm. "Ha, great minds. I told him he needed to decorate."

"Henry, all your help with the house was plenty."

With a key, he snipped the tape on the bubble wrap and unwound it from the painting, revealing the back of a mounted, unframed canvas. With heavy wire running between two eye screws attached to the stretcher, his gift was ready to hang.

"Here we go." He walked one end of the canvas forward till its entire length leaned against the bookcase.

"Oh, wow." Scottie exhaled the words as much as spoke them.

It was beautiful. The landscape featured muted purple shadows and blazing foliage clinging to mature hardwoods. Beyond the trees, a path wound through rolling golden fields glinting with frost. No people, no animals, just a brilliant autumn day that mirrored those I'd seen every November from the time I was ten until the shooting. I felt the crunch of twigs and underbrush under my boots, saw the pointers dash through those trees, inhaled the clean, woodsy scent of a rural autumn morning.

There in my study, above the painting, on the bookcase, sat the photo of Teddy and me on our horses.

Sounds streamed out of the silence and battered at me. Furious barking. Shouts. Gunshots. All of it deafening.

Images flashed. A black-purple-orange dawn and trees and a silhouette.

And then . . . then . . .

Blood pounded in my ears. My heart slammed. I gulped. Couldn't get enough air. Couldn't breathe. I swayed, staggered backward. A black-edged vision stole my sight. Sweat that I couldn't lift an arm to wipe away trickled into my eyes.

Distant voices. *Philip? What's wrong?*

Hands on me. *Easy . . .*

That was all until, after a time—fifteen minutes? an hour?—I found myself on one end of the living room couch, pressed against its back. Scottie sat beside me, close but not touching. Across from us, Henry slouched in a chair, elbow resting on the arm, hand covering his face.

Sorry, I tried to say, but no recognizable word escaped from my dry mouth. At least I could breathe, hear, see.

Scottie shifted. "Shh."

I leaned my head against the back of the couch and shut my eyes, panting a little, willing my heart rate down, struggling to understand what had happened. My reaction to Henry's gift was irrational. It was a *painting*, for heaven's sake, nothing more. And magnificent. Its size and its stunning colors perfectly filled the one blank spot in my study. Apparently, only I noticed their resemblance to the dusky morning of the shooting. How and why would colors suddenly elicit that kind of reaction?

Or was the tipping point not the colors in the painting but rather its content—the view through the trees, nearly identical to the one I'd seen when Dad, Jamie, Teddy, Henry, and I headed out with the pointers and our shotguns for another day afield? The one I would have seen on November 20, 2005, if Vince Gardner hadn't intercepted us.

The difference was Emily. Or more precisely, the memories our contact had evoked. Not only the painting, but every little thing reminded me of the shooting, Teddy's death, my life, and memories of my family from before that day. Memories I hadn't recounted in years now constantly bubbled up, pushing at me. Prodding for a response.

Well, I'd certainly given them one. Eyes still closed, I rubbed at my face with both hands.

This reaction to a mere painting was unacceptable. I needed to finish this project with Emily, to stop bumbling along with a system I didn't understand, controlled by people like the disinterested court clerk who'd never prioritize the records of a ten-year-old closed investigation. We needed to take charge, to stop waiting for Henry to become more proactive.

But the painting reiterated the bottom line: no matter what we learned, the most critical and most basic facts wouldn't change. Teddy would always and forever be dead. So would Vince Gardner, and Emily would live the rest of her life without him. I'd always be a killer. And

those irrevocable facts, and learning why Gardner ambushed us, would make no difference in the lives of my
family. Now that I'd finished my house, Henry needed to
return to his busy professional and social life. Likewise, I
needed my parents and Jamie to continue on without me.
Scottie was kind, and she'd been immensely helpful, and
for a few hours her presence had seemed natural and fit-
ting. I could handle Dilsey's seizures, and everything else,
on my own.

I breathed deeply, more relaxed now that my heart had
slowed to a normal rhythm, and dragged myself from the
couch into the kitchen. From her bed, Dilsey lifted her
head and gazed beyond me.

Only a second later, Henry and Scottie blocked the doorway through which I'd just entered, one behind the other,
observing me. My newest friend and my oldest, one wedg-
ing herself into my life, the other always there whether or
not I wanted him. Both confounded by my . . . whatever it
had been. I was confounded, too, but not worried. I didn't
know the physical explanation, but I understood the trigger of my reaction. But they'd have to remain ignorant,
because no way in hell was I going to explain the colors,
sounds, and images that had just exploded in my thoughts,
reducing me to helplessness.

"I'm just tired." I retrieved Scottie's coat and held it open
for her. "Thanks for everything."

She caught Henry's eye, and he assured her, "I'll stay
for a while."

At her car, Scottie set her purse on the front passenger
seat before facing me. "I live five minutes away, and I'm a
really good listener."

"Scottie—"

"I mean it. Any time day or night. You have my number. My address is in the Grainger directory." She squeezed my arm, scooted into her seat, and crammed the key into the ignition.

I shut her door and used the remote to trigger the gate. She backed all the way down the drive, and by the time the gate clanked shut, she'd disappeared and already I missed her and wished she were still with me.

CHAPTER 25

WHEN I RETURNED inside, the glass pocket doors to my study were closed, and, to my relief, the painting was gone. The bacon-cinnamon-coffee aroma of Scottie's breakfast lingered. In the kitchen, Dilsey straddled her bed, weaving slightly, staring at me and whining. I knelt beside her and eased her down, and she nuzzled my cheek and thumped her tail.

Henry didn't answer when I called his name, but his jacket still dangled from the coat rack. I sagged into a chair, folded my arms on the table, and rested my head on them. Contrary to what I'd told Scottie—that once I was awake, I was awake—sleeping straight through till Monday morning seemed not only possible, but likely.

An anxiety attack. That was what it must have been. In Henry's painting, the view through the autumn trees into the field triggered emotions so deeply buried, I hadn't known they existed. Emotions that had raced through me that November day only to be dammed up ever since. Even if I convinced Henry and Scottie that the long, practically sleepless night with Dilsey had caused my reaction, I knew better. My project with Emily had placed the shooting in the forefront of my consciousness. Without her, the painting would've been nothing more than outstanding artwork to hang in my study.

I sat up and pressed both palms into the smooth surface of the table, telling myself that my reasoning had to be accurate.

Except for the afternoon in the hospital when my parents told me Teddy had died, all these years I'd smothered all twinges of anxiety. I'd backed away from Sawyer. I recoiled from Emily's first email. But today—content from breakfast, relieved that Dilsey had stopped seizing, and exhausted—I'd dropped my guard.

I could blame my anxiety attack on Emily. Henry would. Our fact-finding efforts *had* reopened wounds that would've remained healed had she remained unknown to me. Did that make Henry and my father right when they said that I should never have involved myself with her?

That question was irrelevant now. I couldn't unknow what she'd told me or how Mrs. Brown had characterized her father or that Henry had, intentionally or otherwise, steered me wrong. I saw no way forward except to finish what we'd begun. Stopping now would leave everything exposed but nothing resolved. An open wound that couldn't be hidden and wouldn't stop causing pain.

We'd learn what there was to learn or, more likely, conclude that there wasn't anything to learn. Then Emily would drift away from Vince to the family that apparently loved her, and I'd resume the life I'd constructed, a life complicated by nothing more than my dog, my house, and my students. And restore my friendship with Henry to its previous footing.

I lifted my head, remembering what I'd originally wanted to talk with him about: his explanation for concealing the residency requirement for the Tennessee records.

I forced myself fully upright when the porch and mud-room doors banged, one after the other. Henry entered, radiating with cold. He popped a coffee pod into the brewer, not asking if I wanted any.

He pulled out the chair across from me and blew on his coffee, his knuckles white around the mug handle, his gaze so intense that I mentally prepared for a verbal lashing for . . . for what? Putting him through the hassle of returning his gift? Making him frustrated with himself for not seeing in the painting what I'd seen and feeling what I'd felt? Instead of delivering the lashing, however, he blinked and swiped a palm across his eyes.

"I'm sorry," we said simultaneously. Everything else, all the unspoken words, hovered between us.

He drained his hot coffee in a few quick chugs, brewed more, and sat again. He peered into his coffee without drinking. Occasionally, his eyes lifted, his gaze flitting around the room, hesitating on the daffodils, before he focused again on his mug.

Uncharacteristically, I couldn't read him, and I didn't know what that meant. So, I defaulted to suspicion and shocked myself by how quickly my resentment escalated. "Why didn't you tell me only a Tennessee resident can request public records?"

"What?"

"You didn't know? You didn't pay attention to what I was doing, even though I asked you several times and finally had to talk with your paralegal? Or maybe you didn't want me to find out, was that it?" I threw out the last question accusingly, watching for a tell that he'd lied.

"Let's not discuss this now, after . . . after whatever happened earlier."

"Nothing happened. I just need sleep. So yeah, let's discuss it *right now*."

"Philip, you're making a big deal out of nothing. You did a shitty job of researching. You could have—"

"Damn it, Henry."

He sighed, and his shoulders drooped. "I didn't know you had to be a Tennessee resident. Some states are like that, some not."

"You couldn't have mentioned that? Rather than letting me find out only because I called them yesterday?"

"They should've contacted you immediately."

"They didn't, and it would have been nice if you'd helped a bit more. Now, I need one of your Tennessee friends to file the subpoena request for us."

"Why don't you drop the whole thing? Like your dad told you to."

I reared back in my chair. "You know that how?"

With an index finger, he traced the wood grain on the table. "It came up one day."

He must speak with my parents far more often than I imagined. Why would Henry and my father even care what Emily and I learned from the records? "No, Henry, it didn't just *come up*. What's going on?"

Again, his eyes focused everywhere except on me. He pushed back from the table and half rose with his mug, then dropped back into his chair as if he lacked the energy to stand. "Tell me again why you have to do this? What's the *real* reason?"

Suddenly chilled, I wrapped my arms around myself. I'd originally told him I wanted to learn how a stranger could pull off the shooting and why he'd want to, that I owed Emily because I had shot her father and that helping her was the quickest way to get rid of her. All that was true, but it wasn't the entire truth. How could I explain, in a way he'd understand, what I'd discovered while I talked with my father that December afternoon by the trailer that hauled away Teddy's horse? My partnership with Emily had shifted everything, including a measure of my trust in Henry. But if I wanted the truth from him, I had to overlook that and assure him that despite his suspicion of Emily, and of what she and I sought to accomplish, I'd be honest with him and in return hoped he'd be honest with me.

And so I told him what I'd sensed a decade ago and now recognized as fact, with that recognition stripping from me any capacity to hide from the agonizing truth.

"When Teddy died, my parents changed. Either they stopped caring about our family or—and this is what I believe—they *dropped* any pretense of caring about us. They—"

He grimaced. "Why the hell would you think something as asinine as that?"

I pushed away from the table and paced around the kitchen. "Before I got home from the hospital, they'd buried Teddy, removed every photo of him and all his ornaments off the tree. And they locked up his room. And then they got rid of his horse. *Got rid of him*, Henry, like he was a piece of furniture or a junky old car. And remember when they came back to the farm together, while I was still in ICU, she made you go home. She should've expected, *wanted*, you to stay for Jamie's sake if nothing else. Don't you get it? It wasn't only Teddy they didn't care about. It was—*is*—all of us. And then all these years later, Emily showed up."

Without a word, Henry fled into the hall, stopping with his back to me. Dilsey struggled off her bed and followed him. He brushed her head with the tips of his fingers.

Saying the words aloud should have invigorated me. They didn't, though, and I sank into my chair, exhausted. Deflated. "I need to know why Vince Gardner's actions affected my parents to that extent. The sooner you stop giving me partial information and help me find someone to file for the subpoena, the sooner I'll have answers and be able to finish with Emily. But with or without you, I'm doing this."

He trudged to the kitchen, carried his mug to the sink, and zipped on his jacket. "I'll call you later."

"You're stalling."

"I'm not. I need to think everything through, especially considering your meltdown."

"I told you—"

"You're tired. Yeah, I heard you. Get some sleep. I'll call you."

When he banged shut the front door, I dropped back into my chair, my eyes burning with exhaustion. Dilsey laid her head in my lap, and I traced the groove between her eyes, questioning whether Henry's lack of response meant my revelation about my parents' behavior following Teddy's death shocked him, or whether he'd already guessed the same thing and hadn't known what to do with the information. Or something else.

CHAPTER 26

ON TUESDAY AFTERNOON, I ignored a text that pinged while I guided a student through points of grammar he should've learned in middle school. Ignored it while I dashed to the departmental office to thank Scottie for the cookies she'd delivered on Sunday when she stopped by to collect her dishes and check on Dilsey and me. Ignored it while I counseled two more students about a shared presentation gone awry.

Still recovering from the effects of her cluster, Dilsey had accompanied me to campus but remained in my office. I felt confident that I was close enough should she have additional problems, but I didn't expect any. Students in all my classes asked about her, and I promised she'd return to class on Wednesday.

At four on the dot, I closed my office door and opened the message from Emily.

Important!!!! Call me!!

Hmm. Multiple exclamation points suggested news of far less importance to the receiver than the sender. We hadn't corresponded since Friday, when I'd emailed her about my conversation with the county clerk in Tennessee. I couldn't imagine what was so urgent.

She answered my call right away and didn't even say hello. "The TBI didn't investigate the shooting. The *FBI* did."

Her words, when they registered, shocked me out of my chair.

"That's impossible. Henry would've told us." I paced the room, disbelieving. "How do you know?"

"I called the TBI."

"You did?" Why hadn't I thought to do that? Maybe Henry was right about me conducting shitty research.

"Last we talked, you said you needed to talk to Henry about the subpoena request. I had no idea how long it would take, so I went to the source, to get the TBI to tell me exactly what to do next. Except they're not the source."

"What did they say?"

"That I wouldn't learn much even if a subpoena succeeded in releasing the records, which was unlikely anyway because the FBI took over the case from them. I asked why they took it over, and the clerk or agent or whatever said because one of the victims was a sitting US senator."

I collapsed into my chair, hot with anger, not doubting for one second that Henry knew that critical detail as he also knew—I was positive now—that nonresidents couldn't access Tennessee records. He should've told me. My father would have known, too, and he'd lied. No, not lied exactly. He'd failed to tell the entire truth. The rural authorities had turned the investigation over to the TBI—that was technically true; the article Emily had attached to her original email confirmed it. So, why hadn't my father mentioned that the TBI also relinquished control of the investigation? Like me, he'd been hospitalized when the investigation began, so perhaps he hadn't known immediately. But unlike me, he was a criminal defense attorney. He knew how those things worked, and he'd sure as hell followed the case to its end. He'd misled me, and his deception could only have been intentional.

And his misdirection and lies could have had only one purpose: to conceal something. He purposefully lied to me. How could he? And why?

I got up again and paced again, with Dilsey trailing me for a couple of passes until a quick scratch behind her ears settled her. I wasn't as easily placated.

"Emily, hold on. I ne—"

"But we need to—"

"I know, I know. Give me one second." I squeezed my eyes closed, and a new question blazed across my mind, printed words glowing in an afterimage that I'd never actually seen before. Why the misdirection and lies now? The shooting was years ago.

The longer Dad and Henry stalled us, the longer Emily and I would take to learn the truth. It might take so long that we'd quit. And that was what they'd wanted all along, for Emily and me to drop our questions. To stop—no, not Emily and me. They could ignore Emily. They had ignored Emily and could easily suppress her questions. The intent was to keep me from asking questions about the day I was shot, the day I killed the shooter, and the day my little brother was killed. My father and my best friend were deliberately working against me. I slammed my phone against my leg and then did it again. What the hell kind of family plays these games?

"Stay, Dilsey," I said when she whined and headed toward me. "Not now."

With a jolt, I recalled that someone *had* mentioned the FBI. *Ross* had said the FBI asked him the same questions I asked. I hadn't picked up on his words at the time, and if I had, I'd have assumed he misspoke. But that made perfect sense. The TBI most likely wouldn't have crossed state lines to interview him. At the very least, wouldn't investigators from South Carolina's equivalent agency have accompanied TBI investigators? But Ross hadn't said that. He'd said the FBI.

Henry would explain his deception right now.

"Emily, I'll get back with you."

I didn't realize I'd snapped at her till she said, "*Wait. What are you going to do?*"

"Sorry." I sucked in a breath. "I'm asking Henry exactly what's going on. I'll call you back, okay?"

He answered on the fourth ring. "I know, I know. I'm still thinking."

"That isn't why—"

"Right. You're calling to remind me we have theater tickets. It's on my calendar. I need to go. I'm about to head into a meeting."

"Why didn't you tell me the FBI took over the shooting investigation?"

He took way too long to respond. "Who told you that?"

"The TBI."

"You called them?" His voice was flat, quiet.

"You and my father have lied to us, and I want to know why."

"You knew they investigated the shooting. They interviewed you."

I rubbed my forehead, searching for a memory that didn't exist. No one interviewed me. I was in the hospital, and then I was home. "No—"

"Look, Philip, I have a meeting. I'll call after—"

With a surge of confusion, frustration, and rage at him and my father for their treachery, and at myself for being oblivious or naïve or just plain stupid, I slammed the phone facedown into the desk. Unable to stand, I slumped into my chair. Dilsey left her bed and thrust her head onto my lap. I squeezed my eyes shut until the emotional vertigo passed.

Since Emily's first contact, Dad and Henry had discouraged me from having any association with her. Digging into the shooting shouldn't have been complicated, even ten years later. But it was, and I realized that Henry had duped us, essentially encouraged us to flounder instead of assisting us as he'd promised. Apprising him of our progress—what a joke—gave him the advantage he needed to further obstruct us. Plus, when I'd been open with him last Saturday morning and explained why our search was so important, he'd left my house with a promise to call me later. Which he didn't do. And there was the matter of his apparently frequent conversations with my parents.

He should have told me he didn't want to be involved. *But he had*, I remembered. I'd insisted he help because I believed I needed him.

Well, screw him.

His role ended now. He'd betrayed me, and I needed to apologize to Emily for dismissing her intuitive distrust of him. She and I would finish alone, or I'd hire an attorney or private investigator to work on our behalf.

Dilsey slid onto the floor and rested her head on my shoe. "Good puppy-girl," I murmured. I googled the FBI FAQ page and spent half an hour scanning the records request process. We could submit a Freedom of Information Act request or a Privacy Act request—once I figured out the difference. But getting the records might take months. Or the FBI might deny the request. The appeal process added more months, and the appeal might be denied. And the law exempted many records from release, and, for all I knew, the investigation of our shooting was among them.

I shut down my laptop, questioning whether the search—learning the details—was worth the hassle and whether Emily might feel the same way. I stood and stretched, running options through my head again, trying to kick my frustration aside before I called her back.

She answered on the first ring, her voice cheerful. "A positive outcome of knowing about the FBI is that we can bypass the whole TBI subpoena thing."

I hadn't considered that. The FBI records would likely include information from the TBI's initial investigation. "We'll need every bit of the time we save." I relayed what I'd learned from the FBI website. "I need to warn you that if we have to deal with appeals, we might be talking about years before we know anything."

"Oh no," she said, clearly dismayed.

"I guess our next step is to scour their website, make a list of questions for them, and go from there. And I'll find a PI or another attorney to advise us."

"Did Henry quit?"

"We just fired him. You were right." I steadied myself for her reminder that she hadn't ever trusted him. I wouldn't defend him or my trust in him. I couldn't.

Emily paused. "He withheld information, didn't he?"

"Yes."

"I'm sorry."

Her sympathy stung more than *I told you so* would have.

After a moment, she continued, "There's something else. My parents think it's super nice of you to help me, especially considering the circumstances. They want to meet you. They were miffed when I didn't bring you by the other weekend."

"Your parents know?" Was her adopted family so open she didn't need to hide Vince, her notebook, and everything else from them? "I thought—when Henry asked whether they knew, you told him it was none of his business."

"Because it isn't. But they've known what I wanted to do since I was fourteen, since the day Kim—she's my mother—since Kim caught me adding an article to my notebook. She and Alex promised that if I concentrated on school till I was twenty-one, they'd help make it possible to find out what happened with Daddy. They don't do anything to help exactly, but they let me keep living at home, give me moral support, financial support, and don't hassle me about finishing my degree, that kind of thing. They gave me a year, which is up in August. And yeah, I'm an adult and I can do what I want, but they kept their promise, and I'll keep mine to finish school."

A support system and a long-term goal. That was how Emily had maintained her focus on Vince all those years. The two people who might have been most envious of her loyalty to him instead opened a world of possibilities to her. How fortunate she was to have them. How different, in a good way, they were from my parents.

"Anyway, we want you to come to my birthday dinner. It's February 27, a week from Saturday. Kim's cooking. No gifts, very casual. You, me, Kim, and Alex. And Dilsey. Kim said to be sure to bring her."

"Emily, I—" My default was to decline. Her home in Greenville was a long drive. The trip would consume an entire weekend or at least one extremely long day. And what would I talk about with her parents? I couldn't imagine discussing Vince and the shooting, and certainly not my family, with strangers. Our mutual familiarity with the

Greenville–Spartanburg area? Maybe. At least we had that in common.

On the other hand, the couple that had rescued a teenager, apparently stabilized her life, and now supported her in reconciling questions about her previous life intrigued me. Surely their desire to meet the guy who shot their adopted daughter's biological father wasn't as simple as thinking I was nice for helping her. Nothing ever was as simple as it appeared; Henry was proving that. Did the Warners have an ulterior motive that Emily didn't recognize? Or one she knew about and chose not to mention?

All that aside, because of Henry's deception, I kind of owed her. And that was in addition to the other reasons for which I already owed her my support and my time. Attending a family dinner might make me feel slightly better about having set us up for failure. "Okay, I'll come."

"You will?"

She sounded shocked, and I hoped I wouldn't regret my acceptance.

CHAPTER 27

THE ELEVEN DAYS between my terse phone conversation with Henry and my drive to Greenville passed without so much as a text between us. But no matter, since plenty of classroom tasks demanded the mental energy I'd have spent considering his duplicity and scrutinizing his every syllable.

Although I hadn't thought much about the Warners' house, I hadn't expected their great room to resemble a sports club's trophy display. Human figures frozen in a variety of athletic poses stood atop walnut and marble bases on floating shelves and bookcases all around the room. Action photos of the family cluttered what little wall space remained. In every solo picture of Emily, she gracefully smacked a ball with a racket or bat or stick, which, given the drive and single-mindedness she'd shown during the two months I'd known her, made perfect sense. The absence of even a fleck of dust on anything proved the value of the mementos to the family.

I couldn't help but compare them with the walls and shelves of my parents' house at the farm, walls and shelves that once bursting were now empty. Not empty in the sense of unoccupied—artwork, vases, and attractive knickknacks filled the space. Merely devoid of proof that the family I'd once believed we had been ever existed. How strange that the same event that destroyed my family—or the illusion of it—created a loving family for Emily. Or were the Warners also an illusion? I scanned the room again. Its warmth enveloped me, and I felt as if I'd known and liked them all my life. No illusion there.

An L-shaped sectional sofa and a recliner faced a TV tilt-mounted over the fireplace. A multicolored "Happy Birthday!" Mylar balloon was tied to a softball trophy on the mantel; the balloon was so large that I expected the trophy to take flight. Another balloon, tethered to a chair at the unset dining table, proclaimed what I presumed was Emily's spot.

"I had no idea Emily came from such an active family." I didn't know much about her that didn't concern Vince Gardner except what little she'd revealed during our visit with Mrs. Brown. I'd shared nothing personal with her either. And she'd never even asked how Henry fit into my life and why. Of course, I hadn't planned on sharing any personal information with her. Standing in her home, clutching the icy Michelob her father had given me and about to eat dinner with her family, my previous lack of interest bothered me.

Alex Warner grinned. "Yup. And she's particularly adept at whacking the hell out of things. Just so you know."

No surprise there. "Thanks for the warning."

"What's your sport?"

Used to be riding, shooting, a little tennis. "Teaching."

He laughed. "Yeah, I hear ya." He motioned toward the sofa with his beer bottle. "Have a seat. The girls will be out as soon as they finish primping." He raised his voice to carry beyond the room. "I long ago quit trying to understand the fuss for every trip from the house, even if it's just to go bowling."

"I heard that," a female voice that wasn't Emily's yelled from the hallway as, incredulous, I echoed, "*Bowling?*"

"Emily's friends' idea. A surprise birthday party for her at the bowling alley."

"Adults have parties at bowling alleys?" So much for the quiet family dinner I'd expected. The thought of maneuvering through a mob of Emily's friends at a dark, noisy, smelly venue made me want to chug my beer and scurry back to Grainger.

"Who mentioned adults? We're talking about Emily and her friends." He settled into the chair opposite me and read my discomfort. "Don't worry. You probably won't be the worst bowler."

"I probably will, but it's not that. I doubt I can bowl at all. I have an old shoulder injury."

"Oh, right." Alex nodded. "From the shooting."

I shifted, taken aback at his casual tone that relegated the shooting to a common event, like the weather or a sports score.

"Use a lighter ball, or I'll show you the best arm swing for you." He advised me like the coach Emily had told Mrs. Brown he was. "Or use your nondominant arm. Or skip bowling altogether. You won't be the only one. You'll have fun anyway."

I wasn't so sure about the fun, but this was Emily's birthday, and she'd invited me. I should at least attempt to blend in. I swallowed a mouthful of beer and felt better.

The woman who whisked into the room reached me before I had time to stand to greet her. "You must be Philip. I'm Kim, Emily's mom. Thanks for coming."

Emily followed, pulling a fuchsia rolling bag that resembled a misshapen airline carry-on. Her ponytail tie and her shirt matched the bowling bag.

"Hey, Philip!" She abandoned the bag and surprised me with a quick hug. "Where's Dilsey?"

"In the truck." It seemed the best spot for her until I got a feel for the Warners. "Happy birthday. But bowling? You forgot to mention that."

"I didn't know, not till a couple of hours ago. It's a miracle they managed to keep it quiet. And not just my friends. Kim and Alex couldn't keep a secret if their lives depended on it."

"Ha," Alex said. "Okay, let's load up. We gotta pick up the cake and at least try to arrive before everyone else." He carried our empty beer bottles to the kitchen.

"Should I follow you or meet you there?"

"Neither," Kim said. "You're riding with us."

"Thanks, but—"

"No buts. Parking's a bitch, and you've driven enough today."

"I'll need to check on my dog. She has some medical issues."

"She does?" Emily frowned. "You never told me that."

"We'll only be gone a few hours," Kim said. "But Alex can leave his keys with you so you can zip back here to check on her."

I could live with that. Besides, I'd rather leave her in her familiar and comfortable crate in my truck parked in the quiet driveway of a safe neighborhood than in a strange parking lot.

Before leaving, I let Dilsey out in the Warners' driveway. They surrounded her, petting her, and her tail beat against my legs.

Kim peered into the Expedition. "Baby bumpers? How sweet."

The Warners loaded their bowling equipment and a box of party gear into the van while I walked Dilsey around the front yard in the encroaching dusk. Then a gentle beep from the Odyssey urged me to crate her. I adjusted the bumpers and checked the water level in her bucket. She circled twice and nestled into her fleece blanket, relaxed and unperturbed, and my concern faded.

An old warehouse park seemed an odd place for a bowling alley, but when we rounded a curve on an interior passage wide enough to accommodate two contiguous semis, a sign for Bowled Over indeed appeared at the far end. The logo depicted several humanoid bowling pins lying on their sides and two humanoid bowling balls high-fiving. A first grader could've drawn better.

At the entrance, I offered to park the van while Alex and the girls carried in the cake, bowling bags, and box of party stuff. Kim had been right about the limited parking. I found a spot three buildings over. I suspected I wouldn't get even that close when I returned from checking on Dilsey and was glad I'd left her at the Warners'.

Inside its heavy glass doors, Bowled Over was indistinguishable from the handful of other bowling alleys I'd visited. I steeled myself against its gloom and obnoxious din, and, worse, the combined smell of stale beer and grease, wax and shoe spray, and sweat so very distinct from the aroma of clean horses and hay and sunshine I grew up with. A burst of what the place apparently considered music blared over a sound system that deserved better.

The reception area jutted out from the front wall in the center of the building. I passed it and Alex simultaneously.

I handed him the keys and told him the location of the van, and he pointed me past the bar and café toward an alcove. Kim fussed over the cake at the end of a stretch of covered tables against the wall. Emily sat alone on a barstool at one of the high-tops, her feet on her fuchsia bag, her chin resting in her palm, and fingers cradling her cheek.

I slid onto a stool beside her and folded my hands on the table. "What happened? For a birthday girl, you suddenly look awfully glum."

"Daddy and I used to bowl here, and like I told Mrs. Brown, I've been here a lot since he died. But that last year, 2005, we came here for both our birthdays. No party, just us. I hadn't thought much about it, though, till Alex carried my cake through the door. Just like Daddy did."

Her admission jarred me. "I thought I was the only one with spontaneous memories."

She pushed up from the table. "That happens to you too?"

The gate to the farm. The tree houses. Henry's painting. "More often than you'd imagine."

"You never say anything about it."

I was about to tell her that some things you couldn't talk about, when Alex appeared between us.

"Okay, you two. This is a par-tee. No talking shop." When Emily started to deny it, he said, "And what else could you possibly be so intense about in this bastion of American sports?"

He plunked a yellow smiley-face token and two blue poker chips on the table in front of me. "For your shoes and drinks. We're in lanes one through six. And you . . ." He tugged Emily's ponytail and set an opaque plastic jar of tokens in front of her. "Your first two guests just arrived. Time to mingle."

Emily hopped off the stool. "C'mon. I'll introduce you."

I pocketed my tokens and followed her. After the couple's birthday greeting, Emily pulled me up beside her. "This is my friend, Philip, from Virginia. Our families have known each other for years, and we recently reconnected."

Friends? Wow. When had we become friends? The moment I accepted her birthday invitation? At Mrs. Brown's house, when for the first time she and Vince became three-dimensional to me? Or was "friend" her uncomplicated way to excuse my presence among her real friends?

We all nodded and expressed the usual niceties. Emily shoved the jar of tokens at me. "How about you distribute these? You'll get to meet everyone without needing me."

So, for fifteen minutes I ambled between the alcove and the six lanes reserved for Emily's party, distributing drink tokens to everyone and shoe tokens to those who needed them. There were thirty people, including the Warners and me. Most were Emily's age. The rest seemed to be her parents' friends. I followed Emily's lead and introduced myself, awkwardly at first, as an old family friend, until I warmed to the idea. By the time I'd met the final guests, I almost believed it was true.

Kim relieved me of the jar. "Ten minutes to the first game. Go get your shoes and ball."

At the reception counter, each of the three college-age employees wore a navy polo shirt with Bowled Over's awful logo stitched in yellow over the breast pocket and name tags just above. The name of the girl who clinked my token into a can on the counter was "Bowling."

"That's really your name?"

"Yeah. Family name. My grandfather used to own this place, so it was kind of a joke."

I gave her my shoe size and carried the pair she handed me back to the party. Despite Alex's claim that not everyone would bowl, the entire group had jammed into the pit area below the half wall separating the lanes from the spectator concourse. I sat at one of the upper tables to change shoes. Then from the racks along the concourse I tested ball after ball. Unfortunately, the best option was hot pink with lighter pink swirls.

Abashed, I carried it down to the return rack.

Alex signaled a thumbs-up. "Ya gotta do what ya gotta do."

To my surprise, the friendly laughter that followed put me at ease. Everyone was there for fun, and my bubble-gum bowling ball was part of that. Emily's friends welcomed me with their laughter and invited me into the celebration. For the first time in ages, I felt comfortable, even among strangers. When the overhead monitor brightened a moment later with our blank game scorecard, my name appeared last. Last, but I was part of the group.

Emily bowled first, and she was good, confident and fluid, and smashed the hell out of all ten pins. Not everyone else was as expert, but they were all way better than me. My shoulder twinged at each roll of my pink ball, but I ignored it. For the first game, at least, I'd stick it out.

Between frames, on the curvy vinyl bench, I chatted with Emily's friends about nothing. They called me Phil, a nickname I detested, but I didn't correct them. Being "Phil" stamped me as part of the gang, and in surprise I found myself enjoying Emily's friends, her birthday party, and even the bowling itself as Phil, a guy far different from the real-life Philip.

One frame into game three, my right shoulder bolted an electrical pain through my arm and into my hand, and I dropped the ball hard on the foul line. "Oops. I'm out." I called to my teammates. "Consider it an opportunity to improve our score."

I returned my shoes and, at the bar, exchanged a beverage token for a fizzy draft Bud in a clear Bowled Over cup. In our alcove, I perused the food: fruit and cheese tray, crackers, various pizzas, wraps, and plenty more. The chocolate sheet cake with its twenty-two candles forming a capital *E* would come out later.

With a full plate, I settled at a small round table in the concourse overlooking our lanes. The fingers of my right hand tingled, and I rolled my shoulder and flexed my elbow to ease the mild discomfort. It hadn't hurt so much in ages because I constantly protected it. I probably should've skipped bowling. Still, I had to admit it had been fun.

I ate my fries and sipped my beer, lulled into contentment by the sounds, lights, and even the odors that only a short time ago had rankled me. My peripheral vision caught sight of a blue shirt as I bit into my wrap.

"Quitting so soon?" the girl named Bowling asked. She toted a large dishpan half-filled with cups, candy wrappers, and other trash.

"I got hungry."

"Uh-huh. I saw your score."

Kim came up from the pit and saved me from a retort I hadn't yet formulated. "Hey, there, B. I hope you can get away to have cake with us later."

"Not sure, Mrs. Warner. We overbooked parties tonight, so they begged Grandpa to come in to help. He's here, but he's not happy about it."

Kim laughed and pitched a balled-up napkin into the dishpan. "Bring him too. Chocolate cake will cheer him right up."

Before long, the entire party assembled in the alcove and sang the birthday song. "Make a wish," several friends called.

Emily leaned over at the cake, then looked so pointedly at me that more than a few heads swiveled in my direction. I suspected our wishes were identical.

She blew out all twenty-two candles, but when the whoops started, they flared to life again. Trick candles. Her friends cheered. "Gotcha!" someone yelled.

Still facing the cake, Emily stood motionless, then hunched her shoulders. I didn't know whether she was superstitious, but if she'd wished what I'd have wished, how could she not help but sense a foreboding of failure?

Without thinking, I edged past the guests between us. At her side, I laid my arm across her shoulders. She wiped her eyes with the back of one hand. I handed her the cake knife, and with the silly candles still burning, she slashed the first slice free from the rest of the cake.

Several hours later, while Emily escorted her friends to the front entrance, Kim, Alex, and I relaxed at a high-top table. We'd boxed up the gifts and leftover party stuff and stacked everything beside the cake. Soon we'd be on our way back to the Warners' house.

I'd left Dilsey over four hours ago. The evening had sped by, and inexplicably, I'd not made time to check on her. Her seizure cluster just two weeks ago almost guaranteed she'd not seize this soon, but I still felt anxious. And guilty.

An older man—seventyish, bald, and shaped like a duck-pin—entered the alcove. "Too late for birthday cake?"

"Not at all." Kim slid off her stool. "Where's Bowling?"

"Busy. Been a helluva night. I promised to take her a piece."

"You got it." At the buffet table, Kim flipped open the lid of the cake box and lifted two huge slices onto plates. She set both in front of the man where he'd hoisted himself onto the stool beside me.

"Jess Bowling." He offered his hand. "You must be Emily's friend from Virginia."

"Yes, sir."

Emily entered the alcove. "Hey, Mr. Bowling. You made it."

"Couldn't miss sharing cake with the birthday girl."

Alex pointed toward the counter. "We're off to settle the bill and load the car. Emily, you and Philip keep Jess company. I'll text you when we're out front." And they were gone.

"This was super fun." Emily's smile extended all the way to her eyes.

Jess returned her smile. "I'm glad. Like old times. Like the birthday you had here once before."

She nodded. "Not a party, though, just bowling and dinner. You have a good memory."

"Your daddy was a regular. And you too. I never forget my regulars." He ate two bites of cake.

"You used to bring me a ketchup bottle if I ordered fries," Emily said. "'Have some fries with your ketchup, girl.'"

"I've seen that in action," I said, and Emily giggled.

"He loved to come here, hang out with his friends *and* with you, all at the same time. When he let you take his turn, even in league play, it pissed off the guys because you always threw gutter balls. Till you started throwing more strikes than them, and *that* pissed them off more. No pleasing some folks."

"I remember." Despite her grin, Emily's eyes teared.

"Yup, we surely missed him when he died. Don't know what got into him, shooting that senator. It's like when his brother died, he became a different man."

"What do you mean?" Emily scrunched her face. "He seemed sad, but of course he would. Uncle Mel was his only relative other than me."

"Oh, you know. Got drunk when he came here without you a couple times. Bitched and moaned to anyone who'd listen that his brother was innocent and never shoulda been in prison in the first place, and he could prove it. And if his brother wasn't in prison, he wouldn't have died. That sorta thing. I always took his keys and one of the boys drove him home when he'd had too much to drink."

My interest more than piqued, I straightened in my chair. "Why was his brother in prison?"

"Armed robbery, assault, something like that. It was all over the news."

"Really?" Emily frowned. "Huh."

She'd mentioned her uncle at our McDonald's and Cast Party meetings, and even then she'd claimed to barely remember him. I believed her.

"You'd a been little. That was . . . mmm . . . late nineties? His big-name lawyer couldn't even get him off."

Emily and I looked at each other. "What lawyer?" we asked simultaneously.

"No idea. Anyway, I figured his brother was guilty no matter what Vince said. A real son of a bitch. Bowled here before your daddy started bringing you. Kicked his ass out the day I caught him selling drugs. We might not be high-class, but I wasn't putting up with that shit."

Emily's phone buzzed with a text. "Alex says they're out front waiting for us."

Mr. Bowling stood. "Good to see you again, girl. Happy birthday."

En route to the Warners' house, Emily and I rode quietly amid her parents' post-celebration chatter. Mel Gardner seemed to have been quite different from his brother Vince, but something was off. How did someone like him afford a *big name*–meaning high profile, meaning expensive–defense attorney? And if he had been able to afford one, who had it been?

Was this the link we'd been looking for?

CHAPTER 28

AT NINE THIRTY, Alex parked his Odyssey beside my Expedition in their driveway. I told them I'd join them inside for decaf after I walked Dilsey.

When I lifted the hatch, she stretched and banged her tail against the wire of her crate. Her water bucket was still full, and her bedding was no more rumpled than when I'd left her. Relieved, I clipped her leash on her collar and eased her to the driveway.

I needed her to pee quickly so I could re-crate her and get into the South Carolina courts database. Researching on my phone would be awkward, but I was unwilling to wait to connect my laptop with the Holiday Inn Wi-Fi. I'd check all the counties of this area, starting with the two largest, and if they yielded nothing, move on to the smaller outlying counties.

But Dilsey wanted to lick me, not take care of business. She reared, wrapped her forelegs around my waist, and flicked her tongue toward my chin. I pushed her off. "Hurry, Dilsey." I wiggled the leash, and she flattened her ears and finally peed. I returned her to her crate, slid into the driver's seat, and pulled out my phone.

In the various fields of the Spartanburg County database, I tapped in *Gardner* and *Mel* and set the dates at January 1, 1990, through December 31, 2000. Nothing. Then, on the presumption that his first name was some version of Melvin, I typed in *Mel** and searched again. The resulting list, most recent cases first, filled the screen. Reaching the end required scrolling to a second screen.

I pushed back in my seat. Took in a long, long breath. Tapped one finger on the steering wheel as the implications whirled.

Melvin Gardner was quite familiar to the South Carolina judicial system. And this was only one county.

I scrolled to the bottom of the second screen, the oldest records. As I read the second entry, a minor drug possession violation to which Mel Gardner pleaded no contest and received a month in jail, the front passenger door opened. Emily hoisted herself inside.

"You can do that in the morning."

Still reading, I said flatly, "Why wait? We know who your uncle's defense attorney was. Let's get it over with."

What my gut didn't tell me was *why*. Why would Dad, who defended only people accused of white-collar crimes, accept as a client a low-income guy charged with a violent crime? I was counting heavily on Mr. Bowling's memory about a big-name attorney being correct.

I tapped one by one through every case number that wasn't a traffic violation. When I found the first link, I summarized aloud. "This is April 1996. Charges were five counts of murder, one count of arson, various drug manufacturing and distribution charges, and more. He was acquitted in a jury trial."

Emily waited, giving me space.

"Defendant attorney: Rutledge, Bennett." I read the words as they appeared in the record—formally, coldly, a fact without emotion that nevertheless set my heart pounding.

As if placing as much distance between me and the facts could change them, I mashed the seat adjustment button until I was as far as possible from the phone propped on the steering wheel. I turned the key in the ignition and lowered my window all the way. Still, I could barely breathe.

"But he was acquitted of everything, right?" Emily said. "That's a good thing. What am I missing?"

"There's lots more." I continued clicking, reading silently. Emily flipped on her seat warmer against the chill from my window and waited.

The last entry, the most recent one, yielded the second relevant link. "February 1998. Charges: armed robbery, assault with a firearm. Disposition: Guilty, jury trial. Sentence: 25 years, no parole. Defendant attorney: Rutledge, Bennett."

"The case Mr. Bowling mentioned."

I paused to corral bits and pieces of memories and align them in a comprehensible way.

That was the year my father stopped going to his office downtown. He spent inordinate amounts of time in his study, sometimes with suited strangers, sometimes alone. He even abandoned family meals and instead carried his plate into his study and ate alone. When Jamie cheekily reminded him of his and Mom's rule about eating as a family, my father, for the first and only time I recalled, sent him to his room without supper. Even incorrigible Henry stayed quiet, forking his food around his plate, glancing furtively at each of my parents, for once seeming afraid to be noticed. At last, Dad told us what was going on.

"My father said he'd decided to switch careers. In March that year, 1998, he filed to run for governor, and in June he won his primary and resigned from his law practice. He campaigned full-time till he won the election in November."

"Wow." Emily twirled the end of her ponytail around her hand, "But what does Uncle Mel's conviction have to do with any of that?"

"Look at the timing, Emily. How could it not?"

That was the big question. Why would the loss of one case, especially for the type of client I couldn't imagine my father defending, drive him from a profession at which he'd thrived and excelled? Why would he give up the law, even for the power of political office? That wasn't the man I'd known. Then again, neither was the man who gave away Huckleberry and urged me to move on from Teddy's death.

We jumped when right outside my open window Alex said, "Coffee's ready, girls and boys. Bring your dog in with you."

"Okay," Emily replied.

Neither of us moved for several minutes. I'd never expected to find any link between my family and Emily's. The gulf between us—social, financial, emotional, educational— rendered a connection impossible. From the beginning of our collaboration, I'd believed we'd find nothing and that I'd return, with no answers and few regrets, to my quiet life.

I visualized my father visiting Mel Gardner in the sort of place in which a man like him would be held while awaiting trial. I couldn't picture it. His usual clients were educated, financially comfortable, well-dressed. At worst they'd get house arrest. Or perhaps I was naïve. And for him to lose a case? Wouldn't I have heard rumblings from my parents? I'd been at boarding school during Mel's trial in early 1998 and during most of my father's run for governor that fall. But even as a young teenager, was I so oblivious? Or did I assume such a change was normal? And what bearing did my father's defense of Mel have on Vince?

Confounded suddenly, I couldn't stay there, couldn't face the Warners' candor, kindness, and love that amplified my family's reticence and coldness. "I'm leaving, Emily. Thanks for inviting me. Please give my regards to your parents."

"Where are you going?"

"My hotel." But I had no intention of going there. I wouldn't sleep now anyway.

"No, you won't," Emily said, speaking louder than was necessary. "You'll drive home in the dark and stew about this and rationalize why it can't be true, even though this info—this connection between Dad and your family—is *exactly* what you've wanted all along."

I started the Expedition.

"You're afraid," Emily said. "And running from the facts won't change those facts."

"Get out, please." My words were harsher than she deserved, so I added, "I'll call you later."

"I'm afraid too, Philip. Don't you think it's been easier to believe that Daddy went crazy than that he *intentionally* set out to hurt someone? Yet neither of those—crazy or evil—was the man I knew. So, who was he really? How can I love someone so much that I never even knew? How'd he hide in plain sight from me?"

I hadn't realized Emily was as afraid as I was. "You were just a kid." I stared out the windshield at the Warners' brightly lit house.

She sighed. "I never thought we'd find anything."

Shocked, I turned the truck off and faced her. "*What?* That's not what you told Henry. If you didn't expect to find anything, what the hell has all this been about?" Why did you upend my life for nothing?

"Because not trying was a regret I couldn't live with."

The house's front lights flicked on and off, beckoning us inside, a theater announcing the end to intermission. Emily tapped the digital clock in the dash. "Come on. You came here for my birthday, and we still have ninety-seven minutes left to celebrate."

On the coffee table in the great room, three empty over-size mugs surrounded a round tray containing a carafe, creamer, a bowl with various sweeteners, and a Diet Coke. I settled at the end of the sofa closest to the fireplace. Dilsey lay on the floor beside me, her muzzle on my foot. When I adjusted out from under her, she shifted to keep her head right where she thought it belonged. I could barely reach the mugs without disturbing her.

Alex poured coffee, handed Emily the Coke, and settled at the corner of the sectional sofa between his wife and daughter, one arm around each. "Good birthday, yes?"

"The best!" Emily's serious expression belied her words.

"Then why, when you two walked in here, did something suck all the air from the room?"

Emily drank her Coke and eyed me over the top of the can. I couldn't tell whether she was silently requesting permission to tell them what we'd found or warning me she was going to. Or something else.

I beat her to it. "We're just tired."

Alex chuckled, and Kim said, "I'm calling bullshit on that."

When I tried to meet Emily's gaze, take her cue for how to respond to the bluntness that differed so much from anything my parents would say, she focused on something above and beyond me. Then she opened her mouth.

"We think we might have found out how Philip's family and mine are connected."

"Emily, stop," I warned. "Now's not the time to talk about this. We don't know enough to draw conclusions." Or to share them. Perhaps that might come later. Perhaps not.

She ignored me. "When his father was a lawyer, he defended Daddy's brother."

"How on earth . . ." Kim leaned forward and peered across Alex toward Emily.

"Something Mr. Bowling said. That's what we were doing in the car, researching a lead."

Unease constricted my chest so suddenly, I coughed. Dilsey, in one motion, popped up and levitated onto my lap.

Emily untangled herself from Alex's arm and leaned forward. "If not now, then when?"

I had no experience on which to base any answer other than *never*. "We don't know that there's anything to this. Just because my father defended your *uncle* doesn't mean he had anything to do with your *father*."

"You don't believe that."

She was right, I didn't. Not one bit. I couldn't talk about what we'd discovered, though, because . . . Because why? Because after the shooting, Mom and Dad had never allowed discussions about anything important? Was that the single pathetic reason?

I flinched when Kim said quietly, "Emily, maybe he wants to talk with his parents first."

I shook my head, incapable of finding words sufficient to describe the inexcusable silence that consumed my family after the shooting. Across the space occupied by Dilsey, I fumbled for my decaf, but when I wrapped my fingers through the handle, the mug trembled, and I pulled away. I stared at the top of Dilsey's head, weighed down by the Warners' eyes on me, with the Warners waiting for me to say what I suspected they'd figured out.

It took me a while to get started. I rubbed Dilsey's head. I drank some coffee. I met Alex and Kim's compassionate eyes more than once.

I focused on a frame on the wall across from me.

"Till Emily found me, my family never, *ever* discussed any aspect of the shooting. Not as a family, not one-on-one. Not the day itself, not my brother Teddy, not even my father's and my recoveries. Taboo, all of it. We ignored the fact it happened." Except, I realized now, the silence itself was our dysfunctional way of acknowledging that some truths were too monumental for words. "Emily's first email forced us to broach the shooting, but only on the surface, nothing beyond that. I was advised explicitly and repeatedly not to get involved."

"I didn't know." Emily's voice drifted so quietly from the couch, I barely heard her.

"And then when I did get involved, my old friend Henry . . ." Did I dare acknowledge his duplicity aloud? "Henry intentionally misdirected us."

Kim shook her head. "Surely you had someone—some other relative, a counselor, a friend?"

"No." I'd discarded my college friends and others who'd known me—known *us*—before because, unless they could explain what had happened to us, and there was no way they could, they'd never again understand anything about me. I cut them off and withdrew increasingly deeper into the cave of silence that became comfortable and safe, like home. Like the way home was supposed to feel but didn't. Even Henry, my longest and closest friend, was part of the covenant of silence. I'd never needed to cultivate others who might fit into my new world, not even in friendly little Grainger. I'd tried to push Scottie away too. But tonight, for the first time, my self-imposed isolation manifested in a longing so intense that my head and chest and every muscle in my body ached.

"Would you *like* to talk about it?"

I snapped my head toward Alex. No one had ever asked me that. My family's silence about Teddy had kept him dead for the identical period of time that Emily, by talking about Vince, collecting even negative press about him, had kept her father alive in her heart and mind. Ten years was a long time. Too long for us and for Teddy. Yes, I would like to talk. "It's too late."

Kim left her spot beside Alex and pushed in beside me. "It's never too late, hon."

"I don't know your family," Alex said, "but I know their stellar reputation. Your willingness to help Emily showed Kim and me how extraordinary *you* are as well. You didn't ask for advice, but I'm a coach, so I can't help but give some. Talk with your folks. Push them to tell you what they can and acknowledge what they can't or won't. Accept with compassion whatever that brings and repair your relationship as best you can."

I was thirty years old, but in that moment, enveloped by Alex's words and Kim's embrace, I felt like a six-year-old being consoled about the monster under the bed. I sat rigidly still, not sure what to say or do next. To my surprise, I longed to reveal the monsters to them and devour whatever comforting words the Warners offered me. But the lessons from my family constrained me, and I couldn't open up, not even to these kind, sensible, and straightforward people. I trusted them, though, because I trusted Emily. They cared about her and, amazingly, they cared about me. I hadn't trusted anyone so completely in many years.

"If you want to talk, we're here. Tonight. Later. Anytime." Kim hugged me. "We won't judge you or your family. God only knows how we'd have reacted."

I cleared my throat. "Thanks."

"I want you to consider something. It doesn't diminish the loss of your little brother or the struggles your family, and Emily, too, have endured. It's just our perspective, Alex's and mine."

Kim stopped, awaiting my permission to continue. I nodded, still leaning against her and patting Dilsey, who hung half off my lap.

"The chain of events that placed Emily in our lives, a chain that includes Vince's death, was a miracle. Her finding you because of the fire at your school, another tragedy, was a miracle too."

I watched Emily. She blinked, but a tear escaped anyway, and she sniffled. "Pretty sucky miracles," she said.

"No denying that." Alex hugged her.

"What I'm getting at," Kim said, "is that maybe there's a miracle in all this mess for you and your family, too, if you open yourselves up to recognize it."

It was a decade too late.

CHAPTER 29

WHATEVER EMILY DID overnight while I drove home in a mental tempest of *what-ifs* and *hows* and *whys*, it wasn't sleep. When I opened my email just before noon, my account spilled messages from her with URLs, cut-and-pasted articles, and attachments about Mel. About my father and Mel. Sitting in my study, I drowned in them.

The 1996 trial was a big deal because of the extreme violence of the crimes with which Mel was charged. The 1998 trial was a big deal because my father lost, and he never lost anything. His courtroom opponent both times was his friend Adrian Wells. A few articles hinted at a post-verdict controversy involving withheld evidence, but none explicitly accused my father of anything or substantiated the claim.

Senses humming, I finished Emily's final email, gulped three ibuprofen tablets for my pounding headache, and called her.

"We weren't searching far enough back." Her voice rose in excitement. "And not quite the right things."

"Yeah."

"You don't think your father really did something wrong, do you?"

"Absolutely not. Impossible." Despite our difficult relationship, I'd stake my life on his professional integrity.

"And wasting time following that line of thought will lead us exactly nowhere. *Again.*"

"Okaaay . . ."

She stretched out the word, and I didn't blame her for questioning me. I'd professed the same confidence about Henry, and I'd been wrong.

"Maybe Daddy *thought* your father withheld evidence? What if we call the reporters who–"

A *no* popped out before I could stop myself. Publicly reaching out to anyone would cause one big mess for Emily, me, and our families. "I'll call the guy who prosecuted the trials."

"You will? Do you know him?"

"Yes."

She let that hang, silently reminding me she'd assumed all along I had connections. Even if I'd considered them, I wouldn't have thought they mattered, because we had Henry. And we hadn't known then about Mel.

As soon as I arrived home from campus the next afternoon, I phoned Adrian Wells, expecting his assistant to answer and surprised when his worried voice asked, "Everything all right with your family?"

I hadn't considered that a call from me would concern him. "Yes, sir. Everything's fine." As best I knew.

"Thank God. What can I do for you, then?"

"I'm researching a guy you prosecuted twice in the mid-to-late nineties. My father was his defense attorney."

"Melvin Gardner," he said immediately.

Mel must have made quite an impression. "Yes, sir."

"You're interested in him why?"

Wells was at least as talented a trial lawyer as my father had been, and even from three hundred miles away, I didn't doubt he'd catch any lie or half-truth I concocted, though I considered doing just that. I also suspected he'd relay our conversation to my father, but if I were going to talk with him at all, I had to accept the risks. "At the end of his armed robbery and assault trial, the trial you won, he claimed my father withheld evidence. What can you tell me about that?"

"Answer my question."

Okay, avoiding his questions wouldn't work either. "Because I want to know if his defense of Mel Gardner had any bearing on Vince Gardner's attack on us." My intuition had already answered the question, I realized. It just hadn't explained why.

"What does your father say about it?"

I should have expected that question. "We never discuss anything remotely related to the shooting."

He was quiet a moment. "I suppose that shouldn't surprise me. And I guess I shouldn't be surprised you'd want to know. How'd you even hear about the withheld-evidence allegation?"

Mentioning Jess Bowling would raise too many questions, like why Mel Gardner's name would come up at a bowling alley—and why I was even at a bowling alley and with whom—so I skipped that part. "Archived news articles." I pressed him. "What was the withheld evidence?"

"There wasn't any."

"What did Gardner *claim* it was?"

He answered almost before I finished asking. "I don't remember."

"With all due respect, Mr. Wells, I don't believe you." Like my father, he made remembering *everything* his business.

"Listen to me, Philip. Your father was thorough, honest, and dedicated to his clients. That includes Mel Gardner. In the many years I was the chief violent crimes prosecutor for this area, Mel Gardner was *the* most evil criminal I prosecuted. If I hadn't screwed up the first trial, the second one would've been nonexistent because he would've been on death row. You need to discount any rumor of withheld evidence, because there was no withheld evidence. Your father did his damnedest, always, to ensure even the worst among us received a competent defense. Your parents—all of you—went through a lot. Don't dig where nothing's buried. I shouldn't have to tell you how detrimental any misconduct would have been not only for your father's career but for his personal life as well."

I couldn't let go, not yet. "What about *Vince* Gardner, then?"

He sighed. "He had a record, but nothing recent or violent. He harassed your father after the second trial. I guess you could call it a threat, but no one took it seriously, and your dad refused to press charges. I think he felt sorry for Vince Gardner, having Mel for a brother. That was the end of it. Next time I heard his name was nearly eight years later when he attacked y'all. So much for your dad's sympathy. Bad blood ran in that family."

"Did you and my father ever talk—"

"Our conversations are private."

"But . . ."

"This is ancient history. All four of you, and Henry, have moved past it and built very successful lives. Both Gardners are dead, and neither deserves your attention. Let it go."

For an instant, I considered telling him about Emily and almost as immediately dismissed the thought. He'd finished with me; mentioning her wouldn't lead to additional information. So I promised him I'd consider his advice, thanked him, and called Emily.

"You don't really believe he doesn't know anything, do you?"

"I don't know what I believe."

"You say no every time I bring this up, but don't you think it's time to go to Tennessee?"

"No."

"We can talk with the police or the people where you sent the subpoena request. The caretaker that some of the articles mentioned—maybe he's still there and will show us around the property."

I tuned her out. After my recent anxiety attack, sparked by a mere painting, I couldn't imagine climbing the front steps to the cabin. Or entering the great room with its huge stone fireplace and the wide archway to the eat-in kitchen, the last place I'd seen Teddy. Hearing the pointers in their kennels fifty yards away begging to work. Baffled about how Vince Gardner had surprised us that morning. Wondering why he wanted to. I couldn't explain all that to Emily, though. I didn't know how to explain in a way I could bear to say it. "There's nothing to find there."

"You don't know that. If you won't go, just tell me where it is, and I'll go alone."

I won't say I wasn't tempted. She'd drive all the way there, learn nothing, and check Tennessee off her list. But all the while I'd imagine her walking where we'd walked, standing where Dad and I had fallen, listening to the dogs barking and the wildlife skittering and chirping as they'd done ten years ago. Just thinking about that place sent my heart pounding. I switched the phone to my other hand and wiped my sweaty palm on my thigh. "No."

She blew air into her phone. "Fine. What's next?"

We had bits of information, but we needed an expert to locate the missing pieces and complete the puzzle. "Time to hire a private investigator," I said. "It'll be touchy because it involves a sitting US senator, so let *me* find someone. Next week's spring break, and I'll devote as much time then as it takes to find the right person."

Immediately after we disconnected, my phone pinged with a text from Henry. We hadn't communicated in the two weeks since I'd discovered he'd concealed the FBI's involvement. Anger at his betrayal, which I thought I'd suppressed, constricted my stomach, and my finger hovered over the delete button. The first few words of the text caught my attention.

Don't delete me!

I sighed and, amused despite myself, opened it.

Don't delete me! Look, this is stupid. Let's talk. Tomorrow night. Dinner, then theater. Same as always.

I'd ignored the note on my calendar about the play, had planned to let the day pass without acknowledging it and expected he'd do the same, but I recognized his words as a gesture of reconciliation. He was wrong, though, about "same as always." Nothing was the same. Part of me still wanted to delete the text, but the other part replied, *See you at the usual time.*

CHAPTER 30

AFTER REPLYING TO Henry's text, I wasted more energy convincing myself not to scrap the evening than Henry and the play deserved. *Let's talk* meant he intended to explain himself. Or at least that was what I assumed he intended. Not that, given my waning trust in him, I'd necessarily believe what he'd tell me.

In the end, our long friendship and the expectation that he'd set things right propelled me to Richmond after my office hours the next afternoon. While I awaited his arrival, I fell into the theater-day routine I'd begun during the months I lived there: meandering with Dilsey through Henry's neighborhood of historic row houses, and then medicating and feeding her. When Henry trudged through his front door, Dilsey scooted her stainless bowl toward him in greeting, gulping her food as she went, rattling the bowl with her vigorous full-body wagging.

As she inhaled the last bits, he said, "I thought you might stand me up."

"So did I."

He looked like he might say something else but instead just handed the empty bowl to me and, accompanied by my dog, went upstairs to change clothes. A few moments later, Dilsey bounced back into the kitchen. By the time

Henry returned, I'd washed her bowl, wiped the floor of food dribbles, and walked Dilsey on the patch of grass out front. She settled in her usual spot under Henry's dining room table.

I leaned against the counter and crossed my arms. "You going to fill me in?"

"Later. Let's go."

Henry's Mercedes wasn't as challenging to park as my Expedition, so he drove. We left the coupe at the theater and strode down the street to our favorite steakhouse. All in silence. After we ordered, he ignored me and played with the magnetic attraction between his knife and fork.

"Henry."

He attempted to raise the fork with the knife, but it skittered to the floor. When he bent to retrieve it, his phone pinged, and he frowned when he checked it.

It pinged immediately with another text, then rang. He stuffed it into a pocket.

"Take it if you need to."

"I'll deal with it later."

Always later. "Why didn't you tell me the FBI conducted the shooting investigation?"

"You never asked."

"That's a bullshit answer."

His gaze followed something across the room, and determined not to lose focus, I didn't turn to find out what. "*Henry*, answer me."

He didn't, though he did try to broach our jobs, the upcoming college basketball playoffs, the weather, anything unrelated to the shooting or Emily. When I responded at all, I rewarded him with a single word or a shake or nod of my head, refusing to play along with his disregard of the only subject that mattered. Eventually, I paid the bill, and we maneuvered the crowded sidewalk to the theater. His phone pinged again. And when it rang after we settled into our seats, he finally answered.

He listened for a moment, his expression unreadable. "Because I didn't know. He's right here; ask him yourself." He listened again. "It's not that easy." He ended the call.

Before he could pocket the phone, I snatched it from him. The last half dozen calls had been from my father. "Henry, what the hell's going on?"

"You're asking *me*? Why'd you call Adrian Wells?"

His words caught me completely by surprise. I expected Adrian to call my father, but I didn't expect my father to relay my call with Adrian to Henry. "What?"

In the orchestra pit, the musicians tuned their instruments, and Henry raised his voice over the discordance. "It's one thing for you to dig around on the internet. It's something else entirely to harass your parents' friends, especially someone like Wells, about the past."

"What else am I supposed to do? I've practically begged you *and* my father for information. You withheld it or lied outright or both."

"Just leave it alone."

"I didn't go looking for this."

"Then stop. You can't change anything any–"

"I'm *sick* of that excuse–"

"And you're hurting everyone in your family, including yourself, by–"

"I'm not hurting anyone."

"Thinking you should even try. That damned Emily." He slammed a fist into his leg. "*Stop upsetting everyone*."

"*Upsetting* everyone?"

The house lights blinked and dimmed, and the couple in front of us turned to glare. Henry forced a smile at them, and the overture enveloped us.

I gazed unseeing at the stage, tuning out the story and the music, perturbed by the coziness between Dad and Henry that seemed to have developed for one reason only: to shut me out. Henry disregarded the musical too. He fidgeted with his phone, its brightness muted, his mouth set in a straight line.

At intermission, without a word to him, I escaped up the aisle, through the lobby, and outside. I paced among the smokers, knowing without a doubt that my father, Henry, and possibly my entire family were hiding something big from me.

Henry joined me. "Should we leave?"

I whirled on him. "Did you know my father was accused of withholding evidence in a trial?"

"That's absurd."

"Is it?"

He yanked me from the cluster of gawking bystanders. "No way would your father do anything like that. Where'd you even hear such a ridiculous thing?"

"Emily and I—"

"Emily. Of course." He sneered and thrust his phone at me. "Ask him."

I swatted it away. "I'm done with his bullshit. And yours."

Henry stalked off. I stared after him, flexing my fingers to ease the tension in my arms, aware of my limited options to learn about the allegedly withheld evidence. The hell with it. I *would* phone my father, and I'd challenge any word he uttered that smacked remotely of evasion or untruth. I concentrated on controlling my breathing and punched in his number.

"Hi, Philip. Play over so soon?"

Of course he'd know where we were. Of course he'd know the play couldn't possibly have ended. "Did you screw up Melvin Gardner's defense in '98?"

He wasn't even caught off guard enough to pause. "I believe Adrian set you straight."

"He lied." I paced down the sidewalk. "And from the time I first mentioned Emily, so has Henry. And you. For all I know, Mom and Jamie—"

"You're responsible for what you choose to believe."

"I don't need a damn sermon." Infuriated by his calm tone as much as by his words, I squeezed the phone so hard, I cut him off. When I called again, his voice remained level.

"Philip, settle down."

"Don't you dare tell me to settle down when you—"

"Now you're just acting childish. I'm not discussing any of this until we can talk civilly and in person."

I pivoted and retraced my steps. Was he bluffing? He had to be. "I'm on my way."

I expected him to backtrack, but instead he said, "See you soon. Drive safely." Only after he hung up did I remember I didn't know where he was. As that thought formed, a text from him pinged.

Washington.

I looked around for Henry as I pocketed the phone. He slouched by the theater's door, hands in pockets, watching me, and pushed upright when I approached. "I'm going to DC. Give me your keys."

"We'll get your truck."

"That'll take too long. I'm leaving right now."

"I need a way home. And Dilsey's there."

"Take an Uber. And you can handle Dilsey for a few hours."

"What if she—"

"She won't, because she just did."

He slapped his keys into my hand. "Fine. Good. Maybe he can finally jolt some sense into you."

I abandoned him outside the theater and tore from the parking deck and north up the interstate. My phone's GPS indicated traffic would delay my arrival by at least fifteen minutes, but I intended to prove the timing wrong. Dropping the phone into the console, I focused on clinging to the road now leading me to answers, while simultaneously believing that the lies and evasions would continue.

CHAPTER 31

TWO HOURS OF imagining everything my father might say, and rehearsing every possible response, ended when I slammed the Mercedes's door in the driveway of my parents' Washington house. On the porch, illuminated by floodlights as if he were on stage, my father leaned against a brick pillar, arms crossed.

I stopped well before the steps, maintaining the distance that separated us, and choked out, "I won't believe anything you say."

He stared at me. "Then why are you here?" Without waiting for my reply, he pivoted into the house and firmly shut the door.

In the ambient hum of the city, I remained alone on the walkway, once again cut off from him, battling between barging inside to confront him and barreling back to Richmond to collect Dilsey and go home, once again leaving everything unsaid.

Then why are you here?

He wanted me to listen, and if he wanted me to listen, that meant he wanted to talk. *Finally.* Suddenly terrified of what he might say, I rang the bell. He opened the door immediately, and I brushed past him into the entryway. The grandfather clock midway down the hall chimed. Ten forty-five.

"Where's Mom?"

"She's out."

"I want her side of this."

"You don't get to make that call." He pointed toward his study.

The room was big, though not as large as his office-study at the farm, and darker, more formal. It had a wet bar, a fireplace, and tall shuttered windows overlooking the side yard. The furniture was the same as when I'd last been there during my surgery and rehab, newer than at the farm, and all leather and oak and dark.

He leaned against the bar, studying me. I hesitated midway between him and his uncluttered desk. The door remained open, meaning we were alone in the house.

We eyed each other for so long that one of us inevitably had to break contact. It was me. I dropped into one of the chairs by his desk.

He relaxed then, dropping his arms to his sides, uncharacteristically slouching a bit. "You have no right to bother Adrian with questions pertaining to me, to us. Who else have you spoken with?"

"No one."

"Good. Don't."

I chose not to mention my decision to hire a private investigator. "What else am I supposed to do? I've tried to get answers from you and Henry, but—"

He stopped me with a raised hand. "I'm about to tell you everything you need to know. Then you can drop the inquisition and send that girl on her way, and these discussions will be over."

His gaze was so intense that I lowered mine. *Everything you need to know.* I swallowed hard.

"Vince Gardner had an older brother named Melvin, whose criminal record dated back to when he was eight or nine. Shoplifting. Animal cruelty. Larceny. Assault. It escalated. He did work, but he'd get convicted for something and go to prison and consequently get fired. This pattern repeated continuously. He and a guy he met in prison found work together painting the interiors of renovated houses. The job paid well. Gave them more money than they'd ever had doing a job they were good at.

"But the other guy couldn't stay away from meth. Mel viewed drugs strictly as a business venture—and it's a violent business. He convinced his friend to set up a meth lab in his own house, a place the guy shared with his wife and two kids, a little boy Teddy's age and a four-year-old girl."

Dad turned to the bar and poured what looked like bourbon into a rocks glass. Instead of drinking it, he left it on the counter and faced me again.

"One evening, Mel and his friend fought, apparently over the meth business. Mel shot the guy and then the witnesses—the wife and kids, even though the kids were too young to be a threat to him. The neighbors heard the ruckus, but no one called 911 till Mel set the house on fire. As meth labs will do, it exploded. The incident terrorized the neighborhood and became high profile statewide."

Mel was Emily's uncle, and she'd said she never knew him. No way she knew what he'd done, or she'd have suspected that her father intentionally kept her away from him. By never allowing her to meet him, Vince had protected her. I could admire him for that.

Dad reached for the bourbon and gripped the glass in both hands, still without drinking. Despite everything we'd been through as a family, I'd never seen him so rattled. I sensed he'd never told this story.

"Mel disappeared after that, but a few days later an anonymous tip led the police to him and he was arrested. That was early 1996. Mel was barely older than you are now. In addition to my private practice, I worked rotation at the courthouse, assisting the overloaded public defenders. My name came up for Mel's case. Even though he had a weak alibi from someone willing to lie for him—or more likely, afraid not to—I knew to my core he was guilty. And he knew I knew. Under normal circumstances, I wouldn't have taken Mel Gardner's case, but even slime like him deserves a competent defense. And so I gave it my best shot.

"The jury deliberated for nearly a week. Adrian's prosecution—which overall was solid—had several pinprick holes. I punched right through them and provided the jurors enough reasonable doubt for them to acquit Mel. I don't blame the jurors for his acquittal; they did their job. I blamed myself." He drained his entire glass and stared at the floor.

I clutched the arms of my chair. That was the weirdest thing I'd ever heard him say. His job was to defend Mel. He did that, defended Mel better than Adrian prosecuted him, and had won. He always won.

I rose and accepted an empty glass from him. The expensive bourbon was made the same year Teddy died. I poured a generous three fingers and returned to my chair.

He refilled his own glass and paced, his breathing and voice ragged. "I was sick about setting that monster free. I couldn't sleep or eat or work. Couldn't interact with you kids. Couldn't think about anything except that I'd turned Mel Gardner loose. Every time I shut my eyes, images of those two little children innocently eating dinner looped endlessly through my head. And then there were the actual crime scene photos. There wasn't even enough left of the place to make the photos gruesome. And worse, every little thing about Teddy reminded me of those children. I could hardly stand to be around him, my own baby. Mom suggested counseling, but I couldn't bear the platitudes they'd lay on me. Then she suggested a trip, but I could never escape."

As he grappled with memories from two decades ago, I forgot to be angry and began to feel sorry for him. I'd never viewed him in any role except as my father. I'd never thought of him as a man. Would never have seen him as a decent, conflicted man suffering for having done his job extraordinarily well.

He swallowed another mouthful of bourbon. "I realized for the first time what a bullshit profession mine was. As a first step, I removed myself from the courthouse rotation."

A first step toward what?

"Mel resurfaced in the fall of '97, this time for armed robbery and assault at a convenience store. He asked me to defend him. I declined. He begged, even threatened. Still, I declined. He couldn't afford to hire anyone, and he refused a public defender. I figured he'd defend himself, lose, and rot in prison. Most likely someone would appeal his conviction, but it wouldn't be me, and the appeal wouldn't get far.

"Mel swore he hadn't committed those crimes. Said the witnesses putting him at the scene were lying. Told me he'd prove it. Vince corroborated his claim and brought me his answering machine with a time-stamped recording of a message from Mel during the time of the robbery. The message was little more than Mel's verbal assault on Vince for delaying plans to help fix something in Mel's house. In the background, however, an announcer gave the score at what clearly was a football venue and proved Mel was nowhere near the store during the crime."

Dad returned to his spot by the bar. "Right there with Vince in my office, I had an epiphany. I'd atone for my role in Mel's earlier acquittal."

I shifted uneasily, sensing his story was about to head somewhere I might not want it to go.

"I told Vince I'd defend Mel, then I visited Mel in jail and told him the same thing. Vince had left his answering machine with me, and after I listened to the recording a few times, I took it home, set it on the credenza in my study, found a hammer, and smashed the shit out of it."

I gaped at him. "But he was *innocent.*"

Adrian had pointed out how detrimental any misconduct would have been for Dad's career and his personal life. Now, Dad's admission of violating every rule of his profession, knowing he'd lose everything if anyone exposed his transgression, stunned me. Never had I considered him corrupt or incompetent. Lightheaded and dazed by his revelation, I clutched my glass and forced myself to breathe. "You destroyed evidence. You can't do that."

"I did do it. And make no mistake: Mel Gardner was never *innocent.* He might not have committed *those* crimes, the armed robbery and assault, but he was never innocent."

He stared at me without blinking. "I gave that son of a bitch Mel the best nondefense ever. And when the jury convicted him, I didn't ask the judge to override them in favor of a new trial or acquittal. Instead, to keep from laughing out loud, I envisioned those toddlers. It was easier to let my colleagues and the jurors and news media think I had lost than to let them know I had actually won."

Dad never lost. Even now, warped by something I'd never have imagined and didn't understand, he remained undefeated and secure in the belief he'd done the right thing. I was stunned. "How did you get away with it?"

He shrugged. "Easy. No one knows."

"Adrian?"

"Absolutely not."

So, assuming Dad was telling the truth, Adrian *hadn't* lied. "Henry? Mom? Jamie?"

"No, not Henry. Not Jamie. Not even your mother. Only me. And now you."

The weight of his revelation nauseated me, and the room spun. To keep something so damning a secret from those closest to him attested not only to his astounding self-discipline, but also to his awareness of the destructiveness of his secret. What did it mean that he'd shared it with me? He was far too savvy to assume I'd not expose him and equally aware that my better judgment would prevent me from doing so. "Why are you telling me this? Why now?"

"So you'll stop bothering people like Adrian."

"Even though you're safe now because the statute of limitations would've expired?"

"South Carolina has no statute of limitations on criminal offenses." He squared his shoulders. "Even before tonight, I'd never have been home free. And now?" He shrugged.

And there it was: the cost of my knowing what he'd done, that as long as one other person knew his secret, he was at risk for being turned in to the authorities, tried, convicted, and jailed. But I couldn't think about that now. "Emily wonders if you did something. The articles she found . . ."

"Let her wonder."

I shook my head, still incredulous he'd double-crossed a client, even an evil one. "Surely Mel told someone you didn't present the recording."

"He did, after the conviction. Once Vince gave me his answering machine, Mel and I never discussed it. He tried to raise the issue with me before closing arguments, but I brushed him off. When he brought it up later, I denied knowing anything about any recording. No one believed him. Vince complained to the media, and it generated some buzz, but no one believed him either. My colleagues laughed about it. The word of a Mel Gardner against the word of a Bennett Rutledge and his impeccable, scandal-free record? Figure it out."

Unbelievable. "How did Mel die?"

"In prison he was always in trouble. In mid-October 2005, more than seven years after his conviction, a group of gangbangers killed him. He had eighteen years left to serve, so those guys gave the South Carolina taxpayers a windfall."

His callousness astonished me. This was my *father*, a morally upright man who had defended the law for years. Unable to fathom his attitude or his behavior, I shifted my thoughts to the Gardners.

Mel had been the crazy one, not Vince. Mel had also been a true son of a bitch.

"Okay, Vince was pissed, but he'd have known Mel's character better than anyone. Besides, he had Emily to take care of. So, why come after you?" Would his answer reveal Vince Gardner's motivation? And would that answer be enough for both Emily and me?

"With Mel's second trial, I'd started along the proverbial slippery slope toward corruption. Having once violated my professional and personal codes of conduct, I knew I'd do it again if necessary."

He waited until I looked into his eyes before adding, "*Because getting Mel convicted was worth what it cost me.*"

I gawped. I couldn't help it. "*Dad . . .*" I felt like a child begging his father to make sense out of the senseless.

After reading my face, he turned away, adding, "Or it was worth what at the time I thought it would cost." He swished a mouthful of bourbon like mouthwash. "I decided almost immediately to give up my law practice. Your mother—and everyone else once I announced my run for governor—assumed I just couldn't accept losing my first case. I didn't care what they thought. Knowing what I was capable of and how I could justify my actions to myself, I had to get out. Had to remove myself far from future temptation. I won the primary and immediately resigned from the practice. I dove headfirst into the campaign. My political ambitions kept our family in the news—and on Vince Gardner's radar."

"What happened?"

"The week after Mel's conviction, Vince threatened me. He was arrested, but I refused to press the harassment charge, so he was out after a night. He was way better than Mel, had a few minor infractions years before, nothing violent. He held a good job, was raising his daughter. He was mostly just angry—"

"You *did* know he had a daughter."

"I learned about her during the second trial."

My face burned. "You lied to me. About Emily. About Vince threatening you. About nearly everything."

He sipped his bourbon and pressed on as if I hadn't spoken. "I forgot about Vince's threat until he showed up

the Sunday of our hunting weekend in 2005. Do you remember what he said right before he shot me?"

The room darkened, and I pressed back against the
chair. I could not have an anxiety attack right now. I
would not.

"He said, 'Remember me, Senator?' I learned later that
Mel had died a few weeks earlier. Vince wanted revenge
for my withholding of the answering machine recording, for not keeping Mel out of prison and thus not keeping
him alive. I recognized his voice immediately. Later, in
the hospital, the FBI questioned me several times. I
didn't remember Vince's initial threat, the one from right
after Mel's conviction, until the FBI asked me about it.
They interviewed Henry and Jamie. They interviewed
you, too, but I doubt you were coherent enough to give
them much."

I bowed my head, scouring my memory for an interaction with investigators, which Henry had also mentioned.
I might have had a flash of two men in suits, but I might
not have.

"I don't remember anyone questioning me."

"In the end, everything pointed toward simple revenge.
By early January, the investigation was closed."

The question Emily and I had both wondered about
popped into my head. "How did Vince find us?"

Dad walked to the bar and picked up the bourbon bottle.
Yet instead of refilling his glass, he left the bottle on the bar
and sat behind his desk. He slid his cell phone off the blotter and folded his hands in its spot. Slipping back into his
politician's persona?

"Although it was never definitively determined, the authorities concluded he followed me, Jamie, and Teddy

from the farm. Our November hunting weekends were no secret. He could have attacked at any point along the way but apparently had no intention of harming your brothers. He waited till they were out of the picture and we were far from any kind of medical or other assistance."

I spun my glass in my hand. Gripped by my father's story, I still hadn't even sipped the bourbon. Vince's intent be damned. He didn't make Teddy any less dead by following them for over three hundred miles before striking.

"I'm telling you because I need you to understand how complicated the situation is. The simple answers you and that girl seem to think exist don't, and you need to back off. If you won't take my advice, take Henry's."

I shot up and gripped the edge of his desk, leaning over it. "Henry—your confidant! Do you tell each other *everything*?"

"*Sit down.*"

Dad whacked his open palm so hard on the desk, I jumped. After a tense and silent showdown, I collapsed back into my chair.

"If you hear nothing else tonight, hear this. Do not insinuate anything negative about that boy. He cradled Teddy while he died. He tried to manage Jamie's panic, and he and the caretaker, Driscoll, worked their asses off to save us. He's a major reason you and I are alive. When the EMTs arrived, he was so covered in blood, they assumed he'd also been shot. He stayed at the hospital with us till your mother arrived, then took Jamie home and stayed with him until Mom and I returned. He'd have stayed longer if Mom hadn't insisted he go back to his parents. And later, when you got pissed off at us and disappeared—and made your mother and me feel as if we'd lost a second son and Jamie feel as if he'd lost his other brother—Henry's the only reason the police didn't show up at your door with a contrived warrant to return you to us. He's the keeper–generous and loyal and devoted–that you apparently need. Have you even once looked, *really* looked, at what the shooting did to all of them, *especially* Henry, who saw nearly everything start to finish? Have you ever asked him about how those moments and hours and days impacted *his* life? In some ways, he's been far more a son to us these past ten years than you have."

His words gutted me. No, I'd never considered the impact of that November morning on Henry. As with everyone else in my family, he never raised the topic, always acted as if the shooting never happened, and so I assumed he was fine. Or would have if I'd thought even that much about it. In the years between the party he'd arranged at the farm that February and my departure for California, I never recalled him ever acknowledging the shooting, and if he had, I'd have shut down the conversation. Even when he convinced me to return east, it never came up. The first time we discussed that day was right after Emily initially emailed me. Even when I first mentioned her to him, he never acknowledged the shooting, and I'd assumed, as with my parents, it had affected him only negligibly. Never once did I consider his reticence to be the means by which he tried to forget.

And perhaps silence was the means by which Jamie and our parents, struggling in their unassuming ways to fathom the event that had altered the trajectories of all our lives, tried to forget too. Struggling to endure not just the loss of Teddy, but the loss of me as well.

I bit back a groan. How could I have not recognized the additional damage I caused my family? How did my own grief, anger, and desperation to run from memories I'd never escape so thoroughly segregate me from everyone else's grief, anger, and desperation?

At the farm the Christmas just after Teddy died, my father said that one person's actions could irrevocably change other people's lives. I'd assumed he was referring to the man who shot us. I knew now he meant himself, and his decision to destroy evidence. And now I recognized my own ripple as part of his, as part of Vince's and Mel's and Emily's. Everyone affecting everyone else.

My first sip of bourbon punished my throat all the way down and perhaps gave credibility to my hoarseness. "I didn't know you cared. About Henry or any of us. About Teddy dying."

His head snapped back as if I'd slapped him, and when he spoke, his voice quavered. "Why would you say something like that? Teddy was my youngest, my baby boy. You, my oldest, almost dead too. Jamie and Henry traumatized."

"You and Mom cut us off from Teddy. Right away, you locked his room and left his ornaments off the Christmas tree and took down not just photos of him but any family photo with him in it." My words gathered momentum as they spilled out. "You got rid of his horse. And when I tried to talk with you about it, you said that Teddy was gone, that we needed to put him behind us and focus on moving forward. Focus on returning to normal, you said." I blinked my eyes clear. "How could you put Teddy behind you? How could I? He was the best, the sweetest . . ." I coughed to clear my throat, but I couldn't erase the anguish. "He was perfect and then he was dead, and you didn't want to remember him."

He froze, not blinking, maybe not even breathing. The only sound was the pendulum of the grandfather clock logging the seconds. Bourbon sloshed over my hand, and I set the glass against my thigh to steady it. I hadn't revealed anything new, but somehow I'd released a dark secret.

He rose from behind his desk and sank into the chair across from me. "My God. All this time, that's what you thought?"

"What did you expect me to think? You did all that, said those things."

He inhaled deeply, needing every molecule of oxygen in the room. "We *did* want to make Christmas as normal as possible. But it wasn't possible, and we shouldn't have tried. Mom and I were foundering, trying anything that might make the nightmare stop. Someone put up a tree for us, but Mom and Jamie couldn't bear to decorate it, so the Riggses did. But Jamie begged us to remove Teddy's ornaments. He cried every time he saw them, and we couldn't bear it. We never told you or Henry about that because we didn't want you teasing Jamie or blaming him for anything.

"All that happened while you were still in the hospital. Against medical advice, we sprang you early so we'd all be together for Christmas. That's why you were barely mobile, but we thought if we were all together, we wouldn't hurt as much. Your mom . . . She's strong, Philip, you know she is, but she couldn't bear for you to be in that place and away from us. She'd wake up crying every night . . ." He leaned forward, hands locked together. "Unfortunately, when you sneaked out in the golf cart, the first thing you came across was Teddy's horse being moved.

But we couldn't keep him. I pictured Teddy every time I saw the horse, and I couldn't stand it. And your mom . . . she . . . All I wanted was to heal our family, but I made things worse. Then, as soon as you were able to get away from us, you left, and we didn't know where you were or how you were. Or even why you'd gone."

So much pain. So much I'd misunderstood. The weight of his revelations kept me unable to move or speak. I couldn't look at him or explain or apologize.

"Philip, I'll tell you now what I couldn't then. No matter how angry you are at your mother and me or how hurt you feel by what we do or how wrong you think our actions have been, we will always care about you and always worry about you when you're gone. We will always be here when you return. And Teddy will always be part of this family. We love him and miss him. We always will." He nodded. "I always will."

Emotions battered me, each playing out within seconds of one another. Shock that he acknowledged that he cared about all of us—*loved* us—after all. Amazement that he'd admitted it aloud. Anger at him because all these years he'd held back when his simple explanation might have made all the difference. Anger at myself for pulling away when I should have pushed back at him, forced him to confront Teddy's loss and all that went with it. Sympathy for the difficult judgment call he and my mother had made to help Jamie cope but that backfired for me and perhaps for Jamie and Henry as well. They'd acted in our best interests, and they'd been wrong, and had no way to know that until it was too late. For that, they deserved my admiration and my sympathy. And one day I hoped to be able to share both with them. Today, however, wasn't that day.

The fallout from the shooting was only one part of the storm that had broken over us in my father's study. His admission of deliberately tanking a man's defense was earthshaking. And I used that admission to bring my turbulent emotions under control.

After he had resigned from his law practice, my father campaigned for governor with a laser focus I'd not previously noticed. That focus, I realized now, was his resolve to never again place himself in a position to violate his core beliefs. That resolve had guided him for years. And he'd worked so diligently to do the right thing for his constituents, he neglected to do the right thing for his family.

His cell phone vibrated on the desk, and when he lifted his hands to reach for it, his cheeks were shiny. His softened expression told me the caller was my mother, and as he answered and listened, he looked directly at me. He spoke so quietly that I couldn't hear his words.

When they finished, he handed me the phone. "Henry's been calling you." His voice was grim. "It's your dog. He says it's an emergency."

I'd left my phone in the console of Henry's Mercedes. Almost panting, I tapped in his number as Dad watched.

"You need to get here ASAP." Henry's voice was gravelly. "We're at the emergency vet near my house. Dilsey started seizing at about ten fifty and after the third one, never came out of them. And then it got worse. She . . ." He stopped.

I checked the phone to make sure we were still connected. "*What?*"

"She's still alive, but it's bad. You need to come while . . . while she . . ." He could barely force out the words.

"Henry–" But the dead air in my ear told me he was gone. Setting the phone and glass on my father's desk, I said, "We'll have to finish this later."

He followed me outside, and when I reached the bottom step, he called my name.

I turned and raised both hands, like a traffic cop. "Yeah, I got it. Don't speed."

"No . . . Please let me know how she is."

CHAPTER 32

FURIOUS AT MYSELF for abandoning Dilsey, I sped through the DC traffic, laying on the horn incessantly. The flow improved on the southbound interstate, and I leaned forward, urging the Mercedes like a horse—faster, faster—and blasting the air conditioner into my face to freeze my anxiety and fear.

To freeze my shame.

I'd been so distracted by Henry and my father that I had left Dilsey without giving specific instructions, *any* instructions, to Henry. I hadn't expected her to seize, but that wasn't an excuse, because I never knew when she would or wouldn't. Her Christmas seizure proved that, but I'd been angrier at my father and Henry than I was concerned about Dilsey.

During the two-hour drive, which seemed to last two days, Henry answered exactly zero of my calls and texts, and I fumed, strangling the wheel so desperately that my hands ached. Even if the emergency vet clinic blocked cell signals, he could step outside to talk. He'd know I'd be frantic for details, for updates, for *anything*. The gist of my one terse response from the vet was *she's stable, but get here as soon as you can.*

I expected Henry to wait, but at 2:06 a.m., when I wheeled his coupe into the parking lot, my Expedition was nowhere in sight. Maybe he'd parked around back.

The waiting room was empty except for a loudly complaining woman at the reception counter with a cardboard cat carrier at her feet. No Henry. He must be in an exam room or with Dilsey. Instead of waiting politely behind the woman, I joined her at the counter.

She elbowed me. "Wait your turn."

I ignored her and said to the receptionist, "I'm here about Dilsey."

When she directed her attention to me, the woman yowled. "Hey, wait your turn. I was here first."

The receptionist tapped the laminated sign on the counter. "Please be patient. Some pets' emergencies are more critical than your pet's emergency."

"My friend who brought my dog in. He's here?"

"Haven't seen him in a while."

"He left?" He'd deserted Dilsey? And me? We *needed* him. *He couldn't wait for two damn hours?*

The receptionist shrugged. "Nothing he could do here. Meet me over there." She inclined her head to the door on her left.

From the interior hallway, she ushered me through the first door into a small exam room with a single plastic chair and a second door on the opposite wall. "Dr. Hollins will be with you in a sec."

Neither her expression nor her voice divulged anything. "Can you tell me how Dilsey is?"

"Dr. Hollins will talk to you."

To her, Dilsey was a job. Another sick pet. They came and went, lived and died, and she wouldn't get too involved with any of them.

But Dilsey's different, I thought, panicked. *Dilsey's exceptional.* Her intuition about people who needed her had landed her on CNN and YouTube. That confirmed, as Scottie had pointed out, how extraordinary she was. I wanted the receptionist to know that Dilsey had a special role in my classroom. People terrified of dogs, like Nicole, sought her out. That proved something too. And Dilsey got to sleep in my parents' house! My mother had never granted any other dog that privilege.

But the receptionist left me alone before I said a word about Dilsey's exceptionalism. I stood by the exam table, hands in my pockets, bouncing my keys in one hand, wanting to follow her, worrying that I'd missed a message from Henry in the past few minutes. The phone hadn't rung, and no text message had pinged, but I pulled out my phone anyway. Nothing new from him, just all his missed calls from when the phone was unmonitored in his car. I paced the small room, rechecked my phone, paced again, was tempted to open the door into what I presumed was the treatment area. As soon as the thought formed, a middle-aged man in lime green scrubs and running shoes pushed open the door with his shoulder as he wrote on a clipboard. His nametag read Dr. Andrew Hollins.

I blinked at the scrubs, not sure he was a serious enough doctor for Dilsey. Their color was more appropriate for roadside construction or trash collection. He should have worn a white coat. Something official.

He laid the clipboard on the table between us and extended his hand. "Our Miss Dilsey is not in a good way. You've spoken with your friend?"

"A few hours ago. All he said was to come. Same thing you said."

"He was pretty upset. He recognized quickly when her seizures were too severe for him to handle and got her here within an hour of the first one, which is far sooner than most people do."

That was good. But why hadn't he stayed? What if, unconscious or not, Dilsey had needed a familiar presence till I showed up? She'd never been alone during a cluster. A twinge of guilt reminded me that Dilsey's situation circled back to me. She was my responsibility, not Henry's, and I'd left her.

"She was in status epilepticus when she arrived. He'd given her one dose of diazepam, but she was seizing nonstop and so violently, he couldn't do more. Wouldn't have made any difference. Quite frankly, as severe as her seizures were, I'm surprised she's still alive."

The room was suddenly sweltering, and I gripped the edge of the exam table to stay upright.

Dilsey and I had been through rough times, but except for the one occasion I'd mentioned to Scottie, she'd always had at least a short break between seizures. In that one instance, Dr. Emerson had pulled her through without a word about Dilsey almost dying. She'd said little, actually. I knew Dilsey *could* die, of course—I'd read about other dogs that had—but they weren't Dilsey, and their owners weren't me. That night, I'd been there to medicate her, to assess when she needed more help than I could provide, and to meet Dr. Emerson at the hospital.

Unlike tonight.

I sopped the sweat from my forehead with my sleeve and backed into the chair.

"Right after she arrived, as we wheeled her to the treatment area, she went into cardiac arrest. We resuscitated her after about six minutes—that's a long time—but as soon as we did, she seized again. We gave her a loading dose of levetiracetam and have her on IV diazepam now. Diazepam depresses respiratory and cardiovascular function, so we're monitoring those, and all her vitals, closely."

He glanced at the clipboard but didn't seem to be reading anything. His voice was quiet. "Honestly, her chances of survival aren't great. Even if she does survive, there's a question of whether she'll have normal brain function. We don't have a way to determine that here."

"I'll take her anywhere."

"I've spoken with your vet. Only rarely do we allow owners in the back, but she assured me you were one of those rare exceptions."

I dreaded seeing Dilsey in the condition I imagined her, but I dreaded not seeing her even more. She needed to know I hadn't abandoned her.

"Once the seizures stopped, she got cold, so we wrapped her in a warming blanket. She's unconscious, and she's connected to various monitors. She's intubated, and we've lowered her head a bit so the fluid in her lungs will continue to drain. She's got IV catheters in two legs. And other emergencies are going on with other pets. Can you handle it?"

My weak "yes" didn't convince even me, so I tried again. "I can handle it."

I followed him into a huge treatment area pungent with disinfectant and animal musk. Counters and sinks and banks of cages, some occupied, lined the walls. Stainless steel tables were scattered around the room. Everyone wore blindingly bright scrubs that failed to mitigate the life-and-death aspects of their jobs.

Dilsey's head poked from a blue blanket at the far end of the room. The gauze strip tied around her upper muzzle secured the endotracheal tube, and her pink tongue dangled out. The monitor displayed her vitals all on one screen, and the beeps, for an instant, threw me back to my own ICU stay. I stopped and gathered myself. The fuchsia-clad vet tech sitting with Dilsey met my gaze, then tinkered with an IV line.

I slipped my hand under the blanket and stroked Dilsey's shoulder. She felt normal, solid and warm. With my other hand, I scratched the special spot behind her ear. She'd always loved that. Even at nine weeks old, the first time I met her, she'd separated herself from her ten littermates and bounced to me as if she recognized me, cocked her head when I rubbed her ear, and pushed her head into my hand. She chose me, but if she hadn't, I'd have chosen her. From that moment, I'd loved Dilsey. I needed her. Why did it take a crisis to make me understand that?

Until Dr. Hollins returned, I hadn't realized he'd left. "Dr. Emerson wants to talk with you. Let's go to the exam room so you can have a little privacy."

Once there, Dr. Hollins punched a number into the receiver of a wall phone and left. Dr. Emerson answered on the first ring.

"I'm so sorry to wake you up at this hour," I said.

"You didn't." She sounded congested. "First, I want to assure you Dilsey's in very good hands. Andy Hollins and I were in vet school together. No one's better in an emergency."

"I wish you were here."

"I don't mean to state the obvious, but Dilsey's situation isn't good."

"I know."

She sniffled. "Talk to me, Philip."

"I don't—" I stopped and cleared my throat. *Tell me how to fix this.* What if there was no fix? No, there had to be. "I don't know what to say."

"How Dilsey's managed to not get to this point sooner is a miracle." She paused. "Not a miracle. It's due entirely to your exemplary care of her."

I should have thanked her, but all I managed was, "It wasn't good enough."

"Some dogs come through pretty well; many don't. We have to worry about adverse effects on numerous body systems, especially in light of the fact she was essentially dead for six minutes. We have to worry about brain function. With an EEG, we'd look at that, but you'd have to go to the vet school."

"I'll take her right now."

"That's not realistic," she said gently. "It's a long drive, and she's unlikely to survive long enough to get there."

I heard what she thought I should do. I did. But I didn't want to hear. "Tell me what to do."

"I won't do that." She blew her nose.

"Dr. Emerson—"

She was full-out crying now, not even trying to disguise it. "If I could be there, I would."

"I know. Thank you. I'll call you." I hung up.

Dilsey was four years old. She had an entire lifetime ahead of her. Years of playing fetch, traipsing with me around Grainger, running full tilt on the quad. Sleeping underneath the footrest of the recliner in my study and years of hanging out in my classes long after anyone remembered the fire. Years of licking my face. Years of preventing me from being entirely alone in my big old house with the huge enclosed yard perfect for a big gamboling dog. Years to age gradually, gracefully, and to die with dignity, even if I had to help her.

If love alone could have protected her, she'd be leaping off the table, pushing open the exam room door, and nudging my hand for an ear scratch. If love could have fixed her, we wouldn't even be at some emergency clinic.

I'd failed her. I should have loved her enough to protect her, to make her well, and yet, I didn't know what I could have done differently.

I opened the door into the treatment area. Across the room, the fuchsia-clad tech rubbed Dilsey's side through the blanket. No. There had to be other options.

But the experts hadn't offered any. How could such educated people be so unimaginative? I mouthed a string of expletives I rarely used, slammed the exam room door, spun and opened the door to the hallway, and slammed it, too, with such force that the puppy poster on the back dropped to the floor.

The experts didn't know *everything*. I needed creative input from someone else and mentally scanned the list of people who might offer it. Definitely not Henry. My mother, Scottie, even Emily, could offer sympathy, but I didn't need their sympathy. Jamie's field was human medicine, not veterinary. And my father's opinion wouldn't have changed since Christmas. There wasn't anyone else. I'd spent a decade making sure of that.

The receptionist stuck her head into the room. "Calm down." She scooped up the poster and ducked out.

This situation wasn't fair. Not to Dilsey. Not to Dr. Emerson. Not to the dedicated, competent people struggling to save her life.

Not to me.

I couldn't repair Dilsey. Not tonight and not ever. My only choice was to love her enough. I collapsed into the chair, and my anger drained to emptiness.

When I opened the door into the treatment area again, the techs and vets looked up, their expressions uniformly sad. They knew, had known even before I arrived. As I approached Dilsey, Dr. Hollins materialized beside me.

"Is there something I need to sign?"

A tech slipped a clipboard and pen onto the table behind Dilsey's head, and I read the document upside down. Someone had already filled in her name and mine and other pertinent information. I spun the clipboard around. *I hereby forever release Dr. Andrew Hollins and the staff . . . for any and all liability . . .* And a check box for what I wanted done with Dilsey afterward. I checked *private cremation with return of remains to owner.* I owed her one final trip home.

Then I scrawled my name, not for one second believing that by disguising the peaks and valleys of my usually neat signature could I claim that someone else had signed her death warrant.

The clipboard disappeared, and a box of pastel tissues replaced it. No bright colors. The tech switched off the monitors that showed proof of life. Dr. Hollins gently unwrapped the gauze tie around Dilsey's muzzle and withdrew the endotracheal tube. Someone rolled a stool to me and when I stared at it, pressed my arm until I sat. I dropped the tissue box to the floor, cradled Dilsey's head in my arms, and rested my forehead against her cheek.

Dr. Hollins stood at Dilsey's hind leg, leaving me alone at her head. In the fat syringe he held, the euthanasia solution, as vibrant pink as Saturday night's bowling ball, was too bright for anyone to mistake for anything other than what it was.

The doctor waited until I nodded.

I shut my eyes, and several seconds later it was over.

I stayed with Dilsey in that room until I finally believed she was gone.

CHAPTER 33

I SHIVERED THROUGHOUT the seemingly endless several-mile drive to Henry's house despite blasting the heat in his little car. His on-street parking space was vacant, and I didn't see my Expedition anywhere. Although he always left lights on whether he was home or away, his house was dark. No exterior floodlights. No interior lighting filtered by shuttered windows. Except for the streetlamps, there was only darkness.

I slipped his Mercedes into its spot and sagged against the seat, trying to muster enough energy not to engage Henry but merely to get out of the car. After ten silent minutes, timed by the car's relentlessly advancing clock, I collected myself and, buffeted by gusts signaling an approaching cold front, trudged along the brick walkway and up the steps to his door. Body hunched against the wind, I turned around and stared at the steps, stared at the street. How had Henry gotten Dilsey outside, down those steps, and into my vehicle? I'd never instructed him to roll her in a blanket, ease her step by step to the ground, and drag her seventy-plus pounds of convulsing energy to where I'd parked when I arrived twelve hours earlier. He'd never asked how I managed. I hadn't thought he'd need to know. She paid for my inattention, my negligence, with her life.

I fumbled for the keyhole, but Henry hadn't locked the door. Nor had he engaged the security system, which I realized when I pushed the door open and no steady beep greeted me. Suddenly, I was uneasy. Maybe someone had broken in. I hovered at the threshold, waiting and listening.

Nothing. No sound. No human silhouettes scuttling among the various hues of darkness. I reached inside, groped for the light switch, and flipped on the outside floodlights and the foyer sconces.

"Turn it off." Three words, slurred together as one, erupted from the living room directly in front of me.

I killed the interiors but not the floodlights. They illuminated the room enough for me to not trip over anything.

At first, I didn't see Henry, because I was scanning the logical places—couch, armchair, even the dining room where I'd left Dilsey panting contentedly. On the second pass, I found him on the floor, head thrown back on the sofa seat, still dressed for the theater but now shoeless and with his stocking feet sticking out from under the coffee table. Along with the usual decorative hurricane lamp, there was a bottle and a mostly full rocks tumbler on the table.

"Henry?"

"Is she dead?"

"Are you drunk?"

He emitted something that might have been a hiccup. "If only."

"I need my keys."

His rushed words urged me out of his house. "They're in the glove box. It's unlocked."

"You left my truck unlocked with the keys inside?" No wonder I hadn't seen it.

"Go."

"Henry—"

"*Get. Out.*" Before I had time to move, he hurled the glass. The tumbler smashed on the foyer tile behind me, and the room instantly reeked of whiskey.

He'd have pitched the entire bottle next if I hadn't dived for it. We wrestled over it until his hand slid off. He crossed his arms on the table and buried his face in them.

I took the nearly empty bottle to the kitchen and chugged the remaining mouthful of whiskey before setting the bottle and his car key on the counter. If he wanted more alcohol, he'd have to get up and raid his liquor cabinet. From the looks of him, moving anywhere anytime soon was unlikely.

Despite being emotionally drained, I was sorry for him. How unnerved he must have been by Dilsey's unrelenting seizures. Although he had the little red tote bag of meds, I'd left him unprepared in every way that mattered. Despite his quick and correct assessment of Dilsey's situation, she died. Did he expect that after he dropped her off? Unlikely. Or perhaps he did, given the tone of our brief phone conversation before I left my parents' house. Did he leave the emergency clinic and not return to meet me there because he couldn't face her dying? Couldn't face me living without her? Neither was reason enough to drink himself into violence. Nothing about Dilsey's death was his fault.

The more I thought about his reaction, the more his dramatics offended me. He had no right to wallow in Dilsey's death. She was *my* dog, and she'd died because *I* hadn't done enough for her.

There was no reason to stay. On the way out, I tossed a dishtowel over the worst of the spilled whiskey, less to absorb the liquid than to remind Henry to put on shoes before shuffling through the glass. I exited the house without bothering to lock the door.

On the stoop, the wind smacked me, and I stopped, unsure whether to turn right or left. But the direction didn't matter. If Henry had parked several streets over, I wouldn't find my truck by circling. You'd find nothing by circling if what you sought wasn't there to begin with. My current options were to wander around the dark, blustery neighborhood at three-something in the morning or return inside and ask him where the hell he'd parked.

A tsunami of regret engulfed me. I should never have stormed from the theater and all the way to Washington. I'd wasted nearly six hours I could've spent with her. Even if Henry and I had stayed for the entire musical, we'd have returned to his house by the time the cluster began. Or I could've collected her and my Expedition from his house and taken her to Washington. Either way, I'd have pumped her full of drugs and perhaps stopped the seizures. Or if I'd ditched the play I hadn't wanted to attend and stayed in Grainger, maybe Dilsey wouldn't have seized at all. I wish I'd figured out what triggered the seizures. I wish I'd found a way to control them. I'd tried so hard. I'd done everything I knew to do, sought the best medical care for her, researched canine epilepsy in depth to improve her quality of life, made decisions without regard to expense or personal inconvenience, and all of it was insufficient and wrong. She was dead, and I wanted to go home.

But I couldn't get home until I figured out where the hell Henry had parked my truck.

I returned inside and sat on the edge of the leather armchair across from him. He hadn't moved, and when he spoke, his voice was muffled. "It's three blocks over, one back. In front of the Starbucks."

"It's not your fault. About Dilsey. It would've happened eventually." As soon as I said the words, I realized I'd sensed for a long time she'd die unexpectedly and young. Realized, too, that I wanted—*needed*—him to understand that her death was not his fault.

"I didn't know they could get so bad so fast. I called you multiple times, but you didn't answer. I thought I did the right thing giving her Valium. I barely waited before taking her . . ."

I stared at the floor and pinched the bridge of my nose. If only I'd brought the phone into my parents' house. "You did exactly the right thing."

"I didn't. Or she'd still be alive. Like she was every time *you* took care of her. My fault. Like Teddy all over again. Totally my fault."

"Teddy?" I leaned forward, clueless as to what he was talking about.

He lifted his head, and the wetness on his cheeks showed even in the dim light.

"Henry, Dilsey has nothing to do with Teddy."

He groped for the absent tumbler. "How the hell would you know? You didn't see what happened." He pounded his fist, rattling the hurricane lamp. "It happened so fast. Yelling and a pop, and it wasn't a shotgun, and Jamie froze, but Teddy"—Henry gulped—"Teddy tried to run out the side door, and I grabbed him, and there was another pop, and a shotgun blast and"—he swept his hand across the table, hurtling the lamp to the carpet—"and he kicked me, not even hard, and I let him go, and he ran out the front door, and he . . . and you . . . and when I got to him, it was too late . . . and he'd still be alive if I . . . but I didn't and he's not and now I . . . I killed Dilsey, too, and . . . and . . ." He dropped his head into his arms and wept.

My anger disintegrated, and I crumpled into the chair, gutted by yet another inconceivable revelation. In our nearly twenty years of friendship, I'd never seen him break, never even suspected he could. At last I understood that his insolence toward Emily, his withholding of information and his misdirection, resulted not from his desire to steer us away from the shooting but from his own inability to face it. Dad was right: not once had I considered the enormous toll the shooting had taken on Henry. He'd held himself together all these years until Emily materialized. That was why he blamed everything on her. She'd forced the memories and feelings to the surface, to be examined and picked at and evaluated. Ashamed, I swallowed the lump in my throat.

And what about Emily? I hadn't yet processed what my father had told me about her uncle and father. *Knowing his misconduct and Henry's emotional state, what should I do now?* I couldn't tell her I'd found the answer she'd sought for so long, could I? Concoct a story she wouldn't believe anyway? Pretend his revelation and Henry's meltdown never happened? Quit without an explanation? No. Her intelligence and fine-tuned intuition would tell her I'd learned something, and she wouldn't let it go until she knew it too.

I smoothed my hands against my pant legs and forced myself not to bolt. Where could I escape? I needed sleep. I needed to tend to Henry. I needed to process Dilsey's death and Dad's secret. Thoughts of Emily had to wait.

I needed to go home.

"Henry?"

When he failed to respond, I reached out, prodded his shoulder. "Go upstairs. Sleep this off."

He didn't budge. Someone should stay with him, make sure he was okay and didn't drink himself into a coma or drive or do something else stupid. I shouldn't leave him in that condition, but I had to get away from here.

Upstairs, from the closet of Henry's bedroom, I grabbed a blanket. I found aspirin in his bathroom cabinet. Back downstairs, I gathered two bottles of water from the refrigerator and Henry's phone from the counter. When I returned to the living room, I righted the hurricane lamp but left it on the floor, then arranged the aspirin and water and phone on the coffee table within his reach. Making one more attempt to rouse him enough to convince him to go to bed or at least to the couch, I shook him none too gently, but he groaned without moving. Not knowing what else to do, I tucked the blanket around him and blinked away the surprise memory of waking to the comforting blanket Scottie had draped over me after what had turned out to be Dilsey's second-to-last cluster.

Before leaving Henry's house, I sopped up the remaining whiskey and swept the glass from the tile foyer. He'd have to deal with the splatters on the living room carpet, but at least he wouldn't cut himself when he sobered enough to stumble into the kitchen. But that might be a while. He remained huddled over the coffee table, his raspy breathing suggesting he'd fallen asleep or had passed out.

I armed his security system and locked the door. My truck was right where he'd said he'd parked it. Once inside, I texted each of my parents to ask them to check on Henry. I couldn't take care of him anymore right then. I needed to find a way to take care of myself.

CHAPTER 34

I ROLLED INTO my driveway about the time that, according to the clock on the display panel, I'd usually be waking. I wasn't sleepy, I was exhausted, and class started in a few hours. I'd show up, of course. Life continued.

Even when everything's changed, a part of you that rebuffs the truth prods you into your routine, and so I raised the hatch to let Dilsey out and stared, shocked, into her empty crate with the full water bucket. The ducky crib bumpers edged the soft bedding she'd trampled into her last nest. She'd have made her final ride, the one to the emergency clinic, in the space beside the crate or in the back seat. No way could Henry have stuffed her, seizing, into her crate. I couldn't have either.

I twined my fingers through the wire on both sides of the crate and yanked. It needed to come out *right now*. Water sloshed over my right hand, and I opened the crate door, unclipped the bucket, and flung it into the yard.

Dilsey was still dead. She'd always be dead.

I realized I couldn't deal with the crate now and shoved it back into its spot, banging on the hatch to lower it. It resisted twice. Not until I smashed the auto-close button did the hatch inch downward.

Next thing was to go inside, shower, and shave so I'd be at least physically presentable for my students, then fix Dilsey's breakfast and mine. No, not Dilsey's. *Shit.*

The wind carrying the cold front bit into me. I lumbered along the walkway, up the steps and onto the front porch, and pressed my key into the deadbolt. But turning the key meant I had to confront my empty oversized house, and so I didn't. I couldn't bear to step over Dilsey's scattered toys or see her ghostly imprint on the cushions in the kitchen and my bedroom, couldn't imagine discarding the home-made food she'd never eat. All those physical things proved she'd existed. All those physical things emphasized that she was gone.

I envisioned myself driving west until blocked by the Pacific, where I would push a button to sprout wings on my Expedition and continue onward forever. But no matter how far I drove or for how long, unless I levitated into orbit, I'd loop back. One big empty circle, and everything would be the same as when I'd left.

Dilsey was gone. My father, by sharing the secret of his misconduct, had simultaneously drawn me to him and thrust me farther away. And not just farther from him but from my mother, as well, because she didn't know what he'd done and should never know. And I'd detached myself from Jamie.

Anger erupted through my exhaustion and sadness. Dad's disclosure ended my search—*our* search—for the reason Emily's father had attacked us. It had been revenge, as simple as that.

The dilemma I'd faced at Henry's confounded me again. I could bow out without telling Emily why. I could tell her the truth without revealing Dad's indiscretion. Or should I tell her what he'd done? What would the short- and long-term consequences be for Dad, for my family, for me? For Emily? Who could I ask for advice? Adrian Wells would be the most familiar with the legal ramifications, but he'd have to act on anything I told him. And shouldn't I want him to?

I pocketed my keys and returned to my truck. Pushing the seat back as far as it would go, I closed my eyes, unsure about what to do next or where to go and unnerved by an unfamiliar yearning for someone to talk with.

I live five minutes away, and I'm a really good listener. My address is in the Grainger directory.

Scottie.

I didn't yearn for someone to talk with. I wanted Scottie.

Her Kia Soul occupied most of the driveway, so I parked on the street. No interior lights shone from her half of the duplex or from the other half either. Why would they at that hour?

After shutting the door as quietly as possible, I crossed the tiny yard. My hand lingered just shy of the doorbell. Why was I there? Scottie couldn't fix anything. But I remembered the comfort of her presence when I woke up on the kitchen floor the morning after Dilsey's cluster. I rang the bell before I changed my mind.

For a moment, nothing happened. Then a light flicked on inside, and almost immediately the lights bracketing the door illuminated the front yard. Not until she opened the door did it occur to me she might not be alone. Once again, I hadn't considered anyone else, hadn't thought about her personal life, what she did on her off time. I backed off the stoop.

The lock clicked, and when she pushed open the glass storm door, I stepped backward again.

"Sorry." Heat rose into my face. "Bad idea. Sorry. I—"

In sweats and bare feet, she stood in the doorway. "Philip? Do you know what time it is? What the hell?" She covered her mouth. "Dilsey?"

I nodded. Without another word, she closed the distance between us and threw her arms around me. I stuffed my hands into my pockets, battling the urge to flee.

She pulled away and wiped her face with her sleeve, and when she took my hand, I let her lead me inside. On a love seat, she squished in beside me and tucked her legs under her, still holding my hand.

"Tell me what happened," she said softly.

The only light spilled in from a hallway or kitchen—I couldn't tell which—but it was too bright. "I guess I wanted to . . . I didn't know who else . . ."

She wrapped her free arm around me. We sat leaning against each other, our contact awkward and yet not. I lost all sense of time.

Eventually, I said, "I knew she wouldn't live to be an old dog, and yet I didn't believe it. If I'd taken good enough care of her . . ."

"You took the best care of her."

I wanted to tell her I hadn't, that I'd failed Dilsey, but the revolving images of my blanket-wrapped dog on the stainless steel table, Henry heaving the full tumbler at me, and Dad uncovering his tear-streaked cheeks blurred into a nightmare for which I found no words.

My chest tightened, and Scottie shifted slightly, drawing us closer. "Some losses might be one too many. Maybe one of the campus counselors . . ."

I jerked from her embrace, but she clamped down on my hand, refusing to let me disengage. Aghast at her suggestion, I snapped, "You think a stranger can fix this—fix *me*—by telling me how to feel? You think I'd give them the opportunity when I'm perfectly capable of working things out on my own?"

Scottie breathed in and out, in and out, then released my hand. "I'll fix breakfast."

I wasn't hungry but didn't have the energy to say so. I rested my head against the back of the love seat, angry with her for mentioning counseling and furious at myself for dismissing it so rudely, not because I'd consider it but because she was only trying to help. After all, I'd sought *her* out. When I shut my eyes, listening to the clang of bowls and utensils and the opening and unnecessarily loud closing of cupboard doors—inhaling the aroma of coffee I desperately needed—I melted into the cushions, dozing until I forced myself off the love seat and into the kitchen.

She'd organized her ingredients on a small wedge of counter to the right of the sink. Eggs, homemade bread, spices, milk, bacon. She was making French toast, a treat I hadn't enjoyed in ages. Coffee percolated in a real coffee pot on the other side of the sink. She didn't acknowledge I'd walked up behind her.

"I didn't mean it the way it came out."

She responded by cracking a couple of eggs, then picked shell slivers from the bowl.

"Scottie." I placed my hands on her shoulders, and they stiffened. "Cooking breakfast won't fix anything either."

"You think I don't know that? At least cooking and baking distract me and give me a way to maybe comfort other people. And help *me* feel a little better about all the sadness and hurt I can't fix. It's better than doing nothing. What's wrong with that?"

I dropped my hands, sorry for denigrating a simple act of kindness in which she found and gave solace. "Nothing."

When she turned around, we were in each other's space, and I backed up.

She said, "Don't be so critical of what helps other people cope. Maybe *you* should try cooking. Or, yes, counseling. *Anything* that will ease the pain you've so clearly been ignoring."

"I'm not ignoring anything."

"Of course you are." She brushed past me. "I'll finish breakfast after I get dressed."

I couldn't let her accusation go. I didn't want her pitying me or thinking I couldn't manage Dilsey's death in my own way. Just as I'd managed Teddy's. I called her name just before she disappeared around the corner. "I've got this. I don't need anyone telling me how to feel."

Midstride, she whirled. "*Someone* needs to tell you. Not how to feel but that it's okay to feel at all."

Then she was gone. A few seconds later, I heard the waterfall rush of a shower.

She had no right to say that. I didn't expect her to understand—how could she? I snatched up the whisk and whipped the shit out of the eggs. Into the stainless bowl, I flung cinnamon and nutmeg and clove and salt without measuring them. I splashed in some milk and pummeled the mixture again. My right shoulder and arm and hand tingled. *Good.*

At that very moment, I suspected for the first time the reason I'd refused every painkiller prescribed during the surgeries and rehab of my shoulder, a body part so resistant to healing and susceptible to pain. I'd wanted to feel *something.* I'd managed my loss of Teddy and in its wake the loss of the rest of my family by making physical anguish a surrogate for the emotions I'd blocked. The physical pain gave me something tangible to hang on to. And it only took obliterating French toast batter to figure that out. I stared at the whisk and the eggs, feeling the wholly inappropriate urge to laugh. Maybe Scottie was right about cooking.

Suddenly, I was listening to silence; Scottie had finished showering. I wet a few paper towels and wiped away the yellow goo that had sloshed over the side of the bowl and created a sticky mess on the counter. In the refrigerator, I found a quart of orange juice and in a cabinet, a juice glass the same bright blue as Scottie's car. When she came back, she'd see me calmly sitting at her little table alternating between sipping the juice and rotating the glass.

She returned smelling soapy, fresh, and wearing jeans, a pullover sweater, and a towel wrapped around her hair. She peered into the egg mixture she never should've left unattended and wrinkled her nose. "Maybe I should redo this."

"I'm sorry, Scottie. You're right—about everything."

I talked then, unable to stop, juxtaposing all the events of the past few months into one disjointed monologue. I told her about the theater tickets Henry and I had and how much Dilsey loved strolling around Henry's neighborhood, and about her favorite spot under his dining room table where I left her, even though I'd always worried she'd hurt herself there if she seized while we were out, though, until last night, she never had. I explained my argument with Henry, which forced me to summarize my relationship with Emily— how I knew her and what our "genealogy project" actually was. I told her I'd gotten pissed at Henry and my father and had ditched Henry and driven to Washington to confront my father over issues related to Emily and the shooting and while there had received shocking news—though I didn't provide details and Scottie didn't ask—and that Henry's frantic call had interrupted us. I explained what I'd found at the emergency clinic and what I'd done, and how I'd found Henry when I returned to his house and how he'd linked Dilsey's death with Teddy's for reasons that made no sense. I admitted my inability to face the emptiness of my big house without Dilsey, and so had come to her.

She listened without interruption until I finished, thoroughly drained, and slumped back in the chair.

"You didn't have a choice, did you?"

"About Dilsey?"

"About any of it."

I spun my glass, almost overturning it. "We always have choices."

"But sometimes they're all bad choices."

I sipped the juice and thought about the choices my father had made and the choices I'd made in response over the years and tonight. All bad choices, made mostly for good reasons or for reasons that seemed good at the time. But how did you ever *really* know what was good or right? With an uncomfortable twinge of empathy, I thought of Vince, a man who made a terrible choice out of loyalty and perhaps even love—both good reasons—for a brother who didn't deserve either, at the cost of a daughter who had deserved both.

I didn't have the energy to think about Dad or Vince now, and pushed them from my mind. "I have to go. My first class starts in forty minutes."

"Trish canceled your classes."

I glared at her. "When? Why?"

"I called her." She placed her hands on her hips. "Have you considered that your teaching today would suck? Plus, when your students hear about Dilsey, they'll be devastated."

I hadn't considered my students at all, and she read my expression.

"Just as I suspected. Now, tell me about Teddy."

I plopped back into my chair and rested my forehead on my hands. We didn't talk while she fried the bacon and browned the French toast and set our plates, utensils, and mugs of steaming coffee on the table. I straightened when she sat across from me.

"Eat," she said. "You look like hell."

I sliced the French toast and rearranged it on my plate before drowning it with syrup in a way Emily would have appreciated. After my third bite, Scottie repeated, "Tell me about your little brother. Tell me about Teddy."

I laid my fork on the plate, but at her scowl, picked it up again. "No one's ever asked me to do that." Because those of us who'd loved Teddy never talked about him and no one else dared to ask. Or didn't know to ask, I reminded myself.

I remembered how I'd craved opening up to Kim and Alex—two people far less familiar to me than Scottie—because I trusted them. I trusted Scottie too. If nothing else, she'd proven herself the night Dilsey clustered. Honoring Teddy by sharing him with her might be part of the miracle Kim Warner had mentioned. For the first time in years, I pictured him clearly, mostly his gentle smile that didn't brighten a room as much as warm it. The memory of him warmed me all the way through.

"He always chewed on the nail of his right pinkie while noodling out solutions to problems and puzzles. When he was eight or so, he built a castle of books—fat and thin, hardback and paperback—so intricately balanced that my mother proclaimed he'd be the structural engineer of the family. Another time, when one of our pointers had a litter, he sat through the entire six-hour, nine-puppy delivery. My father and I showed him how to break open the sacs. 'It's like magic, like Christmas,' he'd said, awed. 'Little presents wrapped the same but different when you open them.' The wonder of the puppy packages amazed him, and the slime and blood didn't bother him one bit."

I grinned, thinking about Jamie.

She smiled too. "What?"

"My other brother, Jamie, the one in med school? He's the one with the weak stomach."

"That's not good." She bit into a bacon strip and chewed. "What else?"

"Teddy had a pony, and some nights he'd sneak to the barn to sleep with him. The summer before he . . . When he was ten, Dad and I found his first big horse, his only big . . ." I faltered, and from across the table, Scottie rested her hand on mine. "Huckleberry. They were as inseparable as a boy and his horse could be. The day before we headed back to college, Henry dared Teddy to ride Huckleberry into the house. Teddy was afraid of getting in trouble, but he didn't want Henry to think he was a coward. He rode Huckleberry up the steps and across the back porch and through the door but no farther, because my mother had figured out what was up and was waiting for him."

"Oh gosh. What did she do?"

"She laughed and offered Huckleberry the apple in her hand."

Suddenly, we were both laughing.

Scottie smiled. "I'd have liked him, your Teddy. Your mother too."

"And he'd have liked you. And my mother would—" I faltered and downed the rest of my juice. Mom would love her, in fact, for her kindness and easy manner and generous spirit, all the reasons—in addition to her baking skills—the students and everyone else at Grainger loved her. Not that I imagined Scottie ever meeting anyone in my family. Except Henry, whom she'd already met.

Henry. Concern about him, coupled with the multifaceted anguish of the past twelve hours, crushed me. I stood. "I need to get home."

Then I remembered why I'd come. Scottie's unwavering gaze told me she remembered too and that she still questioned whether I could, or should, face my empty house alone.

I stacked her plate on mine, utensils on top, and carried them to the sink. She joined me there with the serving dishes and coffee mugs.

"I'll go with you." She tapped the towel still wrapped around her head. "Just need to deal with this."

"No need. I'm ˏokay." That time, though, the words rang hollow. I bowed my head. "Actually . . . I'd like that. Thank you."

By the time she returned to the kitchen, I'd washed, dried, and put away our breakfast dishes. She followed me home, through the gate I'd neglected to close a few hours earlier, and parked her Soul alongside my Expedition. In a flash, she appeared at my window.

"How do you want to do this?"

"I . . . could you . . ." I thrust at her the carabiner that held the keys to my house and everything else. "Just put her stuff in trash bags or boxes, whatever you can find, so I don't have to look at it. Please."

She squinted but didn't take the keys. "You're sure that's what you want?"

"Positive." I shook them a little.

"If there's anything you don't want me to touch . . ."

"There's not." I excused my pang of guilt for expecting something of her I didn't expect of myself. "Thank you."

Without another word, she reached for the keys. She detoured to the water bucket I'd pitched into the yard a few hours earlier, and when she reached the steps, she looked back. I pretended not to notice.

It might take her a while to box Dilsey's toys and bowls and beds and stash them in a closet. After she finished, I'd ask her to empty the chest freezer of the special meals I'd prepared for Dilsey and deliver them to the county animal shelter or to the outside trashcan. I didn't care which. Maybe she wouldn't mind collapsing Dilsey's crate and hauling it from my truck to the basement and discarding the crib bumpers into a trash bag. Perhaps she'd even be willing to return Dilsey's remaining epilepsy meds to Dr. Emerson for donation to a client unable to afford them. After Scottie left, I'd vacuum the dog hair Dilsey had shed yesterday, and the last physical traces of my dog would have vanished.

My phone interrupted my circling thoughts. Jamie.

"I need the code to Henry's security system." His voice was tight. "Mom and Dad couldn't raise him this morning. They asked me to check on him, and he's not answering his phone or the door."

In his tone I heard *I can't believe you left him*. Or was that accusation only my own conscience?

I recited the code and listened anxiously to the door open, the steady beeping, the disconcerting silence while Jamie disarmed the system, grateful he'd stayed connected. *I'm sorry, Henry.*

"Okay, I'm in," Jamie said. "I'll call you back."

Through the windshield, the shadows of the hardwoods' bare branches trembled on the dead lawn. I left my window open so the cold wind would keep me awake. I'd sleep later, after Scottie left.

When my phone jolted me awake, only a few minutes later according to the dashboard clock, Jamie said, "Henry's basically okay. *Very* hungover and babbling something nonsensical about Dilsey and Teddy. It'll blow over when he's feeling better. Got him to call in sick. I'll stay till tomorrow morning, get him hydrated, fed, all that."

"Thank you, Jamie."

"I'm sorry about Dilsey. Are you okay?"

I was. I had to be. "Yeah."

We signed off, and I settled into my seat, grateful to Jamie. Grateful to Scottie too. I pictured her disposing of Dilsey's balls, stuffed animals, squeaky toys, well-chewed beef knucklebones, and the oval clay planter we used as a toy box. When she tossed in the floppy pink elephant, it would trumpet, and she'd remember Dilsey shaking it with abandon as we indulged in bread pudding before her seizure cluster.

Knowing I'd never have to see the elephant again or hear its ridiculous noise should've comforted me. What good would come from having to step over it or see it or any of Dilsey's stuff lying around? Everything that belonged to her, everything she loved, was now irrelevant.

No, no, no, something inside me screamed. Nothing was irrelevant unless you made it so, as my parents had done for Teddy however unintentionally. I'd resented them for that, and now I was replicating their mistake.

I couldn't dishonor Dilsey that way. She deserved my sadness, and if the mementos of her life twisted the knife of grief deep into my core, so be it; I deserved the visceral pain her absence left in my house and in my heart.

I strode up the walk, across the porch, and into the house, intent on stopping Scottie. On the kitchen table, she'd stacked two piles of Dilsey's towels and several coiled leashes. Dilsey's bed lay undisturbed in its corner, but the toys that usually cluttered it were gone. At the sink, she was drying a stainless food bowl, and two others drained on a dishtowel.

She didn't seem at all surprised to see me.

"This is hard," she said.

"I changed my mind."

She smiled. "I figured you might."

I carried the towels to their shelf in the mudroom as she continued drying the bowls. From the planter on the floor below the shelf, I rescued the elephant, a bone, and a ball. Not her favorite tennis ball, which remained at Henry's, but a spare one. Back in the kitchen, I nestled them into the depressed center of her cushion, resolved to leave them there for as long as it took to replace my heartache with a smile.

CHAPTER 35

A SHORT WHILE later, as Scottie and I sat at the table finishing the coffee she insisted we both needed, but which I suspected was a tactic to delay her departure, the doorbell rang.

"See what happens when you don't lock your gate?" Scottie grinned. "People visit you."

I opened the door to Nicole and Kate from my eight o'clock class. An enormous bamboo basket overflowing with bright wildflowers almost obscured Nicole. Saying they burst into tears at the sight of me would be a cliché, but that was exactly what happened.

I froze.

Scottie exclaimed from behind me, "How beautiful!" She nudged me from the doorway and invited the girls into my house.

"No, thank you." Kate thrust an oversized manila envelope at me. "We, all your students, we want to tell you how sorry . . . how much we love Dilsey."

I swallowed hard and unclasped the envelope. Inside, on a sheet of cardstock, handwritten notes from what seemed to be all my students filled one side. On the other, a high-resolution photo of Dilsey stretched airborne against the backdrop of an intact Carter Hall, ball in her mouth, ears flying, intent on reaching something across the quad. I remembered the August day the students arrived for the fall semester. One of them must have snapped it.

The something Dilsey had streaked toward had been me.

How had a group of students who frequently begged for deadline extensions managed to get this all together before 11 a.m.?

"Thank you." I handed the photo to Scottie and accepted the basket from Nicole, relieved when she and Kate declined *my* invitation to come in. "I'll see you tomorrow."

Kate shook her head. "Dr. Glover canceled your classes for the rest of the week. We'll see you after spring break."

"She can't do that." The words slipped out.

"She can, and she did," Scottie said. "It's just a few extra days. And the students certainly won't complain."

Trish worries about you, she'd told me the night of Dilsey's cluster. I'd wavered then between anger and gratitude. Now, despite the initial surprise, I appreciated Trish's thoughtfulness. I smiled weakly at my students. "Gives me extra time to mess with your midterm grades."

They laughed a little, told me to take care of myself, and left. I set the wildflowers on the kitchen table where twelve days ago Scottie had placed daffodils. They at once brightened the room and deepened the shadow of Dilsey's absence. If Dilsey were there, she'd rear against me and lick my cheek, and I'd know better than to push her away this time.

"I love your students." Scottie laid the envelope beside the flowers. "If you're really okay for a while, I'll go to the office. Get some sleep. I'll check in on you." She startled me with a quick hug, tight and genuine and not too long. "I'll see myself out."

I followed her to the front door. "Scottie? Thanks for . . . being here." The words were trite but sincere.

She squeezed my arm, and when she closed the door, I trudged upstairs to shower and nap. I'd never lived in the house without Dilsey, and as I prepared to do those mundane tasks, I became acutely aware of her absence. Everywhere I went, she'd gone too, always shadowing me, even into the bathroom, peering through the steamy glass door of the shower stall, often snatching my towel off the rack and presenting it when I slid the door open.

I'd finished undressing when my doorbell rang again. Assuming Scottie had forgotten something or reconsidered leaving me unattended, I threw on a sweatshirt and jeans, and trotted downstairs barefoot.

On my porch, Emily was wiping her eyes with the back of her hand. "Scottie just told me about Dilsey. I'm so sorry."

I stared at her, blank about what might have prompted her to drive all the way to Grainger. "Hi."

"Can I come in?"

I ushered her to a chair in the living room and collapsed on the couch. Had she discovered more facts about Vince or Mel or my father that were significant enough to compel her to report in person? Had she learned about Dad's destruction of her father's answering machine? I wouldn't have minded not having to decide whether to tell her about it, though the ramifications of her knowing made me uneasy.

She gripped the chair arms. "I know it's a bad time, but I want you to take me to Tennessee."

So that was why she was there. I squeezed my eyes shut. "No. I already told you–"

"Hear me out." She rushed on. "We hit dead ends with Henry and the subpoena thing. Then Mr. Bowling told us about Uncle Mel, and we found out your father defended him, but then that prosecutor guy claimed to have no details. For a moment, I thought we were close, and then nothing. We still need to file a request with the FBI, which maybe won't lead anywhere either, or even if it does, it'll take a while. But if we go to Tennessee, we can find someone to talk to, like the caretaker, or the people in the office you sent the subpoena request to. Or the police. *Someone.*"

"No." What I couldn't tell her without revealing Dad's misconduct—and I didn't know whether I would—was that our search was over. I now knew why her father had attacked mine.

But she did not.

"My timing's bad, with Dilsey and all, but I didn't know about her when I left home, and it's not the first time I've asked. I haven't bugged you because I get how hard it'll be for you to go back, but I need you to appreciate how hard it is for me to never go at all. If I can picture where it happened . . ."

"Go with Alex and Kim or one of your friends."

"You're the only person who'd understand. Besides, you've still never told me exactly where the place is."

I had a flash of inspiration. "It's probably a subdivision now." In all our years of silence, I'd never considered asking Henry what had become of the property or whether he or Dad had ever returned. "It's a long drive to find out."

"Two words: Google Earth."

"I have things to do here."

"Scottie said your classes are canceled this week and that spring break starts after that."

"I haven't slept in over thirty hours. I can't drive anywhere."

She sensed me weakening and leaned forward. "*I'll* drive. You sleep. If we leave now, we'll be back tonight."

"It's too far." Despite myself, and hoping the area *had* been developed, I called up Google Maps on my phone and typed the address of the hunting property. No image-capture date displayed, but the satellite view showed the same lush fields and dense hardwoods I remembered. Foliage hid the cabin, but a corner of the kennel poking from a small clearing suggested nothing much had changed.

Emily leaned across the couch and tilted my phone toward her face, tugging it from my hand when I resisted. I'd just given away the address.

"See? No subdivision." Her mouth twitched, and I waited for her to cry. The satellite image was the closest she'd ever gotten to where her father had died. "We can do this. And after that, next week, we send a request to the FBI and you research private investigators like you promised."

I sagged deeper into the couch. I'd forgotten Emily didn't know we no longer needed a private investigator. We needed *not* to hire one.

"Please, Philip."

Overwhelmed, I grappled with whether I had the strength to do this thing for her. She'd first asked at our McDonald's meeting, before I fully understood her intent and determination and the extent of the courage she'd mustered to ask for help from a stranger who had every reason to deny her. How extraordinary, I now realized, that her capacity, and my inability, to seek support for resolving our questions had culminated in this moment. How could I now refuse to help a young woman I'd come to admire and care about? Besides, if I were honest with myself, I'd have to admit that guiding her to the site of the shooting would help assuage my guilt for the likelihood that I'd keep the relationship between Mel, Vince, and Dad to myself. At the very least, accompanying her should cushion the inevitable gut punch she'd be hit with if I ultimately revealed that relationship. It also would buy time to figure out whether—or what—to tell her.

If she could bravely step into the frightful unknown, I could certainly face the frightful known.

And with my house so empty and quiet because Dilsey was gone, and with my classes canceled, I had nothing to keep me home.

I reclaimed my phone and stood. "Okay, I'll go."

She sprang off the chair. "Really?"

"Really. It's a nine-hour drive, so we'll need to spend the night in the area and visit tomorrow. You prepared for that?"

"You know I am. Suitcase is in the trunk."

Of course it was. "Give me an hour to clean up and pack." I sent her to the kitchen to make herself lunch and had reached the top of the stairs when she called to me. I stood unmoving.

"Hey, did you hear me? I asked if we should tell them we're coming."

I couldn't stomach anyone knowing I planned to visit the place. My father's friends, who owned the property—or had ten years ago—lived elsewhere, and to track down the number of the caretaker, assuming he still worked there, would alert too many people in my father's network of spies and, I was certain, he himself. I hoped no one would be there.

"No need." I shut the door to my bedroom. They'd find out soon enough.

CHAPTER 36

WE SPENT THE night in a motel an hour from the property, and when we met for breakfast, Emily devoured her syrup-drenched food and marked time with her foot against the table leg to every song streaming from the speakers. But as she drove through the cold rain, the closer we got to the property, the more she fidgeted. A mile out, she began repeatedly rearranging her ponytail with one hand. When we arrived at the gravel drive to the cabin, she passed it without braking. When I tapped the GPS on her dashboard, she batted my hand away.

"I'm not ready. I thought I was, but I'm not." She snapped at me as if I'd pressured her into being there and not the other way around.

But I understood and shifted in my seat to offer encouragement. Or permission to reconsider. "It's fine if you want to go home," I said, willing to let her think our leaving would be for her benefit alone.

She clenched her jaw and gripped the steering wheel as though it were a life preserver, then braked hard. "All these years I've pictured it—the way the land rolled, the trees, the house. Over the past few years, I've driven all over this county thinking *Did Daddy drive on this road? Am I close? Is this where he died?* I googled the weather for that day and wondered, *Did Daddy dress warm enough?* I thought if I saw what he saw and felt what he felt and breathed the air he breathed, I might understand. And now I'm so close and I see it's not anything like I imagined, and I won't ever understand. What if I learn more things about Daddy I don't want to know? What if everything I knew about him was wrong? What if finding out pushes us further apart? That's crazy, though, isn't it?"

"It's not crazy." It was sad. Touching, in a poetic way. I wondered whether she'd planned for the moments and then the years after this one. When the ordeal was over and questions and events from the past stopped consuming her, I wondered what goal she'd have for the rest of her life. "This whole search is how you tried to make sense of something implausible. Nothing crazy about that."

"I didn't think the place would be so remote." She frowned and waved her hand around. "How'd Daddy even find y'all out here?"

"He followed my father and brothers from the farm."

"Isn't that something like three hundred miles?" She pursed her lips and peered beyond the windshield. "I asked you once how everything happened. You said you didn't remember. Was that really true?"

I lowered my window for the air my lungs suddenly couldn't find and stuck my elbow on the wet sill. I knew she'd ask again. But I *didn't* remember, not the specifics. "Yes."

For ten minutes, we sat in silence, the rub of the wipers against the windshield and the drip-drip-drip from trees keeping us company. Finally, I asked, "What do you want to do?"

"You'll walk around with me?"

I had to, I reminded myself, as consolation for what I had to conceal. "I will."

She made a U-turn, and when we reached the "Private Property–No Trespassing" sign I'd failed to notice earlier, she turned into the drive and stopped. We stared at each other and simultaneously inhaled.

"Let's do it," I said.

Emily's Focus crept through the lanky pines and budding hardwoods to the cabin. We rounded the last curve, and she stopped.

The exterior hadn't changed in ten years: a nondescript, one-story, L-shaped log house with a stone foundation and, at least back then, unexpectedly plush interior amenities invisible from outside. An open porch along the front became a screened porch along the short side of the L, facing the outbuildings where they'd stored tractors and a couple of off-road utility vehicles. From the furious barking that greeted us, I knew that one outbuilding was still the kennel. I raised my window, wiped off the wet door with the sleeve of my jacket, and now chilled, folded my arms across my chest.

The rain slackened to a heavy drizzle.

Emily glided forward and parked alongside an old four-door pick-up truck muddied to fender level and streaked with pollen and rain. I remembered that the truck belonged to the property's caretaker, Mr. Driscoll, a man a little older than my father. He and his wife had lived in a house on the far northern edge of the property.

Emily and I opened our doors. She stepped into the drizzle. I waited for a wave of nausea to subside. The kenneled dogs continued to bark.

"The dogs kept me awake all night again," Jamie whined as he sloshed milk into his Cheerios.

"Anyone else want eggs?" Henry asked.

"Not all night," Teddy said around a mouthful of the Cocoa Puffs he ate nearly every morning. Just beyond his glass of orange juice, Treasure Island lay on the weathered oak table. "You were snoring, so you were sleeping. Same for Friday night. Don't exaggerate."

"I'm not ex—"

"Boys." Dad stretched out the word, a warning.

I flashed Teddy a thumbs-up. The dogs had been uncharacteristically restless. Two of the six were new this year, though, and most likely they'd altered the pack dynamics. Or perhaps deer or raccoons had ventured closer than usual the past two nights.

Dad and I zipped ourselves into our orange vests, which we'd already stocked with ammunition, settled our ball caps on our heads, and removed our shotguns from the wall rack. Once it got light enough to shoot, we'd already be afield with the two dogs we'd chosen for today's hunt.

Emily came around to my door. "You okay?"

I dragged myself from the car. At least the season was different—spring—and the trees were greening and blooming, not blazing the bright autumn colors of death. The air, though cold, was heavy, not brisk and invigorating as it had been that day. *Get a hold of yourself.*

"Yeah, fine."

Emily pivoted, assessing the cabin, the woods, the outbuildings. "It's so beautiful here. So peaceful. You'd never expect anything bad to happen."

I trailed her while she ambled around the cabin, her head swiveling as she took in everything. Something about the cabin's appearance differed from my last visit, but I couldn't pinpoint what. In the kennel, the dogs clamored. We wouldn't be alone for long. I shook the tension from my arms.

Distant but shrill, a whistle silenced the dogs. Someone *was* around.

"What was that?" Emily asked.

I stopped alongside her. "A whistle."

"I know *that*. What's it mean?"

At a pop muffled by the humidity and foliage, we both jumped, and Emily clutched my arm. "Was that a gun?"

Until the shooting, I'd been around guns my entire life, and never before had the sound of one flung my heart into my throat. "A starter pistol. Uses blanks." I crammed my hands into my pockets to prevent her from noticing their trembling. "He must be out training dogs."

Emily clung to me for another moment. By unspoken consent, we retreated to the car and leaned on the hood. After a few moments, she asked, "Now what?"

A stocky man in boots, jeans, and a tan field vest over an orange rain jacket emerged from the trees along the path leading to the kennel. Mr. Driscoll. His pistol was holstered, and two drenched black and white pointer puppies trotted beside him.

"Private property," he called.

Emily strode forward. I didn't budge.

"We wanted to look around because–"

The puppies bounded to her. It hurt to see them, vivacious and so full of promise, as Dilsey had been not so long ago, and I averted my eyes.

Emily ruffled their ears, then motioned toward me. "He used to hunt here."

Driscoll made eye contact with me and frowned, trying to place me. I closed the distance between us and held out my hand. "You probably don't remember. I'm Philip Rutledge. My father—"

"I remember." His grip on my hand was so strong, I flinched. "Your father's good?"

"Yes, sir." One puppy left Emily and curved himself around my legs. He was three months old or so, already learning his job but still all puppy. I couldn't bear to pat him.

I drew Emily up beside me. "This is my friend, Emily. She, we—" I suddenly realized I hadn't planned how we'd explain our presence.

Emily squared her shoulders and lifted her chin. "We're here because of me. On November 20, 2005, my father shot . . . and got shot and died and . . . I needed to see where it happened."

Despite the waver in her voice, her directness unnerved me.

Apparently, it unnerved Driscoll, too, because he stared at her. "He had a little girl and he did that?"

Neither Emily nor I responded. If I couldn't understand, knowing what I knew about Mel and Vince, how could anyone who didn't know?

"Incredible." Driscoll shook his head. "Look around, then." He called the puppies and traipsed toward the kennel.

"Will you walk me through it?"

Driscoll spun. "*What?*" he and I asked together.

"Show me where Daddy came from, where everyone was. Explain how it happened?"

"You want a play-by-play?" My entire body tingled.

"I wouldn't put it that way. It's just that nothing makes sense. Like, how did he get in here in the first place? If he drove in, you'd have heard his car and the dogs barking. Dogs were here back then too, right?"

Driscoll motioned toward the gravel drive. "He stashed his car in the woods across the road and walked in, probably in the middle of the night. The police thought he also made a dry run Friday night."

I shuddered. I hadn't known that.

"And the dogs *did* bark. Both nights, I came to see what was bothering them. We had a couple new ones who tended to bark at everything. Also, lots of wildlife around. When I didn't see anything, I went on home."

Just before 6 a.m., with barely enough navigable twilight, Dad and I left the cabin, our unloaded shotguns broken open over our right shoulders. He stepped off the side porch and angled toward the kennel. I shut the door and joined him. In their runs, the dogs yammered.

"They're wound up," Dad said.

They sounded uncharacteristically eager, frantic even, but I wasn't familiar with the nuances of their behavior.

Emily walked to the front of the cabin, then along the side to where Driscoll and I stood . . . and where Vince had ambushed me and my father. "Where was he? In the trees? Behind one of the buildings? There's nowhere around the house to hide."

I glanced at the cabin's wall, then turned quickly away, unsettled by the realization of what was different. Low azaleas, not yet blooming, had replaced the overgrown privet around the cabin. "He hid in the bushes that used to surround it."

"Hang on a sec, Dad." I bent to tie my boot, bracing my shotgun between my head and my shoulder. He waited a couple of steps ahead.

"Hey!" a man yelled.

I was startled and grabbed my gun to keep it from falling. Who'd be out at that hour? Who'd be out here at all? Mr. Driscoll, maybe, but that wasn't his voice. I scanned the area but didn't see anyone.

"Remember me, Senator?" The male voice was loud but trembling. Scared.

I still didn't see anyone.

Almost simultaneously, I saw a flash and heard a loud snap. Dad grunted. He was standing in front of me, and then he wasn't.

"Drop the gun, kid."

A second snap sounded and something smacked the door of the porch behind me. He was shooting.

Jamie, Teddy, and Henry were inside.

"Don't!" I yelled.

Another shot. Embedded in the wall of the cabin that time.

"Drop it!"

Physically and mentally paralyzed, I couldn't react.

I saw him then—medium-size silhouette, bulky in a coat, barely discernable in the shadows. Eight, ten feet from me. A yard or so to the side of the overgrowth by the cabin's foundation. Both arms extended. Handgun aimed at Dad.

I forced my gaze away from the spot where Vince had materialized from the privet. Despite the cold, sweat trickled down my face and between my shoulder blades.

Driscoll was speaking. Had been for a few moments. "I was in the kennel when he started shooting. Those shots didn't come from no shotgun, and I knew y'all didn't have nothing else. I grabbed my revolver and ran out."

I fumbled at the loops on my vest and pulled off two shells. I loaded both and wedged the gun under my armpit. I'd never shot that way. Had never aimed at anything I didn't intend to kill.

"Don't do it!" he shouted.

I hesitated.

One blast. Or two close together—I wasn't sure. Even before I knew he'd shot me, even before I realized my own weapon had discharged, I was on the ground feeling nothing but surprise. The silhouette had disappeared.

Had I hit him?

My ears rang. *Stop thinking. Stop.*

"The senator was on his back, and you were sitting sort of over top of him. The bad guy was down too and cussing up a blue streak, waving his arm around as best I could tell in that light. And then he stopped and pointed at you."

I gnawed the inside of my cheek and tasted blood.

My heart pounded. What I coughed up tasted like iron. I spotted the shooter's silhouette at eye level. Still too dark and close to the ground to see whether he held his weapon. Too dark to see his face.

*Squinted at him through a narrowing tube. Deafened
by my shotgun blast, I couldn't hear if he spoke.
Couldn't hear if he didn't. Couldn't move my right
arm because I couldn't feel it.*

My heart battered my chest.

"Then the front door slammed, and the little kid—"

"Teddy," Emily whispered.

"Teddy, yeah. He bolted around the corner."

I breathed through my mouth, struggling not to suffocate.

*My shotgun lay across one knee. Left-handed, I
nestled it against my abdomen. Lifted my shaking leg
under the barrel to steady it and give it height. Still
had one shell loaded. Sought the trigger.*

*I coughed again. The guy swiveled his head to his
right, toward the house. He fired, and I fired. His
head exploded, and I lost track of my gun. I lost track
of myself.*

I backed away from Emily and Driscoll and braced myself against the nearest tree, a spindly, budding dogwood.

"The whole thing took maybe thirty seconds. The guy fired five shots." Driscoll ticked them off on his fingers. "The senator, two misses, you twice. I shot him in the head before he got off his last round. You fired twice. Your first shot hit him just below the knee, knocked him down. Your second one hit, you know, your little brother."

Water splashed from the eaves of the cabin and outbuildings. Far overhead, an airplane rumbled. As from a vast distance, I studied us: Emily, Driscoll, the two puppies. Myself.

Why would Driscoll say such a thing?

Emily gasped. One puppy flung himself against her, and she lifted him and squeezed him till he yelped. "Oh God, no."

I blinked, clearing black dots from my vision. What a weird reaction from Emily. How could he accuse me of killing Teddy? But he *was* accusing me. *They* were. Their not-covert-enough glances at each other condemned me. So, I clarified. "Vince Gardner shot Teddy, and then I shot Vince Gardner."

Driscoll, shifting from foot to foot, rubbed his jaw and eyed Emily.

She buried her face in the puppy.

"What?" I pushed away from the tree and approached them. I gripped Emily's arm, needing someone real to ground me, but she sidestepped, pulling away, still clutching the squirming pointer.

Driscoll invaded my space and pressed both hands to my shoulders. "I shouldn't be the one to tell you, son. I thought you'd already know from your father or the cops. A bunch of pellets from your second shot punctured the artery in your brother's thigh."

My stomach clenched. "Impossible."

"You were hurt bad, on the ground, shooting with one hand without aiming. The boy came around the corner so fast at exactly the wrong time. The other older kid grabbed him as he fell. I was there in a second. I used my belt as a tourniquet, but adrenaline pumped his heart so fast and . . ." Driscoll's voice broke, and his face contorted. "There was too much damage. Nothing I could do. He was unconscious in thirty, forty seconds. Bled out inside three minutes."

I tried to back away from him, but he moved with me. My mouth dried up, and I opened and closed it a few times before croaking, "No. That's not what happened. Someone would've told me."

"I'm sorry, son." He released me.

His face blurred, and my world went silent. I watched myself back away from him until the same little dogwood stopped me. Emily lowered the puppy, extended her hand, moved her mouth, but I heard nothing.

My focus cleared when Driscoll grasped my arm. I lashed out, hitting at him, livid that he would accuse me of an unimaginable atrocity and at Emily for believing him, yet with a sudden soul-level intuition that it had happened exactly the way he said it had.

"Philip!" Emily gasped and tried to pull me away from Driscoll.

I pushed her off and fled through the trees and into the fields, not toward anything but away from them. Away from everything I believed about Emily's family and my family and myself, knowing with absolute certainty that no matter how far I ran or for how long, I'd never escape the devastating secret that had just exploded into the open next to that cabin, a secret simultaneously too big to ever come out and too big to remain hidden.

In the end, I stopped only because I landed so unexpectedly in a water-filled hole that I couldn't raise my hands fast enough to break my fall.

CHAPTER 37

I SCREAMED MY agony to the sky, hollering and bellowing until my throat was raw. I pounded the earth until my hands were numb. I raged like a senseless animal until I heard nothing, saw nothing, was nothing.

And then I endured the anguish of all the memories rushing back in.

Minutes later–*hours later*–I still sprawled facedown under a cold drizzle, unmoved from where I'd fallen, now gulping in the heavy wet scent of the switch grass crushed beneath me. Everything hurt. My right cheek where I'd landed. My twisted left ankle. My right shoulder and arm, always those. But mostly my head and chest, burdened with a weight so heavy I couldn't have raised myself if I tried.

I didn't try, though. What was the point?

Strafed by a barrage of images, I scrolled through them frame by frame, searching for what I'd missed in the near darkness and muzzle flashes, in the panicked timbre of Vince's voice, the pop of his weapon, and the blast of mine. Then I rewound them and replayed them. Replayed them again and again.

In no iteration was Teddy present.

After Dad collapsed, my narrowed vision revealed only the silhouette that was Vince. I never saw Teddy–or Henry, who'd been desperate to snatch him from danger—and if Teddy cried out in surprise or fear to Dad or Vince or me, I never heard him. I shot him accidentally, but I should have known, at least sensed, that he was there. I sensed nothing.

Had Henry seen? Had *Dad*?

I read once that you only ever have one memory of an event. Every subsequent recollection is nothing more than the memory of your previous memory, never of the event itself. Was there ever a time when I did remember Teddy rushing into the shooting? In ICU, semiconscious and struggling to survive, did I waste my one allotted memory? Did I alter it so drastically that in every subsequent memory rippling from the original, he was absent? I wanted the memory. I *needed* it.

It didn't exist.

I'd left Teddy sitting beside Jamie on the bench at the kitchen table, slurp-crunching his cereal as he anticipated another day hunting and an evening curled in front of the fire, immersed in the pirate world of Jim Hawkins and Long John Silver and Ben Gunn. Just a normal ten-year-old kid out of his element on his first hunting trip. And I never saw him again. Once Vince appeared, I couldn't have altered what happened. I was as certain of that as I'd ever been of anything.

My exhausted mind emptied. Time, some immeasurable amount, drifted away from me. Eventually, I roused myself enough to dislodge my foot from my stuck shoe, leaving the shoe in the hole, and rolled over, blinking at the unexpectedly bright glare of sunless sky that offered no clue about the hour. I could raise my arm, slide back the sleeve of my jacket, and check my watch, but why bother when I could lie in that spot forever, and dissolve into the earth?

Realistically, I couldn't stay there indefinitely, and I groaned at the prospect of facing them all again. Driscoll and Emily. My parents. Jamie and Henry. If Driscoll and the police knew I killed Teddy, my father knew as well. And what about my mother, Jamie, Henry? They all blamed me for Teddy's death. No apology, no act of penance would ever absolve me of killing the little brother I loved so much. The world spun, and I flung out my arms, clutching the grass to keep from falling off.

My thoughts replayed events and conversations from the past few months. At Christmas, my mother had welcomed me warmly despite my long absence, and Jamie had attempted to reengage me by asking for career advice. Christmas night, when we argued, my father had said, *Your life will always be my concern.* I assumed he was meddling. Two nights ago he'd said, *We will always care about you and worry about you when you're gone and be here when you return.*

They already knew—they'd always known—and yet they didn't blame me. How was that possible? I'd carry the blame forever.

I longed to slip back in time. Not millennia or centuries, not even to the day before I shot Teddy. I couldn't have changed the events that led to his death, not what Mel did or how Dad responded or how Vince reacted to Dad or even what I, in survival mode, did. I'd return instead to the day I chose the path to this moment, when I'd be lying in a wet field after learning the truth years too late: the late December afternoon five weeks after the shooting when Dad and I had squared off outside the barn. Him in the golf cart, pale, gaunt, and more wounded than I'd ever guessed and me, barely able to stand, staring after the departing horse trailer. Huckleberry should have been the conduit for grappling with the upheaval in our lives, but none of us did or could grapple with it, not then and not later. Not ever.

Perhaps I'd been too damaged and medicated to think clearly enough to force the discussion. Perhaps my father was too full of pain as well. And my mother would've been exhausted and struggling to deal with all of it—Teddy's death, my father's and my tenuous chances for survival, Jamie and Henry's anguish, the intrusive news media, the business of running the farm.

In a revised scenario, I'd demand answers until my father no longer evaded my questions. His truth would have confounded and devastated me. I might still have secreted myself away in the company of confusion and anger and fear and grief—necessary and healthy, I knew now—to come to terms with the facts. But at least I *would* have come to terms with them and avoided squandering ten years of our lives.

I couldn't return to that moment, but I had a second chance to choose a path forward. I *could* come to terms with all those ugly facts now.

If I didn't, once again I could turn away, this time in shame, and sequester myself in my empty house behind the iron fence and locked gate, reconciled to live the uncomplicated existence I'd guarded until Emily disrupted it.

But despite my grief and guilt, despite the residual anger, and the awful truth, I *could* return to my family. I'd beg their forgiveness for running from them despite their repeated attempts to draw me back in ways I'd misinterpreted. I saw their attempts at reconciliation for what they were so clearly now, now that the one missing puzzle piece had been slotted into place, bringing focus to the past and completing the picture that had been incomplete and distorted for so long. I'd embrace the painful emotions essential to create the connections I so desperately needed.

Around me, the meadow emerged from the rain. The stream-like rush of wind whooshed through the tall, wispy cover, and flutters, chitters, and chirps broke out on every side. The crude complaints of a couple of crows soared above all until the plaintive *birdie-birdie-birdie* of a lone cardinal drowned them out. All of them were shaking off the damp and resuming their lives.

I struggled upright when the ground under me vibrated. In the distance, a bright green utility vehicle topped a rise and crept diagonally away before U-turning and barreling toward me.

I dumped the water from my shoe, and without untying it, wedged my foot inside. An examination of my swollen ankle proved it was sore but serviceable. I stood and limped forward.

The vehicle slowed a few yards out. Driscoll drove, and even before he stopped, Emily launched herself from her seat and into my arms.

"Philip. Oh thank God."

I grasped her arms above the elbows and pushed her away from my soaked, grassy body. "Emily, I didn't kill your father. And he didn't kill anyone."

"I don't care about that right now." She jerked loose and clutched me. "I was so worried, and then I got your parents all upset. I never meant to hurt you, and this, on top of Dilsey dying, and it's so awful, and we've been out looking for you for forever, and oh my God, I'm so sorry."

Teddy. Dilsey. At the sudden pain in my gut, I jerked away from her and staggered a few steps before doubling over and vomiting. I didn't stop until I was on all fours, dry heaving and gasping, with her kneeling beside me, an arm across my back, like a younger sister sharing the cumulative pain of every loss we'd endured.

I righted myself and wrapped an arm around her. Long before we met, she'd set aside any resentment about me killing the person she loved most and depended on. She'd approached me focused on her mission and with no outward sign of malice. Instead of using me merely as a means to her end, she'd built a friendship that defied reason. I'd known her fewer than three months, but somehow, on a spiritual level, she'd been a part of me forever. We'd both lost so much. We both had so much and never realized it.

When at last she pulled away, her face was wet. I blotted her tears with two fingers. When I finished, she took both my hands into her warm ones.

"You're so cold."

And then I crumbled. For the first time since Teddy's death and everything that followed, I clung to someone else as I grieved, letting another person support me physically and emotionally and supporting her in turn. We sobbed against each other until finally, empty and overflowing at the same time, we had nothing left to do but go home.

CHAPTER 38

I REMEMBERED NOTHING between Emily filling the gas tank in rural Tennessee and me squinting at a set of double gates swinging inward in the glare of the Focus's headlights. The dashboard clock read 10:36 p.m. We must have sprouted wings to reach Grainger so quickly. The car smelled like dampness and fast food, but if she'd stopped, I'd slept through it.

Home at last. My odyssey was over.

Wait. My gate slid sideways. And I didn't have a guardhouse or a security guy to wave us in.

I raised my seat back. "Where are we?"

"Your parents' farm."

I blinked a few times, processing her words.

"They asked me to bring you here. Insisted, actually."

I groaned, wanting only to be alone in my own house in Grainger, buried beneath the blankets of my bed and under the burden of what I'd learned in Tennessee.

Emily sped to the spotlighted front entrance, which friends never used, and braked near the porch steps. When I didn't budge, she said, "Go on."

I switched on the dome light. Her face was puffy, her nose and eyes red, the blond wisps that had escaped from her ponytail damp. Wadded tissues filled the center console, and a crumpled McDonald's bag lay at my feet. "Emily."

She opened her mouth and, when no words came, she popped the hatch on the trunk.

"Emily, please don't leave."

"I'm sorry. For everything."

"But—"

She shook her head without looking at me. "Just talking to your parents on the phone was awful. I can't face them. Please, just go."

They waited on the porch, I noticed then, side by side. I struggled from the car to collect my duffle from the trunk. Emily barely gave me time to lower the lid before racing off.

In an instant of overwhelming regret, I wondered whether I'd ever see her again.

"Philip?"

I turned toward the house. My parents inched down the steps, and I pushed past them. My father grabbed my arm, but I jerked loose and choked out, "Please, not yet."

As quickly as my swollen ankle would allow, I limped inside, intent on a hot shower and sleep, determined to avoid them until I could offer a coherent apology. In my room, someone had switched on the nightstand lamps, but it was a subtle new brightness in the hall that caused me to drop my duffle and whirl around.

Teddy's room was open and lit.

If I'd expected to feel his presence when I entered, I was wrong. The room was clean and dusted, the bed made with a comforter and pillow shams that I should have remembered. Although his stuff was there on shelves, the mantel, the top of his dresser, and in his bookcase, the room struck me as one that might belong to any kid.

My mother materialized beside me. "Looks the same, doesn't it?"

I nodded.

"If only it *was* the same. For many months after he died, I'd come here in secret. Well, I thought it was in secret, till Dad admitted to doing the same thing."

I gnawed on my lip, astounded at how wrong I'd been about my parents. About everything.

"I'd sit on Teddy's bed or at his desk. Touch his things. Breathe his scent. Cry. I believed I'd be closer to him. I locked the room to preserve him, or his essence, at least, but it dissipated anyway, and so quickly. When we were in DC and I couldn't bear to be apart from him, I'd fly here just to be in his room." She took my hand. "Nothing would bring *him* back. So later, after you left, sometimes I'd sit in *your* room and wish for you, at least, to find your way home to us."

"Mom," was all I managed. I swiped my free hand over my eyes.

"Henry's on his way, and Jamie will come tomorrow. And then we'll all talk. We should have from the beginning. Your father and I made the wrong decision not to tell you the truth. But once we decided, we couldn't go back."

"Even the wrong words would've been better than none." I tried not to sound accusing. We were *all* suffering.

"I know that now." She released my hand and, at the French doors, opened the blinds to the darkness. "You have no idea how close to dying you came. We didn't know when you might come home, or if. Dad wasn't much better off. At least you were both in the same hospital, so I was able to bounce around the ICU between you."

When my chest tightened, I sat on Teddy's bed. Just as my father had accused, I'd never considered what my mother endured in the days, weeks, and months after the shooting. In the pings and beeps of the hospital, I'd lost all sense of any other world and every other person. The first I remembered seeing her, seeing anyone, was the day she and my father told me Teddy had died. How had they borne knowing they'd have to tell me when–if–I became coherent enough to process it?

Her back to me, she said, "The investigators told us you shot Teddy. They knew by the evidence at the scene and from Mr. Driscoll, and eventually they pulled it out of Henry." She bowed her head. "We asked him not to tell you."

I ached for Henry. His behavior the past few months made sense now–his shock, which I misinterpreted, when I told him that I knew I'd killed Vince; his insistence he meet Emily before involving himself in our search; his deliberate attempts to mislead us. I also now understood his alcohol-infused incoherence when Dilsey's death plunged him deep into the memory of Teddy's. But I didn't understand *why* he'd colluded with Mom and Dad. As quickly as it ripped through me, though, my anger at him dispersed. He must have had his reasons. Reasons, apparently, just as valid this year as they'd been for the past ten years.

Mom shut the blinds, brushing the tears from her cheeks before continuing. "I made the wrong call with all of you. I demanded Jamie stay here instead of keeping him in Nashville with me. I thought being home would comfort him, but in reality, it isolated him. I encouraged him to return to school, and when he refused, I didn't argue. Henry stayed with Jamie till I persuaded him–badgered him, really–to return to his parents for some relief from what we were dealing with. But I isolated *him* too. In retrospect, everything I did was wrong. But how could I have practiced for something like that? I should have let them stay in Nashville so no matter how bad it was, how badly it ended, we'd be together."

I carried the box of tissues on Teddy's dresser to her. She blew her nose, and I returned to the bed.

"We didn't know what might tip your life one way or the other, so ultimately your father and I agreed not to tell you exactly how Teddy died."

I blinked rapidly, imagining the anguish of their choice. They'd never have guessed their choice would drive me away when their intention had been to keep me close. I could be angry with them, but what would be the point? I could tell my mother now, finally, how my talk with my father after the trailer drove off with Huckleberry, had played into their choice and upended my perception of their love for us. But in doing so, I'd hurt her worse than I already had.

She scrunched her tissue and took another. "Henry bought in right away. Jamie still doesn't know, but we'll tell him. Because we were afraid we'd slip, we found we couldn't talk about *any* aspect of that horrible day. Too late we realized that we'd trapped ourselves in the truth we let you believe."

"Truth by omission isn't any kind of truth." I gazed hard at her—not angry, but needing to make my point.

Her return gaze didn't waver. "We'd dug ourselves into an inescapable hole. Then, this past Christmas, Henry shocked us by telling us that you told him that you had killed Mr. Gardner. We never imagined you'd think you'd shot him. We believed if you thought about it at all, you'd correctly assume Mr. Driscoll had. After so long, we didn't know how to tell you the truth about that part of it without ending up in a discussion we couldn't face."

"Mom," I whispered.

"All we wanted was to protect you. But in trying to fix what no one can ever fix, we didn't say to you, to any of you, what we should have, and we made everything worse. And when you left, we let you go because we didn't know what else to do, how else to show you how much we cared. But, oh Philip, do you know how hard it is to grieve for someone who's still alive?"

I covered my face, too sad and too ashamed to meet her gaze. I ran from the people who loved me because I didn't understand how guilt and love and grief and regret are inexorably bound. My parents had allowed their grief to transform their love into its own secret to protect me from a truth they couldn't bear for me to carry. I couldn't imagine the burden of their decision. I didn't know if I'd ever love anyone so much. Or if I wanted to.

"I'm so sorry, Mom. For everything."

She came to me, gathered my hands in hers, and kissed my cheek. "We love you, Philip. So much. We always have. We always will. Now get some sleep."

Before I let her go, I leaned forward and kissed her cheek too, tasting her tears. I didn't remember the last time that I'd kissed my mother, but I'd remember that kiss.

When she left, I wandered the room, stunned by the complex simplicity of grief. I touched the things Teddy had loved, not to keep him close, as Mom had done, but to finally say goodbye. His flashlight on his nightstand had made reading under the covers possible before we ever heard about e-readers; he would have loved having a Kindle. His books, like mine, were organized by type and author. Adventure stories. Biographies. Histories. No classics; he borrowed those from me. On his desk perched the tree ornament I'd given him for what turned out to be his last Christmas.

I spun his floor globe, and on the wall map of places he'd never see, I moved a Post-it flag from the approximate West Indies location of Treasure Island to Grainger. On the hearth of his fireplace, the oak mantel clock, a real clock, marked time the old-fashioned way, with hands and roman numerals. It ticked softly, so someone had continued to replace the batteries. It was nearly midnight.

I carried the Christmas ornament to my room, set it on my dresser, and stood under a scorching shower long after the soap had swirled away. Enveloping myself in a towel, I stepped into my unexpectedly chilly bedroom.

My father sat in the reading chair in the corner, his cheeks sunken, the hollows under his eyes dark. He'd aged a decade in the two days since I'd seen him. He'd cracked the balcony door open to the peaceful nighttime silence of the farm. On my bed were a T-shirt and shorts, on my desk an entire sleeve of saltines and a bowl steaming with the aroma of soup. My mouth watered.

"Best I could do on short notice was canned chicken noodle."

"Thanks." At my desk, huddled in my damp towel, I stirred the soup, filled the spoon, and dribbled the liquid back into the bowl, unable to eat despite my hunger, unsure what to say to him or whether to say anything at all.

"I'm sorry about Dilsey."

I shoved the bowl away, sloshing soup onto my desk. "At least now you don't have to worry about either of us being sued because of her."

He grimaced, and I allowed my sarcasm to hang between us.

"I'm sorry, Philip. I know she was good for you. I know you loved her. For us, though, she was one more reason for concern. We worried that if she died suddenly or accidentally hurt someone, you'd be too fragile to handle it and we'd lose you again."

"*Fragile?*" I gaped at him, dumbfounded that anyone, especially my parents, might ever have attributed such a word to me. "You can't be serious." But the softness around his eyes, his presence in my room, the clothes on the bed, the soup, and the fact that he'd asked Emily to drive me to the farm proved he *was* serious.

"Eat your soup."

I pulled the bowl toward me and waved the spoon through it, too weary to press him. Only the saltines appealed, though, so I opened the package and stuffed several into my already dry mouth.

Dad got up, went to the bathroom, and returned with two paper cups of water, one of which he set beside the saltines. "We'll get everything out in the open tomorrow."

"*Everything?*"

He dropped into the chair and chugged his water. "That's your choice." He crushed the cup. "But I'm at peace with whatever you do. Nothing that happens to me will ever be worse than what's already happened."

I thickened the soup with crackers and ate it all, imagining dropping the bomb on my family. *I might have shot Teddy, but want to know how we got to that point?*

Or I could approach Adrian Wells. Because South Carolina had no statute of limitations on criminal offenses, Adrian would have to address my allegations. Or I could bypass Adrian and contact the news media, and let both him and Dad, not to mention the US Senate, scramble.

Thinking about my options felt unexpectedly satisfying. Thinking about them felt petty and mean-spirited.

To snitch on Dad wouldn't destroy only his reputation and career; it would ravage our family. We deserved better. Even Dad deserved better. He'd already been punished as much as he could be simply because he'd always done what he believed to be right, or at least just, and this time it had all backfired in ways he'd never have anticipated.

Still, the anger at the pain his one questionable decision had cost me—not my family but me—remained. I reveled in the selfish possibility of satisfying my anger by revealing his crimes. After all, he'd empowered me, ostensibly granted me permission, by confessing, by entrusting his secret to someone who had every motive to disclose it. Alternatively, I could assuage my anger by doing nothing but allowing him to believe that at any time and for any reason or even for no reason, I might reveal it. But I couldn't decide anything right then, not without time to reflect. Not without sleep.

I handed him my empty bowl. "Thank you."

"Good night, Philip." He stood, hesitated a moment, squeezed my uninjured shoulder, and left the room.

Feeling strangely light, I turned toward bed. No worries plagued me, no thoughts beat at me. The silence in me, for the first time in forever, matched the silence of the night, and I slid fluidly into sleep.

CHAPTER 39

I STOOD ON my balcony in the intense darkness just before dawn. The farm was peaceful, and I could hike, or rather limp, a long way before having to turn back. It would be daylight by then. The horses would have been fed and turned out, the farm staff bustling with their usual chores. Meanwhile, at the house, nothing would be normal. Perhaps some time walking outside would ease my stiff muscles and sore ankle, and it might clear my head enough for me to apologize to my family. I owed them not only the apology itself, but the love inherent in the act of apologizing.

Before I considered going outside, though, I had to find a sweatshirt, socks, and pants that fit, something more suitable than the tee and shorts I'd slept in. I opened the door to Henry's room to borrow the clothes and blinked in surprise.

"Henry?"

All the lights were on. Two full-size suitcases lay open on his stripped bed, one overflowing, the other nearly so. Scattered in strategic places around the room—by his desk, the closet, the bathroom—were boxes, some open, some sloppily taped shut. Henry hunched at the desk in a polo shirt and jeans, typing on his laptop. He started when I entered the room. Like my father, he seemed to have aged in the two days since I'd last seen him. But passed out on his living room floor, he'd been in worse shape than Dad at the start of those two days.

His voice was low and expressionless. "No matter how hard I try, I can't escape one basic, irrefutable, unchangeable fact." He pushed the stuff on his desk aside and opened the top drawer. "I'm a total fuckup."

"What are you talking about?" His drunken breakdown aside, Henry was the most brashly self-assured person I'd ever known. I'd never have considered using *Henry* and *fuckup* in the same sentence.

He pulled something from the drawer and held it up. A book. "I even fucked this up."

I strode forward and reached for it, but he snatched it back and raised it so I could read the cover. *Treasure Island*. My copy, the one Teddy would've finished the day he died. Stunned, I blurted out, "Where'd you find it?"

"I didn't *find* it, I took it. Teddy left it on the table when he . . . And I . . ." He tapped his finger in several places on the cover, and I saw when I took the book from him stains that looked like rust. With a mix of fascination and revulsion, I realized they were spots of blood.

"Till Teddy died, I didn't know anyone could bleed so much. The caretaker—"

"Driscoll."

"Tried to stop it, but there was so much blood." Henry squeezed his eyes shut. Like me, he'd never forget the images, different from mine, but surely as vivid. "Driscoll covered Teddy and got right to you and your dad. If it weren't for him, you'd both be dead."

Henry chewed hard on his bottom lip. "The EMTs stabilized you both and got you out to the field about the time the helicopter arrived. After you left, the police interviewed

Driscoll and me in the kitchen. Jamie was in the bathroom, puking his guts out, but they eventually talked with him too. I was so bloody. When I realized I'd gotten blood on the book, I tried to scrub it off, but . . ."

"It's all right, Henry."

"Everything happened so fast, he didn't even have time to be afraid, but he needed to hear how the story ended. *I* needed him to hear it." He covered his face with his hands. "So I told him. I told him the story as fast as I could. Before he–" He bolted from the chair, yanked open the balcony doors, and lurched outside.

I took a moment to shake off the image of distraught, reliable Henry cradling a fading, bloody Teddy and murmuring the end of an adventure about courage and making the right choices. In Henry's situation I'd never have thought about the novel, and gratitude that he had not only thought of it, but had followed through and distracted Teddy, rushed over me.

I laid *Treasure Island* on the desk and joined him. It was cold outside, but not freezing. The sun rose on the other side of the house, and the western mountains already glowed deep purple. The low-slung fog flitted along in the light breeze like a covey of ghosts. Faint, indistinguishable voices drifted from the barns along with an occasional whinny or bark. The early spring humidity mixed the scents of new grass and horse, both overlain with the aroma of bacon, and my stomach rumbled.

He was looking out at the farm. "I used to think this place was perfect."

"Why didn't you tell me the truth?"

He stayed quiet for a few seconds. "The only thing wrong was that I never belonged here."

I glanced sideways at him. His expression was serious. "You always belonged."

"Once—we were twelve or so—I called your mother *mom*. She corrected me, gently, but still. I don't remember her exact words, but they made me feel, I don't know. Conflicted. Angry that she was covering for my parents. Sad because she didn't get what I was saying. Mostly desperate that at any time she and your dad might oust me from your family. Know what she told me? 'Your parents love you. They're just not showing it in a way you understand.'"

Mom's consolation had been total bullshit. His parents had never cared about him. The last time I saw them was the year Mom and Dad had invited the three Lindens to the farm for Thanksgiving. I eventually concluded that Henry's parents accepted only to evaluate Mom and Dad as surrogate parents on whom they could dump the son they never made time for and probably hadn't wanted in the first place. I'd briefly sympathized with Henry, grateful his parents weren't mine, and then promptly forgot them.

Henry hadn't been permitted to forget them.

"I had to either earn my way into calling your parents Mom and Dad or get there by default. Like if my biological parents were no longer in the picture. From then on, every year before I blew out the candles on the birthday cake your mother made me, I wished my parents would die."

"Holy shit." Why hadn't I known that? Why was he telling me now?

"Didn't care how. Didn't wish them pain or suffering. Just wanted them gone so your parents would adopt me. Right away, I saw how different they were from mine. They cared about you. I wanted them to care about me, too, and I didn't know how else to make it happen."

"They cared about you all along. You should have known." But why would he have, when I hadn't recognized it myself?

Henry's knuckles whitened as he gripped the back of the rocking chair that faced the fields. "And then I let Teddy get into the middle of the shooting. While you were still in the hospital, your mother sent me home, and that's how I knew she knew Teddy died because I'd let him get away from me. I assured her it was fine, that my parents were at their place in Maryland, but I lied. They were on a trip somewhere exotic. Jamie called me every day, but all I wanted was to be with you all.

"And so when they decided not to tell you you'd shot Teddy and asked me to keep it from you and Jamie, I jumped at the chance to get back in their good graces. I couldn't keep Teddy safe, but I could keep *you* safe, even if you didn't appreciate what you had, how much they loved you. But I fucked that up too. When I found the job posting from Grainger, I thought if I got you to move closer, your folks would be so happy. But the damned fire and Emily . . . And your dad and I were so sure we'd found a way to pretend to help you while steering you away from the truth. But I failed that too. And then I let Dilsey die."

When he sucked in a shaky breath, I dove in. "You didn't let her die. You didn't do *anything* wrong."

"All I ever wanted was to be part of your family, *truly* part of it, but no matter what I did or how hard I tried, I fucked it up. For *years*. It's selfish of me to keep imposing on y'all, so"—he threw up his hands—"I'm leaving."

"Oh, sweetheart, no."

We spun. My mother stood at the threshold to the balcony, one hand covering her mouth, her eyes wide.

"Shit," Henry muttered. "Shit, shit, *shit*."

I had no idea how long she'd been there, what she might have overheard. I suspected it was almost everything.

She rushed onto the balcony. Henry dodged her, but she cornered him and grasped him by the face so firmly, he winced. "Listen to me, Henry. You never, *ever* had to earn your way into this family. We loved you from the moment we met you. You were always part of us."

Henry bowed his head, and he sagged against the balustrade when Mom gathered him in her arms like a child.

Mom extended a hand when I sidled away. I wrapped my arms around them both and leaned into a warmth I hadn't felt in a long time.

After a moment, she pushed gently at me. "Go. Let me talk with Henry. Dad cooked breakfast. Tell him we'll be down shortly."

I left Henry and my mother, and closed the doors. But I didn't go downstairs. Instead, from Henry's largest suitcase, I plucked the clothing I needed and dressed right there in his room. Then I unpacked that suitcase into his dresser drawers and closet. He'd take the hint and could empty the other one himself.

As I picked up *Treasure Island* from his desk, I noticed the email he'd been composing when I interrupted him. The address field contained all our names—my parents, Jamie, me. "Thank you for everything you've done for me . . . I'll focus on making my own way now and leave you alone . . ." I didn't need to read further. I deleted the text, deleted the addresses, deleted the entire now-blank email. I couldn't imagine us not being in each other's lives. We were brothers.

I examined the cover of the book. Even in the bright room, the rusty smudges were barely discernible, except for the big one on the back. I pressed an index finger to it and came as physically close to Teddy as I ever would. All the things I knew about grief and love and friendship I'd learned only because of all the things Teddy would never know, and I was grateful for the opportunity for that knowledge.

In my bedroom, I eased *Treasure Island* into the empty slot on the Stevenson shelf of my bookcase from which Teddy had removed it so long ago.

CHAPTER 40

IN THE EIGHT days since Emily and I had gone to Tennessee, dandelions, chickweed, and clover had overtaken my yard. I'd need to mow before long. It was Thursday already, and spring break was about over. The list of chores I had to do overwhelmed me. My students' midterm grades were past due, and I hadn't prepped for the second half of the semester or paid my bills. Somehow, I had to summon the mental energy to deal with those; then I could tackle the yard and house.

Before I opened my gate, I stopped at the mailbox and withdrew the one piece of mail it contained, perplexed there wasn't more. It was a business envelope with Emily's neatly printed return address. We hadn't spoken since she'd sped away after dropping me off at the farm, but I'd thought about her, debated whether to tell her about Dad, Mel, Vince, and the answering machine recording, first deciding yes—and then ultimately no. If I wouldn't report Dad's misconduct, I wouldn't out him to Emily, on the off chance she'd do what I couldn't. Assuring myself I was protecting her, though from precisely what I wasn't certain, usually helped mitigate my guilt for withholding the rest of the story she'd sought for so long.

I wished we'd not gone to Tennessee. I wished we'd gone sooner.

With mild dread, I tossed the envelope on the passenger seat beside the white box containing the flowered tin with Dilsey's cremains, which Henry and I had picked up at the pet funeral home a few hours earlier. He'd accompanied me inside—moral support, he claimed—but had rushed from the dim, ornate, floral-scented parlor when the funeral associate lifted the lid on the box. The tin inside was sealed, and she didn't offer to open it, but the reality of cramming a Labrador retriever into a few square inches seemed more than Henry could bear. In the car, I'd assured him for the hundredth time that her death wasn't his fault. His silence told me he was not convinced.

I wished Dilsey were with me now, pushing her head into my hand. She didn't just comfort other people, I'd finally realized. She'd pressed against me every time she sensed how much I needed her. I recognized that too late to appreciate it.

Among the necessary chores was removal of her crate from the Expedition, but I was in no rush. Like her towels, like her bed and the toys I'd placed on it last week, I'd leave it, bumpers and all, for now.

I pictured the wildflowers Nicole and Kate had delivered. They would be wilted and muted to sepia now, but the passage of time and lack of fresh water didn't mute my students' thoughtfulness. *That* brightness would last indefinitely.

I nosed the rented Nissan up the driveway and parked behind my truck. Henry had driven us from the farm and offered to take me all the way to Grainger, but I declined. He needed to be home as much as I did. So after we collected Dilsey, we'd parted ways at the car rental. Midweek we'd meet for dinner at a favorite spot in Richmond. We'd both need the company by then.

I carried my duffle onto the front porch, left it by the door, and sat on the top step with Dilsey's box and Emily's envelope. Inside the envelope were two letters, both hand-written, both dated three days ago, March 7, 2016. One, addressed to me, was folded inside another addressed to Daddy. *Vince?*

Dear Philip,

Nothing I say will make you feel better about what we learned in Tennessee, so I won't say anything except I'm so sorry. Thank you for everything you did to help me. I know you didn't want to and you could have listened to Henry and your parents when they told you not to have anything to do with me, but you helped me anyway. You're a special guy.

I never mentioned that I've been seeing a therapist for years. Thanks to you, I'm ready to quit. At my session yesterday (which might be the last one!!), she suggested I write Daddy a letter. She's said that before, but I never knew what to tell him. Now I do, and he wouldn't like it one bit.

The letter's in a nice box (teal, his favorite color) in my closet with the photo Mr. Brown took of Daddy and me by our tree house.

I was able to write the letter only because of you, so I want you to have a copy. Don't feel weird about reading it. If I didn't want you to, I wouldn't let you.

I'll leave you alone now, though I'll always wish we could stay friends. We shared so much. Thank you for everything.

Alex and Kim send their love. Me too.

Emily

I returned her note to the envelope and smoothed out
the longer letter. She'd copied it in color, dark blue ink on
ivory paper. "Dear Daddy," it started. Uncomfortable reading something so personal, flustered that she wanted me
to, I refolded the letter and tapped it against my thigh.
After a moment, I convinced myself she was right: if she
didn't want, perhaps need, me to read it, she wouldn't have
wasted a stamp. I unfolded it again.

Dear Daddy,

    *I'm writing to say goodbye. I love you, and I
always will.*

    *But when I was a little girl, you chose to leave
me all alone. Ever since, I've wondered what I did to
make you not love me enough to stay.*

    *I get it now. You leaving had nothing to do with
me. You didn't even consider me, us. You were so
angry, and maybe even sad, about Uncle Mel dying
that you selfishly didn't think about anyone else.
Was it just because he was your brother? Even
though I don't remember him much (and knowing
what I know now, I think you were protecting me
from him), I believe with all my heart you weren't
anything like him. The nice things you did, like
building my tree house, helping me with my
homework, and helping the Browns with Cliff,
prove that.*

    *After reading through a bunch of news reports and
criminal and legal records, I'm positive Uncle Mel
blew up that house and killed the family in 1996. He
got lucky then, getting off. The second time around,
not so much, and that was a good thing.*

For all those years, you stayed mad at Mr. Rutledge for losing the second trial, didn't you? Then when Uncle Mel died, you totally lost it. Don't you think whatever happened to him in prison was too good for him? He should have had to die the way he killed the family. Even that would have been way too good for him.

You should have loved me more than you loved Mel or hated Mr. Rutledge. I thought you loved me, but maybe you never had anyone to show you what love really is. So, I'll tell you.

It's Kim and Alex taking me in even though they hardly knew me. As it turned out, they gave me a better life than you would have. Can you believe they found a miracle in what you did? I hope someday I'll see it too. I love them so much.

Here's what else love is: it's the family that you hurt that almost destroyed itself to protect one of their own. They failed, though, because you left me with so many questions that I had to involve them to get answers. You should've seen Philip's face when he found out his gun, not yours, killed his little brother. The news totally shattered him. He'd already carried around the guilt of killing you, even though he had no choice, and then he had to let go of that and trade it for something way, way worse.

When I read my first news article about what you did, I kept believing the reporters were wrong or at least that you had a very good reason, though I couldn't guess what it was. But neither of those were true. You badly hurt some wonderful people. I was one of them. The Rutledges were the others. There's no excuse for what you did to all of us.

I've done everything I know how to do to find out the truth, and I'm finished. I'm pretty sure Philip knows something he's not telling me. But because of what I've already done to him (because of you), I'm not going to push. I hope I haven't ruined his life all over again. I hope his family can help him get through it. Maybe they can all heal now. They deserve that. And I have Kim and Alex, and I deserve them.

I don't understand you, Daddy, and sometimes I'm still mad at you. But I forgive you.
Love,
Emily

When I finished, I sat still, holding the letter, aching for Emily, awed by her strength. Then I slowly reread it before returning it to its envelope. Despite her uncompromising words, or perhaps because of them, Vince would be proud of her.

We were opposite ends of the same spectrum, Emily and I. She'd chosen to forgive Vince for deserting her, even though she didn't understand his motivations. Even though she was still mad at him and hurt. I understood my father's motivations, even agreed with them to some extent, but I questioned whether I'd ever release enough anger to forgive him for initiating the chain of events that forever altered our family. If what was beyond forgiving was not beyond understanding, understanding might have to be enough for me. That seemed fair.

I looked toward the road at the sound of an approaching vehicle. A bright blue car stopped at my mailbox, then reversed and drove through the open gate. Scottie's Soul. She edged around the rental, parked beside the

Expedition, and strode up the sidewalk carrying a bunch of papers.

"You're home," she said. "I know it's presumptuous of me, but I've been collecting your mail. Emily said she didn't know when you'd be back."

"Emily?" I asked, surprised.

Scottie joined me on the top step. "She called the office last Thursday. Frantic. An emergency, she said, and she couldn't reach anyone. She called the English department to get access to your emergency contacts. We didn't divulge them, of course, but I called the two you'd listed. She'd already tried Henry several times, but I called him again, to no avail. I finally got your brother." She glanced sideways at me, then diverted her gaze across my yard, her bottom lip sucked in.

"What?"

"She might have said more than she should have. About where you were and why, and what you found out."

I nodded and hunched my shoulders, crumbling inwardly. Emily had handled the situation as best she could. She'd done the right thing, calling Scottie. But now Scottie viewed me not only as the guy who'd lost his little brother in a shooting, but as his killer. Or worse: as an even more tragic figure than she previously realized. If I still believed I could run from the past, I'd consider resigning from my job, selling my house, and living somewhere far away among strangers who didn't know anything about me.

But I was done running from the inescapable.

"I called her back the next day to check on her and you. That's how I learned you were in South Carolina and figured you might be gone a while." She placed my mail beside Emily's envelope. "Are you all right?"

"I'm fine."

"Liar."

I hadn't planned to say anything about my time in Tennessee or at the farm, but she moved the mail behind her, slid as close as Dilsey's box between us would allow, touched the yellowing bruise on my cheek, held my hand, and I surrendered. I described how my parents had protected me and why, and what Henry had done. I relayed Jamie's broken reaction when, with all of us gathered in Teddy's room, he learned the truth a decade late that no matter what, he couldn't have done anything to affect the outcome that morning. I admitted my arrogance in never considering the full impact of the shooting on the others or on myself.

I kept private the past events that had culminated in the shooting.

And I told her how much I admired Emily. "She's like a little sister, you know? She's barely older than Teddy would be now, and she's, I don't know . . ." My vision blurred.

"She really cares about you too," Scottie said softly.

In Tennessee, Emily and I had shared the most profoundly vulnerable moment of my life, and now she'd entrusted me with her private message to Vince. Those alone would bind us through time and space, but they weren't enough. I wanted to talk with her, take her riding, visit the tree house near the pond, bowl again with her family and her friends. Perhaps together we'd find the miracle that Kim and Alex had discovered in the events that linked us. "Maybe I should call her."

"Not *maybe*. Call her."

Our phones pinged simultaneously. I ignored mine, but Scottie released my hand and tapped her screen.

"Email from President Randolph." She read silently for a moment. "Aww. 'After consultation with many parties, the Grainger University Board of Trustees has determined that Carter Hall will be renovated rather than razed. Its foundation is solid, and its historical significance to our campus and the town of Grainger unquestionable. Renovations will include a memorial to the sixteen students who died in the fire. Work will begin this summer, and I'll keep everyone apprised of its progress as we continue to heal as a community.'"

Fire. An ancient gift. The renewal bequeathed to a forest by a blaze purging the underbrush, sweeping clean the forest floor and exposing it to sunlight, nurturing the soil. What fire doesn't kill grows stronger.

"I'm glad," I said.

We sat in companionable silence.

Scottie caressed Dilsey's box. "What are you going to do with her?"

"I don't know. Nothing for a while." I braced for her to ask if I'd get another dog, and when she didn't, I silently appreciated that she understood me enough not to.

"You probably have a ton of things to do. I guess I should go." She didn't move.

"You know anything about landscaping?"

She narrowed her eyes. "Landscaping?"

I rose and grabbed her hand, and when I tugged it, she resisted at first, but then accompanied me down the steps and out into the middle of the front yard. When we faced the house, I swept my other arm around. "Like nice low foundation shrubbery? Something that won't get too dense. Something that'll liven up the place."

"Mm, azaleas?"

I pictured the azaleas surrounding the cabin and tried not to wince. "That's not very original."

She pulled her hand away and folded her arms. "You asked."

"Sorry."

"How about this: the hardware store's garden shop. Someone there can help."

I hadn't been to the hardware store lately. Maybe this weekend. What was one more thing on my to-do list?

"I'm going home," she said. "Call me if you need a second opinion on plants. Or just want to talk."

We walked to her car. She slid inside and buckled up, and I shut her door. She turned the key in the ignition.

"Scottie? Had lunch yet?" She probably had. It was nearly three o'clock.

"Why?"

"I was thinking we could go to Cast Party; I'd love one of their huge burgers, but I guess you have other things to do."

She grinned. "Actually, I'm starving. Get in."

"I'll drive."

She shook her head. "I'm already in the driver's seat. Why do guys always think *they* should drive? Get in. Besides, it's not like it's a date."

She was right. Just two friends having lunch. One quiet, damaged, and uncertain about navigating the rest of his life. The other vivacious, confident, generous, and compassionate. And so damn bossy. Always showing up when I didn't know I needed her and never asking for anything in return. I remembered the comfort I felt last week when she'd tightened her arm around me, the relief and joy of sharing Teddy with her, and before then, the welcome surprise when she'd baked treats for Dilsey and for me. I recalled the dinner she cooked, the daffodils she exchanged for a simple tour of the house, and the same evening, enduring Dilsey's seizure cluster with me when she had every reason to abandon us. I owed her. No, not owed: *wanted* to demonstrate how much I appreciated her generosity and kindness, how deeply I valued our friendship. I wanted her in my life.

It's not like it's a date.

A smile radiated all the way through me. "Who says it's not a date?"

CHAPTER 41
MONDAY, JULY 4, 2016

DILSEY WOULD HAVE loved our long Independence Day weekend at the farm despite the heat and humidity. She'd have accompanied us—Mom, Dad, Jamie, Henry, Scottie, and me—on our early morning horseback rides into the foothills, streaking ahead of us and looping around to zip past us again before settling into a panting trot beside my new horse. I'd have pretended not to notice when someone slipped her a morsel of forbidden food. I'd have let her swim, even in the pond, if she wanted to cool off or for the sheer joy of it. If she seized, someone would help me rescue her. Or later, in the pool, she'd have joined all of us. She'd loved swimming, but once her seizures began, I denied her that simple pleasure because I feared I couldn't save her if she had one in the water. But keeping her safe hadn't enriched her life or extended it.

That morning, the holiday itself, accompanied only by those wistful thoughts, I jogged along the drive to the front gate to meet Emily for the horseback ride I'd promised her. We'd spoken nearly every week since I received her letter, but I hadn't seen her since early March, when she dropped me off. Although I was free enough for the summer to drive to South Carolina from Grainger at any time, she'd returned to school and loaded up on extra courses, determined to finish in one term what would require at least two of anyone else. She had no free time, she complained cheerfully. Her priorities had changed, Alex said when he, Kim, and I had dinner last month.

I'd invited my family to ride with us, but everyone opted to sleep in—I suspected to give Emily and me space to talk. At five o'clock and still dark, the temperature and humidity were miserable but not yet impossible. The security guy opened a window in the air-conditioned shack and called a greeting. I waved, leaned against the brick column beside the open gate, swatted at mosquitoes, and sweated.

Ten minutes later, right on schedule, Emily drove up in her silver Focus. I hopped in, and our hug lingered across the console.

"I miss seeing you," she said. "I've thought about surprising you in Grainger for lunch one day. Cast Party—you, Scottie, me. Maybe even Henry."

"I'd like that. Whenever you can fit us into your busy schedule, Scottie and I will be there. And maybe even Henry."

When we arrived at the barn, she bounced to the quiet little gelding Ross had tacked up for her, cooed, scratched him under the chin, and offered him a carrot on the palm of her hand. Her excitement sparkled through her face-wide smile.

"Better than a Breyer model?" I asked, thrilled at her joy.

"Pretty much."

By six twenty, sunrise, we'd ridden deep into the farm. We kept to the mowed path. This time of year, the horses stayed out at night, so I didn't risk opening pasture gates and inadvertently letting anyone escape. We moved no faster than a slow jog, but Emily didn't seem to mind. At the pond, we bore left into the trees.

I'd debated about showing her the tree fort built by my great-grandfather and his brothers, concerned she might think I was flaunting it. *Look at our citadel of a tree house compared with your little deck of one!* But no, she wouldn't think that. She'd interpret the gesture as I intended: another connection.

We ducked the low branches and stopped well back from the gnarled old oak that towered among the lesser trees. I pointed up. The thick summer foliage mostly hid the fort, and Emily squinted through the canopy for a moment before spotting it.

"You said you didn't have a tree house."

"I said my father didn't build us one."

Agilely swinging her right leg over her horse's neck, she jumped off like the athlete she was. I shook my head, amused, and her horse didn't care. She ignored the ladder affixed to the tree and circled, peering upward, disappearing behind the oak's massive trunk, reemerging. When she reached her starting point, she tugged on the ladder. It didn't budge. It hadn't been there in February, and I suspected Ross, or Dad, had constructed it just for me.

"I want to go up."

"Go on."

"Come with me."

I'd planned to let her ramble around there by herself, see the sights I remembered by heart, stretch out on the floor where Teddy and I used to read. But now, fueled by her enthusiasm, I longed to see how the view had changed.

By the time my head crested the edge of the fort's floor, she stood in the middle, pivoting slowly and gaping. "You can see the whole world from here."

Our world anyway.

Other than the foliage color, nothing much differed from my last climb up there with Teddy less than two months before he died. The same sturdy walls on either side, the tree forming the back, the open front, the solid floor swept clean of debris.

Yet at the same time, everything was different.

Emily tested the sides, stroked the rough bark, ran her shoe over the smooth floorboards. "You and Teddy used to come here, didn't you?"

"A lot."

"Thank you for showing me." She blinked a few times and turned toward the open, north-facing side. "I thought I saw . . . Is that a cemetery?"

"It is." If I'd considered she'd spot it, I might not have let her go up. I wasn't ready to talk about it.

"Teddy's there, isn't he?"

"Yeah."

"Let's go see him." Her voice rose with excitement.

I cringed. In the handful of times I'd been at the farm during the first year after the shooting, I couldn't bear to see the physical proof of his death. I still couldn't. The heartbreak of knowing he'd always be a ten-year-old little boy was proof enough. When I was eighty and the gap between our birth years had long since ceased to matter, he'd still be ten. The chasm between his life and mine suddenly seemed bottomless, and my heart and stomach plummeted without any prospect of rescue. I braced a hand against the tree to steady myself.

"I can't. Not yet." Soon, though. In private.

"But . . ." She stopped herself. "Okay, I understand. Someday, when you're ready, can I go with you? I just, you know, want to."

I wrapped my arm around her in a quick hug. "Of course."

After Emily left and I showered and shaved and, along with the others, devoured the enormous breakfast Scottie and my father had prepared, I was ready for the nap in which I rarely indulged. Instead, despite my physical inability to swim well or to properly lob the yellow ball, I let Scottie talk me into playing water polo.

"C'mon." She swung my hand between us as we ambled along the walkway toward the pool. "Be a good sport. The teams are uneven without you."

So, I joined my father and Jamie against Mom, Scottie, and Henry in so many games that I lost count. They trounced us, but none of us cared. Our splashing, laughter, and good-natured taunting—impossible-to-imagine activities not so long ago—was all the victory any of us needed.

By shortly after noon, everyone but Jamie and me had surrendered to the mid-nineties temps, with humidity to match, and wandered into the house. We sat on the edge of the pool, dangling our feet into the clear water that begged for ice cubes. A lone horsefly buzzed around us before seeking more appetizing fare down the hill. Other flying and biting pests were too smart to venture out.

"Wanna bet Mom moves supper inside?" Jamie asked. Thankfully, he was less gaunt than he'd been at Christmas. "So blasted hot out here."

"Not a bet I'd take."

His right foot traced an indecipherable design in the water. A spiral maybe. "I'm deferring my residency for a year."

"I heard."

He kicked at the water, splashing us. "You think it's a mistake, don't you?"

He hadn't been glowing with accomplishment at his medical school graduation six weeks earlier. He plodded through the ceremony, unsmilingly accepted congratulations, and attended, without really participating in, the celebratory luncheon our parents had arranged. At Christmas, he'd been ambivalent about his career choice. At graduation, he'd seemed terrified of it.

"I think it's exactly the right thing."

He stopped splashing. "You do?"

I cared that he cared what I thought. I recognized his indecision for what it was: his inability to make peace with his perceived failure to save Teddy, to assist Henry and Driscoll with our father and me. Each of us would struggle for the rest of our lives with the role—perceived or real— we'd played in those events. The huge ripples from Mel's actions, and my father's and Vince's, the smaller ripples gyrating from the actions of the rest of us, would never completely be stilled.

But he'd find his way. We all would.

"I absolutely do."

His smile beamed his appreciation. "And what about you?"

"What do you mean?"

"Are you still so ambivalent about teaching?"

I squinted into the sun, picturing Teddy and me reading together and the glow of accomplishment I'd felt as he finished one book after another, each more difficult than the previous. Perhaps memories of that glow had pushed me toward teaching when, after the shooting, my dreams of practicing animal law dissipated. I cared about my

Grainger students, wanted them to succeed. "I think teaching suits me after all."

Our father's shrill whistle, stuffy in the thick air, summoned us to lunch.

"The more things change, the more they stay the same." Jamie rolled his eyes, and I laughed.

After lunch, we scattered to watch the track and field trials for the upcoming Olympics, or read, or nap. In the kitchen, Scottie and I shucked the corn we would grill next to the ribs. I couldn't stop yawning.

Scottie smirked. "Keeping you up?"

"Too much exercise, too much sun."

She snatched a cob from me. "Go. I've got this."

The disquiet of a heated conversation stopped me short at the staircase. Unfamiliar voices tumbled from the open door of my father's study across the hallway, but no one was at the farm other than family.

I stepped in. My father stood in the middle of the dimly lit room, arms crossed, staring at his television. On the split screen, a man and a woman on a political talk show screeched over each other.

"You have to watch that on a holiday?"

He unfolded his arms, and when he clicked the remote, the talkers and their babble vanished. "In my life, there are no holidays."

"What're they talking about?"

"Me."

I almost asked him why, and for a nanosecond, his eyes narrowed. He waited, always would wait, for my anger to publicly fuel the specific accusation that only I could levy.

Part of him would be wary of me for it for the rest of our lives. To my surprise, that bothered me.

Instead of responding, I nodded and left him to go to my room, not to nap but to finish a novel. As I usually did now, on the landing, I savored the family photos, many more than had been removed shortly after Teddy died. My favorite remained the portrait of him with Huckleberry's head hanging over his shoulder.

The door was closed to the new guest room where, when our visits coincided with my parents', Scottie slept. The room had been Teddy's. By unanimous family vote, we'd repurposed, refurnished, and redecorated it, converting it into just another bedroom. We distributed Teddy's most prized possessions among ourselves and donated the rest. His books and floor globe resided in my study in Grainger. And the weekend we'd finished, my family celebrated him at the Riggses' barbecue restaurant, which had been his favorite. In a private dining room, we recounted his life in ours, one recollection kindling another, sparking the inevitable tears but also laughter that exploded beyond the room, prompting a smiling Irene Riggs to ease open the closed door to check on us.

I settled into the chair in the corner by the balcony doors, but after reading the same paragraph six times, I closed the book. Jamie was right, and not only about our mother moving supper from poolside to the kitchen. *The more things change, the more they stay the same.*

For example, there was Henry's parents' apparently permanent disregard of him. My mother had tracked them down and invited them to join us that weekend. Mrs. Linden begged off. "Another year, Laurel," she'd said. "Just too busy right now."

"I'm sorry, Mom," I'd told her when I found out. I was sorry—for my parents, who'd tried, but mostly for Henry.

"I didn't tell Henry I asked them." *Please don't tell him.*

We'd always have secrets.

I thought now, not for the first time over the past few months, how desperately Henry and I craved the same thing: the cohesiveness of family. We'd had it all along, but even if we should've recognized it, neither of us did. I believed in—*expected*—perfection, and when the illusion of it shattered, I assumed none of us mattered to each other and therefore chose solitude over imperfection. Henry assumed his delinquency had driven away his parents and so had to prove his worth to mine. When he believed he'd failed, he chose the pact of deception my parents unwittingly requested of him. We knew now, both of us, that we'd had what we wanted all along.

What *had* changed was my preoccupation with my father's television appearances. For the first time since the shooting, I tuned in at every opportunity, imagining what it must be like to wonder whether each interview was the last one, at least as a US senator and upstanding citizen. What interested me wasn't the information and opinions he imparted but rather his deft manipulation of facts and figures and even of his interviewers themselves.

Periodically, my rage at his handling of Mel, and what it cost us, bubbled like an enormous blister. But while I burned, I'd remember why he'd done it and admit that I couldn't say with absolute conviction that if I encountered a Melvin Gardner I'd not also destroy evidence. I'd remember why he and my mother and Henry had tried so desperately and for so long to protect me, and the salve of those memories soothed me.

In early March, with a towel wrapped around my naked body and my father slouched in the chair I sat in now, my hurt and rage drove my desire to reveal his misconduct to the authorities. And, as that dissipated, to allow him to believe that I might. But over the past few months, when I reflected on what I'd learned and on Emily's letter to Vince and on her need to share it, I'd softened.

During our conversation in Washington, my father had supplied what he believed was just enough information about Mel and Vince Gardner and himself to satisfy me, just enough to end my relationship with Emily and eliminate any possibility I'd discover I'd killed Teddy. He'd exchanged the almost certain guarantee that his transgression would forever remain undetected for the possibility, even likelihood, that I might reveal it. His singular, unselfish motive—his choice—had been to protect me. What more could I have asked of him?

Staying angry with him was my choice. Releasing that anger also was my choice. The flash of concern his eyes had registered a few minutes ago convinced me to begin clearing the way for both of us. To make the right choice.

Later, after we cleaned up from supper and before we drove into town for the fireworks display, I'd find him. He might be scouring the grill or hauling the trash outside or watching the news. I'd ask for a moment alone, and I'd promise him our secret was safe, that he didn't need to ever fear his son. We were family.

I set my book on the floor and stretched out in the chair, feeling more peaceful than I'd ever thought possible. Not until Henry called me from the doorway for supper did I realize I'd slept for several hours.

The aroma of ribs, barbecue sauce, corn, and peach cobbler drew me downstairs to the round table in our homey kitchen. Everyone waited for me. Henry pulled my mother's chair out for her and sat to her right, and the rest of us—Jamie, my father, Scottie, and I—joined them.

My mother tapped her iced tea glass and gazed across the table. "Bennett, will you say the blessing?"

Everyone clasped hands with the people beside them. With Scottie anchoring me on one side, I looked at my father on my other. His hand rested on the table beside his silverware.

"Dad." I spoke so softly, I doubt even Scottie heard.

When he glanced my way, I offered him my hand, palm up.

He hesitated. Then his face relaxed, and he reached for me.

I tightened my hand on his, awake to the realization I was the loved son of a flawed but loving family. I bowed my head for the blessing, knowing that I'd already been blessed beyond expectation. I was no longer alone, unloved, and indifferent to love. I never had been.

ACKNOWLEDGMENTS

THE FOLLOWING LIST was compiled from Karen's notes and emails. It was clear that many people contributed in a variety of ways to the process of writing her book, and to helping her personally, but the role of each person and the extent of their involvement was not always clear. Therefore, many of the acknowledgements below are listed as groups rather than individuals to avoid excluding anyone. Your understanding is appreciated.

On behalf of Karen, thank you . . .

To Karen's parents, Bob and Carolyn Foster, for supporting her love for dogs and books throughout her life and helping her to pursue her passions from a young age.

To Karen's siblings—Lisa Hodes, Nancy Councill, Lori Turley, David Foster, and Beth Carrick—for your dedication to Karen's dream of publishing *Reasons for Waking*, and to your spouses for their unwavering support.

To the entire team at Bold Story Press, especially Emily Barrosse, Karen Gulliver, and Julianna Scott Fein, for loving Karen's novel from the start, for choosing to publish it, and for guiding her siblings through the publishing process.

To Maria Olsen, for your invaluable guidance on book promotion.

To Karen's beta readers, for your time spent reading her manuscript and for sharing your feedback.

To those who assisted with technical research and terminology related to the law, weapons, crime scenes, and other topics about which Karen had limited knowledge.

To Karen's writing coaches and editors, especially Austen Wright, for helping her to make her story even more perfect.

To Karen's writing groups, for guiding and encouraging her to continue writing.

To Suzy Foster, for your talent and artistry in translating ideas into pictures, leading to the concept for the book's cover design.

To Bill Carrick, for your time and expertise in designing the book's website (www.reasonsforwaking.com).

To Karen's many friends who looked after her throughout her illness when her family couldn't be there.

To all who helped Karen live life to the fullest—her family, friends and fellow dog-lovers, neighbors, colleagues, and perhaps most of all, her Springers.

Karen was extremely grateful for all of you.

A NOTE ABOUT THE AUTHOR FROM HER SIBLINGS

KAREN GREW UP in a military family as the oldest of six children—five girls and one boy. Our family relocated whenever our father was transferred by the Navy to a new duty station. Every move required us to start over with schools and friends; we relied on each other as we adjusted to each new home. Relocating had a way of drawing our family together.

We siblings eventually attended different colleges and settled in at least five different states. Over the years, we gathered together whenever possible for holidays and celebrations, but those early years cemented our close family relationships.

Karen was an inspiration to all of us. She was blind at birth from congenital cataracts. Multiple surgeries before she was two years old restored only three percent of her vision. Fiercely independent, she never complained and never sought special accommodations. She settled in the Atlanta area where she spent her career as a technical writer and editor for the Centers for Disease Control and Prevention (CDC), but she considered herself a creative writer first. It was her lifelong dream to write a novel.

Karen was passionate about raising, showing, and breeding English Springer Spaniels, and she became an advocate for maintaining the highest breed standards. Through her endeavors, she had an expansive network of friends and colleagues around the country, and she volunteered to support several Springer organizations.

In October of 2020, Karen was diagnosed with metastatic breast cancer. We siblings took turns going to Atlanta to care for her and her dogs, to drive her to medical appointments, and to do whatever was necessary to make life a little easier for her. She was determined to live life on her terms, and she did that with the help of her family and friends.

In November of 2021, Karen called us, ecstatic that her novel was going to be published by Bold Story Press. Shortly after that call, her health took a sudden turn for the worse, and she was unable to complete the final edits. She told us that her biggest regret was that she would die without seeing her book published—so we, her siblings, promised her that we would do everything possible to make her dream come true.

The book you are holding is her greatest and final accomplishment, and we are honored to be able to support our sister Karen even in death by making her lifelong dream a reality. We hope you will enjoy *Reasons for Waking* as much as we do.

Lisa Foster Hodes
Nancy Foster Councill
Lori Foster Turley
David P. Foster
Beth Foster Carrick

ABOUT BOLD STORY PRESS

BOLD STORY PRESS is a curated, woman-owned hybrid publishing company with a mission of publishing well-written stories by women. If your book is chosen for publication, our team of expert editors and designers will work with you to publish a professionally edited and designed book. Every woman has a story to tell. If you have written yours and want to explore publishing with Bold Story Press, contact us at https://boldstorypress.com.

**BOLD
STORY
PRESS**

The Bold Story Press logo, designed by Grace Arsenault, was inspired by the nom de plume, or pen name, a sad necessity at one time for female authors who wanted to publish. The woman's face hidden in the quill is the profile of Virginia Woolf, who, in addition to being an early feminist writer, founded and ran her own publishing company, Hogarth Press.